Pound Hill

Mavis Cheek was born and grew up in Wimbledon. She began her working life at Editions Alecto, the contemporary art publishers. She then attended Hillcroft College for Women from where she graduated in Arts. After her daughter Bella was born, began her writing career in earnest; journalism and travel ing at first, then short stories, and eventually, in 1988, her el *Pause Between Acts*, which won the *She*/John Menzies t Novel Prize. Her novels include *Mrs Fytton's Country Life*, *ce Gentle Gets Sexy* and, most recently, *Truth to Tell*. She v lives and writes in the heart of the English countryside.

Praise for THE LOVERS OF POUND HILL

' witty tale in which the author exposes the readers to a host of delightful characters.'
Irish News

'Many books are advertised as being funny but few live up to he hype . . . *The Lovers of Pound Hill* is genuinely witty and very, very clever . . . satire at its best.'
Bookbag

Lively, sunny, positive, this is a real cheerer-upper of a book. You'll love it!'
Daily Mail

MAVIS CHEEK
The Lovers of Pound Hill

arrow books

Published by Arrow Books 2012

2 4 6 8 10 9 7 5 3 1

Copyright © Mavis Cheek 2011

Mavis Cheek has asserted her right under the Copyright, Designs
and Patents Act 1988 to be identified as the author of this work

This novel is a work of fiction. Names and characters are the product of the
author's imagination and any resemblance to actual persons, living or dead,
is entirely coincidental.

First published in Great Britain in 2011 by Hutchinson

Arrow Books
Random House, 20 Vauxhall Bridge Road,
London SW1V 2SA

www.randomhouse.co.uk

Addresses for companies within The Random House Group Limited can be found at:
www.randomhouse.co.uk/offices.htm

The Random House Group Limited Reg. No. 954009

A CIP catalogue record for this book
is available from the British Library

ISBN 9780099547495

The Random House Group Limited supports The Forest Stewardship Council (FSC®), the
leading international forest certification organisation. Our books carrying the FSC label are
printed on FSC® certified paper. FSC is the only forest certification scheme endorsed by
the leading environmental organisations, including Greenpeace. Our paper procurement
policy can be found at www.randomhouse.co.uk/environment

Typeset in Sabon by Palimpsest Book Production Limited,
Falkirk, Stirlingshire
Printed and bound by CPI Group (UK) Ltd, Croydon CR0 4YY

GNOME
'dwarf-like earth-dwelling spirit,' 1712, from Fr. *gnome*, from L. *gnomus*, used 16c. in a treatise by Paracelsus, who gave the name *pigmaei* or *gnomi* to elemental earth beings, possibly from Gk. *genomos* 'earth-dweller.' Popular in children's literature 19c. as a name for red-capped Ger. and Swiss folklore dwarfs. Garden figurines first imported to England late 1860s from Germany.

The Blessed, that immortal be,
From change in love are only free . . .

. . . Were it not madness to deny
To live because we're sure to die?

'To a Lady asking him how long he would love
her', by George Etherege (1635?–1692)

PART I

One

THE SUN SHONE out of a clear blue sky and bestowed its gentle rays upon the well-kept exteriors of Lufferton Boney. Lufferton Boney is *remarkably* well-kept, thought Molly Bonner, as she walked down the village high street. Her boots – long, leather, black and shiny – were not country boots; her skirt – short, muslin, pink and frothy – was not a country skirt; and her hair – close-cropped, redder than anything of a hirsute disposition to be found in nature, and bouncy – was definitely, *definitely* not a country haircut. And if one were to continue one could cite other outrages; her car, now parked at the top of the street near the church of St Etheldreda (as instructed by Miles Whittington) was nowhere near the kind of car country people drove, it being small, fast and of startling blueness with a silver stripe down its back; the briefcase she carried was scarlet patent leather, the papers inside the briefcase were of a very potent yellow, and the words printed thereon were printed in something that was dangerously near to puce. Miles had told her that the curve in the road where she parked her car designated the separation of the old village from the new, that the church was the marker between ancient and modern. Its porch faced the end of the village street, its entrance opening towards the landscape beyond. So the church seemed to be set there in a stand-off. Fanciful or what? As she passed the old lychgate she looked up once, raising her eyes to the Hill at the end of the village street. Now she could see that the monstrous figure cut into it, though partly obliterated by thorn bushes, seemed to weigh down upon the village below. Maybe not so fanciful then? With a little hiccup of excitement she hurried on.

You would not, thought Dryden Fellows, as he saw her pass by his emporium, Beautiful Bygones (antiques, ephemera and objects of delight), you would certainly not want your son to bring her home with a view to marrying her into the family . . . Nigel, Dryden's son, was of marriageable age, still single and still silly. His only hope, so his father thought, was to marry someone considerably sillier than himself. But whom? Dryden had a very good reason for wishing Nigel married apart from the usual one of parental relief, and he could only live in hope. It was the one wish he could remember being asked of him by his now dead wife (ten years deceased and mother of the very silly Nigel) and that was made on her deathbed. And for various reasons, not all of them human, he wished to get it sorted out and settle the matter.

The sound of a horse's hooves clip-clopped away in the distance and Dryden watched, thoughtfully, the chestnut's shining, undulating rump and the little jodhpured rump above it that also undulated past the Old Holly Bush and disappeared around the curve in the road. That jodhpured rump was unmarried, had blue blood and was born in the same year as his son. There was a terrible yearning in Dryden's eyes.

Further down the street in Hill View House Miles Whittington flitted and darted around his beamed and much furnished sitting room like a hornet in heat, or so thought Dorcas Fairbrother, his secretary (Miles was old-fashioned enough to call her that rather than the altogether more charming term Personal Assistant). She sat at her desk in the far corner, very still, very quiet, and tried to concentrate on Miles's long letter to the local council. This concerned the Gnome of Pound Hill and money – when did his correspondence with the local council not? And she wanted it out of the way so that she could concentrate on this morning's visitor and – with luck – have a little fun at Miles's expense.

'May as well keep on at them,' said Miles absently. 'Though it is to be hoped that our visitor will have the answer.' He paused, tweaked a curtain (Colefax and Fowler, 1986) and added with a smile that did not go all the way up to his eyes, 'Should she, I wonder, sit facing the window and the sun, or with her face away from the light?'

Dorcas said nothing. This, she guessed, was a rhetorical question. As was so often the case with Miles, Dorcas was right. After a short pause, and a pose with his hand placed to his brow for maximum effect, Miles answered himself. 'When they interrogate prisoners they have strong light shining in their eyes. Dorcas?'

'They do, Miles.'

'Good, good.' He moved the Bishop's chair (oak, 17th century) to a suitable position and then stood back, hands now at his side, and surveyed the new placement.

'Excellent,' he said. 'Excellent.'

With a spring in his step Miles moved closer to the window and looked up and down the street. His gaze fell fondly, even dreamily, upon a newly deposited, steaming pile of horse manure. Such things added to the rural image and might be an encouragement to future visitors – but . . . just for a moment he lapsed and then blinked as if remembering the task in hand. He stiffened his back and stiffened his resolve, turned to Dorcas and clapped his hands. 'The horse, Dorcas, has left a deposit. It might give our visitor a bad idea of the place. Would you take the shovel and . . .'

Dorcas, who also smiled, and whose smile did not reach up to her eyes either, said, 'Miles – what do you think our visitor would make of it if, on arriving, she saw your secretary shovelling up shit?'

Miles winced. Sometimes Dorcas betrayed her origins. He looked out of the window again. 'Well,' he said, 'I suppose this is the countryside, warts and all. I could have done with it for the vegetables.' He stood thinking for a moment longer, regret in his eyes. Then he shook his head and went over to Dorcas's desk and stood, hands on meagre hips, looking down. 'Now. This is where you come into your own.' His secretary duly removed her hands from the keyboard of her computer (Dell, 1997) and waited. 'Refreshments. Your department.' He strode over to the chair by the fireplace (empty), it being towards the end of March, and absent-mindedly picked up the cat, Montmorency, to put him down on the rug. Montmorency opened one eye, shuddered, and waited. Miles turned his back and Montmorency resumed the chair. The cat had been his absent brother Robin's cat and for some reason Miles felt he could not dispose of it. Not yet, anyway. Soon, he would croon to himself, soon.

'Dorcas, should I – we – offer her tea or coffee? Or should I suggest sherry. Or beer . . .?' He turned to the empty Bishop's chair and posed as if lost in thought again. Then he twirled in Dorcas's direction. 'Beer would be very good, I think,' he said, malevolently. 'Put her nicely in her place. I have looked her up on the Internet and the family originates from nowhere. A hundred years ago they were nothing. Well, not in the paternal line. Better on the distaff but only just. Money from trade. Beer it is. That will show her. Do you agree?'

'I think beer would put her in a place, certainly,' said Dorcas.

'Good, good, *good*,' said Miles and he clapped his hands once more.

Susie and Pinky Smith toiled up Pound Hill towards the Gnome. Pinky, so called for his tendency to go pink in the sun, in the shade, in the pub – and generally anywhere – puffed. Susie, stout and draped in a not very well put together kaftan, snorted through her nose in the determined way that Pinky had come to dread. He looked back down the Hill, past Miles's house, to the village street and all its serenity.

'Come along, Pinks,' said his wife. And carried on upwards snorting all the way. She made the same noise when they were having sex. It was the noise of determination. The Smiths had been married for nine years and Susie was determined that this year, the year of their tenth anniversary, would be the year of pregnancy. So far this had not occurred, hence their toiling towards the Gnome. You could almost, thought Pinky through his puffings, see the path our feet have created over the years. His own personal belief, one he kept to himself after the unfortunate occasion, eight and a half years ago, when he voiced it to his new young bride, was that by the time they got to the Gnome and his vital organ, they were both so knackered that the likelihood of conceiving anything short of a snooze in the grass was minimal. Eight and a half years ago, after he spoke these words, Susie had stopped cooking and taken to sitting in the garden with a book, not so much reading it as gripping it as if she would choke the life out of it. And when she did come round, with a dire warning that if he ever showed that kind of defeatism again she would be off, he knew who was boss and what the boss required. It was the same with her crystal garden. He dug the soil over in readiness, regretted the loss of cabbages, and said nothing. Best not.

Over the years and unobserved from time to time he had slipped out of Chrysalis Cottage to the village street and stared up at the offensively rampant Gnome, and shaken his fist at it. He had sent it a telepathic message, scattered with curses, some of which were very obscene and the upshot of which was that the Gnome had ruined his life. What had once been a gentle art had become a marrow-sucking demand that left him weak and unhappy. His wife's once desirable and luscious curves left him pale with fear. Sex was a nightmare, and the nightmare was the Gnome's curse.

After these bouts of secret rebelliousness Pinky went back indoors and gave himself up to whatever would come – for he was a married man and he had married for better or for worse. And here was the worst he seemed to have married for. On seeking the advice of a therapist in Woolmington (thirty-five miles away to avoid discovery) a few years ago, Pinky was overwhelmed with silence when the therapist leaned forward and said, 'Trouble in the bed department?' He had a strange and totally unnerving vision of himself involved in a punch-up in Beds-R-Us. He found his voice enough to say a very faint, 'Yes' and was then treated to a long and sympathetic discourse on how to arouse his wife. Since that was very far from the issue he paid his fee and never went back.

Funny, though – in all those years of going through puberty and beyond when he wanted a randy woman more than anything in the world – any woman – when his thoughts strayed hourly to all kinds of wonderful wickedness – it had never occurred to him that to find one might not live up to his fantasies: not at all, nowhere near, in fact. But then, Susie was not *randy* in the way he had imagined, no, she was randy in a businesslike way. The Gnome saw to that. Their visits up the Hill were frequent and deadly. She had even taken him up there once in the snow but luckily what it did to those parts of him that were required made this inappropriate in future. Alas, none of the constant demands from this concupiscent wife now felt nice, rude or naughty. It felt – how could he describe it – deadly and determinedly proper. Nor did it help that Pinky was a plumber. The analogies with his craft simply *would* enter his swirling head.

Susie was sure the fault lay with Pinky. So, despite going pinker than ever, he'd had a thrill in the fertility clinic when the nurse put on her white plastic gloves and looked up from her tray to give him a lipsticked smile. Thank goodness Dr

Porlock had suggested laying off for a while, and not going at it. Dr Porlock had a straightforward way with words – conserving your potency, he called it. Which they did for short (too, too short) periods of time. Otherwise, Pinky was quite sure, he would have been dead within the year. To die from excessive shagging had been his hope and aspiration for much of his early life. But when it so nearly came upon him he found it strangely unappealing.

The Gnome and his very dreadful member were partially hidden by the thorn bushes and gorse and other hardy verdure that clung to his edges. But the land being mainly chalk, these game bits of foliage scarcely hid the upward thrust of his massive shape. The Cerne Abbas Giant had nothing on him for masculinity. It occurred to Pinky as they clambered over the last few tussocks of grass (for some reason the sheep simply would not graze anywhere near the Gnome – Farmer Braddle constantly tried his best to persuade them but they clearly found the idea offensive – and, looking at it again now, Pinky could hardly blame them) that if Miles Whittington had his way this might be the last time they could enact their marital requirements up here on the free basis that had been the villagers' right since time immemorial. Miles had more than hinted that he had a plan to have the Gnome restored to his full . . . impact, and then to charge for the privilege of visiting him. Well thank God, was all Pinky could mutter, though he had little faith.

On he toiled with Susie's happy snorting trumpeting behind him. It was at this point that Pinky always felt a sense of panic; kaftans were strangely unalluring items at the best of times, and none more so than Susie's. How he longed to tell her that he had *never* favoured purple, but – fortunately – looking down towards the village, he saw the distant figure of a young woman striding along the main street, wearing long black boots with quite a lot of knee and thigh showing and not a purple billowing in sight. It'd have to do.

Nigel Fellows, Dryden's son, was deeply in love by the time Molly Bonner had reached Miles's door. Being deeply in love was his accustomed state and one that he relished. Love had happened to Nigel very frequently over the past few years, mostly, it should be said, induced by young women whom his father considered highly unsuitable.

It was the sound of the girl's footsteps ringing out so loud and clear that first caught his attention. It was the bouncing redness of the hair and the other accoutrements that held it. On the whole the people of Lufferton Boney did not have footsteps that rang out. On the whole Lufferton Boney was a quiet village whose passions and turmoil raged silently within.

The children of the village lived mostly in the two developments of modern houses on the newer edge of the village, round the curve of the village street and beyond the church. There was a playground there, tucked behind a row of may trees, and that was where they made their noise. Like corralled baby animals, they were kept away from the lower part of the village and – it was to be hoped by their parents – from the sight of the Gnome. If this had a little to do with the superstitions of the ancients about evil eyes and suchlike, it was largely because the modern parents of Lufferton Boney did not want to have to answer the kind of questions that might be asked by their offspring should their houses be set too close to Pound Hill. They were perfectly happy to be sited well out of the way. That this was also convenient for the older, more established members of the village was not a concern.

All modern amenities were to hand for the newer inhabitants. Beyond the church was the post office and stores so it made convincingly practical sense that the housing developments grew up close to that (sweets, cigarettes, local eggs, milk and bread, newspapers – mostly the *Mail*, *Express* and *Telegraph*) and the playground and the new, rather brutal (post-Lasdun but with none of his spirituality about it), village hall, erected (thrown up, some preferred) in 1966. Some who lived beyond the curve at the top end of the village occasionally ventured down the street and into the Old Holly Bush, but most were content to drink and meet together in the social club attached to the Lasdun-lite village hall.

To the men of the village the Gnome with his monstrous appendage was not a sight to be encouraged, being somewhat alienating to the masculine mind. And disturbing to the female one. Once up the street and beyond the church the Hill was quite hidden. Happily the primary school was three miles away in the larger village of Bonwell from where the Gnome, in all his terrible glory, could also not be seen.

Thus it was strange to hear bootsteps ringing out, and Nigel was brought to the upstairs window of Beautiful Bygones where he was polishing the lock escutcheons and little brass handles of a small George II sideboard, an enjoyably rewarding job in an otherwise unprepossessing sea of meaningless meniality. He went to the window, loving one woman, and returned in love with another. He stood there transfixed, spellbound by the vision as it bounced and swayed along the street. She, this creature in her pink and leather, with her shining red hair (totally and wonderfully artificial in its hue) was everything he had ever wanted. Suddenly. His eyes followed her as she passed and continued to follow her as she made her ringing way down the street. Above her – outlined on the Hill – sat the Gnome. It was as if she were walking defiantly towards him in acknowledgement. Nigel felt a twinge of something very profound which had nothing to do with the pleasures of polishing brass. Julie Barnsley at the pub was no more. This was it. No, no – this really was *it*.

The Gnome seemed to wink his approval as the girl in the

boots (Russell and Bromley, vintage, £22 in Sue Ryder) made her way to the little iron gate fronting Miles's front garden. Now that the figure was well past the shop, getting smaller and smaller, Nigel saw how she swung that skirt and swung that red bag and swung – well – swung everything – and he was certain. Whoever you are, he vowed, whoever you are – it is you I have waited for. But *Miles?* She knew Miles? Now that was very odd and highly unlikely. Were Miles to be receiving a visit from a young lady, Nigel Fellows would have expected her to be wearing something that covered her knees and did not move in the slightest as she walked, in quiet and demure fashion, up to his gate. Miles? *Miles?* Nigel must find out who the, what the, why the – and quickly. He returned to his rubbing with tremendous brio – as if showing the girl how committed to anything he chose to do he could be.

In The Orchard House Winifred Porlock sighed. Donald Porlock did not respond. There was an utterly entertaining article in the *Lancet* about DNA and testing for racial/ethnic identity, which backed up all he had ever thought about commercial meddling with such information. Winifred sighed again.

He put the magazine down slowly and gazed at her sternly.

'Winnie?'

'Yes, Donald.'

'Why are you sighing?'

'Am I, Donald?'

'I think you know you are.'

'Ah well.'

'And when you add an Ah well, you know very well that you are.'

'Well, perhaps I am.'

'No perhaps about it. If you got any more wind up and out of yourself you'd be cooling my tea from over there.'

'Well, I *am* sighing.'

'That much we have established. Now we want to establish why.'

The strange thing about doctors, thought Winifred, was that in their surgeries they were the very essence of charming interest. If a woman sat down and sighed they would not rattle their medical magazine at her and put on a sardonic voice, no, they would lean forward and ask in a low, warm, enquiring tone, 'Now, what's the problem?' Or, if you were Donald, lean forward, use a warm, enquiring tone, and have already made up your mind. Between the ages of 15 and 25 and female – hormones. If male 15–25 it would be sex. 25–40 both sexes, it would be the need of iron and more sleep (children) – with, possibly, the odd pick-me-up in pill form. After that – if female – it would be hormones. If male it would be blood pressure and lay off the fried foods.

Donald's once enquiring mind had been replaced over the years with something more dictatorial and his patients were, in the main, rather a nuisance. Partly, Winifred told herself, this was the natural consequence of spending so many years in a profession, and partly it was the seduction of status. Least said soonest mended, was the proper working spirit, according to Donald. Nowadays if anyone came to him with anything of an emotional nature and became strident about it (women) or determined (men), he would class it as Mental – and pass it on to his partner, a woman. Oddly, most of those he saw went away from Donald's surgery feeling better than when they went in. Perhaps because his diagnosis and remedies were so simple, so comforting; if a little confusing occasionally. Like the time Mrs Webb went into the surgery and put her hand on her bosom and said she had severe pain and Donald prescribed a little muscle relaxant called Valium. Mrs Webb, who also had housemaid's knee, had been fearful that an operation might be necessary (the offending joint had never been right since she tripped over her fishing gnome on the front path) but once she got home and took a pill, all such fear vanished. The knee still hurt but she cared not one jot. Nor did she again until the bottle was empty.

All so very different, sighed Winifred, if the doctor was your husband and you were sitting in the breakfast room of a large old house in a small village in the heart of the South-West. She loved The Orchard House, she loved the landscape – she was just not sure if she loved Donald. Or, indeed, if he loved her. If she asked him he'd probably say he had wax in his ear and leave the room rapidly. Sighing again she remembered how, when they first met, he was radical, fired up with notions of medicine helping the dispossessed and out to change the world. She was thrilled by this. Feminist principles and the making of documentaries for the BBC were set aside for the greater good. But where would they go? Why, they would go anywhere. And then, of course, the newly wedded Winifred became pregnant. Never mind. Honourable activity was still possible. Doctors of conscience were needed everywhere, even in England. Rural poverty was the keynote now, Winifred counselled her husband, only too happy that he seemed to accept her pregnancy with good grace; even – she thought – with something that looked like, but could not be, relief.

And so they came to Lufferton Boney where they arrived full of the thrill of having made the move from sophisticated town (London) to very rural country and dared to do it when she was pregnant with their first child, the sweet and docile Charlotte. And she herself was sweet and docile, with Donald taking charge. How sweetly she became a mother and a doctor's wife – with two more children arriving it was all so perfect. How she forgot her years as a maker of documentaries – a rare profession for a woman in the mid-seventies – though its reminders were all around her since the filming for her last piece – *Ancient Landscapes* – had taken place in the surrounding countryside near Lufferton Boney.

She fell for the place then, knew enough about the hard times experienced by those who lived on the land to consider it a good place for Donald's practice, and so it was. But Donald had drifted. Donald found the honour in which the doctor was still held in rural society to be to his taste and succumbed. Winifred, getting on with the domestic side of things, failed to see it grow and extinguish his social conscience. Now he was too old, too set in his ways. Why he could not even, as he proudly told anyone who would listen, boil an egg. It was too late. And Winifred had let it happen. She had fallen for the place and she had loved living here. Now it seemed to admonish her. You loved me once, it seemed to say, why not now? She did not know. Doctors cannot be everything to everyone (as Donald said to her waspishly and increasingly often), which was true. She soldiered on. Donald was a good man. But she sometimes found herself staring up at the Gnome with a tender ache that she couldn't, quite, describe. Now that Donald had taken on a brand new surgery with other doctors in Bonwell, she saw him even less. And she had no idea, absolutely none, if this was a good or a bad thing.

She looked back at the immaculately laid breakfast table and had an overwhelming urge to break things. The young woman who became so proud of her nice china, nice tablecloths, nice vases of flowers, nice children, nice husband, had given way to the middle-aged woman who was stick thin, energetic, never wore make-up and wished she had thought more about life and less about china, napery and the arrangement of blooms. A Winifred who was now as far removed from the woman whom Donald first met as Lufferton Boney was from tribal Africa. Glancing over the middlebrow perfection of her table setting, she thought of the last programme she'd made. It was almost the perfect ending to the series. They were filming Iron Age burial sites in the surrounding hillsides which had yielded up serious jewellery. You learned on the hoof in those days. At the end of the assignment words such as torque and fibula tripped off her tongue as if she were born to them. It took her breath away, as it did the breath of the audience. It was a good moment to leave the stage.

The jewellery was now safely in the British Museum and, on occasion, when Winifred went up to London for dentistry or to visit her sister, she would pop in and have a look at it. Among the golden ornaments and swan-necked clothes pins were some black, polished beads – made from shale, also called cannel coal, usually cracked or damaged with holes bored into them – and she always felt she was like these broken beads – plain, unadorned, overshadowed – and ultimately mysterious even to herself. What were they? Who was she? The beads were brought from the coast, the archaeologist had said, and valued despite the state of them. He rather thought that this part of the world was included in the Mesolithic Causeway, the great road that was used for thousands of years before the Romans arrived. Ritual sites existed on every bit of the landscape around Lufferton Boney, except, it seemed, on Pound Hill. So far the Hill had shown no traces of ritual sites, except of course the Gnome. Perhaps that was why. Whatever the date of the figure it was enough for anybody who wanted to recognise a message. No one knew for certain what that message was, of course, beyond the obvious one of fertility. Winifed felt it was all a mockery, that Gnome: suggestive of promise, yielding nothing. Just like life.

Well, Charlotte was now well over thirty, of a pierced mien, with her pale hair done in dreadlocks, very strong opinions and given to wearing stout boots when she came to visit. She'd been the last one of the three to leave and was the least conventional. Her mother harboured a warm admiration for her of which she did not speak to Charlotte's father. Donald could barely manage a 'hallo' before the phone was passed to 'your mother'. Winifred saw in her firstborn something of the girl she once was. Where did she go?

The desire to break things subsided. Winifred surveyed the room. The little carriage clock on the mantelpiece tick-tocked away, the slightly tilted gilded mirror hanging above it reflecting the two of them, both with rather more grey in their hair than brown, both with decent garments on, even for breakfast. There was the Spode set on the table, as usual; there was the silver toast rack and the butter dish; there was the little silver stand for the marmalade pot lest one drip should dirty the pretty Belgian tablecloth. Wedding presents, all. Nothing out of order, all very tasteful, all as familiar as the rings on her hand. She sighed once more, quite involuntarily. Barefoot in the kitchen, she murmured. Or rather, comfortable in Marks and Spencers slippers in the kitchen – which only made it worse. Out loud she said, 'I am very, very bored, Donald. Very. Bored.'

'Yes. So you keep saying. So you keep *sighing*.' He laughed, amused at his wit. His wife mimicked his little laugh. She looked at the teapot and then quickly looked away.

'Not amusing, my love. Not amusing at all.'

'So why get the feeling of boredom again all of a sudden?'

'Well, I can't be a country lady – I can't sew, knit, cook, garden or find a flair for paint colours – and I'm past child-bearing – and I seem to be past my sell-by date in the bedroom nowadays . . .' She paused and tapped her finger against her teeth as if sunk in thought. 'In fact I really can't remember—'

'Yes, yes,' said Donald Porlock quickly and sharply. 'But none of that is new.'

'No,' she said, taking up a piece of dark toast and nibbling around the edges. 'It is not new and it is like a pulled thread on a woolly jumper – it keeps unravelling. Eventually I shall not exist at all.'

'Rubbish,' said her husband. 'Absolute rubbish.'

'I was once one of the leading young BBC film-makers, or in line to be. I am now your wife, mother to three grown and confident children, all of whom have left home, member of the WI where I have seen, at first hand, my chocolate brownies being fed to the ducks, and was also – until recently – the clearer up of extensive dog's mess due to our elderly Jack Russell's kidney and bowel malfunction. When it came to it, you administered a shot of something into that same elderly Jack Russell, and that was that. I wonder, Donald, would you do the same for me.'

Donald, who had returned to his DNA by now, only heard the half of it and assumed that his wife was asking if he would do it again to a dog, if they obtained another one. 'Like a shot,' he said. 'Without a blink of hestitation. Best way to go.' He might have retracted those words had he seen the light that appeared in the eyes of his wife. But he read on until the fascinating DNA article took on an oddly opaque quality as that same wife stood over him and gently poured the contents of the teapot over his head. Fortunately, since it had been made over an hour ago, it was scarcely warm.

Julie Barnsley sidestepped the calling card left by the passing chestnut with distaste, paused on the steps of the Old Holly Bush and turned to watch the last flick of the pink skirt as it disappeared through the door of Hill View House opposite. The girl in the pink skirt had stood for a moment, looking up at Pound Hill, as if mesmerised. That in itself, thought Julie Barnsley, was not strange – many a visitor was mesmerised, if not downright shaken by the view up the Hill – but this girl had given a definite laugh. She just put her head back and gave a very throaty chuckle. It was the kind of throaty chuckle that Julie Barnsley would like to cultivate for herself. Not the usual response from someone new to the Gnome and his protuberance. And to be visiting Miles was also unusual. Miles was not one to receive visitors – especially not young women of high – or perhaps odd would describe it better – fashion with a bounce in their step. Odd, thought Julie, very odd, in every department.

She walked on towards the pub entrance. But something, or someone, made her turn and look in the direction of Beautiful Bygones and raise her eyes to the first floor, where she saw, just before he swiftly hid from her gaze, the owl-like stare of her beloved (secretly) betrothed. His expression, seen and noted before he vanished, was that of a starving man offered meat. Julie Barnsley did not like it at all, that expression, on his usually bovine features. He looked lively. He looked like he'd woken up to something. He looked, in fact, just the way he had looked at her, Julie Barnsley, not so long ago when she took him up Pound Hill and made a man of him . . . But she did not think the look was directed at her. She waited but Nigel's face did not reappear. Eventually she pushed open the door of the Old Holly Bush and stomped in. That was not part of the plan – not at all. Nigel was supposed to be enraptured by her. Fortunately – she slammed the door behind her and made the ancient walls shake – fortunately a young woman who looked like that was unlikely to be hanging around for very long. But it did not bode well, not at all. Things must be hurried along before Nigel managed to stray.

Peter Hanker, the young man who owned the Old Holly Bush gave her a cheerful grin. 'Something got your goat this morning?' he asked. 'I've got a cure for that.' But he knew that she would show no interest. Once it had been different, but Julie, it seemed, had different aspirations.

On the ground floor of Beautiful Bygones and not dodging out of sight of anyone, stood Dryden Fellows, duster in hand, staring at the now closed Hill View door. He shook his head as if in disbelief and turned away – catching sight, as he did so, of the still pausing Julie further down the street. His face, not usually very kindly, took on a darker hue than usual. Julie smiled, pouted, put up two fingers (she reserved one finger for exceptional circumstances) and then opened the pub door.

Dryden Fellows shook his head, and his duster, for the second time that day. Julie Barnsley would not insinuate herself into the Fellows' family. She might think she was being clever but she was not as clever as Dryden. If he must leave the business to his son and heir, and also fulfil his dead wife's wishes, then his son and heir (he winced, as usual, at the prospect) must marry good stock. Very good stock. If silly. Dryden felt this combination would not be too hard to accomplish. His son must continue the upward haul towards good connections – and secure fortune. Then Dryden could treat Beautiful Bygones as a hobby and relax into his old age, knowing that he had a place in society and that the trials and tribulations of only managing to produce one son and heir, and a not very bright one at that, would not matter. In fact, in the light of Dryden's marital ambition for his son, not being very bright could be seen as an advantage. He hoped for a bride from the social top drawer, someone who would bring respect to the House of Fellows. And he had his eye on just such a one. If he achieved this then surely, surely Lottie would show herself no more?

Marion Fitzhartlett, who that morning had ridden her chestnut mare from the Old Manor to the village street, as she did every morning, and was even now curving round the bottom of Pound

Hill on her usual riding circuit, was Dryden's goal. He saw her with her straight back, sturdy thighs, in all her well-bred glory and at her best on a horse. It was, of course, a shame that when she smiled she did so with a rather lopsided wink that could be a little unnerving for the uninformed. It was all to do with that wretched figure cut into the Hill. Up the Hill she had gone alone for the first time, riding her pony with tremendous skill and confidence though only ten years old, when the pony – obviously owning far less of each commodity – reared – and off she came, landing firmly on her head at the very top of the Gnome's manliness. The nervous tic of a wink had stayed with her after the event.

There were some that said it was the fault of the Gnome that the pony stumbled on the edge of the cutting, that it was shocked to its equine core to find something so much better endowed than itself, but no one could be sure. What was known was that Marion should not have been up there riding alone – that her nanny or a groom, or one of her parents should have accompanied her – and the ensuing rows and recriminations in the Old Manor left Marion disinclined to ride up the Hill or go anywhere near the Gnome ever again. But she was of old Norman stock and her riding continued. She could not think of a life without it. The nanny was dismissed, the groom sulked for weeks, and Marion's mother was never the same again. As to her father, Sir Roger, it was hard to say if he was affected by the incident or not. For he was also of old Norman stock where teeth-gritting was the best you'd get in a severe situation. Ever afterwards Marion skirted the Hill on her various mounts. Nor did she, as she grew into her teens, give up her love of horses for the love of young men. No. Marion stayed faithful to the equines in her life – and left the young men to dash about, snigger at the Gnome, and admit defeat where the possibility of getting Marion up the Hill and on to her back was concerned.

Nigel, when asked by his father if he liked Marion Fitzhartlett, said that in his opinion Marion Fitzhartlett looked like his infant drawings of his now dead mother: hair sticking out straight and untamed, face asymmetrical, eyebrows all over the place – and that peculiar facial tic. Come to that, she had no bosoms whatsoever. In vain did Dryden point out that she had a fine, curvaceous bottom (from many years of hard horse riding). Nigel did not see a fine, curvaceous bottom in the same light as the fine and curvaceous bust revealed to him atop the Gnome one moonlit night by his secret fiancée.

Until this morning, Nigel would have been perfectly happy to marry in secret and own that bust for the rest of his life. Until this morning Julie Barnsley, who might not have been the first love of his life but whom he was very happy to make his last, had been everything he wanted. And then, in a moment, just a moment, all that had changed. Julie Barnsley, the most perfect little woman in the world, the love of his life, the (secret) bride of his choice, was as dust in the street since the advent of Molly Bonner and the exciting pink, red and black of her. He did not know how he was going to effect this new relationship – but he knew that he would begin trying at once. He also knew that – unless he kept well out of her way – Julie Barnsley would not take it lightly. She had once told him that, should he stray, she would take it upon herself to make a gelding out of him. The laugh she had emitted after this statement still rang in his ears.

Nigel, turning away from the view which now held nothing of interest for him, nor would, he vowed, until the girl in pink re-emerged, caught sight of Mrs Webb out in her gnome garden, inspecting her little men. Nigel thought them rather sweet and liked their brightness. The houses at this end of the village street for the most part being rather dull and good and respectable with traditional colours, Nigel thought the gnomes added a bit of fun. Fun was not paramount in the hierarchy of the village but Mrs Webb, though much frowned upon with her garden of gnomes, was tolerated, since Mrs Webb was part of the occasional staff of the Old Manor and therefore untouchable.

Two

DORCAS FAIRBROTHER REMOVED her hands from the keyboard, placed them in her lap, and waited for the visitor to be shown in. She closed her eyes momentarily after watching her employer exit the room. In the matter of Miles's prathood, she thought, Oh My Giddy Aunt does not come near it. If there were a bigger, meaner prat living in Lufferton Boney, then Dorcas had yet to meet him. Miles took the laurels. Prat of Prats. She put her hands to her mouth to suppress a laugh, which was a shame as laughing did not come very easily to Dorcas these days. But Miles must never suspect her true feelings about him. That would never do. Unfortunately for Dorcas, she relied on him for a living and for the little portion left over that she put away in her building society account every month.

Dorcas Fairbrother sometimes, but not very often nowadays, considered how different it might have been. Almost five years ago she had been engaged to Robin Whittington, Miles's brother. And if giddy aunts did not come into it, chalk and cheese certainly did. It was hard to imagine two less similar human beings, and that they were brothers made it all the more remarkable. Miles, the younger by two years, was tall and thin, not given to kindness, pale of eye, thin of lip and of a waspish temperament. Robin had a cheerful, easy nature, willing to help anyone and on the whole always thought the glass was half full. Miles was a musician by training, a pianist and a violinist, neither of which instruments he played with any great feeling or warmth; in consequence, they produced for him a very thin living. He had not touched either instrument since he gained his parental inheritance. Robin, who in most regards was a loyal brother, said once (when he'd had more than two pints of Old Romany) that his brother was to music what an accountant was to poetry (and Dorcas, who had not had more than half a pint of Old Romany) did not like to point out the flaw in the argument called T. S. Eliot. But so it was. The little baby grand sat under its dustsheet in the small music room at the back of the house, and the violin was wrapped in faded brown velvet and stuffed inside a trunk. Dorcas might have played the piano but it was valuable and – as Miles said – best not to tinker with an heirloom. Miles, however, did tinker with anything that met with his disapproval or blocked his finances in any way. And currently, at the top of the pile was that contemptuous word *heritage*.

Robin, to whom *heritage* meant something positive, might have been found in a basket on his parents' doorstep, so different was he from his brother. To Robin, nature was all and he had trained as a doctor of medicine; after qualifying he specialised in tropical medicine. He started to conduct his research in South America and – almost inevitably, as he told Dorcas – graduated to becoming more of an explorer, a bit of a botanist, and a touch political seeing that the world was under attack from human greed and corruption.

He was a young man with a heart and a mission and he recognised early on that the planet he loved was in trouble and that its wildlife, its whole life, depended on people like him publicising the fact. He knew that the more he found to prove that the key to survival was natural resources, the better for all. The greatest excitement in his professional life was to discover, at the age of only twenty-nine, that the bark of a tree deep in the Peruvian hinterland contained the possible cure for Winterton's Disease. He travelled to far off places and he wrote newspaper articles, books, pamphlets – he gave lectures at the Royal Geographical Society, he talked on television and on radio. He was full of energy and hope and governments and businesses without consciences would have quite liked him to disappear off the face of the earth. He had even had threats. But still he continued. One national newspaper called him Superman, which had made Robin blush and Dorcas puff up like a boastful toad. Here Dorcas paused to allow a smile at the memory – and not a bad looker, either. Shorter and more muscular than his brother, he had crisp reddish curls that could somehow never be tamed, and a bright, open face that Dorcas – entirely inexplicably – once found it impossible not to kiss on a fairly regular basis.

How Dorcas tried not to kiss that face and how she forced herself to walk away from that face on at least two occasions! But she failed. Robin was the last thing she needed: a traveller like her parents, crazy about landscape and green cultivation, a man without dust on his shoes – no moss on any part of him – but – it seemed – he was the first thing she wanted. And despite her doubts, she got him. He was the first stable adult she had ever dared to be close to. And look what happened.

Dorcas was the child of neo-hippies; she was brought up – or rather brought herself up – largely in the back of her parents' old .VW van as it traversed what her mother and father liked to call Glorious Albion. Dorcas had no formal education, no formal health care, no formal parenting and, as many who have been left to their own devices in such matters will, she developed a strong set of rules for herself, a set of moralities and a way through the confusions of life that helped her grow into a remarkably sane and balanced young woman. A young woman who had seen the side of life called itinerant and riddled with fecklessness and would have none of it. No. What Dorcas wanted was to be settled and calm and ordinary. To do this she needed an income, and to get that – she must have a job. But of course she was a young woman without any qualifications whatsoever, unless having read an enormous number of books counted as a qualification which of course it did not. Even so, at the age of seventeen she said goodbye to her parents (somewhere on Barra) and went south.

Over the years she had saved a small sum in her Post Office account, from fruit picking, helping out at stables and the like, and now she withdrew it, stayed at the YWCA in London, and paid for six typing lessons. The Geographical Society was looking for a clerk typist. Dorcas applied, talked at the interview about aspects of the British landscape instead of her typing speeds – and was successful. The rest, as you might say, was history. For almost immediately, bouncing into the office with a request for an envelope, came Robin.

Shortly after the envelope incident, and after Dorcas had attempted to remain aloof for a considerable amount of time – at least a week – Robin told her that his most exciting moment in all the world was finding the tree with the bark for the Winterton's until he met her. That moment, he said, was even more wonderful. He could never bring himself, he said, to use the envelope that had brought them together. He said this in a very surprised voice. And Dorcas received the news in a very surprised way. For she instantly said that she, too, felt the same and that, as far as she was concerned, he could have as many envelopes as he wanted from her.

So Robin loved Dorcas and she loved him and he understood her doubts about the roving way of things. 'My parents . . .' she began to say, apologetically, but he put his finger to her mouth. 'I know,' he said, 'and in any case it's probably about time I stayed in one place.' For Dorcas he was prepared to set aside his long absences and dangerous pursuits and become more circumspect. 'You,' he told her, 'are too precious to stay so far away from.' One of Dorcas's favourite books was *Sir Gawain and the Green Knight*. She was hooked. Sadly it became much more akin to a romantic history as Robin never returned from South America.

Of course, Robin had said, there would be other, smaller trips over the coming years, but this one, funded by the Bolivian government and designed to get his advice and help on land settlements for peasants along its borders, would be his last big expedition. The peasants were better at looking after the land than the greedy landowners, and these areas of South America were precious. He would then come back and after they married he would do more broadcasting, more writing and more gentle film-making, and he would leave the big stuff to the next generation – it was time to settle down. Robin was thirty-three, Dorcas was twenty-five and the future looked wonderfully golden for both of them.

So, while Dorcas went down to stay at Lufferton Boney, and lived in the Squidge, a tiny house on four floors, but just one room and a passageway wide, built in the space between the The Orchard House and what was now Beautiful Bygones but was then the butcher's, Robin set off for his last great adventure. Robin had inherited Hill View House from his parents, and Miles owned the Squidge. You could not fit a baby grand into the Squidge, so Miles continued to live in the parental home and the Squidge was let to seasonal holidaymakers who wished to see the Gnome and the tumuli and other ancient sites all around. Miles made a decent profit from the letting, lived free with his brother who paid most the bills, and resented the whole situation like fury. This he kept to himself.

While Robin was away Miles asked Dorcas to help him with sorting and cataloguing or dispersing his parents' library which – he hoped – might be valuable and was, unsurprisingly, made up of books on music (his mother was a music historian) and the flora and fauna of the world (his father had been something of a naturalist which is how Robin's interest had been kindled). Miles found Dorcas very useful. She found Miles astonishingly unlike his brother, but who cared? It would not be for ever. She was engaged now and soon she would be mistress of the house.

And then, one day, almost five years ago, the news came that Robin had vanished. The jungle, it seemed, had eaten him up. One moment he had been investigating the viability of setting up farms without hurting the amazing biodiversity in Central America: the next it appeared to have killed him. If not the jungle, then another malign force. The threats of earlier years were remembered. It was known that a handful of rich Bolivians owned more than the rest of the poor peasantry put together – and wanted to keep it that way. There were bandits who worked for them, and bandits who worked for themselves. Who knew what or which was the source of Robin's disappearance? Dorcas preferred to think it was Nature rather than Man that took him from her. If so, being jungle, there was nothing of him to send home to England but his equipment left back at base which went to the Geographical Society, a boot that was found near where he was last seen, his well-used leather hat, ditto and, tellingly, Dorcas's photograph. These last three items arrived with Dorcas some weeks after the announcement that he had disappeared.

For the first few years, while the Foreign Office and newspapers took up the story and looked for Robin, she kept the boot and the hat, into which she tucked her photograph, ready for when he walked back through the door. Then, on the first day of this New Year, she put them away and admitted that he was gone for good. Or at least, gone for good insofar as the FO was concerned. But Dorcas would not entirely accept the disappearance until she had travelled to where Robin was last seen and had stood in that place herself. Only then, she thought, would she know. Hence the small amount of savings she put away each month. Unfortunately, Miles did believe Robin was gone for good and immediately raised her rent.

Nothing much mattered after Robin's disappearance except the hope that she would one day, at the very least, get to see where he last had trod. Once she had done that, she felt, she could move on. So, for now, Dorcas remained in Lufferton Boney, which she found suitable for her mood, being a village of disparate beings none of whom seemed really happy – and she continued to live in the Squidge, and went on working for Miles, for a (not very big) salary. After years of living like that, she thought it was probably how she would end her days. The library in Hill View had long been sorted out, but Miles was now wealthy enough to indulge himself in whatever fool's errand took his fancy, to enjoy having a secretary to shore him up in all his money-making fantasies, and Dorcas – who took a sour view of such pomposity – simply carried on. That Miles stood to inherit Robin's not inconsiderable estate, and did not offer Dorcas a share of it, was something that had not gone undetected by the rest of the village. They took Dorcas to their troubled hearts (even eating her chocolate brownies which were little better than Winifred's). Miles made sure that her rent to him was a tad lower than his salary to her so that she could survive but never be free. I am like Rapunzel, she thought, and immediately – because the thought was so fanciful – had her very long hair cut short.

Miles's greatest annoyance came from the inclusion in the family inheritance of the Gnome of Pound Hill and the requirement, through some agreed codicil, to keep it in good order. He had not done so and the powers that be in his despised world of heritage were making noises. It was part of his duty. And if he did not look after the site properly, they would do it for him and send him the bill accordingly. It would be substantial. Or they would buy the Hill for the nation. Perish the thought. Miles could imagine the armies of heritage-seekers trotting past his window, chucking their crisp packets and drinks cartons and who knew what else over his garden wall. Not to mention the infuriating sight of them queuing up to buy tickets. Money that should and could be his. It seemed there was no way out of it. Though Miles fumed and fought, he was stuck. As Dorcas pointed out, he was in a lose–lose situation. If he sold the Hill and its priapic incumbent once it was provenly his, he would have to sell the house, and vice versa. And he did not wish to sell the house. That was a socialist government for you. In Miles's opinion all British governments were socialist and much of the current cabinet were next in line to Lenin. No, it was a terrible dilemma. But at least Dorcas had stopped saying that it would all be resolved when Robin came home. She seemed to have given up on that one at least.

Dorcas watched this struggle of Miles's with the hard eyes of something considerably less than Christian charity. In fact, not to put too fine a point on it, she enjoyed every minute of his predicament and – where possible – dripped a little lemon juice on the wound from time to time. Not much made her smile nowadays but this fed a newly discovered vein of sour amusement within her. Miles had tried, and failed, to find a way to make money out of the Hill, but the Gnome was said to be an aid to fecundity and he was, by custom, free for access by the public at large. Therefore Miles could not charge admission. If they could do it at Kew Gardens, he raged at Dorcas, why couldn't he do it here? One day Kew was the National Botanical Gardens, a so-called lung for poor Londoners at a penny a go, the next they had changed all that and it cost a fortune to get in. Clever. Very clever.

It saddened him that there was money to be made and he longed to make some, but it needed not only capital but endorsement. The heritage people would find a way if they took it on. They would put up a visitor centre and open a shop selling tea towels and there would be a paying car park. Miles could not compete with an investment like that. It was a case of people before property all over again and it seemed he was stuck with it. Filth, was what he thought it all. Plain filth. 'Where there's muck there's brass,' said Dorcas, and suggested that he get an ice-cream van and sell lollies and whirly-whips at the foot of the Hill. She then watched with delight as he did exactly that. His fury at having a visit from Health and Safety who immediately shut him down was highly satisfactory.

This morning she had him well wound up before the expected visit of Molly Bonner, by telling him that the county heritage people had voted to take on the upkeep of Curling Castle – the part of an Iron Age fort that remained on the Brandon Estate some ten miles away – without requiring a penny from the owners. Miles turned quite pink and Dorcas was quite pleased and composed a letter on his behalf to complain. She knew very well that Miles had not done right by her but there was precious little she could do about it except enjoy this status of gadfly. She suspected, as the years went by, that her once kindly nature was turning into something sour and sharp or troubled – as troubled, it seemed, as everyone else's appeared to be in Lufferton Boney.

Contemplating these things, Dorcas waited for Miss Bonner to arrive and looked around the room. How different things might have been, she thought. How Robin would have laughed at his brother for all this miserly prudery, for had he not promised that one day – when they were married – he would carry her up to the Gnome of Pound Hill and make sure of their family's future expansion? Or, at least, she smiled, make sure of *her* future expansion. Now she patted her very flat stomach with her ringless hand (the engagement ring was to be made smaller and, mysteriously, never came back to her). No, she had not grown rounder with the years, if anything she had grown more angular; her nose was becoming decidedly beaky, her lips, once nice and curved and full seemed to be shrinking, and her cropped hair, that had once been thick and dark brown, now showed flecks of grey. She might not yet be thirty but a body responds to love, she thought, putting her hands back on the keyboard, and if a body does not receive love it dries up and eventually floats away like dust. Which is what, she guessed, she was doing. And with no real desire to stop the process ... But for now and for a while she had something amusing to occupy her: Miles's pursuit of the Gnome of Pound Hill. She hoped Miss Molly Bonner was not going to scupper that little diversion.

The expected knock came. Miles took a deep breath, squared his thin shoulders, marched out to the hallway and opened the door. Whereupon he blinked.

'Mr Whittington, I presume?' The visitor looked up at him from the step and laughed a bubbly laugh. Miles did not. 'May I come in?' said the visitor.

She brushed past Miles, who remained totally silent and gaping. He turned. Molly gave him a smile of unsurpassed good humour and put her head on one side as if questioning where she should go now. Just at that moment out rang the querying voice (for she knew how to raise her voice when she wanted) of Dorcas Fairbrother from the sitting room.

'Miles – did you want to call it a penis, or would you prefer something a little more vernacular? John Thomas, perhaps? Winkie? No – no, winkie sounds a little bit small and it's not at all small, is it? I mean that's the whole point of writing this letter – because it's absolutely *huge* ... Big winkie? What do you think?' Dorcas, convulsed with silent laughter, could not go on.

Hearing this as if from a far-off land, Miles struggled to talk over her piercing voice with equal loudness. Instead his voice was but a squeak. 'Not now, Dorcas,' he said. 'We have a visitor.' And he gestured towards the room whence the voice had rung.

Obediently Molly stepped along the passageway and through the door, just as Dorcas began to call out anew. 'Sorry, Miles, didn't quite catch that – which adjective did you . . .?' Then, mercifully, she ceased to speak. Someone vibrant and full of vitality had entered the room.

'Hallo,' she said, 'I'm Molly Bonner. And I just love the idea of a Big Winkie. Puts that butch old Gnome in his place. Fancy advertising himself like that.' Both women laughed.

Dorcas was both astonished at the visitor and astonished at the laughter between them. She had longed for this moment to arrive. Longed for it. She had imagined a tall, thin spinster with an earnest expression and an odd assortment of garments, mostly cardigans, of earthy hue. She had expected the woman to be shockable, or at least, sensitive, and for the whole silly thing to become a farce and a failure. Now here was Miss Bonner, of approximately the same age as Dorcas, with nothing of the earnest expression or earthy hue and certainly no shockability about her. Suddenly Dorcas was having trouble with her diction. Fleetingly she wondered why Miles had not informed her that Miss Bonner was young. He must have known it from looking up her family tree. But Dorcas realised that he probably only searched for her bloodline, not her birthday. This must be so, because he looked just as surprised as Dorcas.

Both women ceased laughing and Dorcas attempted to sound businesslike. 'Miss Bonner?' she said, sounding quite hoarse in her attempts to sound serious, 'Are you—'

'I am,' said Molly Bonner happily. 'Miss Bonner the archaeologist's granddaughter . . . My grandmother always turned Miss Bun the Baker's daughter into that when we played Happy Families.'

Dorcas smiled, feebly. This was not going to progress in the way she had expected. Dorcas had expected to run rings around both Miles and Miss Bonner, to wind them up, to have a bit of fun. Now she felt ashamed of herself. It was mean, unkind, *sour*. She must revert to being a nice person again. She *must*. It was never too early to begin to avoid becoming a sour spinster. Life dealt its blows and you must survive them, she reminded herself, and take pleasure in the little happinesses. And today – she looked at Miss Bonner the archaeologist's granddaughter in all her colourful glory – today might have brought her quite a big happiness. She would try again.

It was as if the newcomer could read her thoughts. They both seemed to draw breath and to make a decision to like each other. The two women shook hands, Molly firmly, Dorcas firmly, and they smiled.

Miles was still standing by the doorway and gaping. That was nice, thought Dorcas, he'd scuttled himself. The visitor, removing a pile of old parish magazines from a little Victorian armchair and putting them carefully on the chair that faced the window and the sun, sat down. 'Don't mind, I hope,' she said. 'But these boots are killing me.'

Miles, who had swallowed and swallowed and now felt in command of his speaking faculties again, arrived back in the centre of the room only to see the visitor's slender outstretched leg, quite naked from well above the knee and with the boot half dangling from its foot. He immediately lost the power of speech again.

'Nice boots,' said Dorcas, admiringly.

'No gain without pain,' said Molly.

'I know what you mean,' said Dorcas, with feeling. The two young women exchanged a conspiratorial glance. Against the ancient faded petit point covering of the chair, the newcomer looked as radiant as a tinkerbell fairy. Dorcas gave up all thoughts of mischief and decided that she liked her. It really was very acceptable to have a little vanity where footwear was concerned. Painful footwear was part of being a woman, like childbirth. How Dorcas would love a pair of boots like those.

'I think,' said Molly Bonner, 'that aphorism might be applied also to the situation here?' She slid her eyes sideways to indicate Miles and then looked back at Dorcas. Dorcas, still smiling, nodded. If this young woman was a prude or a protectionist she disguised it surprisingly well. But then, the only thing Dorcas knew from their correspondence was that Miss Molly Bonner was an archaeologist, her bona fides all provided, and she had money. Lots of money.

Probably, thought Miles feeling both sour and wistful, the girl had more money than he would ever have. It pained him even to consider it.

All villages, no matter how small, like all families, have their secret scandals, their hidden skeletons in their polished cupboards. Lufferton Boney was no different. The village was not entirely proud of its ancient monument and it might have remained more or less unacknowledged for hundreds of years had not its presence been abruptly betrayed by an upstart squire in the early 1800s. The Gnome of Pound Hill, quietly forgotten by all decent, Christian folk, spoken of only as legend by the locals, was cleared of its grasses, emptied of the waste that had been dumped upon it over the centuries, and outlined in beautifully hewn lumps of local sandstone, the correct shape taken from a mediaeval woodcut that the upstart squire located among the papers in his attics (now lost). Since he was an upstart squire and had little pedigree of his own (money from emergent industries bought him the place) he thought having such a grand piece of landskip on his manor somewhat made up for the lack. And it did.

By the time the upstart squire bought into the landed gentry the Age of Enlightenment was surely over. The squire was free to make a feature of the Gnome in the landscape, much as one might build a grotto, and he spared the blushes of no one. The originators of the design, none knew for certain who they were, had not sought to spare any blushes as they cut through the turf to the chalk and flint, so why should a mere squire? The figure he discovered was more than one hundred and fifty feet long and, apart from his cap, which stood very upright, the Gnome was perfectly and shockingly naked. In the words of the squire of the time, he was equally upright in areas other than his cap – and a very fine example of My Lady's Whim. Decent local folk looked away and kept their eyes downcast when going about their business, but incomers were delighted to see such vulgarity. It was known to be a very good place to bring a party of young ladies, who could be relied upon to swoon sweetly upon their first sighting (and their second, third and fourth, too) of the figure.

If the locals hoped that the fame of the figure would wither and be forgotten, they were disappointed. In the years following its rediscovery a legend grew up, that the figure had magical properties for the relief of barren women. The locals now had something else to avert their gazes from: the couples who went up the hill to find out if the Gnome would oblige them in such matters. Some, though not the collector of rhymes and fairy tales James Orchard Halliwell-Phillipps (1820–1889), suggested that the function of the Gnome made it likely that the nursery rhyme about Jack and Jill going up the hill was based on its supposed powers. Whatever the truth of it, the village bent beneath the weight of its notoriety – and the publican of Ye Olde Hollybushe, as it was then, grew rich. Reviving young ladies with a little brandy and water and burnt feathers being one of his specialities.

But then came the agricultural downturns of the century and

with the advent of a fresh, young, no-nonsense queen, the old squire was buried and a new squire arrived who had no truck with such pagan amorality. The Gnome fell almost entirely from sight and from use. The villagers breathed a sigh of relief and went back to being unremarkable again. Until, that is, a certain Arthur Bonner, archaeologist, arrived with his party of helpers in March 1914. In his quiet way he was seeking a touch of glory and he had chosen the Gnome not in spite of, but because of, its notoriety. Arthur Bonner thought there was a great deal more to the figure than met the eye – so to speak.

Molly's grandfather was certain the Gnome was genuine but not understood. Arthur Bonner told the Royal Society his theories – but he wanted to investigate fully before he would enlighten them, or anyone else. The Gnome was not a prestigious site and permission was given. He raised the funds to make the clearance and the investigatory dig, and set about it. He used a party of local helpers initially but they had scarcely begun their work when the rains came down. It was said that the vicar of St Etheldreda's had thundered against the vulgar thing from his pulpit and urged his parishioners to invoke their saint and pray for bad weather to stop the dig, and she had obliged.

The story was possibly true for St Etheldreda was a saint much prized by Lufferton Boney though no one could remember exactly why. Some said it was to do with her releasing all the bondsmen from her land, some said – though less firmly – that it was to do with her happy mixture of love of life and piety. The church contained an anachronistic depiction in stained glass of a wondrously handsome and fair husband of Etheldreda, Egfrith, whom she had married to please her father, but to whom she refused to yield her virginity. His handsome, manly fairness with the sun shining through him on golden days, gave many a village girl something to fantasise over when the parson held forth on Sundays, and many a young woman was moved to whisper that Etheldreda was a bit of a gudgeon and that if she'd had half a chance ... Some saw St Etheldreda's as the great bastion against such a pagan and vulgar monstrosity as the Gnome, the building (fifteenth century and built over something much older) facing up to the figure as if it would like to box its ears. Well, supernatural or not, there was no doubt that the rain did wash away the first encampment of the Bonner party and they could not begin to set up again until April.

On Arthur Bonner's second attempt in early spring the rains stayed away and the dig began in earnest. Or rather the clearing of the intended area began. Villagers stood at the bottom of Pound Hill, some in curiosity, some in dread, and watched as the overgrown site was carefully cleared by a selection of their neighbours. It took time. Bonner himself was said to have decided on the plan to expose the Gnome when he learned that the Ancient Monuments protection people had started poking about and making noises in connection with the Hill. There was talk of an official purchase from the then owner which would have made the permission for such a project much less easy to obtain. In those days Arthur Bonner did not altogether care for the Ancient Monuments people, and they did not especially care for him. Nowadays it would be quite different. Indeed, Molly Bonner had much to thank the conservation powers that be for their agreement to her proposed new attempt on the Gnome.

In his time Arthur Bonner was seen as a renegade. He was not admired by his well-bred peers for he came from mining stock, and had his choice of site been more important they would certainly not have given him permission when there were other, much more worthy grandees of the profession available: Edward Warren, for example, whose knighted brother Herbert happened to be the President of Magdalen College, Oxford and a very good egg. But the owner of the Hill in 1914 took to

Bonner and was persuaded that the Gnome, like any other arte-
fact from ancient times, was something that should be investi-
gated.

Alas for the project and alas for the world, 1914 was renowned
for something a great deal more catastrophic than too much
rainfall in early spring; and by the beginning of August, after
war was declared, the site was abandoned. Tents were removed,
coverings packed away, marking stakes were gradually lost and
the impetus of preserving the nation's heritage gave way to the
impetus of preserving the nation. The Gnome himself, though,
became the charge (or some might say victim) of yet another
enterprising publican. Tommy Hanker (great-grandfather of Peter
who now ran the pub) saw the possibilities and privately funded
the remaining clearance.

After the Great War the new owner of Hill View House, who
had rather ignored the codicil pertaining to the upkeep of the
figure, immediately said that all trespassers would be prosecuted
and thought that would be that. But English villagers are a
cussed lot. Once they were told that they could not go up the
Hill and sit wherever they liked on the Gnome, they adored it
and said that they *would*. They spoke of the figure as their very
own heritage that no one should take from them. And a solicitor from the nearby county town (a new thinker) was brought
in to do what he could. He surpassed himself and found that
the clause stood and that said dwellers and their families in the
village of Lufferton Boney could never be denied access to the
Gnome. It was theirs by ancient rights and could not be denied
them. Not ever.

Each successive owner tried to stop the locals applying this
ancient tenet but, as anyone with a youthful daughter or son
will know, the more you forbid something, the more desirable
it becomes . . . People crept up the Hill by moonlight, nobody
prosecuted anybody, and the village remained reasonably well

populated. Try to take something away from the English villager and you will have a fight on your hands.

Miles Whittington knew this very well but Miles Whittington wanted the thing covered up. If you wanted to visit it you should be made to pay. It was too precious a resource to be so public and available. It was also vile. Miles Whittington knew that to plan to cover the thing up would bring protests from all over the nation (mostly, he thought sourly, from those who lived far away and had never visited the place in their lives, nor would, unless they could carry a placard and wear those offensive woolly hats and be against something) so he tried various means to do the deed discreetly. None worked. He asked the council to put a fence around the most visited part of the thing so that it could not be available except by appointment: Turned down flat. 'You are the custodian of the countryside, Mr Whittington, and as such you should take a pride in the monument,' said Mr Monk (who lived some eight and a half miles away very comfortably in the county town). Mr and Mrs Whittington senior, two in a long line of owners, had signed all the paperwork accordingly – and Mr Whittington junior must oblige.

Health and Safety would have none of it: Oh yes, they were very ton of brickish when the ice creams were up for sale but when Miles said that people were deeply, deeply offended by what they saw, Health and Safety said that was not the case as the activities connected with the place were generally conducted by night and therefore hidden, and anyway that was not their department. The police, in the form of PC Brown, community officer, simply rolled its eyes and winked at the prospect of mounting guard. When Miles said that sooner or later someone would die up there, or at least be badly injured in a fall, Health and Safety said that was highly unlikely as the activities allegedly connected with the ancient monument were generally carried out on the horizontal and very low down.

Health and Safety went back to the more immediate task of removing the village's conker trees. The danger of falling and damaging yourself on the hill was, they considered, nil. The danger of a conker falling and killing an old lady passing beneath the tree with her innocent little shopping basket was, they considered, high. The case looked hopeless. Miles owned a valuable resource, something people would pay good money to see, and he could not exploit it.

The only chink of light in the whole proceedings came from Dorcas who, after the ice-cream suggestion, wondered whether if Miles were to propose a project whereby there would be a proper little museum tracing the history of the Gnome and some artefacts from other local sites, and a visitor centre, and perhaps a small car park at the foot of the hill, he just might get away with it. 'After all,' she said, 'although you are not permitted to deny locals access, it does not say that you cannot charge for the privilege.'

Miles was so ecstatic at the thought that he did not notice the glitter of mischief in Dorcas's eye as she spoke. 'Dorcas,' he said, 'you are a woman after my own heart.'

What Dorcas thought at this statement was possibly unrepeatable. What she said was that he could have the Gnome covered by a protective erection (she used the term advisedly) and then charge quite a high entrance fee (for maintenance) if he got the proposition right. They could provide a viewing platform (she really was having fun here, and Miles, blind to anything but the hope of success, was easy to tease), which would sort out the flagrant locals' misuse of the place. Never again would anyone demand their ancient rights. Of course, he would need to build the museum and visitor centre and have staff there, lay the asphalt for the car park, staff that, too with at least one attendant – and provide literature – though in time all these costs might be recovered.

Miles spent several happy hours plotting and daydreaming and told Dorcas to get on to it. She most obligingly came up with some carefully adjusted costings. On reading the costings, Miles required an ice pack for his head, which Dorcas provided, and suffered a sensation akin to losing the will to live for several days. Miles was not poor, but neither was he *that* rich, and anyway it would hurt far too much – even when Robin's inheritance was finally his – to spend that kind of money. But Miles was also, unfortunately, a man with too much time on his hands. The fight would go on.

Dorcas wrote letters dictated by Miles, Dorcas made telephone calls at the behest of Miles, Dorcas attempted to get local radio interested, as Miles requested. All came to naught. And then a miracle happened. One beautiful February day, a gift of a day, with sunshine and hints of warmth and a light breeze that lifted the budding branches of the trees, the sort of day when hope can be rekindled in the most jaded of souls, Miles Whittington received a letter from Brewer and Gould, solicitors, of London, saying that if he were the owner of Pound Hill then they would be obliged if he would be in touch with them in the light of a request made by their client, Miss Margaret Bonner. Miles did so. Miss Bonner had a propositon to put to the owner of Pound Hill which, if agreed upon, would be paid for by Miss Bonner. A further letter from Miles to the solicitor produced no more detail except that the Miss Margaret Bonner in question was the granddaughter of Arthur Bonner, the archaeologist, who had once worked on the site of the Gnome.

An appointment was made. Miles was half ecstatic, half demented. The Bonner name was looked up on the Internet and found wanting, as Miles informed Dorcas. The assumption was made that any grandchild of Arthur Bonner's would be elderly and therefore malleable. Miles flexed his (very) metaphorical muscles. He would wrap her around his little finger. He would extricate the last drop of blood from her stone, the final squeaking pip from her lemon. That is what he dreamed about each night as he waited for the appointed day. And now this person had arrived and stones and lemons were as ash in his dreams.

This Miss Bonner was no malleable spinster, fluttery and unsure of herself. Here she was now, in his house, and it was all quite wrong, obviously. Although the Bonner person had not set out her plan, Miles's hopes for he knew not what were dashed on the rocks – this was by no means the kind of person he had been expecting. From the way she spoke about the wretched thing, whatever she was about to propose would be very much on her terms. Negotiations regarding covered erections, turnstiles, staff, tickets and car parks seemed a long way off. Miss Bonner did not look like the kind of young woman whom Miles could persuade, some might say bully, into submission. Dorcas, he noted, was looking equally astonished. He doubted if even her charms could win this one over. Damn. He was extremely tempted to turn Molly Bonner down flat, even before he had heard the full Monty, but a delicate word from Dorcas stopped him from making the statement. 'Wait and see,' she counselled, and the two women exchanged yet another look of understanding. It seemed, as he listened, that there was nothing this young woman wished to say to him that would help him one iota with his quest to get the Gnome of Pound Hill out of the public domain for good. Nothing. Well, nothing yet. One must, he decided, go forth in hope.

The wind had got up and cooled Pinky's burning face as he and Susie made their way back down the Hill. He had no idea where she got her energy from but it was disturbing (and flush inducing) to recall how her cries had caused a riot among Farmer Braddle's braver sheep. Most had kept a good way off as usual but, in the way of sheep, familiarity in one or two of the bolder variety bred the ability to ignore so that the rest came closer to the site. They could be heard happily tearing grass and munching away, very close to Pinky's ears, when Susie made a particularly blood-curdling cry which had the munchers jumping four of their even-toed sheep-feet right off the ground before launching themselves over and away at an astonishing rate. Straight into the knees of Farmer Braddle they ran, knees that were not so firm as they once were and knees which, if punched repeatedly by the blindly panicking heads of heedless bovids tended to give in gracefully. He and his knees collapsed. It was an experiment for the sheep to be up here at all and it was not a successful (or strictly allowable) one. Miles's charges were not peppercorn and the damage to the frightened animals made it pointless.

The ensuing scene had not endeared the couple to Farmer Braddle, nor had their helping him up off the ground assuaged his wrath. Susie's cheerful parting shot that he should 'never mind because they would make him a godfather' extracted the kind of suggestions from that potential appointee that had more to do, in Pinky's opinion, with the Marlon Brando approach to the role, than with the humble servant of God and babe. He could well imagine rage like that embracing the idea of a sheep's head tucked into the divan.

'That is *it*, Susie,' he muttered as they tottered down the Hill. 'That is the *very last time*.'

'Over my dead body,' said his wife.

'That could be arranged,' he nodded to himself, but he kept his voice very low. 'That could be arranged.' Pinky was upset. Until that moment he had never wavered in his love and admiration for Susie, even if he had wavered in other respects. But now he felt something almost akin to hatred for her. A feeling new to him and a feeling that, once experienced, justified his being upset. Life was not supposed to be like this for a married couple. They were in love, they had all the time in the world to indulge that love, but there seemed to be only one manifestation of it preoccupying his wife. He began to think of himself as *duped*. He began to think that he no longer loved his wife after all. But still he kept his counsel.

In Beautiful Bygones Nigel took his father his morning cup of coffee, with biscuits, on a tray and properly presented in a cup and saucer that might have graced the table of Jane Austen. His own morning beverage was made in a very large blue and white striped mug. You could, he thought, as he set the tray down, construe from its contents the natures of the two men. While his father enjoyed two bourbon biscuits, Nigel's piece of sustenance was a Wagon Wheel. He had never been able to give them up and Julie Barnsley, by way of showing her love, added a box of them to the pub food order from time to time – Peter Hanker did not notice – and Nigel was never without.

He looked at the wrapper of chocolate wheel: yes, there the covered wagon with its two rearing horses, there was the cowboy whipping them along in what looked like a race against certain death. It was a picture full of adventure and daring and always cheered him up, though he knew that he could never get that close to a horse. Horses frightened him. His father had attempted to get him involved with the hunting set but at the first kill, when he saw the purplish pink entrails being pulled from the fox, he fainted. Since the horse was fifteen hands high it was a painful experience in every way. He looked at the Wagon Wheel again and had only the most fleeting regret. In abandoning Julie Barnsley for his new love he would lose the endless supply of these delights. His new love did not look like a woman who would understand Wagon Wheels. He thought of that pink flouncy skirt again. But what was one small sacrifice to gain all that?

In The Orchard House Donald had slowly and with some dignity removed himself from the breakfast table and made his way to an upstairs bathroom where he sat down heavily on the edge of the bath and slowly began to remove his clothes. He left these in a heap on the floor and stepped into the shower. He took with him the copy of the *Lancet*, which he dashed under the water to see if he could remove the stains.

Extraordinary behaviour, he thought, Winifred must be losing her marbles. All over the tablecloth and the carpet the tea had gone as well as all over himself, and lucky that it was stewed. Through the steamy shower door he stared at the pile of clothes on the floor: almost new dogtooth jacket, a light blue crease-resistant shirt, a pair of good grey twills, one vest, one pair of pants, two socks and his dark tan brogues. Of all the items, these last were the only objects to suffer very little – he kept them polished – or rather, Winifred kept them polished (hah – foiled by her own hand!) and the tea would brush off easily enough. He thought the jacket might be all right, the trousers would certainly come up if Winnie got them to the dry cleaners in time and the socks would wash, but as to the others – it was to the bin for them. She'd have to get him a replacement shirt as well. He shook his head under the stream of water and realised that he had kept the *Lancet* there for too long; not only was it nearly clean of the tea, but it was rapidly disintegrating in his hand. So much for the fascinations of DNA.

As he stepped out from the shower he wondered if that might be a metaphor for his life? Disintegration. Winnie had never done anything like this before. She had – it was true – occasionally sat sighing at breakfast and he had – it was true – tried to avoid noticing it. But he was not a bad husband, after all, he had given her status in the village without her having to earn it in any way whatsoever; and if, like this morning, the sighing went on too long, he always enquired what it was about. And, it was always about the same. It was to do with Winifred being bored – he had enough of that in the surgery to know that this was a common problem among women of a certain age – and short of shaking his wife, and his patients come to that, and saying just get on with it you silly girl, he was stumped. He wished now that he had never taken Winifred to the local school's production of *Comus* . . . They had met Dorcas Fairbrother coming out and she'd said that ridiculous thing about it not being spiritual at all, really, but more a comment on Milton's sense of entrapment within his marriage. Winifred had got rather excited about this and sent for a copy of the text and read the damn thing, cover to cover, at breakfast without so much as one sigh. 'You should read it, dear,' she said, when he asked if she could bring herself to participate in the passing of the marmalade. 'It is full of a subtext that I think you and I might recognise rather well.'

Pills, he thought, going into their bedroom. As he walked over to the wardrobe to find a change of clothes he observed himself, naked as the day he was born apart from, obviously, some surface hair, but – Oh damn and damn again – he was still wearing his watch. Which dripped malevolent drops on to his foot. Buggered. Good watch, too. Pills would do it. He would have to persuade Winifred, as he might any patient, that removal of some of the surface tension from everyday life was A Good Thing and not likely to become addictive. Not if you were careful, anyway.

Later, as he left the house for the surgery, he heard his wife in the kitchen declaiming poetry. Pills, he thought, as he quietly closed the front door, to the fading sound of 'Milton! thou shouldst be living at this hour: Winnie hath need of thee . . .'

*

Miles hovered as Molly sat, barefoot now, boots neatly placed to one side of her chair, scarlet briefcase tidily on the other side, hands folded in her lap and looking most composed. Dorcas jumped up and said, 'What are we thinking of? Would you like tea? Coffee? Something stronger?' She looked at the agonised Miles and added with the slightest hint of amusement – 'Beer?'

'Oh nothing, thanks,' said Molly Bonner. 'Let's get on with the business, shall we? Crack on, as my granny used to say. I'd like you to take me up the Hill and show me this famous priapus at close quarters. It is a bit overgrown, isn't it?'

Miles sat down very heavily on the pile of books that Molly had removed and placed on the other chair. They and Miles tumbled to the floor. Montmorency opened one yellow eye and looked profoundly satisfied before closing it again. Dorcas, suddenly caught in a persistent bout of coughing, went to help him up. He almost batted at her with his hands, and his curt refusal of assistance was decidedly waspish. Molly did not take to this man. But she needed his agreement. She would be vigilant. She kept her face as straight as she could.

Three

IN THE OLD Holly Bush Julie Barnsley was slowly taking the cloths from the pumps with her mind on other things. You did not see much pink in Lufferton Boney, nor did you see much knee and thigh – except her own occasional and honourable exceptions. Come to that you did not see bounce and smiling very much either. And she had definitely seen a shadow of a movement from the window of the room above the shop. The room in which Nigel spent much of his time tinkering, restoring, polishing and anything else connected with the business that did not bring him into contact with either the customers or his father very much. Nigel, she knew, was hot-blooded. The wearer of the pink looked as if she, also, might be hot-blooded and might induce hot-bloodedness to surface in another. And Julie did not like this at all. Nigel was made weak by the feminine, this she knew, which is how she had pinched him from the Braddle girl, but he had prospects, excellent prospects, and Julie planned to keep those prospects in the vicinity of Julie Barnsley.

She took the last cloth from the pumps, folded it and bent to put it away beneath the counter with the others. As she did so she heard a noise behind her and managed to straighten up and move sideways just in time. Peter Hanker, she knew, still found her curves irresistible and although she did not blame him, neither did she feel it was right to allow him access when she was betrothed to another, even if it was secretly. True, she had once been engaged to him, so it would almost be like keeping it in the family, but it would not do for any word of scandal to creep around her until that wedding band was safely on her finger. Nigel was many things that did not make an entire range of sandwiches in the picnic basket, but he was not completely stupid. He was also fickle. She must do nothing to allow that fickleness to raise its ugly head. Peter was the past. Who wanted to be a publican's wife? Nigel was the future, and she would be a high-class antique dealer's wife. And have her own cleaner.

'Morning, Peter,' she said crisply, then went to open up. Across the way she could just make out the shape of Miles Whittington sitting looking out of his window, and the other pink person to one side of him, her face in shadow. It looked for all the world as if he were interviewing the visitor. She hoped to Jesus that he was not replacing Dorcas with a newer model and one who would hang around so temptingly.

'What's taken your eye?' asked Peter, coming up beside her. He too peered at the house across the street. 'That all looks a bit formal,' he said. 'Wonder what's going on. Looks like a meeting of some sort. I don't trust that Miles. Never have. He's up to something and it'll be something to do with the Hill and the Gnome.' For a moment his cheerful face darkened. 'Our birthright.'

Julie turned away from the door and went back to the bar counter. 'Well, I don't care what happens to that thing up there,' she said. 'It's not worth bothering about.'

Peter smiled. He did, she thought, have the nicest smile, sort of lopsided and cheeky . . . 'That's not what you used to say,' he said meaningfully.

She threw a cloth at him. 'You be quiet, you,' she said, and quickly removed the pleasantness of the memory from her mind. He peered out again. 'Looks like they're deep in conversation about something,' he said.

Ten minutes later Julie heard the clack of those boots back on the street. Leaving Old Jim Parsons to hold his half-full cider glass, she rushed to the door again. The three of them, Miles, Dorcas and the mysterious stranger, were about to walk up the

Hill, but not through the little gate at the side of Miles's garden: they were accessing it from the street, where everyone else began their ascent. Indeed, they had paused and were looking very carefully at the access point. How curious, she thought. I wonder why? When she returned Old Jim Parsons held out his empty glass. 'You were about to oblige?' he said, with a wink. She refilled it, still pondering what she had seen.

Up they went on this beautiful morning, taking the climb quite slowly for the sheer pleasure (in Dorcas and Molly's case) of being out on a balmy spring morning, walking on the newly springing turf of the season with the breeze in their faces and the sun on their backs. In the distance the last of the sheep were being nosed off the Hill by the Braddle working dogs. 'I thought there was to be no using the Hill as pasture?' said Molly.

'It's a new arrangement,' Miles cut in quickly.

'Well, it will have to stop,' said Molly.

And Dorcas, pointing to the last scrubby rump as it ran off to its fellows, said, 'Looks like it already has. Perhaps it's less a question of frightening the horses than shocking the sheep.'

Molly looked at Dorcas curiously. She looked back at Molly, wide-eyed. No one is ever that innocent, thought Molly Bonner.

On they climbed. If this is work, thought Molly Bonner, give me more of it. The Hill reminded Dorcas of happier times but she put away the little sadnesses that came creeping when she (rarely) climbed here and smiled for the pleasure of the day. Miles smiled back at her, thinking she was being conspiratorial.

'How long did you say you would want access for, Miss Bonner?' he called.

'Several months I should think,' she said. 'We'd hope to film it, too.'

'Of course.' Miles very nearly rubbed his hands. They could sell the DVD in the shop, he dreamed. He had been quite wrong

The Lovers of Pound Hill

about the lady. She might look confident and alarming, but she was just a little pussycat who rolled over and put her paws in the air. As soon as he suggested that the money on offer would be spent on protecting the site, Miss Bonner had agreed. 'Once I've cleared it back to its origins,' she said, 'it would be good to keep it that way. I will help you get the necessary permissions if there are any objections.'

'Have you any idea what you are looking for?' he asked.

'Oh,' said Molly dismissively. 'Just the original outline, I think. Not much more than that.'

Dorcas stole a look at Molly. She was wide-eyed with innocence.

No one is that free from guilt, thought Dorcas.

Miles walked on and dreamed some more; he would have his car park, his entrance turnstile, his staff – and his protective erection over the Gnome's most vulgar (and most interesting) part. No more trespassers committing unspeakable acts. All visits to be paid for. And everything to be funded by someone else. Miss Bonner's grandmother, it seems, had been a very wealthy woman. Arthur Bonner might have come from nothing but he had married a lady of fortune all the same. Some men had all the luck.

Just for a moment in the village below, the vicar, coming out of the bungalow that was now the vicarage, looked up to the Hill and saw in the far distance (the bungalow was at the far end of the street near the church) a man and two women pottering around what could still be seen of the Gnome's shape – a particular part of the Gnome's shape. He absent-mindedly hummed the tune to 'There is a green hill far away', thought better of it – wished it were far away – and refocused. Even though it was distant he knew that two of the figures were female as they were wearing skirts, one of a particularly bright hue – and the tall thin one was a man in trousers. He closed his eyes and – without much thought – crossed himself. He prayed to his Maker that those up there were not about to perform heinous acts in full daylight – and together. It could hardly be construed as seeking the gift of fecundity in any moral sense, not if whoever the man was had taken two of them up there. *Two*. Something must be done about the pagan thing. And quickly. He was very much on Miles's side in this.

The vicar of Lufferton Boney bestrode, he felt, two worlds. His bungalow, set near to the church, marked the demarcation line of the village Old and the village New. From there, all down the street and towards the Old Holly Bush was the old part of the village, representing hundreds – some might say more than a thousand – years of its existence. The two parts seldom mixed and their vicar privately considered them to be of two categories – hoi polloi and society. Very few from either elevation looked at the Gnome, let alone walked on him.

The vicar, despite wishing to bestride things like a Colossus, was a very short man and like many very short men (Napoleon, Joseph Stalin, the Marquis de Sade) he had a rather elevated notion of his place in the world. It did not help that his very fine and much loved by the villagers pulpit was of a height that made him stand on tippy-toes, but the bungalow added further insult. The new houses, the awful village hall, the noisy playground, the frightful new pub and the shop were all built on what had once been the garden and house and outbuildings of the vicarage.

The vicar, who longed to be in one of the older, more refined houses, curled his lip as he locked his door (you couldn't be too careful) and set off down the street without delay in the direction of Hill View House, giving Marion Fitzhartlett a little bow as she tottered towards him. 'Oh vicar,' she said. But, as she seemed in danger of turning round and seeing what was going on up the Hill, he did not stop. Here was opportunity. 'I have an appointment, Miss Fitzhartlett,' he said. 'But I will call at the Old Manor later today.'

'Very well,' she said, a little sadly he thought, and they both moved on. 'But I wouldn't make it much later than twelve. Not if you want to talk to my mother, that is.'

Marion's mother, Dulcima Fitzhartlett, lay on the grass among the first crop of daisies and turned her face to the sun. Her admiration for Dryden Fellows would never, ever, ever be requited, of that she was quite, quite, *quite* sure. He was everything that Harty was not. Erudite, calm – perhaps a little obsequious (Harty's pronouncing) but sensitive to her moods and desires. She loved talking about elegant furnishings and fine things with him. Next to her in the grass nestled a half-bottle of white burgundy. An empty half-bottle of white burgundy. Half-bottles, she had told herself as she removed this one from the cellar a short while hence and opened it, half-bottles were notorious for going off. Especially the ones with real corks. She was just helping out, really. There were so many of them down there.

She winced as she heard the sound of a gunshot. Harty was shooting the pigeons again. Good. They had already ruined the early lilacs. She hoped he would not get cross if he missed them because that was when he was moved to try for bigger targets – something to get your teeth into, as he put it – and he would not wear his spectacles. That was how old Sally the Labrador had met her end (merciful, really) and Nelly Braddle had only just escaped when she was pegging out the washing behind the beech hedge. Neither of which targets could be construed as items into which to get your teeth.

Dulcima rolled over once more, enjoying the unusually warm weather and picked up the bottle, holding it up to the sun. It *was* empty. Another would be nice. But dratty-drat-drat, just at that moment she heard the clop, clop of Sparkle's hooves. Marion had returned. With unerring eye, Lady Fitzhartlett hurled the half-bottle into a distant row of bay hedging. Not for nothing had she and her team won the cricket cup at Garminster all those years ago. It landed where she wished it to land and there was the faintest of cracking and tinklings. Spot on. Exactly where she had aimed all the others. And from where, discreetly, from time to time they were scooped up and removed by the butler and man of all work, Orridge.

On arriving at Hill View House, knocking several times and receiving no answer, the vicar dared to raise his head and look towards the Hill again – whence, very definitely, came not his help. Indeed, whence came great hesitancy at looking at all. Then he saw that the figures were familiar, or two of them were, and he sank on to the top step of Miles's home, got out his handkerchief, and wiped his face. Relief. They were not strangers in search of unspeakable acts, but Dorcas and Miles and a visitor. The sooner something was done about that terrible thing, the better. Pagans. Pah! They had nothing better to do, obviously, than celebrate that which should remain hidden. Lust, thought the vicar, lust was a frightful curse upon the land. Though it did, of course, give him scope for a very fine sermon.

Molly Bonner stood enraptured by the sight. 'My grandfather,' she said, 'wrote several long letters to my grandmother about the work he was doing up here. She was still at school, boarding school, at the time and he pretended they were from her Uncle Harold. She was only seventeen and he was nearly thirty – she was high born, he was low born, she had prospects, he had none but his teaching and his brilliance in his field, and they were in love . . . deeply in love. It was all very secret and *very* romantic.'

'Rather young,' said Miles.

'Girls married younger then,' said Molly. 'Not much else for them to do. But at least they were in love.'

Dorcas, touched by being on the Hill with all its memories and touched by hearing the word love spoken with such candour, said, 'How did they meet? If their worlds were so different?'

'He gave a lecture on Darwin in Edinburgh and my grandmother's class attended it. The teacher who accompanied the class liked what he said and the way he said it and persuaded the headmistress to employ him for a further three lectures. My grandmother was fascinated by it all, loved the idea of science making sense of things that the Bible said, and – well he began teaching at the school and they did that very terrible thing of meeting in secret and falling in love.'

'How romantic,' sighed Dorcas.

'Almost underage,' said Miles. 'She was a minor. He took advantage.'

Molly laughed. 'My grandmother says it was the other way around. She reckoned that she took *great* advantage. Anyway, it was real love. And then, in her last term as a schoolgirl, he came here and started the work on the Gnome – and he wrote to her as Uncle Harold – until that August when war was declared. In the autumn he enlisted and was due to go out to the Front in the following spring. My grandmother telephoned him at his training camp. Arrangements were made. When he next had his leave he raced up to Edinburgh, they rushed off to Gretna Green, and were married. He went off to the Front, was killed, and my grandmother gave birth to my father in 1916. My father married my mother, late in life, and here I am. In the steps of my famous grandfather.'

'Is he famous?'

'He is to me,' she said stoutly. 'And the world of archaelogy, *now*. But I don't think he wanted fame. He wanted to do his job and he wanted what he found with my grandmother – he wanted love.'

'Don't we all,' said Dorcas, half to herself.

'Not like you to get all sentimental, Dorcas,' said Miles.

She shook her head. 'Some of us, Miles,' she snapped, 'can distinguish between sentiment and love.'

Molly looked up at the monumental priapus that spread before them. 'Or love and lust,' she said.

He shrugged. The two women smiled at each other and Molly nodded. 'Grandfather wrote her some beautiful letters while he was here on the site. She left them to me. And his notebooks. I was only a child when she died so everything was put in trust but they let me have those things. I think they were more precious to her than her fortune – at any rate they have been read over and over again. I've always wanted to continue the excavation and now I'm old enough, wise enough and I can afford it.'

Miles all but rubbed his hands. 'So you want to return the Gnome to his original shape?' he said. 'Clear the edges, so to speak?'

Molly nodded.

'And why do you think this isn't his original shape?'

'Instinct. And my grandfather's preoccupation with it. I want to finish the dig,' she said. And quickly added 'Clearance' as if to correct herself.

Miles shrugged again. What was it to him if a young woman wanted to be so self-indulgent? At the next opportunity he slid beside Dorcas and whispered, 'Cheer up. I thought you would be pleased now we've got what we want.'

'Did you,' she said, and marched on towards the Gnome's hat, leaving him puffing behind. She caught up with Molly

Bonner. 'So you said you think the original Gnome might have been a bit different from the way it is now?'

Molly seemed not to hear the question. They had reached the outer circle of stones and were standing on the tip of the Gnome's hat. Molly Bonner gave the scene her absolute concentration and Dorcas decided that any further questions would have to wait. Eventually, having paced around the hat, Molly came to a halt and nodded. 'Different? Considerably different? Yes,' she said. 'Almost certainly. I'd like to find out how he really came about. Gnome is quite a modern name for this kind of figure – not even mediaeval, really – but we can probably solve some of the mystery with this excavation. Different originally. Do I think that? Yes I most certainly do.'

Four

DULCIMA FITZHARTLETT PRESSED her nose up against the glass of the large front window of Beautiful Bygones. She could just about discern the shadowy shape of Dryden moving around in the back of the shop, and she sighed. In the window was one item, a very pretty Georgian sideboard with polished handles, and set upon it was a little blue and white dish. She already had a perfectly delightful George II sideboard, probably a better one than this, yet she looked at the polished wood yearningly and wondered if Harty would notice if she brought yet another piece of furniture back to the Manor.

There had been an incident a few months ago when he entered the library and tripped over a pretty little footstool (Hepplewhite style, mahogany, *c*.1790) and had his foot in tight bandaging for more than a fortnight – he went down very heavily, did Harty once he was going – and had asked on several occasions with increasing irritation what yet another footstool was doing in the library. Dulcima had bought one or two others over the years from Dryden; it seemed the least she could do when he was so nice to her and talked about elegant things. Harty pointed out plaintively that they had far too many knocking around the place as it was, and as he only had two feet at the best of times, why should he need more of the things cluttering up the library? Why was yet another one there and – worse – come to think of it – where had it come *from*? Still Dulcima gazed through the shop window yearningly.

Footsteps came up behind her and stopped by her side. 'A penny for them?' It was Dorcas Fairbrother. In the days following her walk up the Hill with Molly and Miles she had been in altogether better spirits than for a long time. Something was shifting, she felt, even though she was not sure what.

Dulcima steadied herself against the glass and turned round, laughing. 'It'd take more than a penny for that,' she said. They both looked at the sideboard.

'How beautiful,' said Dorcas. 'What a lovely piece of furniture. How covetable.'

But Dulcima was seeing something quite different as she stared. Something she vaguely envied. She put her arm through Dorcas's and said, 'When George II's wife, Caroline of Anspach, lay dying, he slept in a cot by her bed. At the end she told him that he must marry again. He said that he would not, he said he would prefer just to take mistresses. And his wife rallied enough to sit up and say very loudly "Good heavens George, marriage is no impediment to *that* . . ."'

They both laughed.

'He never did marry again, though. He was that rare thing – a Hanoverian who loved his wife.'

'Well, he made very fine furniture all the same. I suppose I might be able to afford the little dish on the top of it,' said Dorcas. 'Just. If I paid for it on the never-never.'

'It's Spode – a bonbon dish. Do you like bonbons?'

'Love them,' said Dorcas.

'Then I shall buy it for you.' And without paying any attention to Dorcas's insistence that she should do no such thing, Dulcima entered Beautiful Bygones closely followed by a protesting Dorcas.

Dryden was in the workroom at the back when the two women arrived in the shop and, unusually, there was only Nigel in attendance. Up he came, wearing the smile his father had taught him to smile, and making Dorcas flinch as she was given the full benefit. As a smile it was not entirely successful. It might have been more successful as a grimace of bravery under immense pain or even a malevolent look of murderous intent. It reminded Dulcima of one of the leaden gargoyles that sat atop the down-pipes at the manor – a thought she found no stranger than the many others that tended to float in and out of her mind from time to time.

'I am so glad to see you,' said Nigel.

'And I am glad to see you, dear,' replied a slightly puzzled Dulcima.

'Not you –' he said, oblivious to the rudeness. 'I mean Dorcas. Dorcas – I haven't seen you to speak to for ages.'

Dorcas stared at him. He saw her every day as she crossed the street on her way to Hill View House. From the shop he could – and did – see everything. They never spoke, having nothing to say to each other whatsoever. They might exchange a hallo if they passed in the street, or a nod if they saw each other in the pub, or a shuffle of acknowledgement in the queue for the post office, but conversation was not something that had ever entered their relationship.

'How can I help you, Dorcas, hmm?' He moved nearer. Dorcas stepped back. Dulcima slid into the space between them and looked, birdlike, over Nigel's shoulders from side to side.

'Is your father here?' she said wistfully. 'I need some advice from him. I think one of our little seascapes is a Boudin. I like Boudin.' She paused for a moment, her blue eyes becoming misty and sad, 'When I told Sir Roger he thought I was referring to a blood-pudding.'

Nigel did not take his eyes from Dorcas. 'He's in the back,' said Nigel peremptorily. But he did not move out of the way.

Dorcas blinked herself back into action. 'We're only browsing,' she said.

'Oh no we're not,' said Dulcima.

She pushed Nigel to one side and wiggled her way around the furniture to the back of the shop, then went through the archway where she knocked on the door to the workshop. There was no reply. She knocked louder. Above the sound of the knocking Nigel said urgently to Dorcas, 'That girl, the one who visited you yesterday. Who is she?'

But just then the door at the back was flung open and Dryden stood there, looking thunderous, holding a shotgun, thankfully broken in the middle. In a voice of fury he called, 'Nigel? Nigel? What the—?' Then he saw Dulcima, went very red, retreated and put down the gun, returned and took her arm and brought her back – carefully – to the front of the shop. 'I am so sorry,' he said, his voice soft again. 'But I am not supposed to be disturbed when I am working on a gun.' He glared at Nigel who did not notice since he was staring imploringly at Dorcas.

After he had shown them the gun and it had been admired by the ladies – silver chasing, very beautiful, most rare, possibly the sort of gun Sir Roger would admire? – and it had been properly put away in the workroom, Dryden, adjusting his mien from rage to bonhomie smiled upon the visitors.

'We want to buy the Spode bonbon dish,' said Dulcima. 'I want to buy it for my friend Dorcas. *Not* a footstool this time,' she added with a roguish twinkle and a little push of his shoulder. Dryden felt honoured at the touch.

'You are the kindest of women, Lady Fitzhartlett,' said Dryden, lifting the item from the sideboard and holding it aloft as if it did, indeed, contain bonbons. 'It is an exceptional piece, exceptional. Set off by the very fine piece of furniture upon which it sits.' He gave Lady Fitzhartlett an encouraging look. 'Oh do call me Dulcima,' she said. Dryden froze. Dorcas covered her laugh with a cough. In a slightly less obsequious voice he said, 'And how, D—, Lady Fitzhartlett, is your . . .' he hesitated: 'lovely daughter?'

'A very happy girl. Practically a horse herself. And do call me Dulcima. I've bought so much from you over the years and we have talked of beautiful things so nicely . . .' She paused for a moment to dwell on thoughts of beautiful things. Her eyes, engaged with his, went swimmy, 'I think I can grant you that.' Taking the dish from him and handing it to Dorcas without her eyes leaving his face she was vaguely touched to see that he had a definite hint of blushing about him. How elegant, she thought, how delicately he colours, so unlike Harty who went the colour of fish livers under the duress of strong emotion.

'Thank you – Dulcima,' he said. It did not sit comfortably on his lips but he was immensely pleased to be asked. 'I'm so glad Marion is well. Aren't we Nigel?' But Nigel remained silent.

As Dorcas, after much demur, finally capitulated and accepted with thanks the bonbon dish, the son of the emporium, apparently unable to contain himself, interrupted her words with barely contained emotion; she could feel his urgent breath on her cheek. 'The girl?' he asked again, a little more forcefully. He very nearly grabbed Dorcas's arm and shook her, but since he retained his demonic salesman's smile and his father was standing at his side, he did not dare. 'The girl in the pink skirt,' he said through gritted teeth and in a stage whisper. 'Who is she? Dorcas, Dorcas – I have to know.'

Dorcas blinked and came back to the world of reality. She had been wondering what it must be like to see something beautiful in a shop window and to want it and to go in and buy it. Just like that. Amazing. Why, she even had to save up for her underwear. It was at moments like these that she tried very hard not to think of Robin. A woman without a man (or woman) tends not to get given many little treasures in her life. The Spode dish had set her thinking again. Treats, rare things, often did.

There was that lump hovering in her chest, ready to rise, and her heart was beginning to be just a little bit achy. Snap out of it, she told herself and looking up said, 'Sorry, Nigel?'

'The girl?' he asked in a strangled voice. 'In pink.' He had a wild look in his eyes but since Nigel's pashes were legendary in the village Dorcas did not take it too seriously. 'The one who was here yesterday, visiting you and Miles. Tell me who she is.'

'Oh her – she's an archaeologist,' said Dorcas soothingly. 'And she wants to finish the work that her grandfather, Arthur Bonner, the archaeologist, began on the Gnome before the First World War. She may need some helpers from the village . . .?'

'Oh yes!' said Nigel, clasping his hands as if in prayer. 'I shall be there at her side, digging for victory.'

'Oh no,' said Dorcas, hardly thinking about it. 'She won't be digging. Only clearing stuff away from the top.' She paused for a moment, had a thought, seemed puzzled by it, and then dismissed it. 'Clearing,' she nodded, 'that's all.'

The group stood in silence for a moment, each in their own way consumed by various kinds of desire. 'How interesting,' said Dulcima, eventually managing to remove her gaze from the slowly retreating pinkness of Dryden's skin. 'We should all help, shouldn't we? I mean, it is special to the village and all that. Has Miles agreed? How odd. I thought he found the whole idea of the Gnome rather disgusting.'

'She wants to continue her grandfather's work and pay Miles for the privilege. I think she hopes to film the dig, too . . .' Dorcas looked thoughtful again, frowned for a moment and then went on, 'Yes, film the – er – clearing process and pay him quite a lot, I believe.'

'Ah – money and Miles – *now* it makes sense.' They all laughed knowingly except Nigel who was enjoying visions of himself on his hands and knees with a trowel and close to heaven.

'Money. Quite,' agreed Dorcas. 'Otherwise he would never have agreed. But I trust her. She seems to know exactly what she's doing. Her curriculum vitae is impeccable.'

I'll bet it is, thought Nigel. 'So when does the excavation begin?'

Nearly dropping the Spode dish, Dorcas appeared to have a sudden revelation. 'Excavation?' she said sharply to a startled Nigel. 'Digging? Finish the dig? But that's not clearing the Gnome – it's –' Dorcas stood thinking for a moment, as if spellbound. Then she said very slowly, '*I want to finish the dig*, was what she said to Miles, not *I want to finish the clearing* . . .' She moved closer to Nigel who bore the brunt of her interrogation. She clutched his arm. 'What is there to dig up? What?' Her eyes flashed, her nose twitched, something was not right. 'What does she mean?'

'God knows,' he said, terrified. 'Would you like me to wrap the bonbon dish?'

Cautiously Nigel disengaged himself and crept towards Dorcas, fixed his hand around the Spode and took it away ever so gently to make it safe in bubble wrap. Beside him he heard his father and Lady Fitzhartlett draw breath. 'Talking of money, Dryden, shall I pay you in cash?' she asked softly.

'As before,' he replied, with equal softness. She nodded. He ran his hand, a little regretfully, over the George II sideboard. She was his best customer but the disappointment of her not buying it was eased just a little by her invitation to address her as *Dulcima*. Besides, if there were going to be a film crew floating about the village, business might well be looking up and it did no harm, no harm at all, to have one good piece residing in the window.

'I hope we shall see Marion here before long,' he said coaxingly. 'She does not seem – yet – to have inherited her mother's eye.'

'No,' said Dulcima, reluctantly following Dorcas to the door of the shop. 'It was the accident. Up until then they were fine. Though I rather like the slight offside nature of her gaze. I think it gives her an air . . .'

'Oh I did not mean – that is . . .' He turned a shade of blush again. She laughed. He was so very sensitive. Dulcima gave him a nod of goodbye and went towards the exit. Dorcas was holding open the door.

Dryden pushed Nigel forward and nudged him, rather too hard, in the back. 'Perhaps Marion will help the archaeologist in her digging, too?' said Dryden.

'I doubt it,' said Dulcima, 'Now if it were one of those white *horses* cut into the hillside, she'd be up there like a shot . . . But not Pound Hill. She's never been up there since . . .' Her eyes went shiny and sad.

'Ah well, er – Dulcima –' said Dryden boldly, 'I expect she will be thinking about young men as well? Wedding bells one day?'

Lady Fitzhartlett smiled vaguely again. 'She is but a girl, Dryden.' Then she paused and thought. 'Goodness. Perhaps she *should* be thinking about them. Yes,' she nodded, 'why yes – my little girl is a woman.'

'More or less the same age as my dear son Nigel.'

Lady Fitzhartlett nodded vaguely. 'You're right, Dryden dear, of an age . . . definitely of an age . . .'

Dryden looked hard at Nigel. Nigel looked at the floor. Lady Fitzhartlett and Dorcas prepared to leave and Dryden, with a look of irritation at his son, darted to the door to see them go.

'Useless,' said Dryden, when he had closed the door behind them. 'Absolutely useless. Can't you find one nice thing to say to Lady Fitzhartlett about the young lady? Oh, go back to your polishing.' Nigel needed no second bidding. He had just spotted Julie Barnsley coming in their direction and fled to his sanctuary upstairs.

When the barmaid reached the shop Dryden gave her a horrible smile, one that topped his son's to Dulcima by a long way, and turned the open sign to closed. Julie peered through the glass of the door but saw no sign of her intended. Now she knew something was up. Well, that was all right. Forewarned is forearmed. She strode off. Dryden came to the door and switched the shop to its open state. As he turned from the window to go back to the gun, he did a most peculiar thing. He grabbed the edge of a Victorian burr walnut card table (*c.*1870, damage to central pedestal £600) for support and, much as he had flushed earlier, now he drained to white. 'I'm doing my best,' he said to the empty shop. 'I'm doing my *bloody* best.' And looking fearfully over his shoulder he returned to the small back room.

Outside Beautiful Bygones, Dorcas just about managed to recover her good graces to thank Dulcima again for the pretty dish. 'Don't mention it,' said Dulcima, 'The pleasure was all mine.' But, Dulcima thought, Dorcas did not look the happy recipient of a delightful and unexpected gift. She still wore a doubtful, puzzled look on her face and it might have been possible to enquire what the problem was if Julie hadn't interrupted them. Julie did not look her usual cheery self either. She looked even less her cheery self when Dorcas told her who the girl in the pink skirt was and why she was here and that she would be around for some time.

'I expect she'll be staying at the pub. Good for business.'

'How long?' demanded Julie.

'A few months, I think. And we're all going up the Hill to help her,' said Dulcima, to try to lighten the conversational mood a little. 'Men and women of the village, all over the Gnome again. Who knows what his influence might not produce?'

Dorcas laughed but in her heart she knew that she had to get to the bottom of it – both literally and metaphorically. Something was not quite right. Whatever it was about, the girl obviously had a Plan B, when she had only told Miles about Plan A. Digs and excavation were not surface clearance. And the clearance of the Gnome's edges was all Molly Bonner had enquired about. Dorcas must, very delicately, find out what was really going on. It was something to live for. To find out the truth. A bit of action, something out of the ordinary. And how she yearned for a touch of that in her life.

Neither Julie nor Dorcas said anything more. They scurried off in opposite directions, taking their brooding faces with them and leaving Lady Fitzhartlett standing in front of the shop, staring at the relic of George II. So Marion was of marriageable age and she had overlooked this? It made her feel suddenly very inadequate. Still, it had been nice to do something nice for someone and be noticed. Dorcas was a good person. Dulcima found that she had tears in her eyes, though whether it was from thinking about Robin and Dorcas who had been so in love, or about her daughter, who had not, she was not entirely sure.

She turned towards the path to the Old Manor, vaguely – but only vaguely – thinking that Marion was now of a marriageable age – and *wondering*, wondering, *wondering* where the years had gone. Time for another little rummage through the cellar, she thought. Or maybe, if she had discovered a project today, maybe not . . .

Five

IN MARYLEBONE, Molly Bonner was packing. Into her enormous case she placed her favourite battiferro trowels (two), her handbrush with the medium bristles, her camera, her laptop, voice recorder, journal and compass. Unlikely that she would need a compass but it had been her grandfather's and she carried it around with her like a talisman. The rest of the gear was in the van: the markers, shovels, pegs, tarpaulins, wheelbarrow, plastics, heavyweight rucksack and all the other necessary equipment. At least, after the first few weeks, she would be working under cover which would help.

She had made a pact with Miles Whittington that, after the initial clearance, there were to be no gawpers or visitors until she invited them. She used the idea of outsiders destroying evidence if they came, but really she wanted complete privacy while she did what she had to do. Being out on that hillside day in day out with the elements thrashing her would make progress slow. When they had worked on Hullington's Roman villa she was wet through from start to finish, almost mad with cramp and steeped in loathing for the public at large. This must not happen at Lufferton Boney where she would not even have the benefit of a professional co-worker to keep up her spirits. Freddy.

Freddy was supposed to be helping and now he wasn't. First he let her down at Hullington. But she understood and forgave him for that. The opportunity was a rare one and he had to go. It is not every day a young geologist and palaeontologist gets invited to work on such a special upper salt water drainage site, so no help from him there. But now, just as Lufferton Boney was set to happen, he was away in South America. How like a man: the minute you really needed him he lets you down. She felt considerably better for saying this to herself although she knew in her heart that it was not true and unfair. He, like her, was committed to the work he did – and for now their work came first. It was a decision they'd made when they first met. But this was the last time that either of them would be allowed to let the other down. This they had also agreed. Love was a powerful invader of ambition. After this they would put their united selves first. After this, just like her grandfather's undertaking, it would all be different.

She hoped it would be a very big After This, one that caused a bit of a stir. Then she would be content. It was another of the wisdoms that Molly had learned from her grandfather's letters. Even if he did not manage to achieve it, he had set out to do his one last selfish deed before he put archaeology in second place to the woman he loved – but the country he loved beat them both. She and Freddy would do the same for each other. This was the last great project for each of them, the name-maker – then they would marry and be – well – different. It was to be hoped that she and Freddy would not follow the same path as her grandfather and grandmother. 'Let's hope the EU holds firm and Germany doesn't go invading Poland again,' she said ruefully, as she kissed him goodbye at St Pancras.

Well, she smiled at her precious packing, she was on her own and she would show Freddy – and who did he think he was to tell her that the whole idea of the Gnome and its mystery was probably nonsense? Men in archaeology always got their antlers out. He was jealous, that was all, and she would definitely, definitely show him by the time he came home. She missed him very much and she wrote that in her journal. One aspect of her life was very different from her grandmother's:

she had a profession to match his – and that would need to be accommodated.

The rest of the suitcase was soon filled with various items of clothing from lightweight cottons to the most heavyweight of outdoor garments she could possibly need in an English early spring up a hill doing a dig; or clearance, she winked to herself. She would arrive there at more or less the same time of year as her grandfather had when he spent his few months at Lufferton Boney; she knew from his writing what to expect. She had them all, both her grandmother's treasured letters from him and his somewhat cryptic notebooks, and into the case they went, carefully protected by a pink Tupperware box. If what he had written was anything to go by it was likely that she would need every kind of outdoor clothing before the project was complete. She trusted her grandfather's words – from the smallest details about oilskin kneeling pads because of the rough flints that could damage a delicate kneecap and the good sense in the sun of wearing neck shields, to the more exciting and more generalised suggestions of what she might find when she began work on the Gnome.

Her grandmother had never doubted that she would fulfil the task her grandfather began. 'All it needed, Molly,' she whispered to her one night, 'was someone who was as passionate about the work as he was. Someone with intelligence and who loved a challenge. No one took much notice of him because he was not the right sort. He wasn't a general like Augustus Pitt-Rivers, he wasn't knighted like Arthur Evans, he wasn't a consular official like Frank Calvert nor was he a formidable woman of means like Gertrude Caton-Thompson. He was a miner's son – and his brilliance could never balance that out. Wouldn't it be fun if you could do that for him now?' The little girl thought that the word fun was a good one, the rest of it she did not entirely understand. But she got the gist and she did love digging things up. Perhaps there was mining in her blood. 'Oh I know,' said her grandmother, 'that they have since made all sorts of reparations for him – but there would be none better than completing the investigation he started. For me and my memory of him as much as anything else. And you'll continue the name of Bonner in his chosen world – which will be one in the eye for any of those professorial dinosaurs if they're watching from on high.'

Her grandmother had laughed very heartily at this and though, again, Molly was not sure why, she joined in with the chortling and never forgot those words.

At eight years old Molly was already bringing in pipe stems, and sometimes the pipe bowl from the garden, or the odd shard of pottery that might (or might not) be very old. These little trophies she kept on the shelf in her bedroom, reminders of what she would do when she was a grown-up and able to choose. Her parents, for whom she was a late arrival and something, she eventually realised, of a surprise and then an experiment (they were both scientists and pragmatists), had privately thought that Molly's grandmother was getting a bit old and a bit wandering in her ways whenever she brought up the subject of grandfather Bonner's unfinished project. Molly's father had not, as her grandmother hoped, followed in his father's footsteps. He was not the least bit interested in digging up the past, he was a scientist who built on it. 'I never look back,' he said firmly, 'I only look forward.' Molly heard her grandmother mutter, 'Well more fool you.'

But Molly did show an intelligent and enquiring mind when it came to the history of the earth. And although her parents hoped she would direct this talent towards their own chosen fields of chemistry and physics, she did not. The past held her interest, even her heart, and the whispered words of encouragement from her grandmother went deep. But she did learn

73

MAVIS CHEEK

the art of applied intelligence from her parents, and applied intelligence when you are investigating the past is extremely valuable. When you are looking for an ancient needle in a carbonised haystack, it is advisable not to get sidetracked by the dimensions of the structure.

Molly Bonner very soon dispensed with the study of dinosaurs, considering them to be a very feeble attempt by her school to make archaeology exciting, and chose instead the more demanding pursuit of the study of the landscape through time. She loved piecing together archaeological puzzles from what the earth had kept hidden, loved the fact that its discoverers had had to fight for its recognition as a science in an age that was still heavy with religious superstition, and even more she loved the fact that they won. This was the passion that her grandmother wanted to see in her. Molly would one day go out into the field and find these material remains and interpret them for herself.

By the time Molly reached this recognition fundamentalists were denying the truth of what archaeology taught, saying that the Bible was right and that so-called evidence, buried in the earth, was the work of the devil. Other holy books were used with equal bias. A state was even declared as given by God, and land grabbed on the basis of the words of the Bible. If ever a young woman needed that final goad to get on with it, that creationist codswallop was it. Which only went to prove that even the most nutty of religious ideologies can bring forth something good, in this case a dedicated Molly Bonner who saw that physical evidence was irrefutable, even if a lot of dangerously potty people chose to look the other way.

Her greatest delight, as she grew older, was to look at the development of human behaviour over the millennia. She would leave the Palaeolithic and the Mesolithic and even the Neolithic to others. Lucy (*Australopithecus afarensis*) was a wonder, Ardi

74

(*Ardipithecus ramidus*) was sensational, but her real excitement began with the Bronze and Iron Ages. She was, indeed, Miss Bonner the archaeologist's granddaughter when it came to that. As she read his words they reflected her own feelings about the world of the past. Molly was hooked. And when she was also properly qualified – and not before, her grandmother warned – she could begin. A sum of money was set aside for this. Quite a large one.

The letters and notebooks, unregarded by her parents, came to light again after their deaths. Her grandmother showed them to her once or twice but by the time Molly was of an age to read them constructively, she, too, had died. The questions they raised must go unanswered. She was only thankful that the books and letters had not been destroyed. Her parents were coolly dismissive of grandmother Bonner's prognostications on the subject of grandfather Bonner's greatness, referring to his work as his hobby. Only after her mother's death, when the old home was being dispersed, was Molly sent the details of a bank strongbox – and there they were: a bundle of letters tied in faded pink ribbon, and two notebooks in her grandfather's meticulous, elegant handwriting – kept alongside a few other papers of importance, such as the deeds of her parents' house, copies of all their certificates and qualifications and some ancient and yellowing and wholly unexciting letters of employment from the fifties and sixties.

Molly was rapidly becoming accomplished in her chosen field of human archaeology but she waited until she was almost thirty before she set about her preparations to begin work on Pound Hill and the Gnome. She waited in the hope that Freddy's brother – a film-maker – would be free to create some kind of record of what took place but he never was and now she had decided that if she went on waiting for him she would never get started. Something would come up, she decided, and if it did not then she would just have to do the camerawork herself. Absolutely nothing was going to daunt Miss Molly Bonner from getting on with the job.

One of the things she found endearing about her grandfather was that he had the occasional lapse in spelling. For example, in one of his notebooks he had written that if he carried on doing what he was doing, and was right about what he would find, then he might be able to '*dispense with Marvell*'. And he appended several exclamation marks. Which Molly assumed to mean, and rather approved of as meaning, that instead of the revelations of archaeology being seen as some kind of conjuring trick or marvel, it would be seen as yet another source of truth. What was more, the film she intended to make would show how plodding and painstaking the process of discovering the past actually was. If the camerawork was a bit wobbly, all to the good.

Money talked, of course. Once she met Miles Whittington she understood the man. For all his protestations about protecting the site and the importance of keeping it safe for posterity, she knew perfectly well that he wanted to make money from it. He had every intention of exploiting its prurient aspect but she might, she just might, have a counter to all that . . . In any case, she would pay him a stipend for the privilege, and she would then be able to control the proceedings. She saw the look of pain that crossed his face when she said that she would pay him in three tranches – on arrival, after an agreed period into her work, and when her work was finally done. That way he would not be able to undermine the project before it was finished. Molly knew enough about landowners who began kindly and enthusiastically enough and who changed their minds along the way.

The permissions were granted, the material requirements were found, her hair had been re-reddened, and all was now in order to begin. She snapped the case closed, swung it off the bed, slung her hoodie over her arm, and dragged her way down the stairs and out of the flat. She was unlikely to be coming back for quite a while. That bed of hers, when she did so, would seem – she knew – like goosefeathered heaven. From now on it would be the hard-looking bed in the small front bedroom in the Old Holly Bush, and either the grinding wet and cold (with occasional sun) of an English hillside in spring, or the occasional baking sun and warm, driving rain of an English hillside in summer.

She climbed into the van (her adored little car was safely stowed away) and started the engine. It fired immediately and jerked forward as if it, too, could not wait to begin on this mysterious adventure. Molly had no exact idea of what she was looking for, she had no idea of where it would be in relation to the Gnome, or even if there was anything to find, but her grandfather's letters and notebooks implied that he suspected something was there, something that had not been discovered. There were hints that he had made a find that would change the whole tenor of the place. '*We should never dispense with Marvell*,' he had written to her grandmother, and Molly thought to herself that she never would. Archaeology was still a wonder to her and she intended to keep the promise she had made to her grandmother. But the first lesson she had learned from her studies, her own practice, and those notebooks, was that before you do anything physical, you should *look*. Sit and look and look and look, before you turn one stone. That was what he wrote. And that was what she would do.

Miles invited everyone whom he considered important to an informal meeting at his house. He wanted to have a very formal meeting in the village hall but Dorcas suggested that this might alert people to the long-term relevance of the proposal. Whereas if he invited people for a sherry and a nibble and told them that he was having the Gnome properly restored over the next few months or so and it would necessitate the Hill being off bounds for the duration – that would suffice. It would also remind everyone that he was the owner; well, almost. Indeed, she opined, it would be taken as a mark of his community responsibility if he put them all in the picture.

She said this last with what Miles considered to be unnecessary relish. He winced at the very idea of being connected in any way whatsoever with responsibility to the community – he loathed the concept – but Dorcas had a way of being right in these matters, so he conceded to her argument. It would smooth the path for the project's success. So far, all that was known was that Molly Bonner would arrive and take up her bed at the Old Holly Bush. Miles had felt it quite reasonable to ask for a small percentage of her rental from Peter Hanker since he had introduced her into the village, but Peter Hanker's response was shockingly unrepeatable. Still, the Lufferton Boneyites were now aware of Molly's forthcoming arrival and they waited to see what would happen, for while the village was used to visitors they never stayed long once the de rigueur photograph of themselves sitting on or by the critical spot of the Gnome was accomplished.

'It will be an exclusive gathering, Dorcas?' asked Miles anxiously.

'Very exclusive,' said Dorcas, who had insisted that Miles should hold a little gathering. Having obtained his somewhat tortured agreement, Dorcas then said very firmly that the sherry he provided should be of two types, medium and very dry, and should be of the very best quality. It would do no good, she insisted, to give them something inferior as it would only rattle them. They needed to be smoothed and soothed into agreement. Miles was still reeling from the bill. While he was still reeling she printed out a notice about the party and slipped over to the pub where she asked Peter to pin it up.

Why Dorcas was helping the scheme go ahead she was not exactly certain. Something about Miss Molly Bonner appealed to her; an integrity, an enthusiasm, a happiness, that she wanted to indulge. And possibly also her hair colour and unusual dress sense. It made Dorcas, who was not yet thirty herself, feel young again just to be around her. Molly made her smile. There was little of any of these qualities in Lufferton Boney and it seemed unkind not to encourage her. Dorcas was also intrigued by the project. The words 'dig' and 'excavate' really were quite wrong in the context of Molly's written proposal which used the words 'clear' and 'restore', yet she had spoken them both, she knew their full meaning when she used them, and Dorcas wanted to see why.

This new interest in the Gnome made her look at him again. You could admire the shocking scale of him but there was no getting away from the fact that he was ugly – a scar of coarseness on the landscape with his immense erection that rose up almost to his ears, and testicles which, had he been a walker, would have impeded his progress greatly. There was nothing of the spiritual about it, nothing of harmony with nature. Quite the opposite. He was, quite simply, gross. If Miss Bonner the archaeologist's granddaughter made him any more vital in outline the spinsters of the parish – of which she was one, alas – would simply avert their eyes or keel over with strange emotion. Apart, perhaps, from Julie, of course. Well – they would see what they would see. The invitation list was duly pointed out to his customers by Peter Hanker and those who did not visit the pub would hear about the gathering soon enough by word of mouth.

The Fitzhartletts strode rather than walked towards Hill View House. Marion had ridden Sparkle and would meet up with them at the end of the village street. Her mother thought that was taking the whole riding thing way too far and tried to insist that Marion accompanied the two of them on foot but her daughter employed her not-quite-with-you stare, and won. Dulcima thought that girls might begin life liking, or loving, horses, but girls should grow up into women who knew the place of their (four-legged) mounts. Besides, it would have been helpful to have Harty on one side and her daughter on the other, to balance her up should she need it. She might not know a lot about much nowadays but she did know that Miles's sherry was likely to be extremely poor, and had taken the sensible precaution of having a snifter or two before starting out, as well as keeping one or two tucked away in her handbag. She was still feeling rather concerned about her daughter's sudden spurt of age and apparent lack of interest in the young bloods on offer. Dulcima had a terrible feeling that she would have to forgo her lovely half-bottles and other stimulating delights if she were to get her head around the problem. Make me good, she thought, as St A. said, only please not yet . . .

As they approached Beautiful Bygones someone called out and Dulcima hoped that it might be Dryden, but it was only the vicar. Her heart sank. That vicar and his blood-curdling humility. At least she could overlook Dryden's deference since he was the only man with whom she had ever enjoyed a cultured conversation.

They had begun with Grinling Gibbons, some of whose carvings could be seen around the hall fireplace – and moved tastefully on. Harty was useless. When, having discovered the Grinling Gibbons, she tried to talk to her husband about him, Harty had merely said that it might be all right for Longleat but it was never going to happen here. To Dulcima's puzzled, 'What?' he said very firmly, 'There will be no zoo for our parkland. And certainly no gibbons!' Ah well. At least she would see Dryden tonight, if only across Miles's crowded sitting room. Though very probably Harty would want to engage him in conversation about guns and old hunting things.

How odd it was that Dryden and her husband got on so well together and how easy that made it to compare them since they were in each other's company so frequently. When her mother said, all those years ago, that Fitzhartlett would make a good husband, being rich, kind, hardly at home and not very interested in women *in that way*, her mother was right. Harty was, according to those lights, an excellent husband. But she had not been assessed to see if she would make him a good wife. She did not like his hunting friends, she did not enjoy vast meals full of meat and red wine, she did not find it easy to tolerate several gun dogs whipping around her ankles when she walked around the house. Nor did she warm to Harty's reading matter, which consisted entirely of the *Shooting Times*, *Sporting Gun*, *Horse and Hound* and *Country Life* (ignoring the articles about anything he considered fandangly such as art). If, as she once did years ago, she mentioned a novel that he might like to read, he hid behind the sofa and appeared to be having a fit. God knew what it had been like for him at school to produce a response like that. Beautiful things to Fitzhartlett comprised, largely, four-legged creatures that could gallop, though he occasionally looked at her across the top of the *Racing Post* and said she was damn fine looking. If she had tried to speak to her husband of Sèvres or Fabergé, which she no longer did, he would probably think they were horses in the two-thirty.

Once, after a conversation with Dryden, she excitedly told Harty that one of their eighteenth-century commodes might be by William Vile and all he said, without looking up from his beef was, 'Well who'd a thought it? Vile Willy. I was at school with him – taken up furniture-making, has he? Amazing.'

And he had been very unhelpful over Marion's fall. Dulcima

had been distraught, distraught. First thing in the morning she could remember the feeling exactly. In the day, of course, it was not so bad. Harty and his stiff upper lip? thought Dulcima. Stiff bally everything. She could have done with someone who knew how to bend occasionally.

Despite her mother's prescient suggestion that she might not be bothered much *in that way*, Dulcima had perfectly properly produced a son, Edward, who was cheerfully away at sea, as well as Marion, who seemed to combine her father's love of horseflesh with her mother's dreamy ways. Marion, while not exactly away at sea, was quite often away to the woods. When she had her little accident Fitzhartlett, on being assured that she was not dead nor likely to be, said that perhaps it would knock some sense into her. He was still waiting to see. He, too, thought his daughter overdid the horses – and that was saying something. It was after the suggestion about knocking sense into his daughter that Dulcima blinked once and once only and immediately moved into the adjoining bedroom.

Marion would have preferred to avoid the Hill, even its lower slopes, and she had certainly not wanted to accompany her parents on their walk to Hill View House. But some innate sense of duty prevailed and she agreed to come. Peter Hanker and Marion had an understanding about horse-tethering. She took him a pheasant or two in season (her father never noticed that a few went missing – skilfully pilfered before the count) and he provided Marion with safe equine stowage and, if required, somewhere to change her clothes. And now here she was, coming round the corner of the pub, looking reasonably well turned out for a party in a decent knee-length skirt (Hobbs, price forgotten, three years old, perfectly presentable still) that Dulcima had bought her and a small black jacket (Kenzo sale, £218) to match. Her wink was a little pronounced but it often was before a social event and usually died away a bit after a quarter of an hour.

Dulcima liked the slightly off-key nature of her daughter's expression. Nothing like being a woman and confusing people a little. Though the few swains that Dulcima had floated past her daughter's confusing gaze recently had not stayed very long to admire it. Rather like her father, Marion tended to open a conversation with something of a horsy nature and not stray very far from it. Her father read this inaccurately and put some of his hunting friends' sons Marion's way – only to find that while she might love her horses, she hated his hounds. It always amazed Dulcima that her daughter should have such long, straight, rather fine legs having spent so much time in the saddle – but then, she was a thoroughbred. The half-bottles floated off into the distance even more as she wondered what was the point of Marion having such gifts when nobody of a romantic persuasion ever saw them?

The vicar reached them, puffing a little. He really was the shortest man of God that Dulcima had ever seen, and his sermons, delivered from a rather fine seventeenth-century pulpit, gave him the air of taking part in a Punch without the Judy. 'What's this all about, vicar?'

'I'm afraid I have no idea at present. None whatsoever, Sir Roger, none whatsoever, but my guess is that it will be to do with the Gnome again. The goings-on tend to get going on that creature from about now . . .'

Dulcima turned her cornflower stare on him and he appeared to become even smaller. 'Goings-on?' she said coolly. 'Why, vicar, whatever do you mean?'

Fortunately for the vicar they had reached their goal and an answer was not required. Dulcima twinkled a smile at her husband, who twinkled a smile back. A rare moment of intimacy for which Sir Roger looked fleetingly grateful.

'No one seems to have any idea why we are all invited to this meeting,' she said. 'Mrs Webb told me about it. She's not coming because of her legs.'

Both men received this statement with as much intelligence in their expressions as they could muster.

'Quite,' said the vicar.

'Only one way to find out what's cooking,' said her husband, and grunted forward to beat the puffing vicar to the gate. He opened it with a flourish that filled the vicar with envy, and in Dulcima swept making a gracious if slightly meandering way up the path.

'Well I have no idea,' she said grandly. As if the lack of knowledge somehow gave her authority. Sir Roger gave another grunt possibly to convey the thought that she never had very much idea of anything nowadays after noon – and absolutely none by dinner – and up the steps to the front door they went. Sir Roger rapped loudly on the old panels with the head of his cane, an activity he enjoyed, never having had enough fun with his drum as a boy. The vicar jumped and the door was opened by an obsequiously smiling Miles. The party prepared to walk in past Miles's bow.

'Don't close the door,' called a voice behind them. The party on the steps turned to see Peter Hanker and Julie Barnsley half running across the road. Miles was not entirely pleased. Those two could probably sink a galleon of sherry and never notice. 'Who's looking after the pub?' he asked waspishly.

'Billy Webb's mother.'

'Who's that?'

'Mrs Webb?' said Dulcima, apparently without guile.

Behind Miles, standing in the hallway, Dorcas let out a snort.

'Billy is the potboy,' she said quietly to Miles. 'And his mother used to run the Happy Rest in Glastonbury.'

'Never heard of it,' said Miles.

'No,' said Dulcima, 'I shouldn't think you have.'

Miles gave her a quick look but, as usual, she seemed entirely innocent of irony. 'Is she the woman with the front garden full of gnomes?' he asked.

'That's her,' said Dorcas, happily.

'Ought to be thrown out of the village,' he said firmly. Mrs Webb's garden was on the same side of the village street as Hill View House and its array of gnomes – windmills, wishing wells and a variety of plastic artefacts connected with gnomery – was often photographed by passing visitors whose laughter awoke in Miles's breast quite the opposite emotion.

'She does for us,' said Lady Fitzhartlett. 'Legs or no legs.'

Miles opened his mouth, thought better of it, looked perplexed, and closed it again.

'Well – shall we come in or shall we stand here all night, Whittington?' Sir Roger tapped his cane impatiently and stuck out his chin. Miles was a very silly name for a very silly man, in his opinion. Might just as well call a man Inch.

Miles quickly popped his head round the doorway and looked back up the street before retreating into his hallway.

'Just waiting for the Porlocks,' he said. 'No sign of them yet. Come in, come in, come in.'

Unaware of being considered silly, in this as in so many other matters, Miles was all warmth and smiles again as he ushered the Fitzhartletts into the sitting room. He left Peter and Julie up by the front door where they belonged. Dorcas gave Dulcima a little smile as she went past, and might have smiled at Marion but she was never quite sure . . . How wonderful, thought Dorcas, for people to never quite be able to read your eyes and know your thoughts.

'You'd hardly expect me not to attend, now Miles,' called Peter affably, to Miles's retreating back, 'since it was my old ancestor who brought the thing back to life for the village in the first place.'

'And I hardly think that's something to boast about,' said Miles without even bothering to look round.

Peter laughed and squeezed Julie's hand as if to say they were going to have some fun, and Julie squeezed his back until she remembered and snatched hers away.

Miles disappeared into the sitting room, Dorcas slipped in behind him, and Peter and Julie followed. But while Peter seemed quite at ease, even with his rejection, Julie looked very far from it as she entered the room. Julie was on the warpath – and wearing her warpaint accordingly. Nigel had been elusive for days now – and it was time to take a stand. If he wanted thigh he could have thigh. Julie had made hers available in the form of a very short skirt indeed.

Donald and Winifred left by their back door and were in time to see Pinky and Susie in the distance stomping down the lynchets behind their house, which was the short cut to the village. 'Surely they're not coming,' said Donald.

'You are such a snob, Donald. Why ever not?' said Winifred, waving at them. 'It's a general meeting. Probably about our famously endowed figure. And given how much they use the Gnome, it would be very unfair not to consult them in any matter that affects him. Despite his singular failure to send them forth to multiply, they are his greatest fans.'

'Ridiculous nonsense,' said Donald, banging the door and locking it. 'Let's be quick or they'll catch up and she'll be asking me even more questions about how to get pregnant.'

'Ah,' said Winifred, leading the way around the garden path to the front, 'Pregnant. What a lovely time that was. You were still ready to change the world then.'

Donald did not know what to say to that. Was she mad? His memory of his wife's pregnancies was far from lovely. Indeed, his memory of most of the women who had passed through his hands with their pregnancies was nothing like lovely. Mostly he had felt very sorry for them, the gap between the dream as sold in magazines, and the reality as experienced in the nine months, being very wide – as, indeed so often were they.

Winifred, he remembered, had one of the largest crops of haemorrhoids he had ever, in all his years as a medical practitioner, seen. Like grapes, they were. Lovely? Lovely was not a Winifred word, nor was the linking of it with the memory of her pregnancies a Winifred-like connection. He gave a covert glance at his wife. She looked bright eyed enough, with pinkness in her cheeks and her hair washed and combed so he could not say what worried him. But ever since the teapot incident he felt that Winifred was changing – and not for the better – and he was slightly anxious about her. And himself. And the safety of his clothing. He had never in all his married life felt anxious about his wife. Until now. She had been the perfect doctor's wife performing her duties quietly and efficiently, feeding him warm and nutritious meals – if not very tasty ones – at the appropriate times and always knowing what he was supposed to be doing and when. And she had long since ceased to mention notions of changing the world. But there was a distinct difference nowadays and he did not quite know how to go about bringing it into the conversation. Despite the fact that she was washed and combed and looked as she ought, there was a restlessness about her, an unpredictability, that did not bode well.

They made their way with rapid gait in the direction of Miles's house. It was not something either of them enjoyed, being late. Donald had a try at relaxed conversation. 'Feeling all right dear?' he asked, as nonchalantly as he could. But Winifred seemed not to hear. On she hurried and Donald had a job to keep up with her. Behind him he heard the unmistakable sound of a 'Coo-ee', and knew that the Smiths had reached the village street. He increased his speed – good for the heart after all – and by the time he and Winifred reached Hill View House he was in far too much of a lather to worry about anyone; teapot-toting wife or barren patient. Up the steps they went. Donald rearranged himself to look the part of the respected village doctor, and in they were ushered.

Reaching for his glass of sherry, Miles was startled by more knocks on his door. He was convinced that the invited were now all assembled and that the talk by Miss Bonner – Molly – could begin. He was eager for this, eager for her to get on with it, eager for her to convince the gathering so that the payments could commence. He was also rattled because Dorcas was handing round another tray of very full sherry glasses and could not therefore be called upon to fulfil parlourmaid duties. Miles sighed, put down his sherry glass, and went out to open the door. There, in monstrous profusion, stood the Smiths. And while Pinky only looked like Pinky if perhaps a little more so than usual, Susie, thought Miles, was like a cloud, a miasma, an escaping emanation of purple. Her hair was tied up in a frothy bow of purple material, her shawl was knitted and of the deepest purple, her dress beneath it was purple to its very foundations, wherever they might be. But the crowning, or rather shodding non-glory of it all were Susie's tiny, purple boots with little black bows all down the front. It looked as if, were Miles so inclined, he could give her a tap and set her rocking, like a wobbly woman in an old toy room. He just about managed to restrain himself.

'You!' he said.

'Us!' they chorused happily, and with a smile and a nod they passed under his outstretched arm, into the passage and down through the door into the sitting room. It was perfectly clear that neither of them thought there was anything untoward in their arrival. After all, as others would attest if pushed, the Smiths were practically the guardians of the Gnome, or at least the couple who kept him most active. Susie smiled around at everyone and when Dorcas arrived with her tray, Susie smiled even more broadly and said, very loudly, that she had better not in case the Gnome had finally done his duty by her. Pinky winced, picked up one glass and drained it, put it back and immediately took another. It was all Miles could do to stop hurling himself at Pinky's florid person and punching him.

Taking Susie's coy comment to mean that orange juice was required, Dorcas asked Julie (out of habit) if she might have one, and Julie (also out of habit) went off to the kitchen, found one in the fridge and returned with it. Almost mindlessly she twisted the lid with one, deft screw, picked up a glass, and handed both to Susie saying 'That'll be one pound forty, please.' And Susie, who was quite as caught up in the whole thing as Julie, delved around within her purple and came up with the right money. Julie thanked her, slipped it into her pocket, and turned back to the group by the fire before she realised what had taken place. 'I am not on duty now,' she said, to nobody in particular and attempted to insinuate herself between Winifred Porlock and Nigel by the fire.

Nigel moved back a little. He could read sparks and he knew Julie was capable of astonishing rage. He had once seen her frogmarch Billy Webb's big brother Lexy out into the night when he had made a derogatory remark about the state of the beer and her part in it. He must be on his guard for although he had forsworn her, he could not quite avoid the uncomfortable yet titillating thought that Julie was dressed to kill. Or maybe undressed to kill was more accurate. He took his eyes off her knees and sought out Molly's wonderfully vivid hair and lips. The rest of her, in his opinion, was a tad disappointing and the pull of Julie's outfit was great.

If Julie's skirt could not match the style and bounce and pinkness of the archaeologist woman's, it was an honourable rival. Made of shiny tan leather it could, so Peter had remarked with a grin, be mistaken for a belt. Above this she wore a gold lurex top, and (to use more delicate language than the coarse phrase) mate-with-me golden shoes. If she had any doubts about the effect of this ensemble, Peter's reaction – a very loud whistle of approval – had dispelled them. The group by the fireplace contained Molly, who was staying at the pub and smiled a smile of recognition as Julie settled herself next to Nigel. Julie was pleased, if a little rattled, to see that this time the Bonner woman (she could not bring herself to think of her as anything other than an alien without a Christian name) was not wearing anything of a sensational nature. If you avoided looking at her hair and her face, she was very plain. Really very plain.

Molly, having judged the gathering well, was clad in an ordinary grey skirt that did not reach above her knees, and a white shirt. Only her vivid, sharply cut hair hinted at something not quite conventional. She was definitely outshone by the lurex and leather. But Nigel did not seem to mind the plainness of the outfit, observed Julie crossly. He – no doubt about it – was gazing adoringly at her – as he had once gazed adoringly at Julie (and, as she was aware, several others before her). A slight sensation of embarrassment suddenly blew a warm blast about her face and her most generously presented chest. In an instant she knew that she was overdressed. The Bonner person was not overdressed. The Bonner person was discreetly cool and wisely elegant. The Bonner person had judged the occasion perfectly. And if the Bonner person had not gained the whole of Julie's wrath before, in her sartorial wisdom she sure as hell incurred it now.

Julie, closing her eyes to the thought of her balcony bra and what it was doing, thought (as she tried hard not to do) of her mother, a Deardon from Wicklow, who married a Byrne had nine children and a dropped womb and ended up in a mixed ward not knowing whether she was washing the copper from her miner father's eyes or winding the cottons for her mother's threadwork. And buried in a common grave for want of money. Julie would not be like that, Julie would not be anything *like* that – and even though she knew that being a pub landlord was a reasonable living, and that Peter was hers for the taking, if her father was anything to go by the proximity of drink to the man was not a wise one for the woman. Money was happiness. A lot of money was total happiness.

Nigel's position was perfect on two counts: he did not own a pub and he did own (or would one day) a successful, respectable business. When she arrived in England Julie had changed her name from Byrne to Barnsley – the Irish not seeming to be overly welcome and, she fancied, the name sounded honest and reliable, just as she was hoping to become. Nigel's father owned the shop that Nigel would inherit, Nigel's father owned shares in all the big companies – in gas, in electricity, in water – everything – and Nigel's father was a gentleman. Now that's what *I* call security, she reminded herself, as she moved swiftly to his side and tried not to think about Peter and his very gratifying whistle. Peter, of course, being her employer, and for a silly bit of time her lover, knew the secret of her past, but he seemed not to think of it as unusual. Only one who had lived through the Tinker and Bog-trotter insults could know that it was.

*

91

Winifred gazed about her at the clutter of the sitting room and the view of the Hill beyond the window. She was on her third glass of sherry and – delicious as it was – she decided that she would merely hold it and not touch it. Sherry went to her head and knees more quickly than anything – except perhaps pictures of Sean Connery when he had hair – and she did not want to fall down. Or rather, she did quite want to fall down which made it all the more imperative that she stay upright. Donald was looking at her a little nervously, not for the first time, and although he seemed to be in close conversation with the archaeologist, she nevertheless felt that he was willing her to be good. Winifred hoped to talk to Molly Bonner about the area and the archaeology of it, but for the moment she kept this knowledge to herself. After two glasses of sherry, large glasses, she might have burst into tears at the memory of those far-off joyous days of having a career.

If she had not been quite so hemmed in by the very large and very hot fire she might have made her way towards Dryden, Dulcima and Sir Roger – who were in the throes of quite an animated conversation – and taken pity on poor Marion who looked extremely bored. Or at least, Winifred *thought* she might be looking bored. On the other hand she might be looking riveted. It was difficult to say. But then Miles was suddenly by Marion's side with that dreadful leering smile of his that was supposed, Winifred concluded, to denote the deepest interest in anything Marion uttered. Which was not, it seemed, very much. Dorcas looked across at the two of them mischievously. Someone had suggested to Miles that though the age gap was considerable, Marion had evinced a very definite liking for him in a way that was not altogether platonic. And while Marion might not be Edward in matters of future inheritance, she was unlikely to be left without a bob or two come the day . . .

*

Miles was definitely struggling. He opened his mouth as if to say something, letting his eyes move from one side of Marion's face to the other, seemingly hedging his bets, and had not had time to utter the first syllable of his suggestion that he and Marion might take a walk together soon. Of course, she would prefer a ride together, but Miles was not very good on a horse and knew he would not look at his best. He would need boots and a hat if nothing else, and such things were costly. True, it might be sprats to catch mackerels again (he looked anxiously around at the way everyone was swigging away, just swigging away) for she was a woman of considerable fortune to come, but still. His thoughts were broken by the vicar who popped up his head between them, somewhere near chest level. Miles glared. The vicar smiled. Marion looked at the ceiling. Miles's face was not entirely good to look at even though it had changed its expression.

Winifred, seeing the diversity and musing at the trio, thought that he really was suprisingly short for a man of God. 'What a pity no one thought to give him any hormone injections when he was a boy,' she muttered to her husband. Donald gave Molly a painful smile, nodded at his wife, said 'Ah well,' as noncommittally as he could, and turned back to his interesting conversation with Miss Bonner, but it was not the same now that Winifred had said something mad. He gave Molly an apologetic smile and Molly smiled back, but she did not seem much concerned by Winifred's non sequitur. A mature and honest young woman, he thought to himself, and rather strange to find such an attractive female bothering about fossils and the like. But just as he embarked on this interesting chain of thought his wife's words came back to haunt him '*Hormone injections?*' he thought. '*Dear God, no.*' Molly wondered, as she described the very first time she ever found a trilobite, what it was that had made the nice doctor suddenly seem so wild about the eyes.

*

Sidling as close to him as she decently could without actually elbowing anyone out of the way (though she might have liked to) Julie looked into Nigel's somewhat anxious eyes. 'Darling,' she said huskily.

'Oh, hallo, Julie,' he said, in the same tone he might use if he met PC Brown in the street. 'How are you?' Nigel could have wrenched his tongue out. He had *vowed* not to engage Julie in any kind of conversation. He wanted to be polite but clipped. This is what his father recommended for tradespeople who came to the shop: polite and clipped. Nigel had fallen at the first hurdle.

'I'm lonely,' said Julie. 'Little Julie misses Big Nigel.'

Nigel winced and would have thrown his hands over Miss Bonner's ears had he not stopped himself just in time. 'And how are *you*?' Julie sidled closer. Nigel sidled backwards and nearly fell into the fire. He righted himself but continued to move steadily away. 'A little cold,' he said quickly. 'Thanks.' The fire was roasting. Miles had been persuaded that if people were warm and had nice sherry then all would be well and Dorcas, oh the profligate, had banked it up.

'Poor Nigey,' Julie gave a little pout. 'I could warm you up?' she said cajolingly. Though cajolingly, she said it very loudly and she said it very close and very purposefully so that Miss Molly Bonner could not help but hear it. Miss Molly Bonner turned her head away from Dr Porlock and looked at Julie. 'Oh,' she said, 'I always get very pink cheeks indoors. It doesn't mean anything at all. I'm just about the perfect temperature, thank you.'

Julie, who, it was often said, had more front than Brighton – hiccuped with embarrassment. 'Sorry,' she said, 'I was talking to the cat.'

Everyone looked at the floor where there was, obviously, no cat. 'Oh flip,' said Julie, 'I thought the rug was a pussy.'

At which point the archaeologist's granddaughter threw back her head and laughed. How adorable. Nigel moved nearer to her; he who had been in love up to a point, now went deliriously beyond that point and was so seriously in love that he broke out in a sweat. Only then did he realise that his trousers were on fire.

He yelled, bent over, beat them – and Winifred, with a smile of alacrity, fulfilled every fear of her husband's by upending her sherry glass all over the smouldering buttocks of Master Nigel the antique dealer's son.

'May I suggest,' said Molly, thinking that very soon everything would fall apart, 'that I begin?'

'Oh please,' said Nigel fervently, holding a cushion which he had grabbed from the nearest chair to his singed and sherried bottom. But it was no cushion, he discovered, when it dug in its claws. It was the much-affronted cat.

Six

DORCAS STROKED AND calmed Montmorency who had never been so insulted in all his life except when the man he lived with – scarcely his owner, despite his real owner not having made an appearance for some time – had told Dorcas that he, Montmorency, was brought to this abode *for the catching of mice*. One more incident like this and he would betake him across the road to Dorcas's house: smaller, it was true, not nearly so elegant nor classy – but with the benefit of being secure in his feline superiority. And his sleep.

Miles stepped forward and, rubbing his hands as if the money were already his, and smiling that extraordinary smile that made so many look away, he began to list Molly's attributes for the benefit of the party. 'She is a friend to the village,' he said. 'So young and yet so full of good intentions . . . I am proud to have brought her here to work on our beautiful village's behalf.'

At which point, with the curious smell of singed cloth all around her, Molly thanked Miles, and began quickly and firmly to explain her mission. Miles kept his mouth open for a moment, realised that the glory had been snatched from him, forgot to smile (which was a relief all round) and was silent as Molly began to tell them about her grandfather's great interest in the Gnome of Pound Hill, how he had wanted to investigate its source and origins – and to make sure it was as accurate in the land as it was when first cut out of it – but that the Great War had intervened. She told them about her grandmother and how he had loved her. And how she wanted this work of Molly's to be like a memorial to him. She asked that they help her with the initial clearing of the space but that, once the covers were in place, they leave her – and the site – alone, until she had finished. Indeed, that was a *sine qua non* of the understanding between her and the village. The task, she thought, would take several months and after that – well, after that – she hoped that she would leave them with a new understanding of the value of the place. Miles then broke into the talk and said, 'Ah yes – after that, it will be ours again.' He said this with such fondness and such a benign expression that it had everyone reaching for another sherry in disbelief – but since Molly stood there looking open and honest and enthusiastic, they had to believe him though they surely doubted, they surely doubted. Miles hated the Gnome. And now he was professing to love it. What was going on?

Susie asked, 'Does it mean that you want us all to stay away for the duration . . . ?' She said it slightly wistfully.

'Yes,' said Molly, as straightforward as the day was long, 'I must insist on it. A notice will go up. But after that it will be restored and ready and maybe made even more – powerful.'

Susie closed her eyes in pleasure at the prospect. Pinky closed his eyes in sheer relief. He moved a little closer to his wife and vowed, privately, to try hard to rekindle his love. He put the phrase 'over my dead body' out of his mind. 'Take your time,' he said very firmly. 'Take your time, Miss Bonner – please.'

'Thank you. And you might all want to know that there is a television company who are very interested in the outcome of this. But that is for later . . . much later.'

'I used to work in television,' said Winifred, even more wistfully than Susie. 'Many years ago. When I was in my prime.' And then she laughed and began quoting a favourite ditty, 'When I was young and in my prime' but the sound of Donald's groan and the look of horror he gave her brought her up short. The next line, the one about wetting one's knickers, was really, she thought, a little strong. Donald said 'Good God' and held his head. She took pity and stopped speaking but she did not stop thinking of herself in her prime and all those assignments she'd enjoyed when she was young, working for the BBC with, quite literally when she visited the North Pole, the world at her feet. 'We used to say all sorts of things off-air,' said Winifred. 'It livened up our on-air performance tremendously.'

Very gently Dorcas put Montmorency down. The cat swivelled his head and took a long, penetrating look at Nigel, before settling his paws, putting his chin between them, and returning to sleep. Nigel saw nothing of this for he was aghast at Molly's words. He moved towards her.

'Don't you want us to help?' he stammered. 'Can't we come and – oh – hold a torch or something?' It was on the tip of Julie Barnsley's tongue to say that he seemed to be doing that all right anyway, without having to ask.

Molly nodded. 'You can certainly all help with getting my equipment up the Hill – it's too steep for the van. And with the clearing, that's really important. But the more . . . delicate work I shall need to do on my own. Still, there's quite a few ways you can help before that.'

Nigel practically melted at the idea of Molly being alone, anywhere in the universe. 'I'll be there for you – every step of the way,' he said. 'Ow!'

Julie had quite a firm pinch on her; very probably she drew her finger strength from pulling pints.

Molly ignored the noise for she was focused on one thing, and one thing only: that she would get her way. She leaned forward, resting her small hands – hands, thought Nigel, as he rubbed at his singed bottom, that did not look as if they could shift earth even in an ordinary garden – on the desk and saying most earnestly, 'Believe me. This is for the good of the village –

and for the good of the villagers. My grandfather thought that there was something innately special about this site of yours and I want to find out – that is, restore it for you. His letters to my grandmother, and his notebooks, will all be available for you to see – for the world to see if they wish to – once the work is completed. Until then, will you respect my request?'

'What exactly is the extent of the work?' asked Dorcas.

Molly's eyes held that shadow again as she said, 'I won't really know until I get up there, but clearing the edges, obviously.'

She gave Dorcas a straight look. 'Obviously,' replied Dorcas, returning it. Molly nodded. 'Obviously indeed.'

There was a finality to Molly's tone that Dorcas decided to respect. 'I see,' she said. And that was that. Later, my girl, she thought. I shall pin you down later.

There was a short silence. Then, gradually, the room became full of nods and smiles and agreement. They would all help and they would all abide by her rules. While the men were impressed with Molly's spirit and charm, the women were impressed with her mixture of authority and amiability. But above everything they were all impressed with her passion and her cheerfulness. There is nothing quite like passion and belief to endow a speaker with great communication skills. When Molly spoke about how excited she was at the prospect, how interesting she hoped it would be for the village when the work was completed at last, even Marion was impressed. For the first time she found something almost as compelling as a horse. What a pity that it was to be up on Pound Hill. Passion was not something that had entered Marion's world very often and she found Molly's passion very engaging. How odd, she thought, that such a stirring should come to her from the loathsome Gnome. She wondered, fleetingly, if she might get involved but decided that she was, perhaps, not quite ready yet to dare to visit the Hill again and finally put away the memory of falling off Tickle. Not *quite*.

Peter Hanker then stepped into the middle of the room. He was not usually one to put himself forward unless there was something in it for him and when he arrived he had planned to take Miss Bonner quietly to one side at the end of the meeting and suggest she pay him a substantial sum; after all, the pub could do with it, for which he would give her something she might want in return. But somehow, and he really could not say the why or the how of it, a little flutter of shame entered his mind and he decided to bypass the first bit. Instead, he held up a folded, creased, stained, rough-edged square of paper, about A4 size, and carefully opened it. He laid it on the desk before the young archaeologist as if it were a treasure he had found for her. And, if her reaction was anything to go by, so it was. She clapped her hands, then put them one on each of his cheeks and gave him a smacking great kiss on the lips. Nigel nearly fainted away. As did Peter Hanker. And Julie Barnsley was involuntarily moved to wish, yet again, that she could scratch the bloody girl's eyes out. *Both* of them now, she thought. Bloody hell, what was the girl *on*?

'Wow!' said Molly when she had released Peter's cheeks, 'Wow!' She was looking at the paper as if she could eat it. 'How did you get it?' Her eyes were shining. Peter felt a glow all about him and said proudly, 'It's my great-great-something-grandfather's map of what he found when he went to clean up the Gnome. Or drawing, I suppose, would be most accurate.' Molly peered at the paper saying, 'I thought this was lost for ever.' The room seemed to hold its breath. The gathering to crane its universal neck. 'This is wonderful,' said Molly. 'Quite, quite wonderful. Oh thank you so much, thank you Peter.'

Peter, with a pleased smile, pointed to some very faint writing in the corner of the paper. 'I think it says that the outline of the Gnome was based on a much earlier document which was in such poor condition that it had to be transferred to this paper. Where he got that from,' Peter Hanker said, 'I've no idea. I held on to this because I thought it would be worth something one day . . .'

'Oh, it is, it is,' said Molly. 'There is a date – faint but definitely a date . . .' She took the paper over to the window and scrutinised it. 'Yes,' she said, her smile so broad that the gathering in the room felt like cheering – but didn't: 'The original paper came from the church which he thinks had held it for hundreds of years. Hundreds of years. I wonder why?'

'He may have been exaggerating,' said Peter. Molly nodded, still thinking. 'Or perhaps the priests liked a bit of dirt now and then.'

The vicar said, 'Oh I say.' And Dorcas was quick to answer with, 'Oh I don't think he means now, vicar.' Much to Miles's chagrin, she refilled the clergyman's empty glass yet again.

Standing by the window, Molly seemed oblivious of anything but the paper. 'Well, it certainly looks as if your man has changed shape on his outer rim. And the Gnome's hat now is much plainer.' She looked out of the window and up the Hill, then back to the paper. Dorcas was at her side and Miles was relieved to see that instead of another bottle of rather fine sherry his assistant was holding a magnifying glass. Molly took it from her as a surgeon takes an instrument, without removing her gaze from the drawing. 'Well, well,' said Molly. 'I think I see a little of what it might, just might, be. But we won't know anything more until I get up there, down and dirty.'

'Oh yes!' came the fervent cry from the fireplace. But Nigel was quelled with a penetrating look from Julie.

'And if the dates fit, then that will be most helpful. Marvellous.'

Molly looked sad for a moment as she returned to the centre of the room. 'I don't think my grandfather saw this – or at least, he doesn't mention it. What a shame. He would have been thrilled.' She threw up her hands in what looked to Nigel like a lovely gesture of abandoned despair and to Julie like a fit of very bad acting. 'But this looks so early, Peter,' said Molly. 'Which is a shame. Your aeons-ago grandfather wouldn't have had a clue about the site. No one bothered to make a proper scientific record of these things until the blessed General Pitt-Rivers arrived on the scene and took the recording of archaeology seriously.' She flapped the piece of paper. 'And that was as late as the 1860s. Until then it was all about digging it up and jotting it down on any old thing – like this church drawing. Nothing scientific at all – more or less done on the back of a fag packet.'

'Good heavens,' said Sir Roger, 'I didn't know ancient churchmen *smoked*. How civilised.'

He looked at Dulcima in amazement. She laughed – and such a true laugh that it reminded him of when she was first at the Manor – and she said, 'Oh Roger, Molly was speaking metatata—' Dulcima took another run at it, 'Metaphosically . . .' She gave up.

'Yes,' said Molly helpfully, 'I was. My grandfather might have been the bridge between the General – whom he admired immensely – and men like Sir Mortimer Wheeler in the thirties – but that futile war stopped his progress. She gave the room the benefit of a particularly firm stare and this time it was slightly less sweet. 'And very possibly his lowly status.'

'Talent will out,' said Winifred. 'Eventually.' She turned to her husband. 'Won't it, Donald?'

She was not holding a glass and there was nothing nearby – so far as he could see – that could be poured. Nevertheless, he backed away slightly. 'Yes, dear,' he said. He did not, quite, like the way she then tapped her lips with the tip of her finger in thoughtful, speculative manner with that faraway look in her eye again. It was when she started thinking that things got into a mess, a damp one, usually. He tried not to think of incontinence apparatus.

'It was also to do with the subject matter of the site,' said Molly, and had the grace to look slightly uncomfortable. 'If you know what I mean. You can only wonder how the church fathers felt with that looking down on them. Very off-putting. Of course,' she added as a little afterthought, 'they might have welcomed it. Being expected to be good all the time. It might have stirred them up a bit.'

At which the vicar began a coughing fit, Dulcima decided that she liked this archaeologist girl and Sir Roger bellowed a laugh. It may have been the implied suggestion that the clergy liked erotica or it may have been that his little legs could not hold quite so much sherry as everyone else's (Miles had decided that the whole bloody village had hollow legs where his drink was concerned), but the vicar's coughing and snorting went on for some time and was only ended by a resounding thump on his back from Sir Roger. His Lordship might not have the living of Lufferton Boney in his gift any more, but he still had a slightly proprietorial feeling about this man of the cloth, despite his size. Bullying the vicar was part of the history and structure of country life as much as any Gnome, thought Sir Roger, and practically his duty. The vicar, while attempting to look grateful and with the purple of his face slowly subsiding, took a very large swig of sherry. Miles let out a groan. 'Better open another bottle,' said Dorcas, and slipped off to do so before Miles could stop her.

Despite the vicar's distress, there was not a man or woman in the room who was not pleased at the advent of Molly Bonner and puzzled that Miles should be so amenable to the scheme. And Molly was pleased with the assembled because they supported her, which was important for the success of any project like this; and she now had her bit of paper. Precious are the artefacts of history. She held the drawing as if it were a newborn baby.

Only Miles and Montmorency seemed unmoved by the archaeological aspect. Miles was agonising over the sound of another sherry bottle being opened and Montmorency was determinedly asleep. Even Dulcima moved a little closer to her husband and squeezed his elbow at the sheer power of Molly's excitement. Maybe there was more to life, she found herself thinking, but what life, and what more, she could not then say. Quite involuntarily, Dryden, caught by the mood, stopped thinking of ways to engage Sir Roger about the sale of the gun, and stopped trying to negotiate Marion towards his son, and gave himself up to the unselfish pleasure of the moment. He found it was rather a pleasant thing to do. Julie Barnsley did not think this, of course. Julie Barnsley thought just the opposite. And when her eyes were damp with emotion, it was more to do with rage than anything else. She thought that if this pretty young upstart was allowed to carry on, she might be a very bad thing for the village. And herself. But she kept her counsel – for now.

At the end of the evening Sir Roger, who had not done a great deal over the years to take the command his position in the village ordained, apart from bat the vicar around occasionally or fall loudly and correctly asleep in his sermons, felt a new heat in his ancient blood, and a certain incumbence upon him to give a speech of thanks to Miss Bonner the archaeologist's granddaughter for bringing something so clearly worthwhile to their attention. This he did immediately – and volunteered his man of all work and butler, Orridge, for any of the heavy work.

Dulcima found that she was still clutching her husband's hand as he spoke – a public display of feeling that would not do at all. She quickly removed it. 'No,' she said firmly. 'We will all help with our own hands. We will all be a part of the grand scheme of it.' Everyone began to feel, most unexpectedly, that this young woman might be the harbinger of something really rather good for them and their village which for too long had suffered from refracted emotions. Sadly, Dulcima noticed that Marion did not look at all enthused by the prospect. Ah well, there was still time.

'It is an undertaking for all of us,' said Dulcima. She looked fondly at Dryden, who gulped, thought of his delicate hands, and said that while he would mind the shop, he was perfectly willing, perfectly, to allow Nigel to participate in clearing the ground up there. Nigel was thrilled.

Julie sighed. The last thing she wanted to do was go anywhere near this project, but where Nigel went, so must she. Dryden, having made his little speech, turned away and looked out of the window and up the Hill. His face paled, it was as if he saw something up there. 'Oh please,' he said. He put his hand to his head and made a little gasping noise and sank into the nearest chair.

'More sherry,' said Susie. 'He's having a faint.'

'Then it will be water he wants,' said Miles firmly. But it was too late. Pop went the cork from the depths of the kitchen. Pop.

While this little drama was being enacted Donald Porlock, looking embarrassed but standing firm, was told, by Sir Roger, that he was excused fatigues on the grounds that his patients might suffer. And Donald said that he thought Winifred might find helping on the Hill a bit much. Winifred said that if she did find it a bit much it would be up to her, not him, to say so. That she still retained a sense of community spirit. The edge to her voice made her husband uneasy. She was beginning to get so many edges to her where once she had been so soft. Donald moved away from her slightly, but she was not looking at him, she was gazing into the fire with a faraway look in her eyes. Please, he prayed, please do not quote any more poetry.

'And me,' said Dorcas. 'I'll be there.'

Not me, thought Montmorency.

'And me.'

'And me,' said all the others.

Susie and Pinky raised their glasses high. 'Here's to it,' they said in unison. And Pinky added, with great fervour, 'And take as long as you like.'

When Sir Roger's brief speech of thanks and good wishes and farewell was concluded the vicar stepped forward and was about to suggest a little prayer for the end of the event, but Sir Roger, suspecting something of an evangelical nature, would not have it: you went to church, you prayed, you got told off, you went home and marked it down until the next Sunday, or Easter, or Christmas or whatever it was, and you certainly did not clap to the hymnal or turn to your neighbour and kiss the bugger. Nor did you go praying all over the place at a short-legged vicar's whim and in other people's houses. Only in a house of prayer did you do that. Why, it was like ordering a piece of fish in a game pie shop. 'Better stop him, don't you think, dear?' he said to Dulcima, in a perfectly audible whisper that would not have disgraced Laurence Olivier. And Dulcima, who had found the sherry most excellent and was in very good spirits, both literally and in the word she could not quite say, squeezed his hand and nodded.

So, as the vicar drew breath, Sir Roger started some clapping which the rest of the party took up and which went on for a considerable and genuine time. Dorcas slipped about offering them all one for the road – and as they were all on foot they were delighted and obliged. Miles took a deep breath and said nothing, but privately thought again of sprats and mackerels. After the final drink they all went out into the night and had their various happy or not so happy ways lighted homeward by the stars. Though it should be said that there were those who were feeling happier than they had felt for a very long time – and those who had yet to experience the change.

Julie Barnsley stood looking up at the moon until she felt a hand tapping her shoulder. Expectantly, happily, she turned – but it was only Miles standing there, with his hand out. 'My one pound and forty pence, I think?' he said. And Julie, with as much contempt as she could bring to the occasion, which was considerable, dug in her pocket and bestowed it upon him as if it were thirty pieces of silver.

Miles closed the door on the last of his guests and turned to Dorcas. 'Well, well,' he said happily, rubbing his hands, 'I think that went off rather well. Don't you?'

'Yes,' said Dorcas, and began putting the remaining glasses on a tray. 'And the sherry went down very well, too. All gone,' she sang on her way to the kitchen, 'All gone.'

'Indeed,' said Miles, determined not to let it affect him. 'And you were quite right. Better to give them something elegant and expensive now, smooth the path so to speak, and there will be takings enough to cover the cost of a hundred boxes of sherry once the girl pays up and does what she wants to the terrain up there.'

'Whatever she wants to do to it . . .' said Dorcas thoughtfully.

They crossed to the window and looked up at the moonlit Hill. In the light the whiteness of the Gnome's shape stood out clearly save for where the bushes grew thickest. 'Beats me why she thinks she can improve on it,' said Miles – 'but there you go. Who am I? Takes all sorts . . . Nice girl, though.'

Dorcas interrupted him before he could get into absolutely

full flow with his platitudes. 'She's passionate about it,' said Dorcas. 'And I envy her that. It's a long time since I felt passionate about anything.'

'Quite,' said Miles, without so much as a blink. 'And it's always for the best. A cool head. You have a cool head. And who knows, Dorcas, once the final payment is made and the thing is set up and the regular income starts, I may be able to give you a bit of a rise. You may get to South America after all.' He turned to her and slapped her on the back. 'You're a clever girl,' he said. 'A *very* clever girl.' He paused, and then his smile died away. 'How many bottles did they drink?'

But Dorcas was looking at him rather strangely. He faltered. 'Perhaps you should cut along now – you're probably a bit tired. I'll count them myself.'

As Dorcas walked along the deserted street towards the Squidge she thought how little times had changed in some respects. A woman with a brain could still be slapped on the back by an idiot and called a clever girl and when she looked as if she might slap him back, he could assuage his conscience at her reaction by suggesting she was tired. She let herself into the little house with a heavy heart. The only good thing on the horizon was Miss Molly Bonner's project – and the fact that Miss Molly Bonner seemed to be honourable, and possibly also fun. However, the terms 'excavate' and 'dig' still reverberated around Dorcas's head, vying with the more soothing word 'clearance'. She made herself a nightcap of jasmine tea. She trusted the young woman. And Dorcas was seldom wrong in such matters. After all – she picked up her mug and made her way up the thin little staircase – after all – she had known Miles was a shit all those years ago from the very moment she set eyes on him. Give her a rise, indeed. As if.

Seven

IN BED IN Chrysalis Cottage that night Pinky lay beside Susie in the dark and listened to her breathing. A slow, creeping, long-forgotten warmth spread over him. His anxiety had melted considerably, though some of it still lurked. He had not, for example, liked the way Susie smiled so knowingly at him when it was suggested that after Molly Bonner's attentions the Gnome would be raring to go again – but if this tender, gentle way of being together continued, then maybe the feeling of being valuable in only one department, about which he felt so disturbed, would melt away. For this, he thought, was how it used to be, when they were first married. This quiet darkness with only the rhythm of their breathing. No pressure.

He stared at Susie's overly tousled head gleaming in the slip of silver light coming through a crack in the curtain, and the hesitant warmth he felt spread to every part of him. It was, quite simply, as if he were being allowed to breathe again. He stroked her hair (though there was far too much of it for the deed to be a pleasure) and she stirred in her sleep but did not wake. He slid down and scooped her pneumatic curves into his body and they were like two spoons nestling in a drawer. Of his own volition he began to caress his wife, as if for the first time. From long ago and far away she made a familiar gesture with her compressible bottom, a little shake, as if it were saying no to him. He smiled. If only it could be like this always, and not just for the duration of the restoration of the Gnome of Pound Hill. If only he were a man who occasionally had to *win* his wife's agreement. If only he dared tell her. And thinking this thought, and closing his eyes peacefully, he drifted off into a gentle, happy sleep.

Donald Porlock was still up, sitting at the desk in his study, reading and making notes from a large book entitled *Mental Health Medications* (NHS, government publications, 1978). In the kitchen Winifred poured milk into mugs and stirred the cocoa slightly absently as she stared straight ahead of her. She wore her nightdress but not her dressing gown and the thin shape of her body showed through the pink roses of the lawn cotton (Debenhams sale, £25). Pink roses, she thought, lawn cotton, she thought, how predictable she had become. She put the spoon in the sink and picked up the mugs, one in each hand. When they were first married Donald had carried her over the threshold of their London flat with the vow that their lives would be of equal value. Whatever they did, they would do it together, as a team. The domestic requirements were to be shared evenly. She had a career and he had a career and when they went off into the Third World (it was called the Third World then), he vowed, it would still be the same. That was the man she married.

Circumstances, she thought, I was a victim of circumstances. But she knew that she had allowed herself to be that victim. If it came down to testing the egalitarian principles that pertained in a household by looking at who washed out the milk bottles – then buy your milk in cartons. She succumbed, just as Donald succumbed, to the might of generations of respectful serfs that had filtered through Lufferton Boney. If they no longer tugged their forelocks, they still respected the local doctor without question. Two paces behind, Mrs Doctor, if you please and only voluntary work . . . And, metaphorically speaking, she had acceded. So much easier to be amenable than to be uppish. Especially when you were floundering from your bed in the night to stick a baby on the tit.

Beware any woman who moves to the country and thinks she is an equal in the sight of men (and women). Beware any woman who is equally, or more, intelligent than the male. Beware any woman who moves to the country and owns property and money in her own right. The natives will not forgive you for that. Man is the breadwinner, ever was, ever will be – if you behave like Winifred Porlock, that is.

With a sigh she left the kitchen, switching off the light with her forehead as she always did when her hands were full. The mugs were nice thin china, with little daisies scattered over them in a very pretty pattern. They came from John Lewis and she felt like hurling them at the wall. The wallpaper also came from John Lewis. It was called Catkin. For a moment she stood at the foot of the stairs and glared at the stylish, tasteful design and then, as if by some miracle, the mugs were lifted from her hands and her husband's face came into view where only Catkin had been. 'Hallo, darling,' he said brightly. 'Shall I carry these up for us?'

How odd, thought Winifred: not like Donald to leave his work to do something of a domestic nature. She looked up at him enquiringly.

'Don't want to spill them, now do we? Hot liquids?'

Idiotic question. 'What would you say, Donald,' she answered crisply, 'if I said Yes We Do.'

He hurried on ahead.

In bed, later, as they finished their drinks, Donald, propped up on his pillows and staring straight ahead, murmured cautiously, 'Did you have enough water play when you were a child, dear?' Winifred looked down into the depths of the mug. It was entirely empty. Just as well. She placed the mug carefully on the side table and heard her husband give a little noise like a sigh of satisfaction as she slid down under the covers. Her muffled voice was indistinguishable as she gave her answer. Donald, had he not known Winifred better, might have thought it was something not very nice that she muttered into the eiderdown, but that was so out of character as to be ridiculous. Ridiculous. 'Perhaps we could put up a small fountain in the garden. Would you like that?' Something else was said but he could not be sure what it was. So he turned out the light and joined his wife beneath the covers.

It was some time before he nodded off. They lay there, side by side, eyes closed, with Winifred feeling very far from saintly despite being named for St Winifred and her miraculous spring. Small fountain in the garden, indeed, when what she wanted was a raging torrent.

In her bed at the Old Manor, Marion pondered on Miles's capacity to smile. He had seemed to be at it for most of the evening. Or was it a smile? Very hard to tell. It could, she thought, as she turned out the light and stared at the moonlight playing on her beloved posters of those historical heroes of the turf Red Rum and Shergar (Oh where, Oh where?) it could, of course, be an indicator that something was not quite right in Miles's body – perhaps it was a grimace of pain? And that might be the answer to one vital question that Marion pondered with everyone: was that why he didn't ride? There had to be a good reason for *that*. Or perhaps there was something of an irritant nature in the region of his neck area – perhaps he had something not quite right behind his mandible, or his maxilla. If he were a horse and pulling his lips back like that she would be able to check it for him: she would just get out her sturdy probang and see whether there was anything hiding in his throat. Over in a trice. Whatever the reason, in the end he had looked dead spooky and the ceiling had been a comforting diversion. Marion found it hard to trust anyone who did not care for horses. Though she pitied rather than distrusted Nigel, who had also had a bad experience and no one to throw him back in the saddle afterwards. Even Winifred Porlock, who did not ride at all, brought Sparkle the odd carrot now and then and knew how to rub his nose on the side. A decent person knew such things.

She pulled up the covers tight to her nose. When she went back to the pub yard to collect Sparkle she had seen Peter Hanker grab hold of Julie Barnsley as she passed the entrance and kiss her on the lips. A very long kiss, fascinating it was. And then Julie seemed to collect herself and slapped him. Then they both laughed and she went on her way. Even more fascinating. She wondered if Julie liked riding. She hoped so. She hoped everyone in the world could have the happiness it brought. Really, if you did not ride how could you say you were *alive*? On the other hand, when her father and mother had introduced her to one or two young men on their horses, she seemed to have done quite the wrong thing by riding better than they did. Odd. You would have thought a wife who could do five bars and never flinch would be just the sort of girl to take down the aisle. She could not fathom those chaps. Not at all. Nor did she like them. They hunted. She couldn't abide hunting. Nigel's little difficulty was to do with hunting, she knew that. She felt sorry for him. She just loved to be up in the saddle. And horses were just so straightforward. She gave a little whinny into her pillow and fell soundly asleep.

Dulcima, so far not having spilled a drop of Orridge's port, was making her careful way along the passage that connected the old servants' stairs with the second-floor bedrooms. Marion's room was on this floor – which had a better view of the stables – and Dulcima paused to listen. She heard the little whinny and sighed with pleasure. Marion was tucked up for the night and happy.

Orridge had been asleep in his chair in the hall as usual,
seeing them in, and had not noticed his mistress quietly remove
the cork from the bottle awaiting her husband, his nightcap.
She poured out a good glassful, replaced the cork and went on
her way. Happy. How lovely. Orridge was happy. Marion was
happy. Dulcima must be happy? And Harty was stretched out
in his favourite wing chair, one leg propped up on Jarvis his
favourite retriever and the other on one of two footstools.
Orridge would waken, and then wake him and they would both
be happy together. What a happy, happy house. Was she going
to have to jumble up all this happiness? Was she going to have
to find a husband for her daughter and thus break the spell of
daily harmony? Very probably she was. Dulcima sighed. St
Augustine was receding rapidly. She must talk to Harty and she
must act. But – well – she sipped the delicious, nutty port – not
tonight . . . She did not look in on her husband. Jarvis had a
tendency to get up and rush with wagging tail towards her if
she appeared, however silently, in the library – which woke his
master – so better to go straight to bed. Had she entered the
library to say goodnight she might have seen a rather sad looking
Sir Roger stroking and caressing his dog as if his life depended
upon it, each of his feet placed on each of two footstools.

Orridge opened one eye and saw Lady Dulcima disappearing
round the top of the upper staircase. He operated a very simple
system: whenever he was to bring up something good from the
cellar he would bring up two of the something goods. Whenever
he was requested to bring up something quite ordinary, he would
bring only one. That way he could sleep soundly in his chair
at night (he seldom made it to bed before about 4 a.m.) knowing
that he was not being profligate. Besides, there was nothing of
very low quality in the cellar, it was just that he had become
something of a discerning bibulator and did not wish to ruin

his health. When you found yourself imbibing an entire bottle of Château Lambert at a sitting, it was as well that it was so fine. The quality stopped the hangovers, and did not harm the liver. Why, it was practically medicinal.

As Dulcima slid into her bed she looked at the door to Harty's adjacent room. She gave a little sigh and a shrug. He wouldn't be up to bed until dawn, she knew. Sometimes – she sipped again (she must remember how much she liked this forty-year-old tawny) – sometimes she wondered . . . And then she stopped herself. Marriage was not love. Marriage was marriage. Harty had told her to have a stiff upper lip when she thought their only daughter might have died. Marriage was most definitely marriage. She knew that, she had been told that, and she accepted that.

She drained the last of the glass, turned out the light, lay on her back looking up into the darkness, and thought about how charmingly Dryden spoke of carved giltwood mirrors and feather banded bureaux, how elegantly he set out his wares. And that rather strange son of his. How hard was the burden of being left wifeless, no mother for his son. Possibly Nigel would be a good friend for Marion. They could help each other with their social awkwardnesses? Possibly. Except he did not ride. Troublesome. She thought of her daughter, drank off the last of the exceedingly good port, and fell back on her pillow returning St Augustine's indulgent smile.

Nigel pretended to be asleep when his father charged into his room.

'Good grief,' said Dryden. 'What's that bloody noise?' He switched on the light and stared all around. Nothing was out of place. The boy (b. 1986) was in bed, asleep; his clothes were in a pile on the floor; the curtains were drawn – and yet – and yet – Dryden had definitely heard something that made him wonder if Nigel had taken up tap-dancing. Very delicate tap-dancing. He was just about to leave the room when he heard the noise again, much nearer this time, a definite tapping. It came from the window.

He strode over, pulled back the curtains, and there, bathed in moonlight, was Julie Barnsley with a very long pole – it looked like the window-opening pole from the Old Holly Bush. Bestriding the situation like the Colossus of the vicar's dreams, he threw open the window and leaned out just as Julie gave the pole another go. It engaged, immediately, first with Dryden's cheek and eye socket, and then his nose. It did not cease for several goes, on the grounds that Julie Barnsley could not see – quite – what was happening up there – and she needed all her concentration to hold the pole at the base.

Dryden reeled back, fell over the end of Nigel's bed, bounced on to his son several times, his elbow connecting with Nigel's cheek, and wondered if he should have had that last sherry. Nigel sat up and held his face and stared at his father. Had he done this to him on purpose? Did he know about Julie and the engagement? His father had never hit him in his life before. But as Nigel raised his fearful eyes towards his father's face, he saw that he had buried his face in his hands. 'Oh God,' said Nigel, 'I am sorry. She threw herself at me. Please don't, please don't . . .'

'Don't what?' said Dryden through his fingertips.

'Don't hit me again. I have broken it off.'

Leaving father and son to continue talking at cross purposes about which part of their anatomy might, or might not, have been broken off in the fray, we return to Julie Barnsley who was still calling, softly, persistently, beneath the window, and still holding the now redundant pole. She waited. No one appeared at the opened casement. Julie realised that all was not well, that the end of the pole (brass) had hit something soft and yielding, followed by a noise indicating that the soft and yielding bit was connected to a human being (well, almost). After a little more gentle persistence in the calling department, which rendered nothing, the window was closed by a pale hand that seemed to float out of the darkness and vanish as the catch was fixed down. She waited silently until, quite horribly, the face of Dryden Fellows appeared at the closed window, and as it shimmered there in the moonlight it looked strangely other, not like him at all, yet it was him – was it? The face opened its mouth and let out a noise. Not a good noise. And – with no wish to go into the details of same – she was off. Racing up the village street, carrying the pole before her.

Julie looked, thought Peter Hanker as he stared out of his own bedroom window at the charging figure coming towards him, like St Joan in all her fiery fervour. He sighed. It was a night for Lufferton Boneyites to sigh, it seemed. Sighing had broken out all over the place. It followed hot on the heels of the post-party happiness.

Not to be outdone, Peter sighed once more and got into his narrow, cold bed. What it was that made Julie so keen on the fool Nigel he could not, for the life of him, fathom. Peter Hanker might himself be a man of business in all things but he was not one to impute such values to golden-haired Julie. Besides, in his reckoning a woman would have to be loony to marry a twit like that for money. No, he reckoned she was in love with the creep. Women were the strangest creatures. Never did what you expected them to do. Nigel! That wimp. And Peter had been so sure that Julie was in love with him once upon a time. How wrong could you be? He had offered his hand, and his heart, and all the other bits as well. He had said that together they

MAVIS CHEEK

could rebuild the business, find ways to increase the profit margin, be partners in every sense. Love would make it work. So much for that little idea . . .

He waited for the bed to warm. He was extremely tired of sleeping alone. He had thought the single bed would help, for he thrashed around too much in the double, but it scarcely made any difference. Yes, what women wanted was a very great mystery to Peter Hanker. His previous barmaid, a woman of forty-five if she was a day, had a T-shirt with Tom Cruise printed on the front. And she thought *A Few Good Men* was his finest hour. She left, never to return, when one of the regulars told her he was very short and wore high heels for the part. Such was a woman. Unpredictable and given to strange desires. Just like Julie. Peter wondered if it had always been like that and decided that back in the mists of time they probably just got on with it, none of that lovey-dovey stuff, and very probably an easier time was had by all.

He turned the light out and his thoughts turned to his guest, Miss Molly Bonner. Strange it was, he thought, that though she was pretty and funny and intelligent and vibrant – with very good legs – yet his heart was not taken by her. Why was that? Why was it that someone who was all those things, and now staying under his roof, and single, or so it seemed, did not give him that special buzz (Peter Hanker was uncertain about the use of the word love from now on and decided it was best avoided – buzz said it all, in his opinion) – whereas Julie . . . As he gave in to the night he began to dream of sitting on Pound Hill and proposing marriage to Julie. And in his dream she accepted. Men, he thought in his dream, dangerously unpredictable creatures and given to strange desires. Like changeable women. Nigel! It didn't bear thinking about.

*

But Julie was not on Pound Hill. She was telling herself that she had been stupid and that she had better not be found out. She flung the pole over the wall into the yard of the pub and ran off home as fast as she could go. She had probably blinded Nigel for life. It was cold comfort to think that he had sufficient in his trust fund to have a live-in carer and that she, as his wife, would not have to push the wheelchair very often. Julie's view – like that of so many of her contemporaries who do not yet even wear spectacles – was that difficulties such as blindness constituted great helplessness. One day, though not for a year or three, she would turn on the television and see a race taking place which consisted largely of blind men on bicycles in a velodrome in France. Not helpless at all. But for the moment, if she had blinded him, she had to make up her mind whether it was worthwhile pursuing financial security with a damaged man attached to it. If it was, then she must do something about that scarlet-headed freak. Archaeology? Finding fossils? What kind of job was that for a girl?

Julie rented a small place off the High Street called the Lamb Shed. And this was what it had once been. It was draughty in winter, too hot in summer – but it was all that Julie could afford. For now The Lamb Shed was at the edge of the village, beyond the Old Holly Bush and try as she might to crane her neck, look around corners, peer around the edge of Pound Hill, she could not see any of the village houses from her window. None. What you could see – she shifted her gaze towards it for a moment and then quickly looked away – was the tip, just the tip, of the Gnome's famous appendage. Best not think about that, thought Julie, as she peeled off her clothes, decided against a shower because it would wake her up, and wriggled into her bed. She blamed the sherry for causing her to bestow upon Nigel such a whack that she had given him the perfect excuse to remove her from his life. If only she could repair the damage.

But how? She closed her eyes, the better to concentrate on finding an answer, but all she could remember was the absurdity of Nigel's smouldering trousers and the light of laughter in Peter Hanker's eyes as they both struggled not to give in to the silliness of the scene. Making sure of your future security did seem to be a serious business. Pity. She liked a laugh. She had also – she could say this into her pillow for who would ever know? – she had also enjoyed that kiss.

Miles stood by his window, bathed in the moonlight, and looked out along the white ribbon of the village street in the direction of the top of the Old Manor (predominantly 1590 with an earlier wing). His jaw still ached from all that smiling and he did not feel ready for bed. He was wearing his blue and white striped pyjamas and his feet were cold but still he stood there, thinking. Perhaps when he had made much more money he could approach the Fitzhartletts? But he knew it was pointless, really.

It cut him to the quick that he, the man of the hour, the man of property (soon, soon) and distinction in Lufferton Boney could not get himself wed to the only single woman thereabouts he considered his equal. But in his heart he knew that unless he rode a horse, and rode it with confidence and pleasure – or at least appeared to – he could never succeed with Marion. A most indelicate thought popped into his mind, one that made his smile all the more like a leer. Any spirits abroad that night would be glad no one human could see it. For the thought was that Marion had probably only ever seen both the Gnome and a horse's private parts. My God, he thought, peering through the window, thinking he saw some movement out there, the prospect of her disappointed face on her wedding night was perfectly hilarious. Such was the humour of Miles Whittington. He must tell Dorcas about this in the morning; they could have a good laugh. Good old Dorcas. Where would he be without her? Most certainly he must stop the silly girl from running off to the jungles of South America in search of Robin. He had persuaded the village nobility, when they thought they might help her financially, that it was a terrible idea, that she would only become more depressed once there, as the FO were very firmly of the opinion that Robin was dead and buried, or eaten. Dorcas needed protecting from herself, he said. And they agreed. Now he smiled and held something up to the moonlight. It sparkled. Rather fortunate, he thought, and not for the first time, that Robin had not returned.

Before he pulled the curtains he saw Julie Barnsley looking like a pole vaulter as she flew past his house and hurled her pole aloft into the yard of the pub. Really, thought Miles, people did strange things in this village. Very strange things. On the bedside table he placed the object he had been holding up to the moonlight at the window. It was a rich and rare solitaire diamond ring set on a band of glowing white gold. Miles polished it and admired it often in the privacy of his bedroom. Robin had entrusted it to him before he went away, and it had been meant for Dorcas. All it had needed was a little adjustment. Yes, most fortuitous that it was not on her finger when his brother vanished. Very . . . He took one last look at the vulgarity of the Gnome. And a horse's private parts, he chuckled again, and dived into bed, as if the dive would wash him clean of the thought.

Dorcas let the light from the moon flood into her room. She did not even rise to find out what all the clattering and running was about in the street below. Molly's delight in life made Dorcas feel shadowy and strange. Only half a person, only half there. She might have been like that if Robin had been beside her. Well, perhaps something would come of the Bonner girl and her project. Something good. Something for Dorcas to relish. How she longed for relish in her life. Molly Bonner looked as if she enjoyed *her* life, even though she seemed to be quite alone: no parents, no grandparents – and no husband or lover anywhere to be seen. If she could do it, why couldn't Dorcas?

The upsetting thing about love, of course, was that it was never far away. Songs were full of it, books were full of it, radios and televisions were full of it – and now Molly was, too, thought Dorcas. That love affair between her grandfather and her grandmother – how he had written letters from Pound Hill and how she had replied, in secret – all so romantic. Dorcas knew it was a story of true love that she both envied and admired, a touch of romance that she could not turn away from. Gawain again, tapping her on the shoulder. Despite Miles's malign optimism about turning the Gnome and the Hill into a money-spinning tourist attraction, and despite her own desire to rile him, she was pleased that Molly was here. Molly would force her to be a better person, even though going up there was difficult. It would, she counselled herself, do her no harm at all to have to confront the past, move on, start anew. After all, the archaeologist's granddaughter was doing it out of love, because of love, so who was she, Dorcas, to hold back? Whatever else she had lost in life, she had never lost the feeling of love, only the possession of it.

A shiver ran down her spine, for she realised that, with this decision, she was taking on the mantle of the permanently single woman living in a village who grew a little more dried up every day and smiled and did good works. Dorcas had never wanted to be a woman who did good works, for that way brings people's pity, but now – she sighed once more – now she was. I will do what I can for Molly Bonner's efforts on Pound Hill, she said to the unmoving Gnome, though she wanted more than anything to leave the place exactly as it was, to let it remain eroded, let it be hidden for ever, along with her memories of being there, held up high by a pair of sunburnt arms with freckles that you could count, and teeth that smiled out of a brown berry of a face ... Love, like relish, seemed a remote and hidden thing now.

She sat there, looking out from her pillows at the Spode dish that glistened in the silvery light. And if the Spode dish had been able to look back at her from its shelf, it would have seen that the same silvery light picked out the trace of a tear on each of Dorcas's well-scrubbed cheeks. Something that no one else knew about, but which was not a very rare event, as the dish could assert – if asked.

Eight

MOLLY BONNER WAS also in bed but she was nowhere near turning out her light. She, too, was considering love and its consequences. She had beside her the pink plastic box in which she kept her grandfather's letters to her grandmother and now, at last, here she was, in the place where it was most appropriate to read them again.

The first letter was dated the day that Arthur Bonner set up camp on Pound Hill in early March. Unlike his granddaughter he put up a tent and lived in that for the duration of the workings – except when rain washed them away so badly that the party repaired to the Old Holly Bush for respite until the clouds moved away. But he had not been given what Molly had just been given, which was the drawing done by Peter Hanker's great-great-whatever-grandfather. There was no mention of it. And even allowing for the fact that Peter's grandfather-much-removed was unlikely to have been a great artist, the sketch must be accurate enough. It was something for Molly to follow. She slipped out of bed and tiptoed across to the window. Whatever the mystery was, if there was one, it was out there and ready to be discovered.

The Gnome lay on the Hill, shameless and even more shocking in the silvery moonlight, his shape bleached by the brightness, and Molly could see at once, even though bushes and undergrowth disguised much of it, that his outline was different from the drawing. Very possibly, if the drawing were to be followed, as she suspected, it might show that something had once been cut to look like drapery over his arm. It might confirm – if she were right – that he was a great deal older than currently assumed.

It was all far too exciting for sleep. And the Lufferton Boneyites seemed a friendly lot, willing to pitch in, which was what she needed. Her main difficulty was that she had no one whom she could trust to secrecy lined up to film each stage. She would have to do that herself after all and it would not be easy. Ah well. Freddy would be the sorrier when he returned and saw how much she had achieved. His short note wishing her good luck and giving a poste restante address was chucked on to the dressing table. The box of letters and the two notebooks were what held Molly's attention now. She looked at the clock: ten to midnight. Oh, she thought as she hopped back into bed and snuggled the covers around her and took another letter from the pile, Oh she could not wait for tomorrow to come and the work to begin.

My dearest girl, [she read] *We are very comfortable up here and getting the layout shipshape before we start. As in life, so in archaeology, a wise man makes sure he is well prepared for any occurrence so we have brought everything but the kitchen sink with us. Laycock says he has one of those in the cart if we need it. The people of the village are wonderfully helpful. Life in this part of England is hard for those who live by the land. We are nearly all pastoral hereabouts, with some root crops grown for animal feed, and recovery from the bad years is slow. Yet they would gladly share all they have. I do not like to tell them that it is their very suffering that has left the site here so pure and so much undisturbed in the surrounding landscape. Unusually it is not a place that has been used for pasture like the surrounding flatland. There are almost no sheep anyway nowadays, poverty and poor practice in evidence, and cattle*

*and pigs don't tend to climb hills. But, by recompense, I
can pay my way, and shall, and it will help. The beer in
the local pub is first class and we are down there most
evenings for a warm by the fire, and a decent meal. The
landlord is full of ideas about the Hill and its tenant, and
a good and cheerful man. The village seems proud of its
Gnome, yet not proud of it – rather, I fancy, like a parent
who does not want the world to think the less of him for
bragging about the cleverness of his offspring.*

*I take your admonitions to heart but you will have to
trust me that my silence on the subject of possibilities is to
do with there being nothing definite to report, rather than
my keeping secrets from you. You will need to accept this
trial if you are to be the wife of an archaeologist, which,
God willing, you are to be one day. To keep a secret from
you, dearest Margaret, would be hard. I might be able to
do so when we are apart, but once we meet – you always
see through me. I do not want to commit my findings to
paper except in the form of notebooks until I am quite
certain of my facts – though I shall probably give a hint
in my letters as archaeology is as much about detective
work as it is about science and I need a little fun to enter
the proceedings to keep my girl happy. But I hope with all
my heart, which you know you have, that our meeting will
not be too far off by which time I will have something
more certain – and – yes, dear girl, – exciting – as you
would have it – to tell.*

*Meanwhile you must, <u>must</u>, think very hard about your
future. If you want to take a man who is nearly twice your
age (it must be said, though you would not let me when
we were last together) and who has very little fortune and
almost no reputation – though a passion for what he does
and a hope that the future will bring good things – then I*

126

am he. For myself, despite your father's understandable assertions as to my motivations (you shock me with your language, my love – to say he speaks of an old man lusting for a young girl is strong! Rather it is an older man full of love for a young woman) I want to state, again and again and again, that I love you with all my heart, and know that you love me and that, despite your youth, you have a brave, intelligent head on your shoulders and one that, should it so take the thought into itself and find it acceptable still, I will marry. I cannot dare think that will be very soon, since you do not finish at school for another three months and have seen very little of the world and there is no doubt that your family will send you off to Switzerland to be finished as soon as school is out. But I will wait. If, as you say, you wish only to see the world with me attached to your arm. Then so be it.

You ask about the Gnome. You are unkind to tease me. You know perfectly well where his fame lies and I can only tease you back by stating that every evening, before turning into the tent, I sit on his most famous part and smoke a pipe before bed. He is, as I write, magnificent in the moonlight, but he needs clearing. I look at him and wonder why he was positioned here. This is the mystery. We will know a little more over the next few days but my guess is that he was originally laid out by Vespasian's chaps rather than the Bronze Age locals. A thought I keep to myself currently, as must you. But odd that he should be placed where he was visible only to a comparatively limited area. We are looking into the uprisings that the locals caused in those first few years of Roman power – if it was Vespasian he was mighty good at suppressing rebellions – the Scots and the Welsh can attest to that and I'd hazard that the South-West showed its mettle, too. Of course our Gnome may

*have been a pagan figure that the Romans adapted. But I
doubt that. They would be more likely to obliterate him.
And that he is referred to as a gnome seems to be out of
the new Latin from the late mediaeval period and he may
well have been called something else before then. But I
have no proof.*

*Oh my darling girl, this is not what you want me to
write. You want me to write that I love you and miss
you and wish to be with you and the foolish stuff of
lovers. So I do. And I enclose a small thing, black and
dull to your eyes, I'd warrant – found up here when I
walked the land first – and you must be content with it
as a love token despite its plainness – for that small and
smooth black article you hold is a little aberrant – that
tells me there is something to know up here beyond what
the Gnome seems to say. This object was brought here.
It was drilled with a small hole. Why? The usual use for
such pebbles was jewellery – beads, mainly – or weaving
– no one is quite sure – but none has come this far before
and none has been found already drilled but away from
a settlement of some kind. I take it as a talisman that I
am on the right track of something – but what, my love,
what?*

*Look after it and I shall collect it from you when we
next meet. I have an inkling, just a faint inkling, of what
I might – I hope – I will – find, but no certainty. The only
certainty in my life now is you. I hold on to that. As I
cannot, yet, hold you. Dearest Margaret, Love is the binder,
always is and, I hazard, always was.*

More anon, your loving Arthur.

The letter, carefully folded, was placed back with the others. It
always made Molly sad to read it, knowing what was to come.

The next time they met it was not for a little love trysting moment, it was to elope and marry. After which he never went back to the site.

Molly lay in the darkness a while and pondered – it was the most informative of all the letters for after that it seemed that the excitement began and Arthur's communications, even with his beloved girl, were shorter and more obscure. The shale piece, which he drew and identified in his notebook, was not kept with the letters and notebooks but she knew the stuff well. Some of the finest polished beads were made from it – though this piece was referred to as being still in its found form, as a pebble, from the Jurassic coast. Her grandfather was certainly right to be puzzled by it. She was, too. Some beads, properly polished and pierced, *had* been found away from the coast, but none had been discovered as far as Lufferton Boney. Another mystery. She liked mysteries up to a point, you would be a fool to take up her profession and not like them, but in this case she wanted to be sure that it would eventually be solved. Of that there was no certainty. Far from it. Now she had seen the site for herself she concurred with her grandfather: it was older than its received history allowed. But just how old?

She turned out the lamp, began the thinking process, and fell instantly asleep. Tomorrow was time enough for mulling, tomorrow when the site would be secured and made ready, after which her helpers from London would be gone, leaving her and the village volunteers to take it to the next stage. But after that they, too, would leave the field to Molly alone. The prospect both delighted and daunted her. She had never worked a site in such singular fashion before. Some (including Freddy) might say it was madness. She smiled. It was love that had done this to her. The love of her grandfather for her grandmother. If it had not been for war he would have reached an answer and Molly would not be here setting up the site. She might not even be an

archaeologist. History, personal or worldly, is full of unpre-
dictables. Love and War – the two great movers and shakers of
history – had been more powerful forces than knowledge. Always
would be.

Nine

So THEN, how did Pound Hill and its ancient site escape being scheduled and protected and ring-fenced and compulsorily purchased for so long? How was it that a private landowner could have such a monument to the past and be allowed a say in its future? How was it that, unlike the inhabitants of other ancient places, the people of Lufferton Boney – and the few trippers who arrived there – still had access to the figure? How was this done? Quite easily. There was no letter sent to *The Times* by William Flinders Petrie as there had been in 1900 on behalf of Stonehenge so that Pound Hill's owner, like Edmund Antrobus, felt shamed into responding with remedial work. No – nothing like that. The site was overlooked for a long time. The Edwardians were slowly waking up to the need for public interference in conservation and there were many grander sites that required their attention. Arthur Bonner wrote in his Notebook 1 that Pound Hill was reasonably high, it was set in the middle of a bowl of land and therefore not widely seen from the surrounding countryside. Most strange, he wrote, for such a bold figure in the landscape to be placed so insignificantly.

Thus the Gnome waited. The locals seemed to look after it up to a point, and up to a point it was left alone. Whether it did the job that many hoped for could not be proven or disproven. Many babies were born, many wishful mothers had visited the Gnome – and who was to say? But not until recent times had the beady eye of the heritage establishment been cast so determinedly upon the site. There would be no houses on the baby slopes of Pound Hill. No removal of the Gnome by stealth. Nor, it seemed, would it be economically viable to make it into a pukkah museum. To which Miles, not unreasonably, might say Just My Luck.

When Molly Bonner came along with her proposal it was the next best thing. Her money would provide. Miles had no fears that the powers that be would refuse him – as he put it – the permission to control the number of visitors and take remuneration for the protection of this ancient monument once the Gnome was restored to his full (some might say too full) glory. Miles would be its protector, is how he put it to them, and they nodded in enthusiastic relief. Another box ticked. They happily acquiesced.

Once it might have been true, indeed it certainly *was* true, that Arthur Bonner was not considered the right sort to be honoured in his profession, but that was the case no more. Archaeology was no longer seen as a personal and expensive quest by the elite, but a democratic way of showing everyone today how their ancestors lived yesterday. Rich or poor, beggar or toff – all were part of the story of the ages. And since his skills and talents were now acknowledged, Arthur Bonner's work in other areas – before Pound Hill – was properly recognised. His conclusions that the Augustan legions had moved much further north than originally thought were honoured at last, as were his various identifications of long-serving temples and what went before them.

He took his place in the Hall of Fame and his work, right up until his death on the Front, was now acknowledged. But no one in his profession gave a thought to his last site, Pound Hill. Too much was going on at the time for anyone to register it – Molly's grandmother had his only records and now Molly had them. They would be given to the right people and put in the right place once Molly had done her job. Her grandmother advised this and Molly agreed. And while she did, of course, invoke the name of her (now) esteemed ancestor in order to set the scheme up, she did not go into any greater detail than was absolutely necessary.

Some grants were available for the project but it would be largely self-funded by Molly. This smoothed the wheels no end. When she needed help or muscle, Molly would use locals, and if she needed more expert help than she herself could supply, why she would call on it. But she did not think that would be necessary. Miss Molly Bonner, as her first appearance in Lufferton Boney's village street had shown, was a woman of confidence, experience and conviction – though her pink skirt and her boots had been tidied away for the duration and she wore rough-cast clothing that, if anything, thought Nigel as he gazed upwards using his father's binoculars (which he held slightly away from his eyes and nose as the bruising was still, despite the passing of time, quite painful), made her all the more attractive. Like seeing a pretty, delicate, fragile little feminine thing wearing army combats. He shivered at the thought and focused more longingly upon the figure scurrying about up on the Hill. Molly did not notice him lingering in the street below; Molly had other things on her mind. But Julie Barnsley, wincing slightly at the degree of bruising she observed, did.

The blinds were drawn in Beautiful Bygones. Dryden lay back on a horsehair and leather chesterfield (ex-Manchester St James' Men's Club, 1870, £700 in need of restuffing/covering) and held the packet of frozen peas even more firmly to the bridge of his nose. He, too, was still suffering. He chose to pull down the blinds and block the sight of the Gnome and all its activity and not to open his eyes even indoors for the time being. Nigel was hardly in a condition to go wooing anyone, especially Marion Fitzhartlett, even if he were up to the task. Though he seemed to be determined to do Molly Bonner's bidding. Oh well, nothing wrong with that, might even put a bit of muscle on him.

Miles, looking up, fingered the cheque, looked again at Molly's signature, and sighed. He was happy.

The Fitzhartlett family made nothing of it. There was no ribbon to cut or speech to be made at this point and so they carried on in their usual way. Sir Roger took his gun over to Biddlecombe, Marion took her second-best horse to be shod over Dunsditton way; and Dulcima made herself wait for her morning's tipple until the clock had struck eleven. This, she smiled, was progress. To celebrate she chose champagne. Such delights were moving rapidly towards an end.

Pinky and Susie put on their rucksacks, stuffed bread and cheese and cider into each one, and set off from Lufferton Boney. It seemed to Susie that while they were waiting for the Gnome to come back to them, cleaner and more potent than ever, they might rediscover the pleasures of the tramp. It used to be one of their special private jokes – Pinky would say 'Fancy a tramp?' And Susie would say 'Why would I want a tramp when I've got you?' They did it again, now, and it made them laugh and laugh, all the way to Binster Rings. Pinky's tentative suggestion that Susie discard her flowing garments for something a little more sensible was greeted with consideration by his wife. This was progress. It was still a bit flowing and fringed on the top half, but the lower half was a very proper pair of jeans. Figure hugging. Nice.

Winifred looked at Donald and wondered if she would ever feel happy to see him sitting across a table from her again. Donald did not seem to know her thoughts. 'I do believe that Nigel and his father have been fighting,' he said. 'Black eyes, they've got, the both of them, in the same place – must have been a hell of a clip . . . Fighting – I ask you.'

Winifred pushed back her chair and stood up with a very odd look on her face. 'Well Donald,' she said. 'At least that is *something*.' She went to the window, pulled back the curtain (Peter

Jones, chintz, three colourways) and stared up the Hill. How free the girl looked. How engaged with the world. That, she thought, is my salvation. My hopes, my possibilities. And then she laughed. 'I will lift up mine eyes unto the hills,' she said to the flitting figures atop the Gnome, 'from whence cometh my help . . .' She laughed again. When she returned to the break-fast table Donald was looking at her most peculiarly and holding on to the teapot so hard that his knuckles showed white.

Peter looked out of the front window, just before he opened up, and saw Julie Barnsley staring at Nigel Fellows who was staring, through a rather fine pair of binoculars, at the busy goings-on up on the Hill. He seemed, noted Peter, to have trouble focusing the very fine binoculars – Peter was a man who enjoyed gadgets and technology and boys' toys and it pained him (almost as much as it pained him to see how hungrily Julie stared at Nigel) to see another man misusing something of such high techno-logical calibre. He threw the bolt on the door, flung it open and dashed across the road. 'Nigel, you prat,' he called. 'This is the way to hold them for maximum effect.' And he thrust the binoc-ulars in the sensible position right up into the other man's eye sockets. So Nigel, bowed down with something, made a not very nice noise, and hit him. Julie Barnsley ran over to the two of them and separated them with fierce elbows and even fiercer eyes. Above them, quite oblivious, Molly Bonner and her team worked on.

And Dorcas? Where was Dorcas? Dorcas was in her tiny court-yard staring up at the pale blue morning sky and the Hill. She did not look up at it very often for, though she would never say it to anyone, it always felt as if the Gnome mocked her in some way – as if he declared to the world that she was a fool for love and that he had won. More than that Dorcas could not explain, but so it was whenever she looked up at him – until now. Now that Molly Bonner was up there doing whatever it was she was doing, it somehow felt that the Gnome had diminished a little, had become less certain in his mockery, that his pride in his member was not quite so clear and strong now that there were people scampering about all around it. 'Good for you,' Dorcas whispered, looking up at the crouching figure with its distinctive red hair in the far distance – the figure seemed to be measuring and hammering and stretching tapes with a determined movement and sound. It rang out, in fact, the hammering, and Dorcas was pleased. If anyone could take that Gnome in hand and control him (a thought that made her chuckle) then Molly Bonner could. The prospect gave her energy, renewed hope even – and Dorcas remembered what she had, in misery, forgotten; something that she once vowed to say every day until Robin came home or she went to find him. She spoke it again now. 'I don't know if anyone, a god, a fate, a will-o'-the-wisp, is up there and listening, but if you are, and if you can, please send him home safe to me. Or let them find his remains so that I can bury them – or *something* – anything. Let it happen. Please. Thank you.' Feeling much better and just about resisting the urge to stick out her tongue at the lowering creature above her, Dorcas then returned to her tiny kitchen, filled with coffee the vacuum flask that had not been used for many a year – and set off to climb the Hill and deliver it to Molly Bonner.

As she walked past Hill View House she saw Miles at his window flapping the cheque, part one of the payments, smiling more broadly than the cat in *Alice*. 'Bank, Dorcas,' he mouthed through the window. She nodded, pointed up the Hill, indicated that she would be five minutes – and went on up.

The geological survey was over and the results were no different from Grandfather Bonner's surmisings and what Molly expected.

Now all was ready for the villagers to be invited to help with the clearing of the site, and then Molly – at last – could begin. So she was in a very friendly and receptive mood when Dorcas arrived with the flask.

'I feel I'm one of the Beaker people,' said Molly, smiling her thanks up at Dorcas and sitting back on a lump of stone to sip from the plastic beaker.

Dorcas sat beside her. 'The what?'

'The Beaker people – lived here around two millennia ago – or maybe a bit less. Someone called Abercromby gave them the name because they drank from pottery vessels. They probably sat up here with their beakers just like us once.'

They both looked about them at the peaceful scene. 'It's good to see it without any sheep,' said Dorcas. 'Feels right. They never were up here when I first came to Lufferton.'

'I should think they're taking a rest cure after all they've seen.' Molly ran her hand over the grass. 'Doesn't look like they've been up here at all,' she said. 'No sign of lynchets or similar. Maybe they simply preferred to rear them on lower ground. There's plenty of good pasture round about. So much to find out still. Of course it could be for another reason they never grazed it . . .' She shook her head as if to remove the thought. 'Time will tell.'

'What other reason?' asked Dorcas.

Molly shrugged. 'There is more to this place than we know,' she said.

'And there's more to you than we know, Miss Molly.'

Molly was looking down and plucking at the grass. She did not look entirely comfortable. Unusual for her.

'You said two words that didn't quite fit,' said Dorcas firmly. 'You said "dig" and "excavate" – both of which are somewhat different from "clearance".'

Molly looked into her beaker as if the answer might be there.

'Clearance?' said Dorcas. 'Or a bit more than that?'

Molly looked up and straight into Dorcas's eyes. 'Dorcas, you are right. I might not be here – entirely – for what I said I was. Not exactly *only* clearing.' She looked about her. 'Maybe it's like the Gnome. My edges were a bit blurred.' She gave Dorcas a sideways glance as if assessing whether or not she could be trusted. Dorcas, staring towards the horizon, nodded as if to say she was not surprised. 'I knew there was something,' she said.

'You have an honest nose,' said Molly. 'So I'll tell you the plan.' She took a deep breath, stared at the ground, and began. 'Now I'll have to tread carefully here. But I decided it was best not to be specific. With laymen, if you say you are digging at a site they expect to see treasure at the end of it. Roman jewels or a Saxon hoard, perhaps. Once in a lifetime things. Usually you find burials, grave goods, the ancient midden heap at best, or nothing. And I have no idea what I'll find, if anything at all. But I judged your friend Miles to be – um – less altruistic than avaricious in this enterprise so I thought it best to cool the idea down. He'd never stay away if he thought I was looking for treasure.' Molly gave her a frank look and put her chin in her hands. 'So?'

Dorcas laughed, touched her nose questioningly, and looked sceptical. 'No one has ever accused my nose of being a telltale,' she said.

Molly laughed. 'My grandmother used to say you could tell a lot about a person from their nose,' she said. 'Small ones that held flat to the face were the noses of people without courage, she said – very large ones that stuck out much more than was proportionate would always be wanting more than they had and poking into other people's business – but a straight nose that fitted its surroundings – she was very firm on the subject – would always belong to a person of balance and honesty. Yours is straight, perfectly in proportion.'

'Careful,' said Dorcas. 'You'll be telling me next that I'm beautiful.'

'Oh I wouldn't do that,' said Molly.

Dorcas turned and looked at her and could not help laughing. 'Why?'

'Because you are not.'

'That's the last time I bring you hot coffee. But I suppose flatterers are generally out for something not entirely good.'

'Do you think you are beautiful?'

'No. Not at all.'

'Neither am I,' said Molly. 'But I'm cute, like a silly dolly – whereas you are dramatic and special looking with your dark hair and eyes and your –' she looked her up and down – 'willowy shape.'

'I think you mean thinness,' said Dorcas. 'And the dark hair is flecked with grey.'

'My grandmother said that I had my grandfather's thighs.'

Dorcas did laugh now, right out loud. 'Your grandmother was a great sayer of things,' she said. 'They look all right to me.'

'They are chunky,' said Molly. 'Short and chunky. Which is very good for what I do which is a lot of crouching, a lot of lifting, a lot of kneeling.'

'They're not that chunky,' said Dorcas amused.

'Chunky enough,' said Molly, laughing. 'For the job in hand.'

Now Dorcas looked Molly very straight in the eye. 'And what is the job in hand? Exactly?'

'I'll trust the nose,' said Molly.

So she told Dorcas about her grandfather's view that there was more to the Gnome of Pound Hill than his gargantuan masculinity. 'He visited it a few times and he felt there was something that was not quite right about the landmark, that the placing of it was odd, and according to his letters it was all much clearer to him on this visit. Mind you, I think you see everything more clearly when you are in love. It's as if someone has wiped the world's windows.' Dorcas opened her mouth. Molly held up a hand as Dorcas was about to speak. 'And before you say something rational or cynical, I should say that my grandmother described him as sensible, feet on the ground, not given to fancy, driven by intellectual assessment rather than instinct, though every archaeologist, every scientist as a matter of fact, has to have something instinctual about him or her. Somewhere beyond our conviction that we are the highest form of life and have left our animal beginnings behind, is a residual connection with things we can't explain and will probably never know but which are real, nonetheless. Mystery. Stuff that can't be proved by evidence . . .' She shrugged. 'Instinctual.'

Dorcas smiled. 'Lecture over?' she asked.

'Not quite.' But Molly smiled back.

'I just wanted to say that I concur. It certainly happened to me that way. It was like everything suddenly had an application of Windolene.'

Molly nodded. 'Exactly. Well, I shall dig a trench at a chosen place. I'll know it when I find it. If necessary, we'll test some soil samples. That should help me date it.'

'Any idea when it might have been cut out?'

'Open minded. Grandfather thought it was probably Roman, but it could be later – or earlier. Late Iron Age. He didn't seem to think it was mediaeval, despite tradition. But as to why he's there . . .'

'But isn't it about fertility? Just that?'

'Who knows? Possibly. That may be all it is. But I've got a feeling, like my grandfather had a feeling, that there's more to that Gnome than meets the eye.'

'I don't think it's the eye you need worry about,' said Dorcas, quite deadpan. At which they both laughed in highly unlady-like fashion. Some of the London team stopped their work and looked up enviously. Molly signalled that she was taking another five minutes. 'Then I'd better get back to work,' she said. 'We all help each other out on various digs but I'm supposed to roll up my sleeves with them. They're only here for a couple of days. But what do you think of the Gnome? I mean living down there and seeing it all the time?

Dorcas considered. Did she trust this young woman? Yes, she decided. Yes I do. 'Look,' she said, 'this will sound bonkers but when I look at the Gnome I get a feeling – a real certainty – of something else, something inexplicable – which may or may not be to do with how much caffeine I've had that morning. But it's the strangest of feelings that he's leering at me – at all of us. Looking down and leering. That he's not a benign guardian or a figure of fun, but – well – the opposite. It's a relief to hear you talk about mysteries and instincts being part of everyone's experience.'

'Exactly,' said Molly. 'If you tell someone else what your nutty thought is then you'll find – ten-to-one – that they think something similar. Happens to me all the time.'

She looked up towards the Gnome's strangely wrought cap. 'I wonder,' she said, putting her head on one side, 'if there isn't something about his head as well as his . . . When you are up this close you can't see him in his full magnitude, which is something of a relief. Could be overwhelming. But from down in the village – well . . . And yet only in the village, really. Not far and wide. Unusual, that.'

She looked down towards Lufferton Boney and seemed to lose herself in thought. Her gloved finger tapped the edge of her nose, which was smaller than Dorcas's and slightly folded into her cheeks at the sides so that one might be forgiven for wondering if she was wholly honest herself. Eventually she came back to life and said, 'I can't fathom why it was put here. Not really. If it was cut out to represent a god or a symbol of power then it might have been put on that hill over there –' she pointed to a higher piece of land in the distance: 'or over there. Where it would be seen by many more people, including travellers. Not this smaller hill which is mainly to be seen by the people living locally and in the valley.'

'Well,' said Dorcas, cheerfully, 'that's what you're here to find out. I'm sure you will. You've only been here for a short while yet you already know so much – instinct and mystery included.'

Molly laughed and tapped her nose again. 'I'm not as honest as you are,' she said cheerfully. 'Much of that comes from my grandfather's letters. It's just that as soon as I read it, it made sense.'

Dorcas looked about her. There were hooks driven into the chalky soil with tapes attached.

'Those indicate where I think the original line was drawn.'

'It looks much the same.'

'It changes quite a lot in some places,' said Molly. 'Goes down about twenty centimetres at the edges but it would have been cut deeper than that originally – probably about thirty. And it's fluctuated over time from previous clearings and general erosion. But oddly enough not on the – er –' She nodded towards the top of the phallus and her cheeks went quite a deep shade of pink. She put her hands flat on either side of her face. 'It's really odd,' she said, 'but the Gnome does unnerve me a little. I have to steel myself to approach that bit of him. Not like me.'

Dorcas said, 'Not surprising, really, given the scale of him. We all feel a bit uncomfortable in his presence. That's probably what we are meant to feel.'

'Oh, I'll get used to it. But that part of him seems to have been more or less left alone entirely. No enlargement there.'

Both women stood and stared at the Gnome's masculinity for a second or two. 'Well, you wouldn't need to, would you?' they said at the same time.

Molly hooked a thumb over her shoulder in the direction of the London team. 'They go back tomorrow – and then I'll need my village helpers. They can remove the rest of the overgrowth and the undergrowth and then I'll crack on by myself.'

To Dorcas it seemed a daunting task. 'Are you sure you can do the rest on your own? We're all very willing, you know.'

'No!' said Molly, perhaps a little too quickly and loudly. 'I'll be fine.'

'You looked distinctly un-doll-like just then.'

'It's just that when the delicate stuff starts you really don't want a lot of people tramping about. It has to be me on my own.'

'I think you are going to enjoy this. And make a name for yourself.'

'That's part of it,' said Molly. 'That's the ambition of any archaeologist in the land. But I also want to complete what Grandfather Bonner started. And when I've done that . .' she bent and brushed off her knees: 'then I can give up for a while and concentrate on having babies.'

'What?' said Dorcas, not believing she had heard properly.

Molly laughed even more loudly. 'You heard. Babies.'

'Have you got anyone in mind?'

'What for?'

'The babies?'

'Of course,' said Molly, 'but he's in Brazil at the moment. He knows everything there is to know about pterosaurs – which can never be enough, apparently – but Brazil has fossils that make new links and throw new light and, well,' she laughed. 'Get involved with a man on a mission and you have to take your place in the pecking order . . . If he were a dog he'd be a terrier. Never give up until he's shaking the answer between his teeth.'

Dorcas smiled. She recognised the type. 'I know all about that,' she said. 'South America must be full of rugged Englishmen doing wonderful things –'

'Welshman in my case,' said Molly. 'He sings as he goes.'

'Do you love him very much?'

'Yes,' said Molly. 'But South America is hugely important from a palaeontologist's point of view – he had to go. I suppose it's one of the last great frontiers. What do you mean "full of rugged Englishmen"?'

And then Dorcas, who was not one to talk about Robin or the past, decided that she would. 'My fiancé –' said Dorcas, and stopped herself. It sounded strange, alien, almost untrue now. 'He was on the border between Bolivia and Brazil. He died out there.'

Molly's curving mouth, usually nearer to a smile than anything else, went down at the corners. 'What was he doing there?'

Dorcas told her about Robin's one last major project. After which Molly shook her head and said quietly, 'I'd heard it was pretty lawless over there. How did he die?' And she sat back down again as if she had all the time in the world.

'That's the worst part of it,' said Dorcas. 'I don't know. I got a boot and a hat and my photo and nothing else. Nothing at all. He vanished. Eaten by animals, perhaps. Dangerous terrain. Or shot. Or kidnapped. Who knows?'

'That border is dangerous for other reasons than furry carnivores,' said Molly. 'It's a drug runners' paradise. And it's policed by some of the richest families in Bolivia – who don't like the plans for sharing the land out more equally.'

'All that,' said Dorcas with a sigh. 'The Foreign Office said that he wouldn't have been kidnapped – which is the other thing that happens – as they never got a ransom demand.' She shrugged. 'So that's that . . . One day I hope to get out there and . . .' She shrugged.

'Where exactly did this happen?' asked Molly.

So Dorcas told her. 'And now,' she said, putting the flask back together, 'I had better go.'

As if to confirm her words, just at that moment from below came far-off shouting. It was Miles. 'Baa-aa-nk, Doo-or-cas,' he called. And he flapped the cheque.

Dorcas pulled a face.

Molly looked sympathetic. 'Don't worry,' she said. 'If we find anything out about this place, we'll slap unbendable rules on him quick as you like. In the meantime –' She put a finger to her lips. Dorcas looked across to the two higher hills. 'Yes,' she said. 'Now you come to mention it, it is odd that they should choose here to put him.'

For the moment that was the end of the conversation. Dorcas, feeling lighter than the wind, ran down the Hill towards Miles and the money. Even just saying Robin's name brought him alive for a moment, and that was lovely.

That evening, sitting up in her bed, Molly wrote a letter. She would have sent a text or made a telephone call, but the intended recipient of the message was not likely to be anywhere near a telephone, or a signal. And the intended recipient would go back to base from time to time, to the poste restante he had sent her, all things permitting, where this letter might be found and collected. She began by writing

Dear Freddy – and she drew a small heart by the side of his name. After which the she wrote – *I know we were not contacting each other unless it was a matter of life and death or bragging about something – and everything is going well here – but today*

I heard a very sad story about an Englishman with red hair and freckles who answers to the name of Robin . . .

When she had finished the letter she sealed the envelope, kissed it, put it under her pillow to post the following morning, and fell happily asleep. There is nothing better in the world than drifting off to dreamland when you are feeling that your little bit of the universe is unfolding exactly as you want it to.

PART II

One

SOME WEEKS LATER, and in the firm belief that looking was learning for an archaeologist, Molly sat for a long time contemplating the current shape of the Gnome, what she thought the Gnome's shape had once been, the various likelihoods of ways that that shape might have been changed, and the drawing of 1789. The people in the village below had mixed feelings when they looked up and saw her, so still and quiet, her chin in her hand like Rodin's *Thinker*. They felt admiration and anxiety about the reappearance of the Gnome. The clearing had been fun, something for everyone to get involved in and – apart from a degree of bossiness by Miles and ribaldry by some of the younger folk – it had gone smoothly for Molly. But now it was her time and with a convincing display of fierceness she sent them all away and said they were not to come back until she invited them. Now she was alone on the Hill, her back to the wind, contemplating the ancientness of the landscape all around her. Molly was taking her time and quite uncaring of what the people below her thought about it. She knew that Pound Hill and its famous occupant were connected in more than a surface way: she knew it, and she meant to prove it.

Nigel was perfectly happy for Molly to be there and be still. He could watch her through his binoculars, and dream. The bruises had all but faded now, as indeed had Julie. Molly was all. Nigel contemplated spending every free hour he possessed at her command. Her white knight – that is what he would be. He'd seen *Extreme Jousting* on the television and liked the idea of wearing favours and rescuing maidens. It was unfortunate that *Extreme Jousting* incorporated the riding of a large and speedy horse, but he put that out of his mind. Fantasies were never difficult to move around, where Nigel was concerned. If real life was somewhat unrewarding, his other life was quite acceptable. Molly would want him one day. There was bound to be something she needed rescuing from while she was up there. He would be prepared.

He heard his father's footsteps on the stairs. Into the room he came just as Nigel hid the binoculars up the back of his sweater. 'I want you to give the wood on that gun a damn good oiling today – delicately, mind – no dripping it or putting too much on at once. If we get it right it will be the perfect gun for Sir Roger – and he might take better care of this one.'

'He does seem to go through them quite a lot, doesn't he?'

'Nobody likes to miss an easy shot,' said his father defensively.

'But he jumps up and down on his gun. That's hardly good breeding, is it?' Nigel gave his father a sly look. He knew perfectly well that his father would like him to get friendly with Marion Fitzhartlett but Dryden ignored the jibe so Nigel continued, 'And a gun like our one is a beauty, collectible you said. Is it fair to future generations to ruin a fine gun?'

His father bristled, as Nigel knew he would. 'The Fitzhartletts come from a long line of great Englishmen; if he wants to jump on his gun, then he is entitled to. If *noblesse oblige* is privilege with responsibility, then a man of distinction can do the opposite sometimes, and behave – behave less nobly.' He pointed to the stairs. 'Now, will you kindly get going with the gun oil? And *only* the oil, mind, none of your fiddling with the workings.'

As he walked past his father Nigel muttered something along the lines that if *he* jumped up and down on a gun – or anything, come to that – and broke it, he'd be for it.

Dryden, following him down the stairs, said that if he married

Marion Fitzhartlett he could behave as badly as he liked – use his guns as stilts if he wanted to.

'I'd have to,' Nigel said mournfully. 'She's not only got turnip hair and a strange look, she's very, very tall, whereas M—'

But he got no further. Best keep to himself where his love now lay, at least for the time being. How wonderful is the eye of a lover; Molly Bonner was scarcely one inch shorter than Marion Fitzhartlett. If you removed the horse.

Nigel might have given up on Julie but Julie had not given up on Nigel and it was with a certain nervousness that he moved about the village nowadays. But it was worth it, he decided, worth the risk of Julie's wrath. He pictured again how Molly sat so sweet and still and thoughtful above him, and with a light heart he picked up the oily rag and began to feel happy again. He looked at the gun. He felt his muscles pump. Why leave it to his father? He could mend what was wrong with it in a twinkling. His father never gave him credit for anything.

Dryden had noticed and approved the new sense of discomposure surrounding his son and the barmaid. You did not spend a lifetime with beautiful objects made for superior people without a good deal of the nobility they had absorbed over the centuries rubbing off on you. He had but one son, and that son must – *would* – marry well. He had made a promise to a dying woman to make Nigel happy and marriage seemed the solution. He was beginning to think that the dead woman would never rest until their son tied the knot with someone acceptable. Julie was not the right material. Not at all. The disapproval expressed on his deceased wife's face at the prospect had said that very clearly.

There had been enough blue-blooded people in Dryden's life – selling off the family silver and other fine old things was the way they kept themselves afloat nowadays – for him to feel almost akin to them. When you have mopped the tears of a dowager as she parts with her last pair of Worcester candlesticks, you may be justified in considering yourself almost one of them. Antiques were not trade, not really, they were about being a guardian of heritage. And what if, Dryden thought, wincing a little, what if he also purveyed objects of a lesser nature sometimes? Objects such as old brooms and flatirons and the like? These were what the less grand visitors to the village could afford, and they were the crumbs from his table that paid the boring little day to day expenses like council tax, insurance and similar mundanities. Though it always beat him how an American could expect to fly back home with a flatiron hidden in his suitcase. Especially now.

Nigel had no mother and so Dryden must make the match. Nigel's mother, Dryden's wife Lottie, had been a sweet-faced country girl whom he loved in his youth; but somehow, and he could not say how, when they inherited the shop and the business she became less satisfactory – he winced at that thought, too – so she stayed at the back of the shop and never raised her voice. And gradually she seemed to just fade away. Dr Porlock might have said gruffly that it was myopathy and not neuropathy and tried various cures that all came to nothing, but Dryden thought he knew better. When Nigel drew his mother with turnip hair and stick arms, it was not very far from the truth. By the time Dryden saw that truth – saw that it was something akin to neglect – it was too late. What made it all the more shameful was that, as he stood in the church-yard (he had already bought a family plot, which he felt raised his status) he experienced only relief. And he heard a little voice saying in his head that now she was gone, he could get on with the pursuit of becoming a man of higher degree. Unfortunately for Dryden, he also seemed to hear another voice, a more familiar one, once so sweet and low but now so pleading, pleading . . . and those eyes . . .

He would never marry again.

And why would Dryden never marry again?

Because he was afraid of ghosts.

In the days after Lottie's death he saw her frequently: on the stair, in the dimness of the shop, slipping down the village street at dusk. And always admonishing. Her appearances became fewer over the years but you never knew. Dryden could never bring himself to speak to her when she appeared, on the grounds that he did not wish to encourage the visits. He decided he could cope with the sporadic ghost of Lottie in this condition. But it was quite likely that if he remarried the ghost of Lottie might change its attitude. Bad enough dealing with the spectre of a dead wife to whom it was daily business as usual, but the spectre of a dead wife who felt a bit uppish about everything was unthinkable. Dryden had dealt in enough old objects to know that they hold their secrets but that someone, if only a ghost, will always be privy to what the objects have seen and known. Therefore Nigel, his son, must take on the task of noble union for him. Nigel, his son and heir, must marry well. Lottie had wished for her son to be happy and Dryden chose to think this would be through a good marriage. The only benefit from Nigel's many liaisons, especially with the barmaid Julie, was that it proved to Dryden that his son was not a homosexual. A very great relief.

Julie Barnsley knew she must fight and she was definitely not happy.

When she confronted him later that day, Nigel denied everything. 'No,' he said, 'I am not ogling her, I am doing what my father has asked me to do, which is to keep an eye on her.' When Julie Barnsley asked him why his father had wanted him to do that, he – who was not known for his quick-wittedness, was fairly convincing. 'Because,' said Nigel, 'she might be up there finding something old and valuable.'

Julie wondered. Could that be the truth of it? After all, they were in business for the selling of old things and it made sense. And although she had seen plenty of interest shown on Nigel's side, the archaeologist woman had shown little in return. Now Julie, who had been so sure that all was lost, was confused. 'Do you still love me, then?' she asked, playing her trump card.

'Of course I do,' said Nigel, keeping his eyes, as they almost always were nowadays, firmly on the figure on the Hill. 'You know that.' So she must be content. Contentment did not sit easily on one such as Julie. It did not seem fair that the newcomer should be so well liked, so absorbed by what she was doing, so supported by everyone, while she, Julia Barnsley, was alone and fighting for her future. Julie gave the sitter on the Hill one more long and unloving look – behind her the Gnome seemed to glitter in the morning sunlight, an illusion perhaps from the dew – and made her way across the road towards the pub.

The funny thing was, she thought, as she pushed her way through the door, the funny thing was that she quite liked being a barmaid. Very often she found that the morning had racketed past and it was lunchtime already. By the time she had laughed at the absurdities of some of their trippers with Peter, taken disgusting compliments from a collection of the retired agricultural workers from round about – gnarled, sunburnt, wet-eyed old men who looked at her and remembered their youth and chasing the girls in the fields – been propositioned by loud young men and pulled the pumps, she felt fit as a flea. And in the evenings, when she took special care with her looks (the more so since the arrival of Miss Molly Toogood) she basked in the pleasure of Peter's gaze, which was always approving, and of being chatted up by all sorts – old and young, rural or town, rich or poor – for the Old Holly Bush was a favourite for five or six miles around. Not only did it breathe a pleasant, easy-going atmosphere and rustic charm (largely made up of old chairs and tables that had seen much service in the last fifty or sixty years and Peter saw no reason to change them) but it had a cheerful propensity to break the law where smoking was concerned. Perhaps breathe was not quite right, perhaps it coughed a pleasant, easy-going atmosphere for it had a little room at the back, a snug, where smokers could go and avoid the chill of the day or the cold of the night and no one let on, and certainly not PC Brown who, it was said, could smoke for England.

Julie wondered, as she set up the bar, what would it be like to be married and a lady of leisure? She decided that it would be grand. Never anything to do ever again. Nigel said, when he first proposed to her, that he would never let her lily-white hands anywhere near work – neither restoring furniture, nor serving in the shop, nor even going to auctions (which he was never allowed to do, actually) and she, though not entirely convinced since her hands were far from lily-white at the best of times, rather more rose-pink towards red from the bar work and a little chewed around the edges, decided that she would like it that way. As she opened the shutters she saw the top of the Hill and the figure once again, still crouching, still thinking. She must be cold, thought Julie, pleased. And damp. Who'd want to do that for a living? She felt cheerful, once more contemplating her future life as a lady of leisure. Nigel loved her. He would keep her in the way she would like to become accustomed to. Totally idle. Julie Barnsley had not, at this point in her life, read *Madame Bovary*. Julie Barnsley was a prime example of why the book should be presented to every new fiancée who fancied that married life would be easy.

*

Winifred, who *had* read *Madame Bovary* and spent the following forty years too busy to remember it, turned away from her window. Her heart was heavy with an ache that she knew was probably envy, though it was not her customary experience. Something about the advent of that girl had quite jumbled her up. She flopped into the soft, fat sofa cushions (antique gold cotton velvet, Premble & Rawlings, 1973) that furnished the cosy television room (Sony HD 22-inch six months old, DVD/video recorder/player ditto), and wondered what could have brought Flaubert to mind now. Probably, she thought, pushing in an ancient video selected from a pile at her feet and upping the volume to drown out her thoughts, it was a matter of age. That was what Donald thought, and he was, after all, a doctor. The picture flickered to life and she put the girl on the Hill out of her mind and concentrated on the girl that she once was . . . '*And now*,' said the agreeable presenter to camera, '*we go to the final part of our story about the history of the making of the British landscape, and head for the South-West . . .*'

Donald did not know whether to be pleased or anxious about his wife's sudden fancy to watch daytime television. On the whole he thought it was a good move. The sort of thing women who were under strain about being women would find helpful. He did not know what sort of programmes she watched – there seemed to be all kinds of things going on – no car chases or sex scenes or noisy violence, which was encouraging – and the actress looked familiar, he thought, as he passed the sitting-room door each morning on his way out. 'All right, dear?' he made a point of calling. But she had the sound turned up very loud. The woman on the screen had a nice voice, though. Calming. Just what Winifred needed. She needed something, all right. He did wonder if he should ask Charlotte to come for a visit but, frankly, the embarrassment of having a daughter who wore enough metal about her person to stick her to a large magnet and who would invariably take her mother's side, was not an appealing thought right now. He closed the door softly behind him and tiptoed down the path to the car, the town and his surgery. Once in the street he straightened his shoulders and raised his chin. He was a man of importance, out here at any rate.

Peter and Marion were standing together in the yard behind the pub and both of them were talking about the Hill and what was happening to it.

'Why,' said Marion, stroking Sparkle, 'if we had to have something on a hill, couldn't it have been a horse instead of a man?'

'Hardly a man,' said Peter.

Marion's eyes lost their customary neutral look, and a light of something similar to amusement shone in them. Peter wondered if he had ever seen Marion's eyes light up at anything other than a horse before. He looked at her questioningly. She said, 'I should have thought it was quite the reverse.'

'Of what?'

'His being hardly a man. The way I see it –' she returned her gaze to the Gnome, 'he's every bit the man, and hardly a Gnome . . .' She shrugged. 'I'll never go near him again, that's for sure. My little tumble was all his fault – and that – that – *thing* of his. Horses,' she said, 'never let you down. I like horses more than I seem to like men. Anyway. Or at least the ones I know. Apart from you, that is.' This was said without guile and with no subtext beyond friendship, and was received as such. Peter and Marion had no romantic thoughts about each other and the world left their easy relationship alone.

'Do you meet many men?'

'Not really. Except Father's shooting pals. And all the younger ones of those are *awful*. And they hunt as well – I can't stand the hunt. I once saw the MFH get on his horse the wrong way round. Too much stirrup cup. It's cruel, whatever they say.'

Peter knew all about these would-be countrymen. Most of them ended up in the bar after a shoot, all loud voiced and given to drinking more than any gun should, haemorrhaging tweed and talking about the sort of hedges that didn't grow in the country. If Julie asked them what they wanted they snorted with knowing snorts and clearly thought they were the first men ever in the land to come out with the old joke about sex and barmaids. Peter had given up saying anything as Julie claimed she never even heard the words they spoke now – just the relevant ones like 'Pint of Old Romany' or 'Double gin and tonic.' Not all of them were like that, of course, but many were. The nicer ones seemed to slope off early.

'Those aren't men, either,' he said.

'They always want to talk about trust funds. And none of them ride, none of them. Though they think they do. Then I take them into Hinterjack Wood and they fall off. And they get very annoyed and swear a lot and – oh well – they've got no stamina. Whereas Sparkle,' she turned and looked up at the horse with love in her eyes, 'Sparkle is the perfect mixture of reliability and risk, modest good looks, and knowing how to treat a lady without going all silly. Doesn't even get jealous when I ride Coco for a change. You wouldn't get a man behaving so well.'

'You and I did a fair old bit of riding when we were children,' he said. 'But I'm not sure I could keep up with you now.'

'I'd slow down a bit for you,' she said.

Peter laughed. 'You'd have to nowadays.'

'We are friends, aren't we?' she said.

Peter nodded. 'I hope so.'

They turned their eyes back to the Gnome and the crouching, contemplative figure of Molly Bonner. 'She's amazing,' said Peter. 'Don't you think?'

'Ah yes,' said Marion faintly. 'Amazing. Perhaps she will marry you and take you away from here.' Her horse gave a little whinny. 'I should miss you.'

'Maybe she would,' he laughed. 'Marry me and take me away from here and all my debts.'

Marion nuzzled even further into Sparkle.

'But I wouldn't go. I just don't fancy her and I can't work out why.'

'She *is* amazing,' said Marion. 'Very amazing. Perhaps it's because you – fancy – someone else?'

It was Peter's turn to blush. 'Oh, I didn't mean . . .'

Marion laughed and patted her horse's neck. 'I never for a minute thought you meant me, silly. I know better than that. And I know who it really is. And I know who *she's* got her eye on.'

'Not me,' he said. 'Not any more. That's for sure.'

Marion patted his arm as if it were an equine flank. 'Who knows what will happen?' she said.

Peter nodded. 'Well – I'd *better* go and open up.'

'And I'd better continue my ride,' said Marion in voice light with what Peter realised was happiness. How amazing, he thought, that a horse could do that for a woman.

'All the same, if I can help I will,' said Marion. 'You've been a good friend.' Up she jumped on to the saddle, and turning Sparkle's head, she rode out of the yard and into the street. 'Faint heart,' she called over her shoulder, and she was gone.

From the window of Hill View House, Miles took his eyes off the girl on the Hill and watched, as Dryden Fellows often watched, the horse's rump as it rolled its muscular way along by the side of the fields, with its tail swaying like a hula dancer and above it Marion Fitzhartlett's slender body also swaying from side to side. Miles might have a sharp mind where money was concerned, but he was not self-deluded. It was highly unlikely that Marion Fitzhartlett would ever consider becoming his wife and there was no one else up to the job. He certainly did not feel that bursting sense of love he remembered Robin banging on about after he met Dorcas, and he was not sure that he wanted to experience it. Robin had gone very peculiar after becoming engaged – whistling and singing and stomping his feet all over the place and never seeming to sleep. What a long time ago all that was. Miles could honestly say – though not to a living soul – that he did not miss him at all. Well, maybe a tiny bit. As someone to be enjoyably aggrieved by. He sometimes wondered what people meant by a heart – apart from the literal meaning of an organ pumping blood around – but he only ever wondered with the slightest shadow of regret. People who had a heart, he observed, usually got stung for it. Miles was a mixer of metaphors just as he was a mixer of truth and lies. Miles was a man one should not cross.

Even four-footed creatures were required to earn their keep. There was no such thing as pleasure without a price. Miles turned and looked at the idle cat, Montmorency, who was as usual asleep in a chair. Robin had been so indulgent. Why, Miles could almost hear the mice squeaking with delight behind the wainscoting. He went over to the chair, grasped it at the back, and tipped the cat out on to the floor. Then, with a none too gentle movement of his foot, he pushed the astonished and affronted creature towards its place – in the kitchen. The cat went, thinking dark thoughts. Miles was cheered by the thought of Montmorency running amok among the rodents, dark thoughts or not. But Montmorency suddenly had a lighter one.

It being spring, and the sap rising and whatnot, the cat also thought along the lines of 'While I'm up,' slid out of the catflap and headed towards the pub and its coarse, but willing, newly procured pub cat called She.

Miles and Dorcas had been working all morning on the likely three-year forecast of remuneration from Molly's scheme, and it looked very promising. Of course, the remuneration would not be huge but – like so many mean people – Miles was also a lover of power. Making people pay for the privilege of a visit would please him very much. Not to mention the nicely growing bank account he had, with joy, already opened in the name of Gnome. He imagined how swiftly the balance would grow. Miles, to be fair, had never read *Silas Marner*.

The vicar, from afar off and seeing Miles at his window, waved. He pointed upwards to the figure on the Hill and nodded approvingly. Miles was glad that he appeared to have God on his side. He was less glad about the vicar, who seemed to be more than a little interested in the amount of money Miles might make from the project. The vicar, Miles knew, had a desire for a new pulpit, something a little less high around the edges and Miles was damned if he was going to offer a penny towards it. He quickly changed his choice of word from 'damned' to 'blowed' – just in case there was something in the idea of an all-seeing, all-powerful God. Though, as he turned his gaze once again to the gross depiction up on the Hill and the charming figure crouching in thinker's pose beside it, he wondered if the vicar's God was the right one to be working for.

The bastion of the Fitzhartletts was atop the battlements – well, the walkway around the roof of the Old Manor – with his gun. On the whole, on the domestic front, it was felt that he was at his safest when he was very high up and only allowed to shoot at things that were also very high up. Sir Roger concurred. Though he did find, as age settled upon him, that his guns all felt a tad heavier than he would like.

He peered at the speck on Pound Hill. It had been moving around earlier but now seemed to be sitting (or standing, hard to tell) very still indeed. It was absolutely forbidden, of course, but could he get it from here? He leaned forward. It might be a deer. Or it might be a fox. A bit of venison would be very pleasant, especially if it were venison he himself had shot and the accolades could go on all through the dinner if they had guests. Dulcima seemed less and less amused by his skills in that department; indeed, Dulcima seemed less and less amused by any of his skills in any department nowadays. Well, for some years, actually. But if it were a fox, then he would be in good odour with everyone. Except the fox, of course.

He puffed his chest for a moment, and raised his gun to have a sight – but just as quickly lowered it again – although, strictly speaking, and he could argue it, he could take a shot because the fox – or deer – was on a level with him so it was fair game. But reality surfaced and he remembered the archaeologist girl. He had been told, very slowly and very loudly, by Dulcima and Marion this very morning, that she would be on the Hill, and moving around, and he was not to fire at her under any circumstances.

As he brought his regretful gaze down from the unmoving figure he saw his wife's back view half hidden by the two mimosas they had planted on their return from honeymoon. Dulcie's choice – against the gardener's advice. But they had flourished, and though they were said to be short lived – ten or twenty years maybe – here they were, all this time later, healthy and alive as anything. Clever girl, Dulcie. Never seemed to get to the other side of her. He turned and started back down the winding little staircase that led to the third-floor attics. When he reached the bottom of the steps he sat down on a broken boot box, rested his gun against his leg and began rubbing the ear of the nearest dog. It really was ruddy heavy, ruddy heavy that gun. He'd talked to that chap in the shop about a new one but nothing had come of it. Something lighter altogether. An older model. He closed his eyes to picture the kind of gun he meant.

Orridge found him there two and a half hours later having searched all over for him to ascertain if he required his luncheon cheese sandwich toasted or not. Before waking him, Orridge put his thumb to his nose and waggled it. Which made him feel a whole lot better. He'd suggest a good claret tonight because that's what Orridge wanted, having got Mrs Webb to make him a nice shepherd's pie.

Dulcima was standing by the overgrown tennis court, the only place in the garden which showed the Hill and the figure perfectly. What a shame, she was thinking, that the village's volunteering had ended so soon. How very much she had enjoyed working on the ground up there, in a team. Harty wouldn't come, of course, nor would Marion. And she'd managed not to drink anything that morning but her break-fast orange juice. Why, when the whistle blew for elevenses, that was what they had, elevenses, out of vacuum flasks, coffee and tea and biscuits – and the like. She'd had her little safety bottle in her pocket but hadn't touched it. Which proved, yet again, the thought she shied away from: that she was not, really, a serious drunk. Can't even succeed at that, she thought, not even that.

Dulcima shook the thought away and looked at her watch. The girl on the Hill had not moved for over half an hour. Now that was dedication. That was serious commitment. Dulcima decided to wait to have her pre-prandial snifter until Molly Bonner stood up. Even more progress, she thought, even more progress.

Dorcas looked up to the Hill, too. But she smiled to herself, with no regrets, no fancies, no thoughts beyond the little bit of a secret that she was privy to. The clearance would certainly be more than that. An actual dig somewhere up there. It would be exciting to see what it produced – if anything. And even though she knew that Molly could not see her, she waved from Miles's window, a wave of good luck. The archaeologist's granddaughter did not seem to consider luck to be a part of anything. Just plain good sense and science, with a little fairy dust mixed in, was what she suggested would make it all work out in the end. Good sense, a good eye, science – and a touch of magic. Not a bad philosophy for any undertaking. If she could only get out to Robin's last known camp, Dorcas thought, she might be able to use it as a blueprint herself. Her determination, which had faded a little over time, was greatly restored at the thought.

Just before she turned back to resume her work with Miles, Dorcas noticed Montmorency with a slinky look about him making his way, with resolute tread, towards the side entrance of the Old Holly Bush. Was it her imagination, or did his gonads look a tad larger than usual? Better not go there, she told herself. A single woman could only stand so much visual masculinity – the Gnome was quite enough without admiring the size of Montmorency's balls as well.

Two

IT WAS IN his first notebook that grandfather Bonner wrote about the outline of the Gnome and suggested that its edges should be checked. He had not been able to find any contemporary, near-contemporary or convincing records of the original shape – but he thought that they must exist somewhere, perhaps once kept in a monastery or in an old attic or library, as his notebook entry went on somewhat mournfully to say:

Detailed examination shows that it is highly likely the figure was not originally this size or shape but I have no proof of the original outline or anything approaching it, alas. Despite searches in the local museum collection and in the archive of the Society and in local sources such as religious houses and old libraries, nothing has come to light. I cannot see the point of this figure in terms of status or power or even as amusement. It is highly localised and I cannot see any religious or ritual significance from the late Neolithic nor the Bronze period that might be appropriate for such a small area of notice. If anything, the figure is naught but a foolish, laughable even, travesty of the well regarded priapic figures that were worshipped on a smaller scale by our indigenous peoples, and on a large scale by our Roman invaders, and taken very seriously. Phallicism was a very important cult of regeneration for most cultures – particularly the Romans, but I have no proof that this figure was cut so long ago, alas. I have an idea that it was – but this is not enough. I hope work on the site will put this question to rest. Of course the prevalence of phallic worship in Italy spread to all parts of the Empire but it was certainly also here before the Roman invasion. I doubt there was a religion in the world that did not want to worship what it saw as the bringer of crops and progeny. Therefore, generally, the totems were given a dignity that this figure lacks. Post-Christian, I very much doubt.

I would, if pressed, say that the figure came to be cut in Roman times, but I have no convincing proof except my instinct and my eye. It could certainly be possible that the figure is more ancient than we suspect, Druidical perhaps, and that its shape was much altered over the centuries but the initial investigation makes this hard to ascertain. This is because the outline shape of the figure has been worked and worked anew over many years by those who sought to exploit its visitor value. I must make assumptions for now about why it was cut in this unlikely position. All I would say is that it may be the case that they chose Pound Hill because of its remarkable shape and steepness, the surrounding hills being smoother and rounder. But it is not of a scale to be seen from much distance, which is most strange. It has certainly not been well-grazed land.

There followed a series of measurements drawn on his own sketched diagram of how the Gnome looked – his measurements being imperial (how apt, thought Molly, given that this was at the height of imperial Britain). She transcribed them on to her own sketch, which she had based on the drawing from Peter Hanker. It was a little changed. Enough for Molly to know that in less than one century the demarcations of the figure could alter even without anyone setting out to do this. Which meant that her grandfather's theory was probably right. If the Gnome was as ancient as he thought, or even halfway as ancient, it was likely to have been very different when first cut. It confirmed what Molly concluded from her observations.

Such an effort for a very small impact is unusual, and unknown to me. Just possibly this is a site of significance, which might make sense of it, but I have no way of establishing what that significance might be. When we have excavated further, particularly around the edges, I hope to be more positive in my suggestions. I also feel that the shocking nature of the phallus, and the rather odd way it sits with the figure, is something to consider. But I will be methodical. Once it is cleared we will begin our search at the feet and continue upwards. I shall bose. Taking two sidesteps on the way – the one to explore the phallus and its peculiar twist – the other to explore his out-thrust arm – which also looks odd to me.

Grandfather Bonner was a man of his time and although there were laboratory techniques, analysis of soil samples, geophysics and all the other brilliantly helpful stuff of modern science available to her, Molly hoped to complete her task and find out what her grandfather came so near to discovering without using anything more modern than he would have used. He had reached a point where he felt he knew some of the answers, so she would be a poor follower if she could not do the same. The new excitement was Peter's drawing and although that was not known about in 1914 Molly decided it was quite justifiable to use it. After all, it was around when Grandfather's dig took place; he just didn't have sight of it.

'Soil samples and the scientific laboratory are wonderful things,' said Molly to the fluffy, pale grey clouds above her. 'As are the geological survey boys but it's time for me to find the courage to begin without them.' And courage it certainly would need, as it always does at the very beginning of a dig, for in the end – never mind all the facts and research and results – someone, some one person, has to make the final decision alone. Where to begin? She always felt rather like a surgeon about to make the first cut. It could all go horribly wrong. Freddy was wonderful at being positive at such times, but no – she was on her own so far as decisions were concerned, just like her grandfather. She and she alone must decide the position of the first trench.

Something about her grandfather's later writing, once he had begun the work, nudged away at her even as she felt delight in discovering the alterations to the shape of the Gnome. He wrote of finding something beyond that, something that touched him emotionally – and, of course, he thought he would come back. Like so many in his field who find a possibility, he did not want to share it with the world until he was sure; he would be no different from the rest of his profession in wanting a touch of glory. What – if anything – was the subtext of his findings? Why was he able to 'dispense with Marvell'? What did that mean? And what about the shale bead? There was a frustrating feeling that it was all there, right in front of her, clues and help – and she was missing it. In which case she must just try harder.

The Gnome's left arm was held out from his body, as her grandfather wrote, and did look odd (though little of the Gnome looked normal) and it was altogether likely, since they agreed on this feature (albeit with nearly a century between them) that it had been covered with something once; something that hung over the extended forearm perhaps, or down from the hand? And the Gnome's hat, which did – just as her grandfather described – look ridiculous, had once been a very different shape: much more ornate. Military, perhaps. Not a cap like now. That must be quite a recent change. A helmet? Hard to tell. She must go carefully and make no assumptions.

What was odd was how hard it was to confront the phallus itself. Indeed, as she told Dorcas, whatever its reason for being there, it was still able to shock even an experienced field archaeologist like her. But then, she counselled herself, if the phallus were placed there not to enhance, but to alarm or disturb, it was merely fulfilling its duty. You could be as modern as you liked, you could think you'd seen it all, but the Gnome was still disturbing. Since no one could read her thoughts, she allowed herself to think that it was – even to her – rather frightening. Molly was no shy little virgin but still it had an effect on her. And this effect was made worse by the peculiarity of its shape.

Whilst perhaps not being a world expert on the human male's anatomy, Molly had seen a great many historical phalluses – from all ages and of all materials and of many and varied sizes with all kinds of meanings. But this one was just *wrong*. Something about its proportions and the lie of it was unusual. Phallic worship might represent the member as gross and disproportionate – but not slightly silly. Mixed messages were not to the purpose, surely. And never in her experience, which was, of course, not as wide as her grandfather's, had she seen one quite so alarming and quite so absurd at the same time. The images were to be worshipped, revered, feared – not mocked. In this case, the end of the phallus – the tip – was placed at a strange angle, as if it had been strained by the creators to get to where it ended. It reminded her of the mosaic floors in outposts of the Roman Empire like Britain, where local and inexperienced mosaic layers were asked to recreate a floor from a pattern book. Invariably they began all right and as they got towards the end of, say, a line of animal medallions they would find the space was wrong and either cramp the last bit, or extend it, to fit. But with a figure this imposing could such a mistake be possible? It hardly seemed likely.

Molly put her head on one side and viewed it critically again. It was a physical conundrum. After all, the figure was not here for the people who saw it to admire its ears. The standard form of all these phallic figures, from the earliest times, through Hebrew phallicism certainly to the Romans – and even beyond in some parts of Europe – was that the massive phallus was supported by the free, right hand and thrust upwards at an eye-watering ninety degrees. This one was made with what she could only think of as a wonky bit on its tip. More interestingly, it seemed as if that particular part of the phallus was scarcely changed from its original size and shape while the rest had been lopped off and added to fairly randomly. Maybe it was simply its connotations that had allowed it to be left alone.

If her grandfather was right it had been created at the end of the first century AD, when Julius Agricola finally quelled the British rebels. But he was not, from his notebooks, certain of this. After that Roman success things became a bit less primitive. But then again, it could be mediaeval and an attempt to dishonour the heathen past. Unlikely. The established Church was not known for its portrayal of manliness, round-bellied women being more in its line. So, earlier? Betwixt and between? But that still didn't explain why whoever made it, made it and put it in such a local setting. If it was meant to be ridiculous like Greek satyrs and their Roman Mutunus Tutunus equivalents, was it just up there for a joke? Molly looked up at the Gnome, trying to see it with fresh eyes. It was hardly what you'd call bitingly funny. She shivered and found herself wishing for Freddy. Which was odd and unusual when she was on a dig. How long had she sat here? Too long. Hours. She walked around for a while swinging her arms to get the circulation going again.

Below her, Winifred Porlock stood at her front door with a thoughtful look on her face. She was wondering about something.

Donald had left her tidily indoors, which is how he seemed to prefer her nowadays, but she was drawn to the Hill, and to the girl. Such stillness and dedication in this cold weather. Oh it took her back, how it took her back. Along with most of the village she had enjoyed the experience of helping up there, but now Winifred wondered whether – if she could get up the courage – she might be able to offer more help. Which would probably be politely refused on the grounds of her being so old and dull, she thought gloomily. But she went on looking hopefully all the same.

Molly was crouching again, this time at the very edge of the top of the phallus. Despite knowing it was soil and chalk and flint and sandstone and anything else that made up the Hill, she found it very hard to touch the shape and she must overcome this squeamishness. The rest of the figure caused her no problems but here there was a restraint. A feeling that it was holy? Sacred? Obscene? What? The cap of the corpus spongiosum, as hewn out of the soil, was quite dramatically – even unpleasantly – disproportionate. It occurred to Molly that if she could feel strangely superstitious about approaching and touching such a place, how much more difficult must it have been for those who lived in bygone times? This is pathetic, she told herself, and with the same enthusiasm she might feel at plunging her hand into a drain, she ran her fingers over the edge of the part first with one hand then with the other, and then both together. Whoever had cut out the figure had given the top of the phallus a slight incline, a cushiony curve, as if it were made of appliqué or quilted slightly – as if it were the real thing. Molly stood up again, brushed off her knees where the soil clung, and decided to begin. And damn and damn again, she thought, for not having anyone to help with the filming. She would have needed to be able to trust the person she used and they would have had to know how to wield a camera. It would be so miserable if any of her discoveries and theories should leak out before she was ready. 'I'll have to do it all myself,' she said to the airy emptiness. 'But before I do anything else, I must decide where to cut the trench.' She was becoming quite skilled in using the auger, old-fashioned as the process was. Rather like bashing down on piano keys, it got rid of frustrations nicely. You put down your block of wood and then you bashed the mallet down on it as hard as you could – and hoped for a hollow sound. No wonder her grandmother said that Arthur Bonner was the mildest of men.

Molly went down to the trailer and pulled back the covering tarpaulins. The weather in April was changeable and she did not want to be stopped by rain or even snow. She also wanted to keep the site from prying eyes so she had put in a good quantity of cloth protectors. Apart from these the trailer contained all the items she thought she needed: her trowel, her shovel, a hoe, wheelbarrow, pick, whisk broom, plumb bob and a great many rubber buckets. It also contained a large mallet, a very large mallet, the auger – which her supplier had handed over to her with an odd look on his face. Molly had not deigned to tell him what it was for. He would have laughed. Technology was all, nowadays. She lifted the mallet out, with some effort. It was wooden and not too heavy – but heavy enough. Good job she was fit. Then, as she prepared to pull the covers back over the trailer, she realised what she had lost. The little movie camera. She shifted things about, scrabbled under everything, threw the cloths out on to the grass – but it was not there. It must have bounced out somewhere. And then she remembered . . .

The trailer had been brought up the Hill when the ground was slightly icy. The last part of the climb was just too steep for Peter Hanker's Land Rover and the trailer had to be unslung and pulled by hand. On being asked, Nigel called stoutly that Yes, he *had* put the chocks under the trailer thank you very much, as Peter unhooked it from the back of the vehicle. Unfortunately, Nigel was not entirely competent in manly things, nothing like, and the trailer had rolled quite a way and half overturned before Molly saw what was happening and dived to catch it. While she and a couple of other helpers dug in their heels and held on for dear life, it crossed her mind that she had never seen a man go quite so red in the face as Nigel and kindness made her decide that it was from effort, rather than shame. 'Everything is fine,' she said, to placate his embarrassment and then felt embarrassed herself at the expression of gratitude which lit up his face.

They managed to haul the trailer the rest of the way. Peter returned to the village with a cheery wave. She wished Nigel would not be quite so chivalric about everything. Telling her that she looked completely lovely in her brown waterproof and clunky, clay-clagged boots was hardly what she needed to hear at that particular time. Nor, she guessed, was it what the barmaid from the pub wanted to hear, if the expression on her face, fully made up beneath its cagoule hood, as they righted the trailer together, was anything to go by. It was with relief that Molly watched the barmaid take Nigel's arm and go back down to the village.

It must have been then that the camera rolled out. Molly walked back down the Hill to where the trailer had overturned. The clearance had not stretched this far as it was well below the figure. There were bushes and undergrowth aplenty where Molly began to search. Eventually she found it nestling in the centre of a gorse bush. Its case open, the camera was useless now from rain, sleet and ice. She shook it and tried it – held it to her eye, and shook it again – but to no avail.

Molly stood for a moment holding the camera. Well, she

would have to get another one – but, she reluctantly accepted, not today. Today she must really begin the work – how easy it was to keep finding other things to do. She gave the camera one last sad look and tucked it into her jacket. Enough of that, she told herself firmly, begin!

She collected the mallet from the trailer, took it back up the Hill, lifted it high and brought it down on the ground several times, so hard that she panted with the effort. That felt better. Much better. Below Pound Hill, in the village, two pairs of binoculars were trained upon her. One pair belonged to Nigel, the other to Winifred Porlock. And for some reason Mrs Porlock, the doctor's wife, observing the business with the camera and then the business with the auger, was nodding and smiling as she watched. 'A little more gently, I think,' she said to herself. 'But I know what you are doing, and I know why. You old-fashioned little thing.'

Nigel was neither nodding nor smiling but looking a little less than dewy eyed. That was not how damsels in distress should behave . . . They should sit down and look sweetly defeated until help, in the shape of a white knight such as himelf, came by. What Molly was doing looked alarmingly muscular. Nigal winced to see it. That mallet was extremely large and heavy and she, whom he had privately vowed to serve, was wielding it in a manner that looked considerably less than damsel-like. Thump, thump, thump, it went as she brought it crashing down on the ground. Thump.

Three

IT CERTAINLY MADE the adventure more interesting to come to Pound Hill and use the same tools as were available ninety years ago. There was something liberating about not having anything technical to worry about. And the auger did the job. It brought her closer to the place, she thought, as if there were nothing and no one between her and the site but a veil of misty unknowns. Field-walking was still a quiet pleasure to the archaeologist, a time to reconnect eye and brain with the land. When the light slanted a certain way you could often see what had gone before without the benefit of any technology. The eye was the most useful tool an archaeologist owned. Molly gave the ground another smite, and another, and another, walking in a straight line back to her site. And as she got into the rhythm of the bosing she felt more confident that she would find out the secret of the Gnome of Pound Hill. If there was one. And if there wasn't? Well, there had to be something, those old notebooks told her that. This method was as good as any. Pitt-Rivers had great success with the bosing technique, so why not Molly Bonner?

Dryden, having ordered Nigel back into the shop and removed his binoculars from him, was now looking up at the figure on the Hill. That girl was altogether too impressive. The village was impressed with her, the village aristocracy was impressed with her, even *he* was impressed with her. And Nigel was downright smitten, though when he removed the binoculars from his son he had looked less like a man in love than – frankly – a frightened schoolboy. Seeing the girl and the mallet Dryden was not surprised. It did look somewhat aggressive. All the same, the heart was on the filial sleeve again, or about to be. Nigel had chosen badly, when did he not? At least this one would not be remotely interested in his son – you could tell that at a glance – unless you were Nigel. He looked over his shoulder nervously. Time was cracking on. Something must be done.

Dryden went back inside and closed the shop. Nigel pushed his way past him as if to leave. 'No you don't,' said Dryden. And then more kindly, 'Now listen, I want to talk to you about Sir Roger and that gun. I want you to have the opportunity to show your gunsmith's skills to the Fitzhartletts – I want you to sell the gun to him. He already wants it so it shouldn't be too hard, even for you. I'll do all the necessary to the mechanism. You concentrate on making it look good. It'll put you – us – in good odour up at the Manor. I think Lady Dulcima likes you already –' He paused briefly as if a thought had just struck him: 'Though she seems to like everybody . . . And Marion is just waiting to be wooed. You'll just have to try to ride.'

Nigel stared miserably at his father's face. Nigel and horses were a three-act drama – you attempted to get on to the horse, you got on to the horse, you fell off the horse. It was hell. But his father smiled at him with just a hint of menace; there was no brooking the order.

'And I shall have to think about making you a partner proper. That should speed things up a bit.'

Nigel blinked. Now he really was sunk. His father was serious. He thought fondly, wistfully of that little lady with the bouncing scarlet hair and the bluest eyes and turned his gaze hillward. Just at that moment Molly lifted the mallet high above her head and brought it down upon the ground with yet another smash. Nigel winced and the thud of it echoed.

Something was beginning to curdle in his brain: the mixture of a milk and water damsel, and that Russian athlete Tamara Press. He felt doubly upset. Even as he attempted to overcome the curdling, another thud made him wince.

He nodded to his father. 'Yes,' he said. 'I'll do it.'

At least that was something, the gun. Nigel could show off his skills at last. He had always, always known he had a craftsman's hands despite his father's views, but his father never let him loose on anything. He put the other bit of the bargain out of his mind, the bit about Marion – and concentrated on considerations of mechanism, wood and silver, gun oil and polish. Above him came the sound of his father saying waspishly, 'Well Lottie – is that acceptable to you?' And it was not for the first time. Odd.

Bosing works best on land that has never been ploughed or grazed. If land has been used for farming then thumping the ground with the mallet and block is less likely to show any hidden differences in underground solidity. But given the unusual nature of Pound Hill, the fact that it had not been used for agriculture, if there were any buried secrets on the Hill, bosing should be up to finding them. But Molly had drawn a blank. Now she was taking the mallet up to the top of the shaft of the Gnome's member, bosing away – trying to be objective – and so far with nothing to hear but the dull sound of soil density.

Molly stopped to rest for a moment. There was not a murmur up here. Not even a bird. Even the clear April sky had begun to cloud over. It was as if the world was holding its breath. She certainly was. For Molly and her mallet had reached the tip of the Gnome's great member, the cushiony area. The very top of the shape. She brought her mallet down very hard, wincing as she did so, and the resultant sound brought a smile of satisfaction to her face. At last. She hit the ground once more, just to be sure. Now she knew exactly where she must dig. Yes. She stood there, leaning on the handle of the mallet, scanning the sky where the clouds had grown darker. A spot of rain fell, then another. Damn. Harder now. This would slow things down. She watched the course of the raindrops falling to the ground and she had her first reward. This was what happened sometimes, if you were lucky. For as the water splashed on to the earth, something embedded was wetted by it and went from dull to glossy – something that was not earth, nor grass, nor chalk. Another piece of the Kimmeridge shale?

The mallet dropped from her hands. She fell to her knees in excitement, slipped off her glove and very delicately, with her smallest trowel, she lifted the little thing from the earth and held it in the palm of her hand. Kimmeridge shale it was, like the piece her grandfather wrote about. Another bead, perhaps? Or – was it a weaving weight? It was an aberrant, it was shale, and it was mysteriously up here. She watched the rain splash on the object in her hand, washing its surface, showing that it had, indeed, been drilled. A central hole, slightly off-centre, in an imperfect round shape. Whatever its original use it was proof that someone from the distant past had been here and dropped it. The link was tangible and encouraging. She raised her head and thanked the rain. This was where she must dig. But now the rain was lashing down, its torrents running down the Hill. Exactly as it had rained in that spring so long ago and doing exactly what it had done then. Stopping the work. And the clouds had darkened even more so that there was almost no light. Without cover it would be foolish to begin her trench. She *ached* to begin. She *ached* to start carefully lifting off the first layer of scrubby chalk and turf. But for now she must cover the place with the tarpaulins, protect it both from the elements and from any prying eyes –

or creatures that might come in the night and poke about. She would get cold and wet enough doing that – and by the time the cloths were up and sufficiently secured to withstand a reasonable amount of wind it would be too dark anyway. The years had taught her patience. Tomorrow, whatever the weather, she would begin to cut.

As she drummed the poles securely into the ground and stretched the cloths over them, struggling against the wind and the rain, she wondered, not without a twinkle in her eye, if this was why her grandfather had seemed slightly cautious – coy, even – about telling her grandmother more about the site and his find in his letters. For Molly, having completed her task, was now standing under the protective tarpaulins which were firmly stretched over the very tip of the Gnome's priapus. Even a liberated Edwardian young lady might find it disturbing to be told about such a thing. Or a liberated Edwardian man might find it difficult to mention such a thing in any detail to that lady. She smiled as she skipped, dripping and red-cheeked from the wind and rain, back down the Hill to the warmth of the pub. Sunshine and dry weather willing, tomorrow she would begin.

Winifred removed herself from the window. Even with the rain and the wind, she wished with all her heart that she could be up there, working away, involved. When Donald returned from the surgery, he found his wife sitting in the kitchen with what appeared to be a very small gardening trowel in one hand, and an old movie camera balanced in front of her. And no hot food in sight.

It crossed Julie Barnsley's mind that it would be very easy to poison Molly Bonner. All she had to do was slip something tasteless and deadly into her half-pint of Poacher's Ale or her ham and chicken pie – and that would be that . . . For a moment she drifted away into these pleasant thoughts but the sound of Molly's voice – sweet and kind – broke in saying, 'And a packet of crisps, please, oh dreamer.' Julie found herself saying automatically, 'Cheese and onion, plain or smoky bacon?' And that was that dream over. Molly, pink and wholesome again having showered and changed, was waiting for her supper in the bar. She was also waiting for Dorcas. Hence the crisps. A day out in the air with only a packet of sandwiches and an apple makes for a keen appetite. So does the excitement of discovery. Nothing was likely to take the edge off her longing for food though the butterflies dancing around in her solar plexus might hamper her input slightly.

At the other end of the bar sat Pinky and Susie, happily slouched on their bar stools. They had been having *such* a jolly time of it, they told her, slurring a little, since she had put the Gnome out of bounds. There being no possibility of Susie being in the family way, Susie could enjoy a drink. And she was doing so. 'That one's on us,' they chorused, as Julie went to take Molly's money. 'And put a short in it.'

'Better not,' said Molly. 'Got an important day tomorrow.'

'Does that mean you've found something?' asked Julie eagerly. She was thinking, the Sooner She Finds the Sooner She Goes. But Molly merely shook her head, put her finger to her lips and went over to her table by the fire.

When Dorcas arrived Molly was deep into reading her grandfather's notebook II – in case she had missed anything. But so far as she knew she had not. 'Marvell?' she said, looking up dreamily, 'Marvell, marvell, marvellous . . . Oh well, he probably meant marvellous. Something to marvel at.'

Dorcas said, 'Miles is very curious.'

'He is,' said Molly. 'Very, very curious indeed.'

Which set them both off.

The fire crackled as Dorcas threw on another log or two. Then she leaned back, wiping the tears of laughter from her eyes, 'No but seriously,' she said, 'he's seen the covers go up. And he wants to know why. Shall I tell him something? Shall I? Tell him something?' Dorcas tried to look innocent but did not succeed. People with honest noses are unlikely to be convincing when in deceptive mode. Dorcas was being appropriately nosey.

'Not half as much as *you* want to know why,' said Molly. Which Dorcas had to admit was perfectly true. 'I'm saying nothing to anyone,' said Molly. 'Until I have something to say. Until then, I work alone and hidden from the world.' Dorcas rolled her eyes. Molly clamped her lips over the rim of her glass by way of conviction. 'But I might let you come up some time if you can do it without anyone else – especially Miles – knowing. Otherwise it will be come one, come all – and that would be disastrous.'

Donald went back indoors and, after closing the front door, leaned on it with a look of painful confusion on his face. He had still not eaten and he had just watched Winifred stride down the village street, in a manner in which he had not seen her stride for many years, and push her way into the Old Holly Bush with a determination that would not have been amiss in Monty approaching Rommel. *Why?* What on earth was Winifred doing going into the pub? She never went into pubs, let alone the local. He feared, very much, that it was hormones again. He feared very much that she would buy a drink and then throw it over someone. Or worse . . . He ran a distressed hand over his forehead. 'My God,' he whispered, 'she's taken to drink.' He took a deep breath and removed his sagging back from the front door and without seeing the irony he went swiftly into the sitting room and picked up the bottle of

Macallan (ten-year-old fine oak, Waitrose) and poured himself a very stiff measure, very stiff indeed. Medicinal. He often recommended it to his patients.

In the pub Dorcas and Molly were embarking on their second half-pint of ale when a voice behind them said softly, 'Miss Bonner. I saw what happened to your camera.' Molly, her mouth still fixed around the rim of her beer glass, turned slowly – as did Dorcas, who was merely holding her beer, and there was Winifred Porlock, eyes bright with excitement, cheeks aquiver and looking slightly mad.

'I'm quite adept with the things, or I used to be – a correspondent who does not understand the art of camerawork is a fool – though latterly I was more involved with television. The last film I ever presented in that medium was about archaeological finds in this region. I've still got the video of it.' She sounded slightly wistful. 'I expect such cameras are even easier now. And I'm discreet. Nothing would be said of the venture unless you spoke of it first. Discretion is my middle name. You cannot be the wife of a doctor without being discreet . . . And I did do a course, quite an extensive course, in digging. One had to get to know the process in order to talk about it.' She held up her little trowel. 'And I still have this.'

Winifred's eyes peered hungrily at Molly as if she had not eaten for a month and Molly was food. Molly put down her glass and darted a quick look at Dorcas, who nodded and then said, 'Winifred, how nice to see you. Sit down. What can I get you to drink?' But Winifred Porlock's bright eyes were still fixed on Molly. Molly, she could see, was considering her offer. After a moment, taking Dorcas's nod as a sign, Molly smiled at Winifred. 'That,' she said, 'would be so very helpful . . . Mrs Porlock.'

'Please call me Winifred. Winnie, if you like. *Anything*. But let me help.'

'Winifred. Thank you. But are you sure?' What Molly really meant was could *she* be sure. She already knew that this was a two-person job, at the very least, and if Winifred Porlock really had done a proper course – if she knew how to use a trowel and brush as well as a camera and how to keep her counsel – how useful that would be.

Winifred nodded. It was a firm nod. A supreme nod. A nod that said it was the mother of all nods. 'You can trust me absolutely. I was a good journalist once, and excellent in my documentaries on television. I also know enough about archae-ological matters to be useful. I would love to be your camera wielder. I would do it for nothing and it would be a pleasure.'

'It's a movie camera,' said Molly. 'Or it will be, when it arrives. They'll bike it over first thing. State of the art.'

'I'm your woman,' said Winifred firmly.

At which point Dorcas got up and repeated her question about buying a drink. Winifred looked up and said happily, 'Why not? Yes. I will. A gin and tonic, please.' Dorcas turned towards the bar. She had never seen Winifred in the pub before, never, she thought, bought Winifred a drink before – or even sat and chatted with her. All these years . . . Well, well. How things were changing. Dorcas decided that they were definitely changing for the better.

The door of the pub opened. There stood Donald looking about him anxiously. Seeing her husband, Winifred put out her hand and touched Dorcas on the arm. 'And if you wouldn't mind, could you make it a large one? Perhaps a very large one?'

Dorcas good-naturedly put aside her annoyance that it was now impossible for her to wheedle anything further out of Molly, and even more generously put aside her little spurt of jealousy at Winifred getting to do something up there while she could only watch from afar, or sneakily when invited, and went smiling to the bar. Despite these little irritations she was beginning to enjoy herself again, which was miracle enough.

Donald assumed he had not been seen and exited the pub as soon as he heard the words 'a large one'. He had no intention of being around when his wife displayed yet another example of high spirits – both literal and metaphorical. What she was doing sitting with the archaeology girl he had no idea. Nor what it was that made her so pink of cheek. That archaeology girl seemed to be stirring everything and everyone up. He wanted to feel very cross with her. He wanted to tell her to leave Winifred out of the equation, whatever the equation was – but there was something about the way Winifred looked as she sat there between the two young women that made him stay silently by the door. The look he saw on his wife's face seemed very much akin to happiness.

Four

A LETTER ARRIVED for Molly the next day, just as she was drying herself after the hottest shower she could manage. She took the hottest shower she could manage because the day had arrived not sunny and dry as hoped for but raw and damp, despite the season. One of her tutors told her that if you began the day at the site warm, you tended to stay that way. It worked. When Peter knocked at her door, Molly slipped a bare arm and shoulder (with a flash of knee) through the small opening she had made between door and jamb, took the envelope, closed the door. Peter went back down the stairs. Just as he skipped down the last few steps, Julie Barnsley arrived at the bar. She was on her way to a shopping jaunt in the town nearby and the bus went at half-past eight. She saw Peter was coming downstairs – and that Peter was smiling. He was smiling in that way even the most decent men will smile when they have disturbed a woman in her nakedness – no matter if it's unseen – and almost immediately she heard a cry of pleasure from the top of the stairs. 'Oh thank you Peter,' sang out Molly. 'That was just what I wanted.'

Bloody hell, thought Julie, the woman is at it with him now. But then she remembered. No business of mine, thought Julie Barnsley, none at all. It is of no consequence (a phrase noted by Julie and taken from the BBC's adaptation of *Pride and Prejudice* wherein the heroine got her wealthy man) – but when she asked Peter for a sub of her wages and saw that he was still smiling, her voice, which was normally rather gentle where he was concerned, was icy and harsh. 'Have you got a cold coming?' he asked, as he handed her a couple of notes from the till. She marched out without a word. Peter was a good-natured fellow and simply shrugged at the unknowability of women. He had long thought that they were a breed which, if you required them to call a spade a spade, would immediately ask why you wanted them to do that and might find any number of reasons why it was a threat to their individuality.

Upstairs Molly was dressing as if for Antarctica. The weather was to be no more kind to her than it had been for her grandfather at first and she intended to be on site until it was dark. At least she would have a companion now, which cheered her up no end. Who would have thought that the doctor's wife had such hidden talents? A reminder, she thought, hearing her grandmother's admonishing voice, that you dismiss the older generation at your peril.

In The Orchard House Donald was peeping over the banisters at his wife. She was in the hall putting on a variety of garments that included mittens without all their finger lengths, earmuffs, a sou'wester and sturdy boots. As far as he knew, this was market day in Bonwell, Winifred always went on market day (he enjoyed the fruits of her labour in that there was always something particularly fine for their evening meal and quite often a treat for their lunch as well) but she did not, usually, dress as Captain Scott for the outing. When she slung a small rucksack on her back with the confidence of a youthful backpacker he had that sensation hitherto only read about in military histories: his bowels turned to water. A rucksack? Why? What on earth was in it? He watched in some horror but he said nothing. What was there to say?

Winifred opened the front door on to the early morning street and called up the stairs, 'I'll be out for lunch if you were intending to come back, but there's kipper pâté in the fridge and bread and tomatoes. I'll be late. Good-byeee.' And the door slammed shut with a definite air of exaltation.

Donald sank to his knees. 'Kipper pâté?' he moaned. 'Tomatoes?' So it had come to this. Cold food. Madness. Winifred had always provided him with something hot when he came home for lunch. Always. One needed decent sustenance after a morning of coughing, moaning, unhealthy people. He was always telling his patients to eat a proper cooked lunch. Apart from which, he could not abide fish and she bloody well knew it.

In Hill View House, Miles was feeling irritated. Dorcas refused to tell him anything. Dorcas said that she knew nothing so had nothing to tell, but he knew that she had been in the pub with Molly the night before, and women always talked – it was their nature. Dorcas, however, remained absolutely mute on the subject he most wanted to hear about. When pushed she began on a minute description of what they *had* talked about which was, amongst other things, the perilous state of the Global Economy, and varicose veins. Miles did not wish to consider the perilous state of anything, or veins, or anything else not connected to the project. But Dorcas remained adamant. So Miles felt he must go to the Old Holly Bush himself that evening and see what he could discover.

He watched Molly trudge up the Hill with her hands in her pockets and a determined air and wished he could be a fly on the wall, or a beetle in the turf. But it was forbidden. If he broke the agreement she would go home. She could invite whomsoever she liked up there, of course. He gnawed his knuckles and watched. As if all that were not disturbing enough, as he watched, he saw – of all people – the doctor's wife setting off up the Hill after Molly at an unusually determined pace. He flew out of his front door and called to her, very sharply, 'Come down at once, Winifred. You are not allowed.' But she paid no attention beyond smiling back at him and continuing. It was Molly who stopped and called out that it was quite all right. And both women continued the climb.

'Dorcas? What in the world is Winifred Porlock doing dressed like a militant and going up the Hill?'

Dorcas merely shrugged. 'I know nothing,' she said, keeping her fingers crossed beneath the desk.

Miles threw on his coat and his cap and raced down the street to The Orchard House. Donald was looking pale and distressed.

'Why is your wife going up that hill?' he demanded.

Donald shrugged. 'I have no idea,' he said. 'But if it's any help she's intending to be up there all day and has left me kipper pâté and tomatoes for my lunch. So it's not good news.'

Miles looked at him for a moment and tried to run his mind over these facts usefully – but he could come up with no connection. 'She must have told you what she's going up there for?' he said sharply.

'I just told you,' said Donald. 'Out. For the whole bloody day. Probably rambling – in more ways than one. And now, if you don't mind, I'm late for my surgery.' And he pushed Miles out of the house and followed him down the path.

Miles returned to Hill View. 'The doctor's wife, of all people, going up there. Why her?' But the question was rhetorical. Dorcas shrugged again and waited to be asked something specific so that she could tease him further, but nothing more was said about Winifred. So she left Miles nicely in a state of suspense and fury and went on with her work. He stomped up the stairs to his bedroom and, as he so often did when in distress, he removed the solitaire from its hiding place and ran it through his fingers a few times much as a Greek will use his worry beads, but it did not calm him as much as it usually did. He felt that something was happening, something out of his reach, something taking place behind a veil of mystery. Or was it a monstrous deceit? He turned to the window and looked out at the Gnome, the monstrous Gnome indeed. Oh my Lord, he wondered, quite beside himself, what the hell have I unleashed?

With the covers in place the two women were quite hidden from view and protected from the wind-blown rain. April was, indeed, choosing to be the cruellest month. Winifred opened her rucksack and took out the camera and a battery-operated power light. 'What is remarkable,' she said, giving the machine a careful inspection, 'is that cameras have become less complicated to use and more sophisticated in their abilities. This will be fine.' Molly pointed to an oblong that she had marked with her tapes. Winifred did not, Molly was very pleased to see, make any comment on the fact that this oblong cut right across the most sensitive point of the Gnome's vital equipment. Winifred merely pointed the camera at the shape, and then up at Molly, who spoke. After which, with much excitement, Molly and Winifred got down on their knees and began, very carefully, to remove the first layer of the shape, putting it into baskets for checking later. Who knew what they would find?

The hours passed cheerfully, the work went well and their hopes intensified as the baskets were filled. Both kept their hopes in check and were rewarded eventually by a find. Molly gave a little gasp of pleasure, for there was another pebble of shale – and this one was drilled with two small holes. Molly handed it to Winifred. 'Kimmeridge shale,' she said. 'What do you think?'

Winifred took the perfectly round pebble in her palm and peered at it. 'Drilled. For jewellery, do you think?'

Molly peered at it again and keeping her voice calm said, 'I hope so.'

Winifred nodded. 'The rain has stopped. Do you want to take it into the light and I'll film while you speak about it.'

It was good to be out in the air again. Molly took the other pebble from her finds box. She placed one on one hand, the other on the other hand, and held them both out to the camera. They were of the same size. A matching pair. Molly, trying to keep her voice even, pointed this out and said it might indicate that they were decorative beads rather then weights for weaving. 'We cannot be certain,' she said to the camera. 'But without a doubt these two pieces of shale have been worked by human hand, and have been brought here for some purpose. Arthur Bonner found at least one of these back in 1914, though it is now lost. There is something profoundly moving about being the first to find them again.'

And, despite all her experience, so there was. To hold something in her hand that might have last been touched by a far-off ancestor never ceased to be a thrill. It was one of the experiences that made up for the weather, the disappointments, the unanswered. 'All archaeologists hope that their work will shine a little more light upon the past. We think we know so much about our ancestors and the way they lived, but we really know so little. But I hope that by the end of this project we might solve the mystery of the Gnome. Why is he here? Who put him here? The Gnome is mysterious. There is no straightforward explanation of why he was placed where he was placed, or why he was made into such a – to our modern eyes – gross image. My grandfather undoubtedly found something – but he was not given enough time to mark it and log it properly. Maybe we will be able to do that. If so, it would complete the work my grandfather began and the laurels would be his.'

At which point Winifred shut off the camera and said, quite firmly, back in her media mode, 'Enough talking. Let's get on with it. But I could do with a pair of knee pads, not being quite as young as I was.'

From below the Hill Dulcima watched Molly skip down to her trailer, fish something out and race back. To her surprise Dulcima then saw the doctor's wife take whatever the object was, appear to attach something to her knees, and crawl under the covers that had appeared overnight. Dulcima watched her heels and her bottom vanish within. Most strange. Winifred was always such an upright sort of a person. Wonder of wonders, thought Dulcima. Catching sight of Dorcas she toddled over to her. 'What are they doing up there?' she asked.

'I couldn't possibly say,' said Dorcas. 'Why not ask her yourself?'

'Do you feel she is a force for good? I don't know why, but I do. And it would be so nice to get Marion to go back up the Hill just once. I'm sure she'd be less inclined to devote herself to her horses if she did. It really is time she settled down with someone.'

Dorcas said thoughtfully, 'Well, Molly's certainly a force for something. I like her.'

'I agree,' said Dulcima, nodding. 'And I'd say it was more likely to be a force for the good than not. An affirmation rather than a negation. Never hurts to consider the past and even to revalue it.'

Dorcas gave Dulcima a look of surprise – and then covered it up as quickly as she could. Dulcima was not usually given to making philosophical statements so articulately. 'Integrity,' said Dorcas. 'She has integrity.'

'Well, *quite*. And I want to know more about what she's doing up there. I shall ask her to the Manor to dine.'

'I doubt you'll get her to come,' said Dorcas. 'At the end of a day spent up there she'll want to have a drink, have her supper at the pub, and go to bed early.'

Dulcima looked sad. She was sad. It had just occurred to her that it was a very long time since she had wanted to invite someone, anyone, to her home for dinner. A very long time. Dorcas saw her disappointment.

191

'Why not come down to the Holly Bush instead? You can always have a little chat with her there. She's extremely amenable. Once she's had a glass of something warming.'

Dulcima thought about the suggestion. Usually, unless something very odd was happening, like having house guests or a Fitzhartlett family dinner, she was a little ragged, not to say sleepy, by the evening and not very inclined to set foot outside the Manor. All the same . . . 'Well,' she said, surprising herself, 'I think I might just do that. I'll come down this evening and ask her myself. I'll bring Marion. She needs to get out more. On her legs.'

And leaving Dorcas at her door, Dulcima walked back towards her home, wondering if she could, possibly, avoid the cellar enough to remain able to make the journey back into the village tonight. She thought perhaps she could.

Despite some frantic waving, she walked with her head down, deep in thought, and straight past Beautiful Bygones and Dryden's determined gestures. So lost in thought and wonder was she that both the vicar and the doctor, who were on the pavement deep in conversation, were not a little shocked when the Lady of the Manor walked straight into them.

'Oh I am so sorry,' said Dulcima.

'Lady Fitzhartlett,' said the vicar,. 'Please do not mention it.' He bowed so low that his little nose very nearly scraped the floor. Dr Porlock was less inclined to go the whole hog in matters of feudal response and merely inclined his head and said, 'Think nothing of it, Lady Fitzhartlett, it was as much our fault for standing there as it was yours for . . .'

Dulcima looked up at him. 'Your wife seems to be having a very interesting time with our little archaeologist, doctor. Has she said anything to you about what's what?'

'Oh I expect she's just up there making a nuisance of herself,' said Donald, trying to sound at ease.

'Quite, oh quite,' said the vicar. 'Ladies of a certain age, eh?'

Dulcima gave him an odd stare, somewhat fish-like he thought, not like her usual melting, doe-eyed self at all, and said, 'Your point, vicar?' A response so unlike Her Ladyship, so requiring of a justification, that he could do nothing but gesture heavenwards with his little hands and say, 'Always busy, always busy,' and hope it hit the mark.

Dulcima, still very fish-like, said 'Better that than stand gossiping in the street like you two oldies, I think. You might get stuck in that position with rheumatism in this weather. At your age. And you, vicar, are dangerously close to the puddles down there.' And she sailed on with more grandeur in her mien than either man had heretofore witnessed in their patroness.

As she approached the Manor the rain ceased. Marion, out in the stableyard, was grooming one of her horses with a vim and vigour that appeared to be leaving the horse somewhat dazed.

'Marion,' called her mother.

'Yes, Mother,' returned Marion.

'It is about time we found you a husband.'

Marion rubbed her ears. 'Sorry, Mother, I didn't quite catch . . .'

'A husband, Marion, is what we must set about finding you. You'd quite like one, wouldn't you?'

Marion thought for a moment. She tried to put the image of the Gnome out of her mind and think about a man on a horse – which she just about managed. 'Well, possibly,' she said. 'But—'

'I know, I know – you don't like your father's young men and you only like young men who ride but do not hunt. Which has restricted us, I admit. So we must look elsewhere, mustn't we? We must find you someone suitable. And someone who is right for you.'

Marion managed a faint, 'Yes. But how will I know?'

'Know what?'

'If he's the right one? I don't know any – young men. Well – apart from Peter – and I'm sure he isn't the one. I've had no practice.'

Dulcima gave an exasperated little shrug. How many of her contemporaries had daughters who were endlessly surrounded with young men? And here was her beloved and only daughter, who had never wished to be near one. 'Basically, darling,' she said, 'if you find yourself smiling when you think of him, that will do.' Dulcima put up a warning finger. 'But not laughing . . .'

At the hairdresser's recently, Dulcima had read an article that said women who ran several miles a day were usually doing it out of some deep inner unhappiness rather than a desire to be fit. Running away from life, so the article said. Well, Marion, thought her mother, was *riding* away from life. And that could not be. She went over to her daughter and touched her cheek. 'A husband is better than a horse,' she said. 'Just.'

The two of them smiled a little guiltily. In the distance they could hear Sir Roger misfiring his gun. Marion plucked up courage and asked, 'How did you and Daddy know that you wanted to marry each other?'

Dulcima thought for a moment. Yes, good question. Then she remembered the tea-tent.

'We were at Great-Aunt Belinda's for the village fête. And it was hot. Your father turned to me and said, "I wonder if there's anything available to drink other than tea." – just as I turned to him and said "I wonder if there's anything available to drink other than tea." It seemed as good a reason as any. He brought me champagne and it did make me smile, despite the heat. And we kept interrupting each other with the same things. I'd say "I wonder if I ought to go and buy something?" And he would say "I wonder if I should go and buy *you* something." So we ended up playing verbal snap. Very funny.' She went off into a reverie for a moment but was brought back to reality by the sound of a gunshot close to the vegetable garden.

'Oh heavens,' said Dulcima. 'I don't mind if he tries to shoot pigeons but Orridge is putting in the potatoes this morning . . . I'd better go and see.' Then a thought occurred. 'Marion – would you like a bit of practice? If we could find you a young man to practise on? Just to get used to being with them. It might be helpful. They are a very different breed . . .' The gun sounded again. 'Quite so,' said Dulcima, and set off in the direction of the vegetable garden. She was already waving a white hand-kerchief. Orridge might be even more odd with her nowadays but he did *not* deserve to be shot.

Marion watched her mother walk away with all the alarm of an infant left stranded on a Spartan hill. She had a terrible feeling that she had just seen – she looked at her watch – her mother absolutely sober in the middle of the day, and strangely, uncharacteristically, *determinedly* mentioning the word *marriage*. She threw down the currycomb, saddled up Coco, rode like the wind and made for Spindle Tor. She always rode to Spindle when the world became too much. From there she could only see the side of the Hill that did not have the Gnome visible – and she enjoyed the little leaps over the little lumps in the ground that she and Coco or Sparkle had to negotiate.

The last time she had heard her mother use that commanding tone of voice to anyone was when they brought her down from the Hill, after her pony trouble, all those years ago, and her mother had told them to Go Very Carefully – She's My Only Daughter – Steady Now, Gently Does It – and so on. But after that Mummy seemed to go bonkers. Some said it was the shock. Daddy said it was nonsense. And Mummy went even more bonkers. But she was a nice kind of bonkers. Very calm and pleasantly disconnected. Now her mother showed every sign of reconnecting herself. Which Marion felt would also require *her* to reconnect herself. Something had changed. Marion wondered what. She remembered how Peter looked when he talked about the barmaid. Maybe she could do something to help him and agree to her mother's suggestion at the same time? Marion was not entirely without good sense, even if she preferred to keep this to herself.

From the top of Spindle Tor Marion looked down on the village. Both she and Coco were breathing hard but whereas Coco was merely breathless from the ride, Marion was both breathless from the ride, and breathless from the thought of what might be to come. Marriage! Frightening thought. Even so, a dim stirring of something calling itself Duty – she had royal blood, after all – whispered its way through her. But it was immediately countered by a bright flash of imagery that incorporated the horrible Gnome and his horrible thing – which she saw in her mind's eye as she had seen it when she and her pony tripped over the hidden edge of his extended arm and she had rolled right over it. Marriage.

She turned Coco so that they could head slowly down the Tor. Well, maybe if she had to get married she could do it as a duty? As Coco made his clever and careful way over the ancient lumps and bumps of the landscape, it occurred to Marion that there was one person of whom she was very fond that she could help by pursuing marriage. Marion was quite taken with the idea of ladies and knights. The attitude of Dame Ermyntrude and Lady Edith in *Sir Nigel* by Arthur Conan Doyle, and anyone at all from Sir Walter Scott seemed to Marion the height of romantic chivalry. And they all rode horses. Given this, it seemed to her utterly fitting for a lady to make a sacrifice for both duty and friendship, and – if she could not have love herself – Ah me – then she could, perhaps, clear the path for someone else's desires. With that satisfying thought she set Coco to trot back through the village and home.

Some hours later Winifred sat back on her heels almost as comfortably as she used to sit on them when a young girl, and said to Molly's very active back view – 'Well, we have got on splendidly. I know it's only a little trench but it will be very indicative and I think we should have the first few layers completely off by nightfall.'

Molly did not look up but nodded as she continued to work. 'You've been fantastic,' she said, 'I had no idea you were so skilled.'

'Comes from a lifetime of gardening,' laughed Winifred. 'And not wanting to disturb the bulbs. But I suppose it's a competence you don't forget.' She took a deep breath before adding, 'This will be the most infuriating of questions – but I'm longing to ask. What exactly are we looking for up here?'

'Oh damn,' said Molly jumping up and putting her head out of the tarpaulin cover. And she thought: Saved by the Rain.

The sky darkened once more and the downpour made hard patterings on the tarpaulin. A rook or two made its raucous way home and the soft sound of water falling on turf and soil drummed in their ears. Molly slipped out from under the covers to stand in the rain and look about her at the glistening emptiness. There was no way of avoiding the question now. 'I honestly don't know,' she said. 'But I'm certain that there is something and I didn't even know that before I started. My grandfather was extremely cagey, even in what he wrote for his own private consumption. "*There are more ways to rebel than using sling-shot and arrows,*" he wrote in the second of his notebooks when he was digging up here. "*And what I think we may, just possibly, discover about the Gnome, is that he was used to counter deeply*

held beliefs and rituals – I find there is something unkindly in
his stance – unlike the phallic warriors and gods of Greece and
Rome. It could be that he was a way of undermining long-held
and cherished ideals – and doing it in the mode that every coarse
soldier, every coarse schoolboy knows. If I'm right what the
Gnome sets out to do is as old as time in terms of insult. As
old as the myths themselves . . ." So he found something that
excited him. You can tell from what he wrote that there is an
underlying conviction.' She stopped and gestured all around as
the rain pelted down on her. 'I'm just following my intuition,'
she said, unusually pathetically.

Winifred nodded. 'You are doing more than that. You are
using your educated intuition.'

'Exactly,' said Molly, firm of voice again. 'Exactly.'

'Well, come back under the covers, dear,' said Winifred, 'or
your educated intuition might get washed away in the deluge.'
Molly did so.

'As I said,' went on Winifred, 'we filmed an extensive dig
over near Bonwell – and all round Lufferton Boney was chock
full of sites of one kind and another. Ritual burials coming out
of its ears. So I'm surprised that there is nothing up here. I
wonder if that's why it's been left empty? Ungrazed?'

Molly nodded. 'According to Arthur Bonner that is significant.'

'But in what way?' said Winifred, almost to herself. 'Obviously
the Gnome is newer than most of the burials and enclosures
round about. An *untainted* site, maybe.'

'So that he could taint it himself?' said Molly.

'I suppose you could also see it as marking the landscape for
the conqueror . . .'

'But in that case why choose this hill? It's less visible than
half a dozen others. Its only focus seems to be the village and
immediate surroundings.'

'Maybe that's all *they* were interested in,' said Winifred. 'Whoever *they* were.'

Both women sat back on their heels, listened to the rain, and pondered the mystery. Then Molly said, 'The only thing to do is to put all these questions out of our heads and keep on with the work and see if that brings an answer. Who knows? If we do find something beneath this layer, something beneath him . . . And those shale pieces are late Iron Age, I think. British. Not Roman. So why would there be such a mixture of the two?'

'As you say, the only way we'll find out is to get on and dig. By the way . . .'

Winifred's voice had a definite edge to it; an excitement, even. Molly looked up from her trowel. 'Yes?'

'I'd say this trench area has been dug up once before. Wouldn't you?'

Which was exactly what Molly had been thinking but dared not voice out loud. Molly – looking quite as rapturous as if Winifred had suggested this was probably another Sutton Hoo – happily said that she thought so too. 'I'm sure this is where my grandfather was working. At least, there's no record of anyone else working on the site. And nowhere had the bosing echo.'

'Come on then,' said Winifred. 'Before the light goes.'

On they went. It was another four hours before darkness descended. Time to get down to another layer. It went well. The buckets filled. They began to think they might be nearing something more interesting than soil and flints and chalk. The strata were changing. They talked no more. Speculation was exasperating and they needed all their energy.

That night both women were almost too exhausted to eat. Winifred crawled to her house, passing Miles on the way. Miles

MAVIS CHEEK

appeared to be standing sentry. He asked her a question that she could not quite understand. 'Tomorrow,' she said to him in a faint voice and with a limp pat on his shoulder she steered him away from her front door. He did not seem altogether sympathetic but complied. In fact, he seemed to be downright *un*sympathetic – but she was quite beyond caring.

Indoors she peeled off the various layers of what she was wearing and then stood, damp, flushed and exhausted at the door of the sitting room. She raised her hand in a weak gesture of greeting and stared rather wanly at her husband. Her husband continued to sit, as if made from stone, in front of the television holding what appeared to be the wrapping of something quite greasy – fish and chips, from the smell of the vinegar. Winifred made her way into the kitchen. There, possibly as an admonition, was the day's cold collation and the three slices of wholemeal bread she had left out in the morning. All untouched. Admonition or not and feeling no shame (as Donald said to himself afterwards) about the fact that he had been forced to buy chips, which he loathed, and fish which he loathed, Winifred sat at the kitchen table and ate the rejected meal. She then crept up the stairs, had a hot bath, and fell into bed to sleep very happily and very soundly. Her last thought being that it would do Donald no harm at all to eat a bit of fish now and then. He might get to like it.

Infuriating behaviour, as anyone with an ounce of decency would agree, thought Donald when he came to bed some hours later. He had gone all the way into the town for the fish and chips, they were cold by the time he got them back, and he had no idea, no idea at all, how to use the fool of an oven. And she had not so much as said sorry.

Molly was in no better condition than Winifred, and just as happy. She declined Dorcas's suggestion that they might eat

200

together, saying that she would see her tomorrow night at the pub but for now she was completely done in. Dorcas did not have to be told, she merely had to look at Molly on whom tiredness and elation sat in strange disharmony. In Dorcas's opinion Molly was practically asleep where she stood, which was at the pub door. 'That's fine,' she said. 'Tomorrow will be just as nice. Now you go straight to bed.' But Molly managed to remain awake long enough to drink a glass of wine, consume a mushroom and rabbit pie, and drink a pint of lemonade before staggering her way up the stairs, into the shower, out of the shower, and into her bed, without quite knowing how she achieved it. As she removed her jeans she heard the rustling of something in the pocket. It was only once she was in bed that she realised what it was. The letter from this morning. 'Oh,' she said out loud, and the image of Dorcas's face floated into her mind's eye. 'Oh I must . . .' But before she could decide what, if anything, she must do about it she fell soundly and smilingly asleep.

In the Squidge Dorcas was sitting at her dressing table remarking to herself that she had definitely perked up no end since Molly came to stay. It takes something fresh and lively, she thought, to show you how flat your life has become. Here she was, brushing her hair (as if she cared), growing older, growing more insular, and living without relish – just going through the motions of day to day living – and it was just not good enough. She saw that now. Molly was alive – even in her extreme tiredness there was a vitality in her face, the pleasure of discovery. Dorcas realised that a little bit of that elation had dusted itself off on her. She might no longer have someone to love, but now she did have something interesting in her life and someone to care about in the person of Molly and her friendship. Even Winifred, whom she had hardly said two words to over the years, was a different woman now – and Dorcas looked forward to knowing her better. How bad of me, she thought, to forget that every person is interesting in their own way, that every person has a story and a life and a right to exist (she put Miles out of her mind), and so forget what it is to be arrogant and alone. So, she had lost Robin, so Robin was the love of her life, so she would never, quite, recover from that – but the world moved on, things happened, other people suffered and survived. And somewhere in all this pursuit of archaeology was the great truth it brought: that the past always has a future and that future, if it is wise, takes its lessons from the past. For the first time since Robin was lost to her, she felt an interest, real interest, in the outside world and its changing shape.

Dorcas dropped her earrings into the Spode dish, touched it for a moment with gentle fingers, realising that it, too, gave her pleasure. How could she have overlooked that? How could she have been so caught up in her own sad experience that she forgot to look for ways to be happy? You, Dorcas Fairbrother, have many years ahead of you and you must seek your happiness in both the small *and* large things of life, she thought, or you will miss them. Time to slough off the coat of many sorrows and get cracking with making the coat of little pleasures. With that resolution under her belt, she slid into her bed. Tomorrow evening she would meet up with Molly in the pub and however exhausted or unwilling Molly might be, Dorcas would wrest from her the information, any information, she might have discovered. And she would not tell Miles one word of it. There were, she thought regretfully, bits of her life in which the small pleasures she experienced came from perpetuating her old insubordination to Miles. She just could not stop it. She supposed that true inner happiness would occur when she no longer enjoyed that rather negative process. She kissed the photograph of Robin she kept by the bed, and turned out the light.

NOT EVERYONE IN Lufferton Boney had slept peacefully. Miles was pacing back and forth at his window the following day. She was there again. What on earth was the ruddy doctor's wife doing up the Hill? He had no idea. On attempting to question the woman when she returned to her home last night he had found that she appeared to be drunk. Beyond speech anyway. Yawning in his face. He must talk to Donald about that. He had seen her part from the Molly girl at the door of the public house and they had each given the other a victory sign before going on their separate ways. What did that mean? It looked like conspiracy to Miles. Perhaps there *was* treasure up there? Perhaps the Molly girl was not as innocent as she seemed. Perhaps there had been no mystery surrounding her grandfather's activities – maybe the Gnome held a clue to buried riches? Gold? Perhaps they were all in on it. Dorcas, Winifred Porlock, the Molly girl – maybe Donald? Could it be another Saxon hoard?

He broke out in a sweat at the very thought. Had he missed something when he slipped up the Hill last night? After the strangeness of the doctor's wife and the lack of information from anyone else he had decided to take the risk of visiting the site despite the Bonner girl's dictum that no one was allowed on site without her permission. That was suspicious in itself, wasn't it? And she looked like she meant it. Nevertheless Miles had known that he just *had* to go. Not that it had produced anything.

Miles, congratulating himself, had climbed the Hill on the side that faced away from the Old Holly Bush. It was a difficult climb – craggy, rocky and not a path that was ever chosen when the Gnome side was so much easier. It took him over two hours. When he reached the site he had tried to peer under the tarpaulins to see what was what – but without a torch to light him he could make out nothing. If he used a torch then the wretched Molly might see (her window in the pub faced, he knew, the exact spot on the Hill) and then all would be up. If he knew nothing much about the girl, he knew one thing: she meant what she said. She was a person, he could see, full of infuriating integrity – and not only that, she was – like all women – *stubborn*. You could bet that if she *had* found a hoard of gold she would own up to it and very probably tell the world – and there were treasure trove rules and export restrictions, were there not?

He had come back down none the wiser. It looked very dull up there. Not a glint or a glimmer in sight. And now he paced. He paced and paced. Dorcas was saying nothing, though she insisted she had nothing to tell. Why did he always feel uncomfortable with the way she looked at him when he asked her anything about it? There seemed to be a strange light in her eyes when he wanted information. He threw the cat on to the floor which made him feel slightly better. He might have kicked it but since it had belonged to Robin and since Dorcas was due any minute – he thought better of it. Montmorency flicked his tail, looked over his shoulder with sleepy, malevolent eyes, and stalked from the room.

Miles, temporarily relieved, returned to the subject. They were thick as thieves those two, Dorcas and the Molly girl. They were probably thick as thieves in the pub every evening. They probably spent hours on the phone – although maybe not, since Lufferton Boney was useless for mobiles – no signal could penetrate. If you wanted a walkabout you needed a satphone which was somewhere in the region of £800. So they all got by with landlines. It was quite soothing, really, to find no one walking along with a phone stuck to their ear, or booming out their personal information while queuing at the post office.

When Dorcas arrived and settled herself down Miles crept up to her and walked his fingers as casually as possible along the edge of her desk. 'Nice morning,' he said.

Dorcas nodded but did not look up from her paperwork. There was that funny smile on her face again. The cat returned, feeling safe now with Dorcas in the room. He returned to his perfect circle shape on the chair by the fire and breathed deep.

'Are you seeing Miss Bonner this evening, Dorcas?' Miles asked casually.

'You bet,' she said, with a rather more wicked smile now. His heart turned over with rage. 'Poacher's pie in the pub tonight. Like you, Miles, I want to know what's what. But I doubt she'll tell me anything. She's keeping it *all* to herself.'

Miles felt this like a further pain and he pondered. Could he? Could he change the habits of a lifetime and saunter to the pub as if it were the most normal, agenda-free act in the world? If he did he might learn a little more about what was happening. If he didn't, then he wouldn't. No contest. 'I see,' he said, and removed his walking fingers to the other side of the room where they fastened themselves around Montmorency and threw him out on to the village street. Which felt much better. But not, obviously, for the wounded Monty who immediately made for the pub with a suitably woebegone expression about his whiskers. Twice was too much.

Marion hoped that the matter of marriage had been forgotten. She was giving Coco another going-over – such a soothing activity – when her mother appeared at the stable door. 'Ah Marion,' she said, very sweetly. 'There you are. I want you to come to the pub with me tonight. I believe it's quite jolly in

there and you can meet up with some people of your own age
. . . and practise with the young men.'

Young men? Practise? The prospect was hell on earth. But
when she looked at her mother's face, instead of that nice, blurry
look about it, she saw a line of resolution around the mouth that
both alarmed and reassured her. Her mother was being a mother
again. She thought of Peter and how sad it was that he should
love Julie and and Julie should prefer Nigel. She could help. Nerve-
racking thought. Contemplating doing something romantic with
divided lovers was one thing when locked away in the stable, but
to have it moved out into the paddock? To find that it had shoes
on its hooves after all? That what was just a slim possibility of
going over the jumps was in fact a definite possibility. Oh.

Uncertainty made her slump against the comforting, warm
flank of Coco. She breathed out through her nose like a frightened horse. Coco nuzzled her. She nuzzled him back. What could
her mother be thinking of? The pub? Her mother never went
to the pub. Had no need of the pub. Indeed probably couldn't
get to the pub by the time evening was upon her. And Marion
certainly never went to the pub. Well, she went to it for the
tethering of her horse, but she never went *into* it – it was simply
not done. No – Peter always came out to talk to her.

'The pub, Mother?' she said.

Dulcima did not slow her pace, merely nodding as she strode
away. 'Seven-thirty. We'll walk. And we'll eat there.' She turned
and gave her daughter a cheerful smile. We'll have chips . . .'
And without waiting for a reply, Dulcima Fitzhartlett swept on.
Marion looked at her watch. It had happened again. Her mother
was walking very straightly down the little brick path that was
lined with spears of early hollyhocks. Her mother's dainty hand
brushed the bouncing buds and it was like watching a new
woman. Amazing. Over her shoulder she called, 'It'll be fun
darling. You'll see.'

Marion made a show of clearing her hearing but she knew she had heard right. They were going to the pub. Actually going inside the pub. Cripes. She gave what could only be regarded by a member of the equine family as a whinny. Bloody hell, thought Coco, who was all nice and relaxed from the grooming: not Spindle Tor *again*.

Up on the Hill the two women were down to the lower layers, and almost certainly there was a gap of some sort just below where they were digging. Molly did not dare speculate. It was quite evident that this ground had been cleared before. They had even found an electroplated button – pretty likely to have been lost by someone on her grandfather's team – or it might even be his – but it showed that their theory was right and that this was not the first time the trench had been dug out. At least as far as where the button lay.

The trench she had marked out was just over a metre wide and about two metres long. It coincided almost exactly with the hollow sound the bosing produced. Winifred alternated her digging with the camerawork and she was so calm and competent that Molly found speaking into the lens easy and natural. She imagined she was talking to someone dear to her, if an infuriatingly long way away at the moment. Only when she spoke about the decision that the ground had been disturbed before did she get just a little palpitation of excitement. 'My guess is that this is where Arthur Bonner also cut his trench. Now we must hope that we can find out why.' Then, her lips twitching with mischief, she pushed her face right up the camera and said, 'But if we don't find anything I vow I shall take the veil.' Winifred's surprised eyes appeared over the camera top. 'Oh – we can erase that in editing,' said Molly. 'I just wanted to let off a bit of steam . . . and frighten someone who ought to be here with me, and isn't. Which reminds me. Will you shout "letter" when we all meet up tonight? I keep forgetting.'

Occasionally Winifred filmed a few shots of the landscape, the way the light changed, and any bits of wildlife that came their way: birds, rabbits – the odd deer on a distant hill; to break up the filming, she said, and to give it a bit of tension.

'Any more tension,' said Molly, 'and we'll be on the high wire. Hoping we are on the right track makes me feel quite tense enough.' But she laughed as she looked across at her small finds box, which contained just the three items: the shale beads or weights and the electroplated button. 'And I hope that isn't all there is to find.'

Winifred, thinking of Donald's thunderous face as she left the house that morning, hoped so too.

Today the light was good and the rain kept off and it seemed that early summer had arrived. Molly was tempted to remove the tarpaulins – but she remembered notebook II:

We made the great mistake of removing the covers as the weather was more balmy – and we left them off. In the night there was a great torrent of storm water and we were baling out most of the next morning. The trench might only be quite small – about forty inches by seventy inches, but it is deep now, perhaps just less than a yard. I am certain we are nearly at our goal, if goal there be. The day before we found another piece of black shale that has been worked which caused us much excitement. By the time we found that piece the light was nearly gone, despite the covers being off, and we held our breath to continue the following day. It was very foolish and neglectful of us to leave the trench exposed. And to return and find it ankle *high in water was frustrating, not a little embarrassing. The kind of mistake a rookie would make. 'So 'ark an 'eed you rookies . . .' to put it mildly. My carelessness badly delayed us. A good lesson: never trust anything, especially an early English summer. I will keep my piece of shale, Margaret will keep hers, and the two will be united some day soon. When we can also, I hope, celebrate this project's success and give those fellows at the Society something to take notice of.*

Winifred was right. There was something good about stopping to film from time to time – it was a way of thinking things through while doing something productive. Facing a camera and a microphone put her on her toes, as Molly said, and focused her thoughts. It also slowed things down, which their work needed from time to time. Winifred seemed to understand and Molly was grateful for her documentary training. The worst thing you could do at a critical point in a dig was to speed up. Speeding up often meant overlooking things or being a little less careful. 'We are at just about the same point as stated in notebook II, a little less than a metre down. So we are not far off breaking through.' She smiled ruefully into the camera lens. 'But through what, and into what, only time will tell.'

Winifred switched the camera off and returned to the dig. Above them the covers flapped a little in the breeze, though the air was still quite warm. The sound seemed to heighten the moment and Winifred's hands were shaking as she cut away gently with her trowel. Molly's breathing, had she known it, was loud and quick and a sign of her own inner excitement.

They worked in silence for the next few hours. And then Molly gave a little shriek. 'Stop,' she said. Winifred did so. 'Torch, please,' said Molly for although they had a bright light shining directly into the trench, a torch would focus its light more exactly. Winifred handed her the torch. Molly kept her mouth closed. Shrieking with excitement was not very professional – yet now she was looking at something that showed how professional she had been. It was a small fissure, a tiny fissure, in the layer of rubble and soil and chalk, and when she shone the torch into the gap, she saw, very clearly, what was hidden within. The pale yellowy gleam of a bone. Not a new one, certainly. Human or animal? Who could say for certain? But Molly had already made up her mind that the little bit of bone, what she could see of it, looked decidedly human.

Nigel had his binoculars trained on the Hill, which was perfectly pointless as all the interesting action took place under those covers. Nevertheless he had seen Molly talking into the camera (most peculiarly held by the doctor's wife) and holding something out. So something had been found. Which meant, he hoped, that there might be an acknowledgement of that fact in the pub tonight. Surely there would? Nigel felt a momentary surge of romance – celebration – and thought he would go there now and ask Peter to put a bottle of champagne on ice – well, cava – but he remembered Julie was on duty today and he did not want confrontation. He could not even telephone through his request. That morning Julie had pushed a card under the shop door. (His father had used very strong language to tell Julie to stop calling on the shop phone and Nigel no longer answered the domestic one. So a card was her only hope of making contact.) It suggested that she and he meet at the bar any time today. Well, he wasn't going to fall for that but he would slip in once he saw Molly slipping in, and then he would request some bubbles. They wouldn't be very cold but he guessed Molly wouldn't mind too much. Nice girl, he thought, quite clearly easy-going and undemanding. Just his sort. He refocused his binoculars on what appeared to be Winifred Porlock's heels and bottom. The evening could not come soon enough for him.

'Are you going out, Dulcima dear?' asked Sir Roger, more soft-voiced than usual and somewhat baffled to see his wife perfectly upright and sitting at her dressing table with a comb in her hand. And what appeared to be a cup of tea where a glass of something stronger usually stood. Orridge had already asked him if Her Ladyship was quite all right.

Dulcima smiled at him from the mirror. 'Yes,' she said, 'I'm taking Marion to the Old Holly Bush to dabble in a little ordinary conversation with the young people in there, a little social practice, and to have something with chips . . .'

Her husband turned to go out, nodding to himself absently until her words penetrated. *The public house?* Perhaps there wasn't tea in that cup after all? 'Good heavens!' he said to the doorjamb.

'Well, I haven't had any proper mother and daughter time with Marion for ages. Do us both good, I think. We might discuss her future. Yes?'

Her husband removed his gaze from the carved wood of ancient heritage (oak, late 17th century, *not* Grinling Gibbons but a follower).

'And will you drive?' He said this in a considerably higher voice than he intended.

'Oh no, we'll walk. That will do us good, too.'

'And coming back?'

'Walk, I think.'

Sir Roger clutched the ancient carved oak to steady himself. 'Quite sure?' She must have been really going some after all. The public house? Marriage? Marion? Show her a man and she ran off screaming . . .

'Quite.'

'Good, good,' said her husband trying to sound confident and bouncing the palm of his hand several times off the doorway. 'I think I'll just go and . . .' He crept out of the room in search of Orridge. He found him looking quite upset, sitting in the hall, regarding the grandfather clock in bewilderment. By now he had usually been let loose on the cellar under Her Ladyship's orders at least *twice*. 'Everything all right, Orridge?' asked Sir Roger. And Orridge said, 'Perfectly, sir.' Both men knew, however, that it was very far from it.

'Better sit down with you for a moment,' said Sir Roger.

'Indeed,' said Orridge.

Neither man moved until Dulcima, in a pale green jumper and brown slacks (and looking very normal) accompanied by Marion – who was wearing a neat black frock and slightly heeled shoes (her father, a good judge of hocks, realised for the first time that she had a decent pair of legs) – picked up their coats and exited through the front door. Then both men rose. 'The '86 Médoc, St Bernard, I think, Orridge. I'll be in the smoking room. Bring two glasses.'

'A fine choice,' said Orridge, hesitantly.

'Second thoughts,' said Sir Roger. 'Bring two bottles as well.'

The vicar, though aware that God Moves in Mysterious Ways, was much taken aback to see Lady Fitzhartlett and Marion walking arm in arm down the high street towards – Good Grief – it looked like the *inn*. The vicar did not care for the shortening of public house to pub (it sounded common in his opinion) and he felt exactly the same way about the church. People would refer to it familiarly as Ethel's, which undermined absolutely everything, he thought, about a church and himself as its vicar. He had hoped to revert to the other name for Etheldreda, St Audrey, for what could go wrong with that? But when the Fitzhartletts asked the village if it were a good idea, that know-all Dorcas pointed out that St Audrey gave her name to the word tawdry and did he really want that connection? He thought it might be a joke but on checking he found that it was true, that the saintly woman in her youth had liked to wear cheap market necklaces and that tawdry was the resultant portmanteau word. So St Etheldreda it remained. Ethel's it was often called, but at least if he had a lower pulpit he would gain a bit of respect.

The Fitzhartletts had shown decorum over that matter but now here they were, down in the village, and apparently going drinking. He scurried after them and had nearly caught up just as they were passing the alleyway that led up to Chrysalis Cottage, from which Pinky and Susie emerged rather rapidly into his path and they all tumbled over each other. From beneath Susie's not insubstantial chest, the vicar caught sight of his prey going – yes, actually going – into the door of the *inn*. He must follow. Perhaps there, in the bosom of the village, it would be a good moment to bring up the subject of the new pulpit again?

Ungodly words emerged from his mouth as he tried to right himself but Susie was laughing so much, and Pinky was laughing so much, that although the latter was appearing to try to pull his wife up and off, he was really doing a very weak-hearted job. Recently the two of them had begun behaving like silly children, as they had when they were first married. Pinky looked down on his wife – at her voluptuous buttocks, her rolling arms, her round little booted ankles – and heard her muffled chuckles, and loved her. He put his hands on either side of her rear, and pulled. Up she came, leaving the vicar red-faced and puffing but alive. Pinky then put out his hand and attempted to pull him upright. Hard to tell if he's upright or not, he thought, and burst out laughing again. The vicar glared up at him.

'I am so sorry,' said Pinky. A suggestion that was somewhat

213

overruled by Susie's explosion of merriment followed by his own.

With some dignity the vicar rose of his own accord. Fortunately he was saved from saying what he was about to say, which was very much less than suitable for a man of the cloth, by Pinky's fiercely shaking his hand and suggesting he join them – 'We are just on our way to the Old Holly Bush for a drink, vicar' – and dusting down the little man's trousers (while trying not to dwell on how little there was to dust down, really). Susie added, 'Do come.' Pinky tucked his hand into the vicar's arm, Susie took the other side, they vowed to make it up to him by way of the purchase of a substantial bibular tribute, and together they marched him towards the *inn*. He could not protest. Besides, the two foremost ladies of the parish were already ensconced therein, and where they went, he must surely follow.

Donald had watched it all from behind the curtain (John Lewis 'Saragon', 1998 reduced to £6 a metre) in the second bedroom. The world, he thought, had indeed gone mad. There was the vicar, rolling around on the street with Susie on top of him, with Pinky at his side, and appearing to find it hilarious. Now the three of them were in the *pub*. Madness, all madness. Why, he even thought he'd seen the Fitzhartlett ladies entering the place but he had not had his eye in at that point and could not be sure. They might have carried on, or crossed the road and gone into Hill View. Or perhaps they had called on Mrs Webb to persuade her to remove her new group of gnomes. These six were dancing gnomes, with their hands linked and one leg raised as if they were doing the hokey-cokey – unedifying wasn't in it. He could see Miles at *his* upstairs window, staring up at the Hill.

The vicar, who had also seen Miles at his window, followed his gaze. It seemed to Miles that the Gnome of Pound Hill looked down on those other dancing gnomes with devilish eyes. Foolish fancy, he thought; still, he quickly switched his gaze to the door of the pub. The vicar noted the change in Miles's interest and, in the way of one who is desperate to restore some kind of order to his universe, decided that the one thing he *could* predict was that Miles would never enter that place. Even if the aristocracy were in there. He was a man of principle and, as he so often said, he was not given to flinging his money about on drink. With regard to such firmness of intent, thought the vicar, Miles was above reproof. As for himself, unable to remove either of his arms from the friendly embrace of Pinky and Susie, into the den of thieves he went, a most reluctant man of the cloth.

Donald's eyes nearly popped out of his head. The vicar appeared to be inebriated and cavorting into the pub. Good God, he thought, the world has gone mad. Mad. Winifred was already in there, along with the Molly girl, whom Donald had rather hoped would be a good influence. But he could not be sure. Not now. A second night, even if they were somewhat apart on the calendar, spent at the public house by Winifred spelt doom in his opinion. He could only hope that she would stop at this vice.

Gambling could be next. He shivered. He'd had enough women in his surgery in a state of high tension due to bingo bills. Apparently you could play bingo at home with a credit card. Iniquitous. But the women he saw in his surgery who drank and gambled were not usually of the educated classes. They had certainly lost the thread of their domestic duties and so, it appeared, had Winifred. Well, she had not so much lost the thread as lost the whole bally sewing basket. He had tried to heat up the stuff she had left him at lunch – he wanted hot food – but something very peculiar seemed to happen to a ham salad when placed in a saucepan on heat. Why you couldn't have it hot he could not think. After all, it was only meat and vegetables. And it was all very well for Winifred to suggest he should come to the pub, too, in that take it or leave it voice, but his pride would not let him. Just then his stomach let out a very loud rumble. So loud, in fact, that he wondered if Dryden Fellows, who was walking – or rather slinking – in the shadows below, and also approaching the pub, had heard. But he looked neither to left nor right, and simply carried on. Total madness, thought Donald. Above him, as if to endorse the sentiment, the Gnome shone harshly in the light of the moon.

Dr Porlock, once a man of humanity, had become a man of little sympathy with humanity. He saw its frailties as weakness, its ill health largely due to its own unedifying ways, and mostly hypochondriacal. What he respected was a proper illness: cardiac arrest or a decent brain tumour or even, at the other end of the scale, the common cold. Winifred said that he was no longer the man she had first met and admired, the man of resourcefulness and goodwill. In his opinion, she was certainly not the wife he had set up home with all those years ago, either. And if resourcefulness and goodwill meant cold food or going to a public house for a pie, no he was not. If Winifred wanted him to cook for himself she should have shown him how to do it. Donald felt very bitter. He decided to stay at the window to take his mind off the mess in the saucepan downstairs. With all this toing and froing, he would not have been at all surprised to see the Gnome himself stride down the Hill and into the pub for a pint. Peter Hanker must be doing very well for himself nowadays if the whole village was going there.

Just as he had that thought he saw another shadowy figure slipping along the shadowy street to the pub. Nigel. He seemed to be following Dryden with the same slinking motion. Perhaps Nigel was worried about his father? His movements certainly looked covert. Maybe he was checking up on Dryden. Why?

Was Dryden also taking to drink? Perhaps there was an epidemic of it? The whole village becoming drunkards, with Peter leading them on to their doom like the Pied Piper.

Nothing had surprised Dr Porlock so far as Dryden Fellows was concerned, ever since the day he had come to the back door looking white-faced, saying that he had seen his Lottie's ghost and, far from being the amenable little thing she was when she was alive, she had wagged her finger at him and told him off about Nigel. Nigel ought to be happy, was apparently what she wagged her finger about. And Dryden was white as a ghost himself. What rubbish. Donald told him so. 'Take a pill,' said the doctor. And prescribed him a very useful placebo of his own making. Later Dryden had pleaded with him when the visitor refused to go away – and Donald told him to take cold baths.

In they went, the Fellows men, into the the Old Holly Bush, casting backward and fearful glances up the Hill where the Gnome still shone bright against the night. Donald was not one to be fanciful, yet somehow, with that part of his Gnomeliness hidden by tarpaulins, he looked less immense, less powerful, than usual.

Across the street and looking downwards Donald saw the curtains of Hill View twitch again. He wondered, in a moment of rare amusement, if he and Miles were watching each the other. And he thought, yet again, that the world had gone very odd since the advent of the archaeologist's granddaughter. Soon he and Miles would be the only ones left at home. The rest of the village would be in the Old Holly Bush by the fire, drinking ale and eating pies and baked potatoes and such hot stuff. Donald swallowed hard. Why, he was even beginning to think he had better go into the pub himself, after all. But he'd be damned if he would have a pie there – no – that would let Winifred off the hook far too easily. He would stand next to her and let his stomach rumble. That'd show her.

Molly, Dorcas and Winifred were surprised at the number of Lufferton Boneyites who were in the Old Holly Bush that night. Since there were several visitors to the village and several locals from round about, it was all very jolly, if a little noisy for conversation. Between the time that Molly had parted from Winifred and both had made their way home to get a hot shower – or in Winifred's case a nice old-fashioned hot bath – and then arrived back in the bar – where Dorcas had already bought their drinks and found a table by the fire – the place was packed. Dorcas drew her chair closer to the two women and raised her glass of wine. 'Here's to it,' she said. 'But to what exactly?'

Molly drew her chair closer, Winifred drew her chair closer, and Molly said in a low voice. 'A grave. I think.'

Dorcas squeaked. 'A *grave*.'

And Molly immediately put her finger to her lips. 'We can only work on it very slowly but I'm quite sure it does not contain animal bones. I am sure that the contents are human.'

Dorcas said, 'Fancy finding a grave buried under *that* particular bit of the Gnome.' And laughed.

'Out of the mouths of babes and sucklings,' said Winifred. Molly looked questioningly at Winifred but she did not add anything else.

'A grave? Are you sure?' said Dorcas.

'There are bones.'

Molly looked at Winifred, hoping for confirmation. Irrationally she felt that as a doctor's wife, she might be more au fait with such things as bones. Winifred nodded. 'I think so, too,' she said, 'but we must be cautious. After all, it might be of very recent origin, the grave, it might be something that we have to hand over to the police.'

218

Dorcas squeaked even louder. 'No!' she said, feeling a wonderful tremor run up and down her spine. This was absolutely, and literally, thrilling. 'You mean it might be a *murder*?' Her eyes were as round as the table they sat at and Molly, in a somewhat excited state herself, burst out laughing. 'I don't really think it's a case for *Midsomer Murders*. I'm quite sure that it's old, very old, judging by the colour of the only bone we've seen so far. But until we have removed the layer concealing it, and brushed it all out, I couldn't honestly say. It's very interesting that it is *under* the Gnome. As you say, Dorcas . . . what a place to choose.' She produced a pen and drew the phallus, rather accurately, on a beer mat, with an X marks the spot. 'And under that particular part of his anatomy – *exactly*.'

Winifred nodded sagely. She had grown used to the indelicate placing of the trench. But Dorcas had not. As the beer mat was pushed towards her and she looked at what would pass muster as a well-drawn, lewd cartoon, she could not stop herself – and although it came as a total surprise, she started to laugh. 'It's like being back at school,' she said and laughed more loudly. She brushed the palm of her hand under her eyes and laughed – and cried – even more. The drawing was ridiculous. At which point Winifred also saw the funny side. She and Molly had been so absorbed in the seriousness of the task that she had not stopped to think of the smutty aspect, but now she, too, began to laugh and laugh. Looking at the beer mat she suddenly saw it for what it was.

Molly looked at them both, saw beyond them to the astonished faces of the other Lufferton Boneyites sitting around in the bar, and – never one to find it hard to be amused at anything – she also began to laugh, and laugh, and laugh.

And then a very strange thing happened. Even stranger since it began with Julie behind the bar (who had just put the cava on ice for Nigel and was about to ask him why). Julie looked across at Dorcas, Winifred and Molly who were in convulsions of merriment, the kind of laughter Julie remembered enjoying as a child, with her brothers and sisters, where one would begin and then all the others would helplessly follow. Domino laughter, one after the other falling for it, irresistible. And Julie's mouth began to twitch, her nostrils to dilate, and then out it came in a tremendous series of high-pitched explosions. Peter, also behind the bar, found himself surprisingly doing the same. He looked at that upturned face, entirely reshaped by laughter of the most catching kind – and then it was Peter's turn. Just the very surprise of seeing Julie laughing at – well – at what? – set him off. Whatever it was, it amused him so much that his baritone began to make deep haw-haw-hawing noises to add to Julie's giggles. The trio by the fire, suddenly aware of the baritone and the soprano joining in, found this even more funny and renewed their own laughter.

Marion, sitting very properly with her mother and delicately dipping her chips into a small pot of mayonnaise (as recommended by Julie) found herself beginning to shake as she looked at Peter. A little noise popped out from her – and another. Peter looked over at them and waved a foolish hand in the silliest of ways to indicate that he was beyond speech: that really set her off. Then her mother, a glass of very acceptable Merlot to her lips, from which she had been practising sipping, had to put the glass down quickly as she too found herself smiling rather broadly and unable to stop the smile turning into something more pronounced.

As if it really *were* catching Dryden – who had noticed Marion, and then Dulcima, both at it and was relieved to think that if they were it was all right for him – immediately let out his breathy crowing. Something not heard for many a year. As he did so his surprised gaze fell on his son. Why was Nigel here? Had he followed him? But with the laughter overwhelming him, instead of asking the question, he merely nudged his son to join in. Nigel needed very little persuading. Which only left the vicar in their group – and the vicar, who would follow Lady Fitzhartlett to the ends of the earth in a hair shirt in the cause of a new pulpit and her nobility – was swift to see the funny side and laughed considerably louder than his stature might suggest him capable of.

Dryden both laughed and watched his son laugh, noting that although Julie Barnsley kept an eye on Nigel, he did not keep an eye on her. Even a laughing eye. Indeed, his son seemed quite uninterested in Julie except in her capacity as a server of food and drink – which confirmed Dryden's suspicions. Not so long ago Nigel had been transformed when in Julie's presence. Either Nigel was up for the Oscars – or he had transferred his affections entirely and utterly to someone else. In between the laughing and the breathing Dryden managed to whisper to his son, 'Doesn't Marion look charming tonight?' But Nigel, always one to go over the top, could only splutter a reply. And sink his head on to the shaking shoulders of Pinky while Susie leaned back on the banquette and held her generous sides. The noise she made could, without doubt, awaken the dead.

'Well,' whispered Dryden in his son's other ear, 'I think she looks charming, charming.'

Nigel, wet eyed, looked up from Susie's pneumatic charms straight into the eyes of the laughing Marion – who appeared to wink at him (though it was sometimes difficult to tell with her) which was quite an arresting sight. He winked back at her, almost as an automatic response, and whispered to his father through gurgles of laughter, 'She looks like Mummy.' Which had the benefit of shutting his father up immediately. It always did.

*

It really was most extraordinary. Measles could not have spread more quickly. Indeed, the entire human content of the Old Holly Bush was laughing. Even the fire perked up in the inglenook and began to crackle joyfully. Peter looked about him in sudden wonder. The place had never seen so many of the villagers, nor had it seen quite so much fun. Nor had he ever seen Julie so out of control. In his opinion she had never looked more beautiful. He threw a drying towel over her head and turned back to serve Pinky who said, 'Better get one in for the vicar. My wife nearly winded him', but could form no more sentences for laughing. Susie, his wife, he thought, as she sat collapsed on the banquette was shaking like a large, purple flower in the wind, and had never looked more desirable. Life had become too serious, he realised, over the years. The only problem was how much he hated the colour purple. But she seemed to love it more than ever. So he *still* couldn't tell her, of course . . .

Gradually, gradually, the laughter subsided and people began to ask each other why they were laughing. Dorcas put her hand over the drawing on the beer mat as Julie came over with their food. Julie was a quick-eyed woman when she was stoked up, and she saw the sketch, but could not make out exactly what it was. She did, however, fix Molly with a gimlet eye and ask her outright if she had found anything up there. To which Winifred said, 'Could you bring the salt and pepper, do you think? I always like a bit of flavour with my game.' Which, for some reason, started Dorcas and Molly off yet again.

Nigel, who along with the rest of the bar had just begun to calm himself and return to normal, thought it was time to go over and join them. But first – the cava. He squeezed past Marion who may, or may not, have patted his bottom, which made him stop and smile at her momentarily and receive a smile back before recollecting himself, gaining a little colour in the other cheeks department, and moving on. Green eyes, he thought, how unusual. Dulcima put down her glass of Merlot regretfully but very firmly. Yes, she had neglected her daughter. 'Marion,' she leaned over and whispered, 'one does not pat young men on the rump as if they were horses.' And Marion replied, perhaps a little too innocently, 'Oh really?' Dulcima shook her dainty head, more in sorrow than disapproval. She'd have to crack on, but how could she teach the girl to go among men? Marion gave Peter a smile and a wink.

Nigel, watched intently by Julie, was now making ox-eyes at the archaeologist person, and although the archaeologist person was only being friendly back – and hardly even that – still, Julie was on the envious alert. It seemed that little Miss Molly had learned an art that Julie had never managed: Treat 'em Mean, Keep 'em Keen. Right then. She picked up the bottle of cava and shook it for all she was worth.

Outside the wind had increased a little. It carried the sound of laughter up and over Pound Hill and made the tarpaulins covering the Gnome flap and slap in a restless rhythm that echoed its reply down into the village. Miles, who had his window open to try to hear what was going on in the pub, was irritated by the way the air whisked his hair all over the place and slapped him about. He looked up at the Hill. The sky was deepest ink, and clouds scudded across the moon bringing strange shadows with them: one minute the Gnome was lit with the bright, white light, and the next he was in moving shadow – with the undignified addition of what almost sounded like clapping coming from the covered portion of his famous anatomy. The Gnome did not look his usual relaxed and arrogant self. Or perhaps, thought Miles, I am having that thing that Dorcas calls transference? Whatever it was, the covers flapping and slapping and the light going on and off made the Gnome all the more obscene, thought Miles. What was even worse was that laughter was coming from behind the bright yellow glow of the pub windows and all in all, from where Miles was standing, it was not a comfortable experience. Miles very badly wanted to know what that laughter was about. Perhaps the Molly person had told them what she had found? Perhaps they were laughing at the fact that she had got one over on him? Suddenly he could bear it no longer. He pulled his window closed and slipped down the stairs and out of his front door.

Just for a moment he thought his shadow had extended further than reality could possibly create, until, on getting his eye in, he saw that the darkness moving opposite him was Donald Porlock. Who also seemed to be bent on visiting the pub, and also bent on doing it discreetly. He looked, thought Miles, like someone out of an Alfred Hitchcock film, clinging to the walls as he slipped along the street, looking from left to right as if expecting a gunshot from a foreign power.

Moonlight, as it had played on the Gnome, also played on Donald Porlock; there was no mistaking that he did not wish to be seen. Miles moved silently along the railings of his front garden, in synchronicity with Donald – which would have been all right had not there come a sudden tremendous shout – a hollering, really – that made Miles nearly jump out of his already jumpy skin – and Donald do the same – with the addition of a little squeal. Miles looked up the Hill, fully expecting to see the Gnome striding down, mouth agape, arms akimbo, but he was still where he always was, if looking a little peevish – perhaps at having his mighty member half hidden by flapping sheets. Miles looked back to the street. The mystery was solved by the appearance of Sir Roger who had nothing Hitchcockian about him and was quite openly striding down the street towards Donald and the pub.

'What are you two fellers skulking about for? Come in and have a drink.'

Miles was inclined to think that Sir Roger had already taken up his own invitation – as did Donald when suffering a beefy red hand upon his shoulder and a blast of Sir Roger's warm breath in his face, not unconnected with the fruit of the vine, and accompanying the arrival of the hand. What Miles had taken to be one of Sir Roger's many dogs tottering along by the wall proved, on closer inspection, to be Orridge. 'No more for my friend on the floor,' said Sir Roger cheerfully, walking on past. 'He's driving.'

Miles, who might have slipped back inside his house had he the chance, gave a weak smile and trotted over to the pair. Donald was glad to see him and said so. 'Very glad to see you, too,' said Miles in a voice that suggested he would like to know exactly why Donald was skulking (Scand. as in *skulke*, 1175– 1225. Norw. *skulka*). 'Just taking a walk, actually,' he said. Miles nodded. 'As was I.'

At that moment there was a tremendous crack from the Hill, like a gunshot, and both men looked up at the Gnome. 'Tarpaulins,' said Miles nervously. 'Wind's getting up.'

Sir Roger, who was looking fondly at both of them, agreed that the wind was certainly getting up and the best place to be in that case was the public house known as the Old Holly Bush for a snifter. 'Lady Dulcima is already in there,' said Sir Roger again, with a sudden childlike expression of surprise 'And if my wife is in there, then so shall we be. She is in there with my lovely daughter. I thought I ought to accompany them home.' He looked at Donald. 'Is your wife in there too, Porlock?' he asked benignly, and with his face less than an inch from the doctor's.

Donald Porlock recoiled a little, enough to nod without giving Sir Roger a header, and said that she was. And that he, too, thought to accompany her home.

Then, after nodding and agreeing and bringing the beefy hand

up and down a few times on the less than beefy shoulder, Sir
Roger turned his attention to Miles. 'No wife in there for you,
eh? No wife, no daughter, no brother . . . Sad, so very sad.' And
he flung an equally beefy arm around him. And thus flanking
the somewhat wasted member of the local gentry, they made
their way to the door of the pub. Orridge, knowing his place,
snuggled up to the foot of the steps and fell soundly asleep. He
had read a lot of Dickens in his time.

Some of the laughter had died away now and those gathered
were beginning to wonder what it was that had started them
off. Something to do with the Hill and the Gnome, wasn't it
. . .? Winifred saw that the natives were getting restless and she
suggested – in the diplomatic way of a good doctor's wife – that
Molly should stand on a stool and tell the crowd what they had
found. Molly thought this was a good idea – otherwise they
might break the rule and go up there to see for themselves, and
so much could be destroyed or damaged if they did. So she got
up from the table, pulled out a stool, mounted it and prepared
to speak. But she was not quite quick enough.

For as Molly drew breath Nigel appeared at her side. He was
wrestling with the bottle of cava, so thoughtfully and enthusiastically moved about a bit by Julie, and trying to get the cork
out in the manner of James Bond. He failed. Winifred, who
found such inefficiency irritating, and who wanted Molly to get
on with it, had no thought that it might be a love libation: she
took the bottle from him and whipped out the cork like an A1
sommelier. Whereupon the scene was magically transformed into
the Formula One championship.

Except that the bubbling spray was pink and somewhat inferior to a jeroboam of Taittinger, it was very similar in its effect.
Most of it – and you might think that the gods were being

particularly fair that night – hit Julie, who stood wet and gasping and rooted to the spot behind the bar. Happily for Peter she had her eyes closed, for the sight of him racked with silent laughter might have occasioned some damage in the gonad department. Julie was not known for her considered reactions which was, in Peter's estimation, part of her charm.

On the other side of the bar Winifred gaped at Julie, who continued to drip and who, on opening her eyes at last, gaped, back. Nigel looked at her, then at Winifred. Winifred looked at the bottle, now almost empty, in her hand. 'Oh I say,' said Nigel. 'That's a bit buggered.' Molly and Dorcas looked at each other, which they should not have done, for they descended into further uncontrollable laughter. At this point the door of the pub opened and Sir Roger pushed his way in, closely followed by Miles Whittington and Donald Porlock. How warm it felt, how lively, how full of light after the darkness of the street outside – and how oddly wet.

Donald, on seeing Winifred with the bottle in her hand, and several dripping personages around the place, let out a groan. Oh God, he thought, she's at it again. 'My wife,' he whispered to Sir Roger, 'has gone mad.'

'Have a Scotch,' said Sir Roger quite reasonably.

'I think I will,' said Donald. 'A large one.'

Winifred was doubly amazed: at giving young Julie a dousing, and at seeing her partner of so many years propping up the bar in a distraught state and slugging back a large whisky with what appeared to be very inebriated companions (though it was hard to tell with Miles, who was a man of infinite self-control. His eyes, however, were very staring which was a certain sign). So this was what happened, she thought, when a serving wife decides to go for a little freedom. Drinking with the boys. And she resolved not to give in to the blackmail of it.

Dorcas stopped laughing the instant she saw Miles at the bar. It was absolutely unheard of that he should enter a place so clearly connected with the proles. 'Miles?' she called across the bar. 'Are you all right?'

Miles turned and gave her what could only be described as a look of ghastly endeavour – with teeth. It was a smile. 'Perfectly,' he said. 'Perfectly.' He picked up his glass and tried to sound nonchalant. 'By the way, the wind is up out there and your tarpaulins are going at a hell of a crack. I hope they aren't going to make that noise all night? I think I'll go up and tighten them for you before I turn in . . .' But before he could finish his whisky Molly was up the stairs and down them again. She went up in her jeans and jumper, and returned in her sou'wester, sou'easter and very probably all points on the compass protective outwear – and she was off, up the Hill, before anyone could do more than blink. Nigel might have followed her if Julie had not held on to his coat collar with something less like affection and more like a gesture of apprehension by a police officer. PC Brown noticed nothing out of the ordinary for he was in the back room having a smoke. Lufferton Boney was a quiet little place where people kept themselves to themselves, and so did he.

'Well, well,' said Sir Roger, 'I'll say it was going it up there. Like a rifle shot. And I'd say that Gnome of ours is exceedingly angry. And frankly, you can't blame him – digging up his – his – thing – like that . . . Can't say I'd like it very much. What about you, Porlock?'

'Same again, Sir Roger,' he said, not thinking beyond what on earth he should do about Winifred. Winifred was looking at him very coldly across the bar.

A voice, somewhere to Sir Roger's right and half hidden, said, 'Daddy?' A shocked voice. And another voice, equally shocked, said 'Roger?' To which he raised his glass, said 'Hallo dears,' and fell over.

Later, with her husband propped up in a chair between wife and daughter (with the help of the vicar), Dulcima thought how undignified drink could make you. While Marion thought that if she also had a father bent on drinking himself into a stupor, she was – frankly – off out of it. Marriage might well be necessary and no sacrifice after all. She smiled at Nigel even more firmly. He gave her a cautious twist of his lips in return.

Pinky and Susie, having wiped away their tears of laughter, were tucked into the furthest corner of the bar – as puzzled as anyone else about why they had laughed so much, but perfectly accepting the communal oddness. After all, as Pinky pointed out, if you were going to become involved in a communal anything, then a communal laugh-in was about the best. And he was moved to remember the words of Pablo Neruda, which someone had read at their wedding, saying into his wife's warm ear, tickling her with his own hot breath, 'deny me bread, air,/light, spring,/but never your laughter/for I would die.'

To which Susie replied, 'When the green woods laugh with the voice of joy/And the dimpling stream runs laughing by . . .' But she forgot the rest of her Blake, being overwhelmed by the strong smell of alcohol, not usually considered by either of them unpleasant but now, suddenly, making her feel a little queasy. And when Pinky said 'Come on, sweetheart, let's have another one for the road,' she could only shake her head with a wan smile and say that she thought she had probably drunk enough, and laughed enough, and that half of shandy was her limit tonight, and as much pink champagne as she could bathe in. Which set them both off again. Pinky hoped that if he walked her home very carefully she would stop feeling sick. He had other plans. And if it ever occurred to him how strange it was that nowadays the marital boot was most certainly on the other marital foot – he kept the thought to himself.

Home they went, holding each other tight and stepping out into the wild, dark night. Above them leered the Gnome but Pinky did not give a fig for him, and Susie did not so much as glance up to acknowledge his presence. Flap his tarpaulins as much as he might, the dwellers of Chrysalis Cottage were entirely absorbed by each other tonight and had no thoughts for either him or the young woman up on Pound Hill attempting to quell his wrath. Pinky, immersed in uxoriousness, decided to put off his denouncement of purple until another time.

One could only speculate whether the Gnome was pleased or not that he should be so ignored. Certainly Molly had to struggle all the harder against the immense strength of a new onslaught from the wind over the hills. Behind it she was certain she could hear a rather disappointed roar. 'Damn you!' she called to nothing and no one, and pulled on the fixings with all her strength, managing, with almost superhuman effort, to bind them to the earth again. They were secure. She crawled under the covers and took one last, longing look, but she could not see the bone in this dim light. Nevertheless it was there and safe and she said to it as she crawled back out, bum first, that it had rested there for many, many years so one more night would hardly matter – and though she was tempted, oh wasn't she just, tomorrow would come soon enough. She would be back to reveal its secrets in daylight.

Winifred and Donald left the Old Holly Bush, at the same time but scarcely together in any harmonious sense. 'Honestly, Winifred,' muttered Donald, 'I do wish you'd control yourself.' And Winifred thought that was a bit thick, and therefore said exactly the same – save for exchanging his name for hers. As they walked back along the windy, moonlit street towards their house, Winifred looked back and up the Hill to where she saw Molly retying the straps and fixings of the covers. In the pulsing chiaroscuro of the night, Winifred thought the Gnome looked dangerous, angry even, but although she reeked of drink she had not touched a drop so she dismissed the thought as so much fancy on her part. She concentrated on getting her husband home and safely in charge of a cup of innocuous cocoa. Double whiskies in the pub? Whatever would he get up to next?

'I'm afraid I'm invaluable to the project on the Hill, Donald,' she said, as she stirred in the correct quantity of sugar for him. 'So you will have to come to terms with my absences for the foreseeable. And if you wish to take to the bottle – well then, you're a fool – but so be it.' And Donald thought: pot calling the kettle. But kept quiet. At least his cocoa was just the way he liked it and for the time being he decided to be content with that. Hot food and a return to normality was his priority, but it would just have to wait.

Meanwhile when Molly returned to the pub Julie was in the ladies' toilets wiping herself down as best she could. And crying. Peter was at the bar mopping everything up. And laughing.

Dorcas had placed a restraining hand on Miles's arm and suggested that he leave Molly to it. To his 'Any idea what they've found up there?' she said, 'Pieces of worked shale.' Which was truth by omission, she told herself, for she need not mention the bone.

'Shale?' said Miles.

'Yes,' said Dorcas firmly. 'It's a sedimentary rock made of solidified mud – with some clay and stuff, I think.'

Over Miles's shoulder Dorcas saw Molly give a little wave, put her fingers to her lips and indicate that she was going to bed. Dorcas gave a very slight nod and Molly slipped away.

'I think I will have that other whisky,' said Miles, deeply disappointed. Clay and stuff was not what he had hoped for. 'I might even make it a double.'

Miles felt even more gloomy as Sir Roger was now upright again and sitting with his family and Miles had to pay for his own drink – and, rather annoyingly, one for the vicar, too, who seemed to be having some kind of turn. Sir Roger, in drink, was not a light man.

'Damn,' said Molly as she undressed for bed. She still had not talked to Dorcas about the blasted letter. But sleep was nearly upon her and – well – really, it did not matter anyway. Dorcas would know sooner or later and one way or another. And that was that. In fact, she thought, it was probably better to say nothing about it at all until she had something definite to say. She stretched and yawned and thought that today had been a perfect day. Exciting, too, with more excitement to come over the next few weeks. Maybe, she thought, trying to fix the image of that one pale bone in her mind, maybe it would be too exciting for her to get to sleep? But as she slipped her wind-blown head beneath the quilt and closed her eyes on the day, she discovered that it was not. Perhaps it is as Shakespeare would have it: truth makes for a quiet breast.

Long after that night, when the work on the Hill and its Gnome was over and done, the people of Lufferton Boney would remember how they all laughed together in the village inn, and how the simple harmony of that experience was as ancient as the Hill itself, as ancient as the Old Holly Bush itself, and should never be forgotten for the beginning that it was. Given what would be found up on the Hill, the Lufferton Boneyites thought it was highly appropriate that Miss Molly Bonner, the archaeologist's granddaughter, should show them the way to a new kind of harmony.

Six

THE WEATHER WAS mixed over the next few weeks and the covers were kept over the site for the whole time. No one was allowed up there unless Molly specifically invited them, and Molly invited only Winifred, her helper, and Dorcas, her occasional coffee and bun provider, but even she was banned eventually. Now, as the days of sunshine increased as they moved into and through May, Dorcas provided them with home-made lemonade and biscuits which they collected from her and took up to the top themselves. Miles was not keen to furnish them with any refreshment at all, but Dorcas said – quite rightly – that if she kept in communication with them she could report back on how they progressed. But all she seemed to report back was that the progress was slow, very slow indeed. Added to the beads was some kind of button. Miles could hardly contain his disgust.

Slow progress was the truth. But only because the trench had opened up to reveal – if that was indeed what it seemed to reveal – something that was so astonishing, so unusual, so unique, that Molly and Winifred must take their time and definitely, definitely not disturb it. They became totally absorbed by the task. People below noted that the two figures who went up the Hill spry as you like each morning, returned each evening shuffling and bent. Truth was, they did that thing that chiropractors and osteopaths and physiotherapists need you to do in order for them to exist, yet order you not to do when you do it: they worked in the same crouched position for *hours*. It is known as archaeologist's back and is one of the reasons why, if you venture into the home of an archaeologist who lives alone and employs no cleaner, it will generally be dusty and unvacu-umed, for the activity of hoovering catches the same band of muscles used when on a dig. Archaeologists' wives, husbands and partners find this very inconvenient. Archaeologists, in general, do not.

One morning Peter Hanker handed Molly a letter with an exotic stamp on it. 'Another one? Now who's that from, I wonder?' he said, winking at her. Molly tucked it away to read later.

'Good news?' he asked.

'I hope so,' she said. But more than that was not forthcoming.

As soon as she left the pub for the day's work, she forgot about everything else – even a letter with an exotic stamp and the possibility of good news. Later would do, even for that.

Now that the weather was more benign the two women took their break outside the covers, leaning up against the trailer, and if they looked down on the village it was always a certain bet that someone or other would be standing there and looking up and waving. Molly thought they showed remarkable patience (having had to learn to be patient herself) and she looked forward to the day when she could show them the secret of the Gnome. She thought they would be very pleased, and she thought that Miles would not be very pleased. Dorcas, who knew just enough about the find to keep her semi-honest nose content, also thought he would not be very pleased and that made her much more cheerful than she had been of late. Somehow the dig and the find, although tantalising, had reawoken her sadness, and she thought of Robin more than she had for a very long time. But look on the bright side, she told herself, and enjoy the moment, which is what she tried to do. And there was enough good humour in the mixture to lift her spirits.

The surprise was Winifred Porlock, who showed herself to

be a woman of strong conviction and iron will and who had not wavered in the face of her husband's persistent disapproval. 'He will just have to learn,' said Winifred grimly, when he accosted her one evening at the foot of the Hill. It was Dr Porlock's belief that his wife's lack of care was doing his patients no good at all. And that it was why he felt weak during the day and inclined to be short with whoever visited the surgery. He was taking iron pills for it. Winifred's answer was to get out the cookery books, pile them on the kitchen table, and suggest he consider them in the same way he considered his medical textbooks. The consequence being that Dr Porlock took it upon himself to learn to cook. Having done so less in the spirit of generosity and more in the spirit of one who has the hump, so far the results had not been results to relish: they were results to eat if starving hungry. But, as Winifred said, it would be unkind of her to criticise. After all, Donald had never criticised her less than cordon bleu offerings. Nevertheless, his conversion had its moments. On one memorable occasion Winifred had to excuse herself and race down the Hill to The Orchard House which appeared to be on fire.

As Winifred told Molly on her return, Donald had been making chips. 'Why can't he go to the pub to eat if he wants pie and mash? Or even something more fancy?' she said indignantly. 'He doesn't even *like* chips . . .' Molly had to agree with her. The food at the Old Holly Bush was now of the quality known in the pub trade as gourmet. All because of the dig. People came to look from below at – well – nothing – except tarpaulins – but come they did and the villagers used the pub much more in the evenings. What Molly noticed when Winifred returned from saving The Orchard House was that, although she was highly indignant at her husband's behaviour, she was also – beneath the crossness – affectionate in her condemnation.

235

'Well,' she said, 'I suppose he *is* trying.' She paused, laughed and appended the old adage, 'Very trying.'

Peter Hanker had been doing such good trade that he asked Julie if she would do some of the cooking. The results were spectacular: wonderful pies, roasts, stews and gammons, with puddings made – as far as anyone could work out – entirely from sugar and milk and cream. Peter saw to the vegetables, which was never Julie's interest for in Ireland, she said cheerfully, it was greens and potatoes only, and he also saw to the cheeseboard (local Cheddar or blue vein with crackers, £2 a serving) – and the fruit. When he offered Julie an apple and winked at her, she took it absently and bit into it without looking up from her magazine. He felt a little touch of sadness for her. The magazine was full of pictures of wedding dresses, pictures that were designed to make any red-blooded male weak with anxiety, he told himself. Nevertheless he leaned on the counter next to Julie and started to look at them, too. Julie had lowered her game considerably. For one thing she was much busier now and had far less time to scheme, and for another she saw no sign of anything untoward between Nigel and Molly. She was not entirely sure why she felt so much more relaxed, but *something* had changed. Only her determination to walk down the aisle of St Ethel's had not. 'That one would suit you,' said Peter, pointing at a particularly gorgeous froth of white tulle. 'Would it?' she said, surprised. 'Yes,' he said positively, no less surprised himself. 'Yes it would.'

There really was no excuse for Donald to take iron pills, said Winifred, apart from his cussedness. Cussed Donald, she now called him. But she said it kindly and Molly saw a tender look in her eye when she recounted her husband's latest attempts at self-management. It was, said Winifred like watching a toddler learning about the world. Donald fell down as often as he got up, but get up he did. There was love hidden in it, thought Molly, love in what he was trying to do for himself, and love in the way Winifred never said a cross word and just let him get on with it even if it meant her mopping up after a long day on the dig. Even the chip pan episode was never referred to again. When Molly said that she admired this benevolent attitude, Winifred just smiled and looked all around the Hill. 'You can be kind as anything if you are happy in yourself,' she said to a passing pigeon.

Nigel had abandoned standing at the bottom of the Hill with his binoculars since there really was nothing to see. He also noticed that Julie no longer trailed him quite so much as in the past and he supposed that he felt relieved. All the same, with the ex-great-love-of-his-life busy making such things as steak and ale pies (very good ones, he was surprised to find), and the new-great-love-of-his-life under a tarpaulin every day, time hung heavy. But he had something to occupy him, something he hoped would impress his father and make him look more kindly on him. It was the obvious solution. Finish off making the gun as sound as new, oil up the wood, bring up the silver, check the mechanism which his father said needed a new part – make it all lovely again – and then sell it to Sir Roger. Unfortunately Sir Roger seemed to have forgotten all about it for now, there being so much else going on all around them. Dinners at the Manor were happening much more frequently, the guests intrigued by news of the dig, and the Fitzhartletts were much taken up with a revitalised social life. Marion told Nigel this when they met in the street.

'I escape whenever I can,' she said. 'And ride out a bit further than I used to in the mornings. I think I preferred it when it was quiet at home.' And then she did something very strange. She took Nigel's hand and put it on the flank of her horse and held it so that they were stroking the coal black hide together. It felt rather nice. Then Marion mounted, turned, appeared to wink at him again though he was never quite certain, and slowly swayed away down the street. He thought it was rather sweet of her. It was the first time he had touched a horse for years.

Dryden was so busy that he had little time to attend to anything beyond restocking his shop. The number of visitors had increased, and with it the number of sales. So the gun was put back into its cover to be dealt with by Dryden later. Nigel had time. In between serving in the shop while his father was away on various errands and at various sales, he began working on the Churchill.

This was the first project he had ever taken on all by himself and it made him feel very grown up. Why, he even began to enjoy exchanging a few words every day with Marion, and even looked forward to it. She made her way down the street each morning as usual but now she regularly stopped by the shop. Not many words were exchanged, it was true, but the few that there were were friendly enough. She had, he thought, a nice voice and a nice smile and was altogether not quite so bad as he first thought.

A few weeks after the laughter incident (as it was known to the puzzled villagers, for they were still uncertain what had brought it about, enjoyable though it was) Dulcima Fitzhartlett entered the shop. For once Dryden was there and he looked upon her with delight. He had not seen Lady Fitzhartlett except in the company of her daughter, for a week or two and he wanted to show her his latest purchase of a fine nineteenth-century wooden saddle horse, still with its original blue-grey paint – most rare, most rare. He rubbed his hands as she approached and then, composing himself so as not to look too keen, he said, 'You have been much missed, Dulcima.'

He found it very strange calling her that but not half as strange as she seemed to find it. Having absolutely no memory of suggesting that Dryden adopt the intimacy of using her Christian name, Dulcima Fitzhartlett was astonished. Had the man lost his senses? Her mouth gaped and her eyes blinked. Dryden wondered for a moment if he had dreamed her invitation. Something was not going right about this. '*Mr Fellows*,' she said kindly, in a voice that emphasised the title. She hoped this implied that he might like to adopt her approach. 'I have something to ask you but . . .' Today, thought Dryden, there is nothing of the swimmy-eyed melting person of old: here is a lady of high bearing, with clear eyes somewhat bright with offence at the moment. He looked into those eyes, which were definitely displeased, and he was thrown. Competely thrown. She was also wearing a tweed suit of severe cut without so much as a ruffle at the neck. She had transformed herself into a lady who appeared to mean business. She raised a questioning eyebrow.

Dryden tried again and stammered over her name – 'D-D-D –' He then saw the light and opted for wisdom, 'Lady Fitzhartlett?' She relaxed and the eyebrow returned to its normal position. Women play games, thought Dryden. I should remember that. And for a moment he stared beyond the tweed-clad aristocratic shoulder to the shop window and his eyes were dark with fear. The phantom of his dead wife – which looked rather too real for his liking – was nodding at him. He nodded twice and then looked rapidly away.

'May I share something with you, Lady Fitzhartlett?' So far, so good, it seemed. 'I have had the most wonderful piece of luck and I found this –' Dryden stood to one side and gestured towards the fine saddle horse. 'Nineteenth century,' he began. 'Still with its original—'

But Lady Fitzhartlett put up her hand. 'I am trying,' she said, 'to wean Marion away from her horses and into more social situations. I have neglected my duties in that direction for too long.'

'Ah,' said Dryden. 'Then she will need somewhere to put her saddle – when she has hung it up, so to speak?'

Lady Fitzhartlett thought for a moment, and then nodded. 'Perhaps. But in the meantime I would like to borrow Nigel for a day or two, perhaps even an evening or two. I would like him to visit Marion, and accompany her to the the Old Holly Bush and anywhere else a single young man goes, and I would like him to talk to her. Bring her into the world of – well – young men, and young women. Marion is happy with the arrangement if you are, even though your son does not ride. Indeed, that may be a distinct advantage.'

Dryden was ecstatic. He put his hands together in pose of prayer and looked, he fondly imagined, like one of those patrons on a votive painting. Possibly beatified. 'What a wonderful idea,' he said. 'With a view to . . .'

'Why *marriage*, of course,' said Dulcima Fitzhartlett, with just a hint of excitement behind the strict tone. 'What else?' And so absorbed was he in the delightful projection that he did not hear her final phrase which was: 'With someone suitable.'

Dryden nodded. He was almost beyond speech. His very dreams coming true at last. He was about to express his gratitude when he looked up – and there again, with her pale face pressed against its glass, was the image of his dead wife. The image appeared to be nodding at him in mournful pleasure. Dryden shook his head to be free of her and returned his gaze to Lady Fitzhartlett. 'Of course,' he said, 'I am sure it is what you, I – we all – wish.'

'Excellent.'

'You are sure? You seem a little pale suddenly.'

'I am more sure than I can say, Dul— Lady Fitzhartlett.'

'Good. That's settled then. And Nigel will contact Marion?'

'Most certainly,' said Dryden.

Dulcima Fitzhartlett was rather surprised at the glow of joy that suffused the antique dealer's face at this suggestion. How nice the people of the village were, she thought, as she turned to leave. But sometimes odd, she thought, remembering the use of her Christian name. Harty would have a fit.

'And the saddle horse?' said Dryden.

'Possibly,' said Lady Fitzhartlett. 'Later. How much is it?'

Dryden, who would once have added a nought without concern, considered his position. Dulcima Fitzhartlett was not quite so – amenable to suggestion as once she was, he felt. Not at all. So he said, 'I think we can talk about that at another time, when Nigel has proved himself worthy . . .'

Lady Fitzhartlett, finding the choice of words rather strange but not inclined to wonder overmuch, nodded, thanked him and left the shop.

'Nigel!' roared his father as soon as she had passed the window (which was quite empty of spectres again, thankfully). 'Come here at once!' And to Nigel's astonishment, for he expected some kind of dressing-down, he was offered the other kind. Dressing up.

His father took him to Lanyon and Lanyon's in Bonwell to buy him some new clothes. And it had to be said that when Nigel saw himself in the cheval mirror at that establishment, in a jacket of delicate checked tweed and a pair of buff cotton drills, he felt he looked the part and did not mind quite so much that he was to be companion to Marion. There were worse uses for his time, he thought, remembering Julie's thunderous face.

The day was so glorious that Susie and Pinky took their lunch out with them. They were surprised to find someone already up on Spindle Tor when they reached the top. There was Marion Fitzhartlett, sitting with her back against a raised mound, her horse gently grazing at her side, and looking with her somewhat strange eyes at the horizon. 'What made you two get married?' she asked. Her mother was right about her daughter's need to practise; Marion was not one for the social cement of small talk.

'We wanted children,' said Susie.

Marion Fitzhartlett shuddered and looked across at Sparkle (Coco had flatly refused to come out of his stable), still grazing quietly. 'That's what I thought you would say,' said Marion. And looked, if possible, even glummer.

Susie sat down beside her with a tremendous thump and expellation of air and pulled her kaftan around her. It was black and purple, this particular garment, something of an improvement in Pinky's eyes, but still very purplish. 'I must be getting old,' Susie said. 'I used to be able to run up here, now I'm done in.'

Pinky was very pink and it was a pinkness born of pleasure. He was beginning to have his suspicions. Good suspicions. He offered Susie a can of beer but she turned up her nose and took out a bottle of water. 'Eugh,' she said, after sipping it. 'That tastes of fish.'

Pinky went even pinker.

They sat in companionable silence for a while, the three of them. The floating clouds occasionally sent shadows across the sun and the landscape showed up its every bump and dip. 'When you look down from here you could believe that nothing has changed for thousands of years,' said Pinky.

Marion pulled at tufts of grass and looked thoughtful. 'I wonder if the people who lived then were the same as the people who live now?' she asked.

'Oh I hope not,' said Susie, 'I hope they were a great deal nicer then, even if they did run around in animal skins and know nothing about salads.'

Pinky added, 'Or plumbing.'

'Both their own innards and a method for piped water,' added his wife. Which they found extremely funny and which Marion did not. 'Oh don't mind Pinky,' said Susie. 'He takes plumbing very seriously, being that it's his profession.'

'Well,' said Pinky defensively. 'Try living for just one day without plumbing. No wonder they all died at thirty-five.'

'Those that didn't die at twenty from having a baby. Dangerous business, babies,' said Susie, who rather enjoyed a touch of lugubriousness in everyday life.

'Does anybody know what's happening up on Pound Hill?' said Marion, very quickly and suddenly appearing to come to life.

'That girl—'

'Molly, Pinky. Call her by her name.'

'That girl Molly says they are coming on a treat and that we should know all about it in a week or two. But I don't think it's treasure. Miles asked her if she'd found anything valuable and she said something about it not being what some might find valuable but that she herself thought of it as archaeological riches. Miles has put his own twist on it and thinks it will be worth a bit.' He shrugged. 'Who knows. It might all be nothing.'

'I think it's wonderful,' said Susie. She sat upright and looked about her and gestured to the landscape with her fat little fingers, then pointed behind her. Both Marion and Pinky looked in the same direction. 'Just think,' she said. 'Around the other side of that hill a secret is being unfolded from the earth. I think that's very romantic. And under his wotsit, too . . . Or very near it. The number of times we've sat on that place – and nothing.

Zilch.' Susie brushed herself down with a satisfied air. 'No one has sat on him as many times as me,' she said proudly. 'We'll get going again when they've finished up there. Maybe the old fellah will be better after a bit of a rest.'

Pinky said nothing and appeared to be much involved with brushing himself down. 'Maybe,' said Susie, 'there'll be a little Pinky or a little Susie this time next year . . .' She winked at Marion. Marion got up and also brushed herself down, though without the appearance of either amusement or satisfaction. 'I have to go home,' she said forlornly. 'I'm courting, according to my mother, or learning how to be courted. At least it's with Nigel so it's not too bad.'

'He's a little sweetheart,' said Susie. 'Losing his mother like that. I hope you'll be kind to him.'

Marion, looking slightly shifty, or possibly not, said that she intended to be very kind to Nigel. Very.

And leaving the two of them sitting there she mounted Sparkle and off she went. Riding, decided Pinky and Susie, like the devil was after her.

In his sermon that Sunday, the vicar dwelt on the doings of St Basil the Great. Who had, he reliably informed his parishioners, been very short. Had the vicar been able to see right over the pulpit and down into the front row, so to speak, he might have noticed that Sir Roger's eyes were closed, and that Lady F. was staring up rapt at the glass in the east window (Victorian, c.1858/59) among which imagery was depicted a marriage ceremony. Dulcima thought it might be a sign. She had never thought about it much before. But then, as she told herself comfortably, she had never really thought about much over the last twenty years. Besides, it was one of those wimpish modern attempts at magnificence that so betrayed the beauties of the mediaeval stained glass it had replaced (small cannonball, courtesy of Oliver

Cromwell, 1645), all heavy-browed lady saints and dismal-faced knights apparently going about God's business with a severe cold and hair cut in a bob.

Nevertheless, the feeling of a marriage was very marked; no man held a girl's hand in that way unless it was either a betrothal or matrimony. Jesus was doing something with jugs and the bridegroom was looking absolutely enchanted with what he had got in his goblet – and so were all the other men grouped about. Strangely, it had the look of a Spanish bar about it, with those jugs. It was obviously the Wedding at Cana and the moment when the water became wine. Dulcima, considering this, was surprised that the sense of craving did not creep into her. Over the last few days she had been so preoccupied with Marion that she had scarcely thought about drink but now, looking at it anew, the bride in the window appeared a touch bored and the setting oddly continental. She nudged her husband in the ribs. He snorted and awoke, astonished to find himself in a pew facing the lower steps of a pulpit. 'There's a wedding going on up there. It looks very odd, don't you think?' Sir Roger smiled to himself. He could see nothing near or around the altar except a couple of servers yawning. Certainly no wedding. That was more like it, that was more like the old Dulcie, seeing things after – he looked at his watch surreptitiously (19th-century gold Longines Admiral) – after eleven o'clock in the morning.

'It's where they usually have weddings, isn't it?' he said happily.

'What, in a tapas bar?' asked his wife.

Sir Roger snorted delightedly again but a pair of eyes, looking slightly strained perhaps because their owner was standing on tiptoe and was not in the first flush, appeared over the top of the pulpit with a look of deep disapproval. This immediately melted when the slightly strained eyes met the cheerfully twinkling eyes of their patron, but Sir Roger nevertheless squeezed his wife's hand, and put his finger to his lips. It was one thing to have Dulcie back in her usual sweetly confused form, quite another to have to deal with the downside of that form, another little outbreak.

Dulcima Fitzhartlett did not mind being shushed. She continued to stare up at the stained glass. And the more she stared, the more she was certain that the woman in the window looked much as her own daughter would look one day – serenely bored. That was the outcome of a so-called good marriage. It was all a woman could expect in the world of good bloodstock. Until the children came along, of course, and then . . . Dulcima had thought it would never happen to her, the dulling of the spirit, but it had. She looked up at the scene in the window set above the wedding. Jesus the baby in his little manger – all fat arms and legs – and gazing down on him the sweet-faced Mary without so much as a clue as to the future pain. Dulcima sank back against the pew. Give me good old Roman Catholic Virgin Queens of Heaven, she thought, for they, at least, showed in their depictions the sorrows the new mother had to come. Still – if you were looking for signs, and you wanted your only daughter to be married, these two images were as good as any.

A sound of scuffling and thumping broke into her thoughts. It came from the pulpit. No doubt it was the vicar making heavy work of his desire to raise the floor of the place. Philistine that he was. The pulpit was fashioned from ancient tawny marble – even the iconoclasts had not harmed it in their brutalities, and Dulcima would be damned if she would allow it to be covered up or removed. It was a darn sight better to look at than the vicar. It was beautiful, it spoke down the generations, it was not to be covered by something grotesque. For some reason that made her think of the Gnome and the work on Pound Hill. She spoke the thought out loud. 'When will it be finished?' she asked the air in front of her. Sir Roger wished there was some way to stop one's vicar on earth going on so long, too. 'Soon,' he said, patting her hand this time. 'Soon.'

'I can't wait,' said Dulcima, sounding alive to the world suddenly.

Sir Roger knew what that meant. 'I've already asked Orridge to put it on ice, my dear.'

Barking, she thought, absolutely barking. All those years of inbreeding. She must get Marion out of it. Fresh blood. She *must*.

In the Old Manor, while her parents were at church, Marion Fitzhartlett was sitting awkwardly on a bench just outside the tennis court. She had been excused church for the occasion. Nigel was standing, with equal awkwardness, by the side of the bench and looking with horror at a tennis bat he held in his hand. On the bench, next to Marion, was a box of brand new, bright yellow balls. Nigel was not, thank God, wearing shorts – but he had borrowed a pair of Orridge's plimsolls (space cut out for bunions, *c*. 1986) and was preparing to make a fool of himself. Marion wore a white skirt, pleated, to just above her knee, and a navy blue cardigan over a white Fred Perry shirt. She looked perfectly correct. Almost, he thought, attractive. She, also, thought it a matter of almost spiritual gratification that Nigel had covered his legs. There was something distinctly spine freezing about a man's hairy legs, in Marion's opinion.

Conversation was not going well. This was not helped by Marion's stating at the outset that she was here to learn how to spend relaxed time with young men and to eventually marry one of them and that he was the nearest her mother could find. Rather a bald statement, in Nigel's opinion. Even he, not known for his seductive arts (unless you considered throwing yourself at almost every available woman under forty an art) thought the statement a bit too direct. Hence the conversation not going well.

'Well, what do you want me to say to you?' she asked. At which Nigel could only shrug. They both seemed to realise that a game of tennis was out of the question. Nigel did not know the rules and kept referring to the white markings on the court as 'the touchline', which Marion found slightly offensive. Then Marion had a brainwave. 'Why don't we go indoors and *watch* some tennis? Queen's Club?' Nigel, having first established that this was not code for something weird, agreed.

After a while Nigel began to find two grown men batting a ball to each other very entertaining and relaxed into the sofa. Marion also relaxed into the sofa, but at the other end. It was a big sofa, big enough for five bottoms, very squashy and covered in something faded and flowery ('Camoensia', Rosebank Fabrics, *c*.1950). And so time passed pleasantly enough. Marion pointed out what was happening, why the feet had to be where they had to be, what deuce meant, what love meant – and had the grace to laugh at the silliness of the word in the context of tennis – which made Nigel laugh too. At some point Orridge arrived with a tray of tea and a plate of thin bread and butter which Nigel wolfed down without finesse. Marion relaxed even more. It was exactly like being with her brother.

When the front door slammed shut and a voice called out 'Marion, Marion?' Marion jumped amazingly high, perhaps a trick learned from a horse, thought Nigel, and as she landed she said, 'Oh heck, there's my mother and she'll expect me to have engaged your interest.'

Nigel looked around the room. It was a nice room. A comfortable room. One of the oldest in the house. It had dusky pink walls with beams running through them, a pair of old dark red rugs on the floor, a huge fireplace with a pile of unlit logs sitting inside a curly iron fire-basket, cheery pictures of hunting scenes and little old ladies in frilly caps hanging above an upright piano, and some watercolours of ducks and pheasants above a table full of games – dominoes, cards, marbles and the like. The two windows were small and the glass diamonds let in very little light. Nigel was comfortable here, he was beginning to quite like tennis-watching, he had been told to come up to the Manor by his father so that was all right – and now it would all come to an end. So it was Nigel's turn to have a brainwave. 'Tell you what,' he said. 'Why don't we pretend to be – well – getting on together? That lets us both off the hook.'

'Brilliant,' said Marion. 'Absolutely brilliant.'

And awkwardly they both moved towards the middle of the sofa and held hands just as the door of the room opened slowly and two sets of parental eyes appeared. Both sets blinked. Nigel immediately stood up and said 'Hallo, sir. Hallo Lady—'

But he was stopped by a hand, held up to still him. 'Sit down again,' said Marion's mother sweetly. 'Go on with what you are doing.'

The expression on Marion's father's face did not altogether match the mood. If he had come upon Nikita Krushchev in the bath with his wife he could not have looked crosser. Nigel smiled nervously and looked away as Lady Dulcimu appeared to nudge her husband. Both sets of eyes disappeared behind the closing door. Marion and Nigel giggled (the noise of which made one of the listeners at the door thoroughly approve while the other bit his tie) and slid back to their seat. Play resumed. Though it might be noted that the couple remained where they were, close together in the middle of the sofa.

Up on Pound Hill the Gnome was giving up his secret – but slowly, slowly. The weather continued kind and the two women were down to the most delicate of brushwork now, and trying to keep their hands steady despite the excitement they felt. By late afternoon one day towards the end of the second week they realised that they had only stopped for drinks of water – and both felt a little giddy from bending, concentrating – and not eating. 'We ought to stop now,' said Molly, with regret, 'We might start to make mistakes if we carry on . . .'

Winifred stood up and made several little groaning noises as she straightened her knees. 'I don't want to leave it,' she said, also with regret. 'But I think you are right. Tomorrow will be the day.'

'Shall we tell Dorcas before anyone else? Tomorrow night?'

'Well, I'd say that's a good idea – after that she could help. Not with the trench work, but if I show her how to use the camera and what to do and where to stand and everything, then Dorcas could make the film while we work on the very last bit. I'd like to be in that final part.'

'So we tell her?'

'I think so.'

'She'll be amazed.'

'Not as amazed as us . . . No wonder the Gnome looked so angry when we started to dig.'

Miles wanted the job done, the silliness over, so that the building of the barriers and the museum and the little car park (good profits to be made from parking, as he had learned from NHS hospitals) could begin. He also hoped that what they had found was valuable, despite the girl saying it was not what one would expect. Miles wanted control back and it seemed he would have to go on waiting for a wretched eternity before he could get it. The only cheerful note in all this was that the other evening in the bar Molly had said that she might have some very good news for him shortly. But when he pressed her to give him a hint, just a hint, of what she might have found, she looked surprised. 'Oh – it's nothing to do with the dig. Nothing at all. It's just possibly very good news, that's all.' And after that, ask all he might, she would say no more.

When Miles brought up the subject with Dorcas the following morning she looked at him in amazement and said that Molly had said almost the same words to her on the previous night. 'Perhaps,' said Dorcas, 'she's just stringing us along after all. Perhaps she's the mistress of smoke and mirrors. Perhaps there is nothing to find and she will do a moonlight flit.' And then Dorcas could not resist adding, 'Or maybe what there is to find is so precious that she'll keep it to herself for ever . . . Or sell it. The word treasure has been used . . .' Miles had to sit down in his armchair for several minutes until his pulse returned to normal. After such disturbing matters, when he went upstairs for his post-lunch ten-minute nap for comfort and calm he took out the diamond ring again, and as he dozed he held it in his hand, much comforted by its sharp coolness.

On the following day Dorcas and Miles were working together in Hill View House. Miles had slept badly and woken early and was not in a good mood. He was growing very impatient – not least for the second payment which would not happen until the investigation of the Gnome was at an end.

'What have they said to you on the subject, Dorcas?'

'Miles, I've told you – they said they are getting on well and will let us know as soon as it is time to make an announcement.'

Miles went back over to his window, pulled aside the curtain and stared up at the two figures who were just beginning their journey back down to the village. They concentrated on their stepping as the steepness of the Hill required, they were in their usual end of the day strictured shapes and it was impossible to tell if there was anything jaunty or satisfied about them. He watched them come down every evening but it was always the same. Immutable motion. And Winifred, according to Donald, was much the same at home. 'Her lips are sealed on the matter,' said Donald – and added that he had not managed to get a word out of her in connection with what was up there, nothing at all. But he did say that she seemed unusually good-natured nowadays, hadn't thrown drink over anyone for a while, and was prepared to eat up anything he prepared. Over a gin and tonic at the bar he said, 'I am becoming,' to Miles who could not resist a free drink, 'as good as that television chef Fearnley something – though perhaps not as vulgar. I follow his advice. I like to think I am quite a success in the kitchen department nowadays.' Miles could see that Donald Porlock was rather enjoying himself, which is always upsetting when one is not enjoying oneself.

'Here they come again,' said Miles wearily. He turned back to Dorcas whose head was bent and who showed no sign of interest. 'Surely they're nearly there with the damn thing now?' Still Dorcas's head did not rise from her papers. Miles strode across to her and rapped the desktop with his fingers. 'Pay attention,' he said. Slowly Dorcas looked up and connected her gaze to his. 'Yes, Miles?'

Miles sat on the edge of the desk and crossed his legs. Unfortunately this showed a large expanse of pale leg between sock top and trouser bottom to which Dorcas transferred her gaze. Dorcas found it a comfort that Miles was so unattractive. Not only was it helpful that she was not reminded of Robin all the time, but it cheered her enormously when she felt a little down about her luck and her life to contemplate some unappetising part of the man. Sometimes it was the ears, sometimes the nostrils with their little sprouting of hair. Today the leg would do it. She continued to stare at the gap. 'I want you to find out what's going on up there, Dorcas. You get on well with the girl, and with the doctor's wife, so pump them for information. OK?'

'Well . . .' she said reluctantly. She was not going to tell him that they had already arranged to meet.

'No – I insist – it's part of your job. In fact, why don't you head off now and meet them at the bottom of the Hill and see if you can persuade them to have a drink with you?'

Dorcas shuffled her papers together, stood up, slipped her apple green cardigan (she had taken to wearing more colours nowadays) over her slightly suntanned shoulders, and nodded. 'Good idea,' she said, 'I ought to offer to buy it for them. What sort of drink?'

Miles thought quite often that Dorcas was a little odd. 'Well, whatever they want. Wine? Spirits. Doubles. Loosen their tongues. Yes?'

'Fine,' she said. Leaning over the desk she pulled out the middle drawer and removed a grey tin.

'What are you doing that for? It's the petty cash tin.'

'I have no money to buy anyone a drink at your request tonight, Miles,' said Dorcas. 'I do not earn enough.' This was perfectly true. She had money to buy them a drink at her own behest. But over her dead body would she spend any money of her own on behalf of Miles. Miles looked defiant. It was not his business to pay over the odds. He watched Dorcas carefully. 'But that's a twenty-pound note!' he said.

'Three of us, doubles . . .' She waggled the note at him before slipping it into her cardigan pocket.

'But you can have a lemonade or something. Can't you?'

He hoped that Dorcas had heard for she was already out of the sitting room and in the hallway and making for the front door.

*

When Molly saw Dorcas she gave a wave and nodded when Dorcas pointed at the pub and made a drinking gesture. Behind her, Dorcas knew, Miles watched like a hungry hawk. So far, so good. She took the £20 note out of her pocket and flashed it at the two women who smiled delightedly. Did she imagine it or did she hear a groan from the window behind her? As she went up the steps to the pub in high good spirits (but not as high good spirits as she would be when she had bought the drink, obviously) Montmorency came slinking past her legs and down the steps as if he had aged to a hundred. Strange, thought Dorcas, and went on her way.

Seven

THE THREE WOMEN could not sit in their customary place by
the now unlit fire, as the seats were taken; or rather, two of the
seats were taken – by Nigel and Marion. They moved a little
apart and rather primly sipped their Coca-Colas when Molly
and Winifred appeared (Dorcas was at the bar finding out what
she could buy for as near as damn it £20). For once Julie Barnsley
was notably relaxed despite Nigel's being in the company of
another woman. For once, Julie Barnsley knew, she was quite
safe from usurpation. Indeed, so comfortable was she that when
she brought the three women their bottle of wine (honeycomb
unoaked, Stellenbosch 06/07 £19.50 and Peter Hanker's best
offering) she stopped to say hallo to Nigel and Marion. She
noticed, but put no great store by it, that Marion's hair was no
longer such a mess, indeed, Marion's hair looked quite smart
in its new bob. She was also wearing something above her jodh-
purs that looked quite pretty – some sort of shirt in what seemed
to be silk. Perhaps, just for a picosecond Julie wondered, but
she soon put it out of her head: it was just an immense relief
that he was not sitting with that Molly person. Nigel and Marion
were looking at an old map together, heads bent over it and
nearly touching, despite the gap between them, and it looked –
well – rather more intimate than Julie would have expected. But
on closer inspection the map they were looking at was so old
and tattered that it held no hint of any romantic possibility. As
Julie slipped back around the bar, Peter Hanker tickled her ribs.
'Not throwing her out?' he asked, nodding in the direction of
the map readers. Julie laughed. 'As if . . .' she said comfortably.
'As if . . .'

Over in the corner, next to but not with Pinky and Susie, sat Winifred, Dorcas and Molly. The wine, they agreed, was excellent; that it had been paid for by someone else made it even more excellent. That it was Miles who paid made it elixir from the gods. Dorcas told them why the wine was a gift from Miles and that he was likely to expire if they kept up the secrecy for too long. 'As will I,' she said firmly. And leaned back in her chair with folded arms. 'And what is all this stuff about having good news?' The attempt to look severe did not last, however, and she broke into a broad smile. 'He's dreaming of relics of gold,' she said, 'to the point that he breaks out in a sweat every time he thinks about it. Have you found relics of gold?' Molly assured her that they had not found anything remotely resembling gold, silver or anything Miles might consider precious.

'We have, however, found relics of something else . . .'

Dorcas leaned back looking – very slightly – disappointed. 'Ah – so that's the good news.'

'Oh no,' said Molly, sipping from her glass and looking as innocent as she possibly could, which was not very. 'It's got nothing to do with *that*. Not at all. It's quite separate from the Hill and you'll just have to wait.'

Dorcas folded her arms and looked severe again. 'Are you playing games with us, Molly Bonner?'

Molly leaned back and also folded her arms. As did Winifred. Both looked with equal severity at their companion. 'I most certainly am not,' she said. More than that on the subject she would not say. 'But Dorcas, there is something we want to show you tomorrow, up on the Hill, something we have found which is extraordinary. It's not fully excavated yet, but we are almost there and there is enough to see what it – they are. I want you to be the first to see it apart from ourselves. I'm going to trawl back through Grandfather's books and notes again tonight to see if I can link it with anything there. Though I have to say he was pretty obscure. Quite clearly didn't want anyone to find out before he had finished the job.'

'All men are obscure,' said Winifred. 'It is their job in life. As teenagers must rebel, so men must keep what they are thinking to themselves. They were not made to share information, merely to dictate it. If only they were capable of saying what they wanted, life would improve considerably.'

'Goodness,' said Dorcas. 'Where did *that* come from?'

'Experience,' said Winifred bluntly, and raised her glass thoughtfully before sipping.

Next to her Pinky sat bolt upright, looked a little shocked, then stroked his chin consideringly, before continuing the game of cribbage with Susie.

Winifred smiled at the two younger women. 'Doesn't mean we don't love them, though. Silly buggers.'

Molly saw the shadow that flowed across Dorcas's face. 'Drink up,' she said cheerfully. 'For who knows what tomorrow might not bring?'

'Oh now come *on*,' said Dorcas. 'This is not fair, not fair at all.'

Molly put her finger to her lips. 'Enough for the moment. I'll see you both at the bottom of Pound Hill at seven thirty tomorrow morning. Now I must go and plunder those books for any help I can find . . .' And, after draining her glass and tapping the side of her almost impeccably honest nose, she departed.

'My lips are sealed, too,' said Winifred.

'And the other piece of good news? The one affecting me and Miles? Molly wouldn't tell us any more than that.'

'Absolutely no idea,' said Winifred. And poured out the rest of the wine.

*

Behind them, Nigel and Marion were still deeply engaged in the study of the map. Old and tattered it certainly was. Nigel had found it in one of the drawers of the old mule chest at the manor, right at the bottom under the strange and antique playing cards and other Victorian games. It was odd, he thought, as he poked about in the ancient dust and crumbling spiders, how much more interesting and alive old furniture and stuff was when you had it all around you in a home and used it. He had begun to enjoy his visits to Marion's house – to look forward to rummaging about in things, running his fingers over silky elmwood chairs or over rough oak – pulling books out of the dark, carved bookcases and generally feeling – well – at home. Marion said that his visits stopped the boredom – which he took to be a compliment – and she had taught him backgammon. She had practically, though not quite, forgiven him for not being a rider. But she did understand that it came from fear rather than dislike. After all, she had her own little fear to contend with.

The map, newly found, intrigued them both. It was of the surrounding area, showing footpaths, and bridleways and tracks some of which neither of them had encountered before; lost, probably, in the mists of time. There were also several places marked as thickets and woodland that were now cleared. The map did seem to be very old indeed and it was Marion's plan to explore these byways and tracks and bridleways but she wanted to do this on horseback. It was the only way, she decided, and far too tiring on foot. Since Nigel felt quite faint at the very idea of getting up on a horse – he had never even liked the up-and-downers at the fair – he told Marion that he was not entirely happy. She merely patted his arm as if it were a fetlock and said no more. Oh well, he thought, as they sat in the pub and studied the various strange routes, Oh well – cross that bridge when we come to it. While his beloved Molly Bonner was unavailable, this was passing the time very nicely, and meanwhile, his father was completely off his back now that he was up at the Manor most days.

Marion's mother was very accommodating and charming to him and kept giving him little taps on the back and encouraging looks, and Orridge brought them refreshments from time to time, while her father continued to look threatening but took it no further. One way or another the Fitzhartletts seemed to favour treating people as they treated their animals. Sir Roger was probably equally brusque with his gun dogs. Well, brusque was how he described it to his father – Sir Roger's actual words on one occasion were 'I have my eye on you and if you step one little toe out of line with my only daughter you shall feel the toe of my boot.' Marion said that this meant he liked Nigel, but Nigel was not convinced. Still, it mattered not because he was certain that when he had finished the gun and presented it to Marion's father, Sir Roger would fall over backwards with gratitude.

'I wonder what these marks mean,' said Marion, peering closely at the map. Nigel rather liked the way she peered at everything. It was rather touching, he thought, as if she were a newly born kitten. He moved closer, and following her pointing fingertip, which – he saw was very pink and rosy, he made out the faded writing. 'It says something like cysts. Cysts? I wonder what cysts are?' they said in unison, and looked surprised. Third time that day, thought Marion.

Julie over at the bar laughed. 'Lumps,' she said, 'that grow on you. A bit like warts only softer.' Marion recoiled and Nigel felt her lean against his shoulder. It made him feel curiously manly. He was just beginning to explore this odd thought when he looked up for a moment and caught the eye of Winifred who was watching him very beadily. 'Nigel,' she said, 'would you mind showing me that map?' Nigel obliged.

*

From her bedroom window that night Dorcas gazed out at the Gnome. It was one of those June nights that seem not to get quite dark and the Hill and its occupant were almost luminous against the deeply lit blue. She had the strangest feeling nowadays that the Gnome was vexed. The sense of threat that Dorcas usually felt on looking up at the vulgar creature was absent, or reduced, and inside herself she felt the faintest stirrings of something pleasant. What was it? she pondered. There it goes again, she thought. And as she slid into bed and saw the moon shining on the Spode dish with its pretty patterning, she knew. It was the second wave of that elusive little thing called happiness. 'Oh sugar,' she said, as she switched out the light and sank her head on to the pillow, for as if called up by some unkind demon, Miles Whittington's face suddenly appeared in her mind. 'I forgot to report back. But if I'm invited up the Hill then I'll have to drop a note through the door for Miles, tomorrow. Or maybe,' she yawned and smiled, 'maybe I'll knock on the door instead. Wake him up. Who cares?'

And with that cheerful thought, she fell soundly asleep. Beyond the window the Gnome also slept, though perhaps he slept fitfully for the edges of the tarpaulins covering his most private part flapped slightly and constantly in the summer evening's breeze.

Molly was sucking on a chicken bone, courtesy of the Old Holly Bush's best coq au vin, and she was deep in thought as she stared at the open pages of notebook II : '*I remind myself that there are more ways to rebel than using slingshot and arrows,*' she read. '*Perhaps our Iron Age brothers were more subtle in their rebellions than I thought? It is odd that the phallus is shaped so strangely at its furthest end. The conquering Romans were so exact in their engineering and measurement. It might have been there already, of course. Or the Romans might have*

*ordered it to be cut out but did not actually do the cutting . . .
This is speculation. Time may reveal all.'*

Molly, too, went to her window and looked up at the Hill,
and she, too, contemplated the rustling covers and thought about
what they covered. It always made her smirk, try as she would
not to, and she consoled herself by saying it was better than
blushing at the sight of him. The rest of the shape was so exact,
so perfectly in proportion – yet it failed at its most important
point. As if the cutters had run out of space. 'We're getting
there,' she said. 'We're on your track now.' She nodded to herself,
removed the well-sucked chicken bone from her mouth and put
it back on the plate.

Below her the pub was silent, except for the low murmur of
Julie and Peter's voices. They often went on talking for a while
after last orders and chucking out. It was a soothing sound,
caressing almost, and Julie seemed to have become a little less
watchful and disapproving of Molly, as if something had
smoothed out a wrinkle of behaviour. This was a relief as Molly
found it positively exhausting having to be warm and friendly
to one who quite clearly wished her off the face of the planet.
'I don't know what I've done to her,' she said once to Dorcas.
But Dorcas only said, 'You haven't done anything except be
yourself. It's Nigel. He falls in and out of love all the time.
Never stops. And Julie's hoping to take him down the aisle.
You've taken her place.'

'But I haven't encouraged him, have I?'

'Oh, you don't have to. It was bound to happen. But I bet if
you asked him the colour of your eyes – if you asked him the
colour of Julie's eyes or anyone else whose eyes he has looked
into and imagined himself in love, he wouldn't be able to tell
you *what* colour they were. He's got a long journey ahead of
him, that boy.'

So Molly lay down to sleep, soothed by the murmur of voices

below, and looked forward to showing Dorcas what had so far energed from beneath that shocking part of the Pound Hill Gnome. And seeing for herself if what she thought they had uncovered could be so . . .

PART III

One

Who knows how in a small village, word had spread overnight about a significant find up on the Hill. Not gold, not jewels, not a Viking longboat – but *something*. The news produced a sense of unity, a collective excitement, of pride even, in Our Hill. Some of the villagers who rose early were clustered by the gate of Miles's house, shading their eyes against the early morning sun and looking upwards to where the distant tarpaulins rippled gently in the air. Molly, dressed for action and waiting at the foot of Pound Hill for Dorcas and Winifred, put her finger to her lips when asked what she had discovered. 'All will be revealed,' she said. 'And soon.' They had to remain content with that. They were remarkably accepting.

Among the passers-by was the vicar. 'Aha,' said Molly. 'Just the person I wanted to see.' She took him to one side and had a quiet word with him. He nodded several times. Put his hands together in delight and looked extremely joyful. Then his little legs took him away as fast as he could go – not in the direction of the church, nor the vicarage, but in the direction of the Old Manor. His greatest joy was to have a reason for visiting his patrons, and Molly had just given him a cast-iron excuse. How nice to bring a little cheer to people, she thought, being of a cheerful nature herself.

Miles was hanging around, trying to look both superior and nonchalant. Not an easy combination: the result was less superior and nonchalant and more like a man with trapped wind. He watched anxiously as the vicar skipped off, and he wondered. But to his enquiring gaze Molly simply did what she had done to everyone else and put her finger to her lips. It confirmed to

Miles that Molly was in a league of her own when it came to resolution. Her determination and much-dangled purse strings won over his loud bluster every time. So he shut up. A little example, though Miles would not own it, of how the power politics of the world could operate with a different financial balance. But, alas, as far as he was concerned the fact that women did two-thirds of the world's work and owned less than 1 per cent of its assets and therefore had less than 1 per cent of its power seemed perfectly acceptable. So he stood by and was comforted, at least, to see Dorcas approaching the bottom of the Hill and being, apparently, welcomed. She was going to be allowed up there today. Clever girl to have wormed her way into their trust. He'd get the full details from her later. The church clock struck half-past seven. Time for breakfast.

Marion was out riding Sparkle – and she looked as if she was echoing her horse's name. Her hair gleamed in the sun, her cheeks shone with health, and her strange eyes glowed as she rode up to the base of the Hill. Molly remembered to check their colour and noted they were an unusual shade of sea green. 'Was the map useful?' Marion asked. And Molly said that yes, it was interesting, and handed it back. 'Oh good,' she said. 'If you really have finished with it, Nigel and I want to follow it about a bit, to see if some of the things that are marked still exist. If I can get him on a horse. Which doesn't seem likely,' she added, mournfully. 'He's afraid of them. And we can't walk – it would take for ever.' She sighed. 'I'll just have to try persuading him again.'

Winifred, arriving just at that moment, said, 'Well, why not put him on a pony instead. His feet would nearly touch the ground then.'

Marion's eyes lit up with a smile and she leaned down from the saddle and kissed Winifred on the cheek – which made Winifred beam with pleasure. Lufferton Boneyites seldom kissed

266

each other in public; or in private, for that matter. 'That's a brilliant idea,' Marion said. 'And I've got just the pony at home. She'd be perfect. Perfect.' She gave an uncharacteristic whoop, turned Sparkle back towards the village and rode away as fast as Sparkle could go.

Winifred touched her cheek. 'Everywhere seems to be breaking out in a kind of happy harmony,' she said wonderingly. 'Donald is going to attempt macaroni cheese today and he spoke for five whole minutes on the telephone to Charlotte last night, without getting angry once. Apparently when Charlotte asked him where I was and how I was, he told her that I was working up here and too busy for domestic duties. And she said About Time, Dad. Anyway, he said this morning that he quite liked cooking. And I said that if he quite liked cooking, perhaps he could also get to quite like the clearing up as well.'

'Hallelujah?' said Dorcas enquiringly.

'Hallelujah indeed,' said Winifred. 'He was consulting a medical book when I left, making notes on the manifestations of guilt in the disturbed mind.'

'For you?' said Dorcas.

'Not this time, no. For Dryden Fellows, I think. Though don't ask me why. Donald has been very dismissive of him in the past.'

At which point a breathless Julie Barnsley ran up to them and asked if Nigel was around as his father said he was already up and out.

'He's not here,' said Molly.

Julie cast a suspicious eye over her as if she might be hiding him about her person. Dorcas said, 'I think he may be taking a ride around Spindle Tor with Marion.' At which Julie hooted with a cross between derision and good humour, said 'Nigel? On a horse?' and marched off.

There was another short delay while Susie, purple skirts a-flying ran back to Chrysalis Cottage to collect some yellow flowers which she then tucked into the front bibs of the three women's dungarees. 'This,' she said, 'is Chase-Devil. You may need it.' Pinky rolled his eyes as if in mock despair but she was only half serious. Molly, however, did seem interested. 'Why Chase-Devil?'

'Oh,' said Susie, 'it's the pagan protection against dark forces. Its other name is St John's Wort. Hypericum. Just in case. You never know – you may be disturbing something more powerful than time.' Molly felt a funny little shiver running up and down her spine, but then righted herself, smiled and said, 'Well then, let's go up there and see if we are . . .' But she tucked the flowers into her pocket more securely, all the same.

As Susie and Pinky turned back together, Pinky took such a deep breath that for a moment he thought he might expire – then he gathered his courage, remembered Winifred's words from the night before, and said to his wife, 'Now – don't go off on one, love – but about the colour purple . . .'

To the sound of the church clock striking the half-hour, up they went, slowly, slowly, higher and higher, away from the clamour of the folk below, nearing the Gnome who was peaceful now, the tarpaulins moving only slightly in the breeze, as if beckoning them. Even at this time of the morning the air was warm. Molly stopped for a moment and looked up at the sky and around at the landscape. 'We'll risk taking the covers off for good today,' she said. 'The weather is set fair.'

She turned to Dorcas and pointing, said, 'According to that old map – which I think is early – you could have chucked down a spade and begun to dig anywhere over there – all around us really – and you'd have found something. It was even more crowded than it looks now. From the Mesolithic right up to the late Iron Age, probably.'

'When we filmed there,' said Winifred, 'it was jam-packed.'

Molly nodded. 'Hugely significant.' She turned back to climb up towards the Gnome. When they reached the trailer, which was full to the brim with rubber buckets of sifted rubble, Molly paused and said thoughtfully, 'All around, even into the Roman period, busy, busy, busy. But not up here. Up here – nothing. All the map showed was the Gnome. Nothing else. Pound Hill is as smooth as a baby's bottom. And – given what we appear to have found – I'm beginning to have a rough idea why. There's a constant emphasis in notebook II about love. I noticed it last night. And I don't think my grandfather was a sentimental man.'

'Love isn't sentimental,' said Dorcas.

'Oh,' said Winifred, marching on. 'Love? That old thing.'

Dorcas who had been attempting to stay cool and patient and respectful could no longer do so. '*Please!*' she yelled, stomping off after Winifred, the sound of her voice echoing all around them. '*Please* can you stop blathering about maps and stuff and let me *see* what you've found – *now*.' Just at that moment Winifred burst out laughing. She was pointing away from the village and the Hill to the lower slopes of Spindle Tor where they could just about make out the distant figure of Marion Fitzhartlett on Sparkle – and a diminutive figure, which they could also just about make out, which was Nigel – trotting alongside her on a very small pony. A very, very small pony. It seemed certain that if he took his feet out of the stirrups they would drag along the ground. But what was very clear, and ringing even, was the echoing merry laughter that both riders gave vent to, and which bounced around the bordering curves of the landscape and came back to the three watchers on the Hill.

'Oh my goodness,' said Winifred. 'What have I done? Nigel has never been back on a horse in his life. He's scared of them. His father once came to Donald and asked if he would do some hypnosis to see if he could cure it, but Donald doesn't hold with what he calls superstitious nonsense. I thought it might have worked . . .'

'Well Nigel looks happy enough about it now,' said Dorcas. 'In all the years I've never heard either of them laughing like that.'

But Molly was looking thoughtful again. Then she nodded. 'Exactly,' she said. 'Exactly so. You can hear it plain as anything. And look – as the day moves on some of the Tor and surrounding land is in shadow and sunlight – do you see how it brings out the curves and bumps?'

They did. It almost looked as if it were moulded. 'That's very ancient workings,' said Molly. 'I've never seen it look so clearly defined.'

'Nor me,' said Winifred.

'Nor me,' said Dorcas.

'Yet where we are remains untouched. Hmmm.'

Behind them the Gnome seemed to raise the wind and the covers began to move more loudly as if they were being shaken. 'I think he may be getting impatient,' said Winifred.

'That makes two of us,' said Dorcas.

'Three,' said Molly.

'Breeze is stiffening a little,' said Winifred, surprised. 'Let's get those tarpaulins moved. I'll crawl under. Did you bring your torch, Dorcas?'

Dorcas pulled a very large item from the depths of her waterproof, and brandished it. 'I can lighten your darkness, and – if necessary – hit the Gnome over the head if he gets too bumptious.'

Molly laughed. 'It won't be his head you'll be worried about.'

The covers flapped once more. The three women set to work.

*

270

Dryden stood at the window of Beautiful Bygones and looked up at Spindle Tor. It held all his dreams. He saw his son, looking silly it was true for he appeared to be riding a long-nosed dog – but he was riding alongside the daughter of the Fitzhartletts and Dryden could have wept for joy. His grandchildren would have the blood of kings in their veins. They had been up there for hours and were taking a circuitous route – in and out of thickets and the small plantations of trees that were dotted around the Tor and they appeared to be happy and engrossed in each other. Dryden's heart leapt in his breast. He tried to rise above the way his son looked as he trailed his feet on the ground. He was happy. Nigel *was* happy for Christ's sake, wasn't he? Dryden looked all around him most fearfully but there was no pale wraith knocking at his window or standing at the top of the shop stairs – none at all. You'd have thought she might have turned up to see that he had done something right for a change. And while he could not entirely believe in Porlock's prognosis – that it was likely to do with guilt in some way – he nevertheless felt a weight had been lifted from his shoulders since spilling the beans in the surgery. Porlock appeared to have changed his mind about dismissing it and had, on the contrary, patted his arm and told him to look in any time if the spectre ever reappeared. 'The best thing you can do,' he said, 'is to make Nigel very happy. Then you will be released.'

'Is that it?' Dryden had asked. It seemed so simple.

'That's it,' said Donald Porlock. 'Do you have a Mrs Beeton in your shop by any chance?'

Perhaps the good doctor was going off his trolley slightly? Dryden considered that the village had changed beyond all recognition lately. And he did not, altogether, disapprove.

Dryden looked up again at the tiny, jogging figure of Nigel – he looked happy enough. And so did Marion Fitzhartlett. She did not seem to mind at all that Nigel looked even more absurd than Sancho Panza. Hardly a swain. In the privacy of his own head Dryden did wonder, he wondered very much, if the two of them would ever – well – manage it. Create any new little veins for the blood of those kings to flow in. Then he looked away and found his gaze resting on the figure of the Gnome, whose disgraceful end-point was currently hidden from view. And on which three women in dungarees knelt. Perhaps if the two of them went up there . . .? He shook his head. Ridiculous. Ridiculous. Yet all the same . . . Who knew if there was anything in the witchery of it? Who knew? He'd try anything. Anything. Oh glory, he thought, oh glory – but just then there was a shadow at the side window and Dryden turned. There it was again, that pale ghost of a woman who seemed so like Lottie and who shook her head, smiling sadly at him as she had done in life. There again was the pain in his heart. He looked away, back up at the Tor, but he could no longer see the laughing pair.

You would not, surmised Nigel, think that Julie Barnsley had so much strength in those little arms of hers. But there he sat, on the hard ground, leaning in dazed fashion against what he thought of as a hummock but which that old map called a cyst – leaning up against it and endeavouring to get his breath back. Even such a short fall had winded him. Julie had borrowed Peter's quad bike and followed the riding couple about halfway up Spindle Tor – curious rather than suspicious – before the quad bike refused to climb safely any more and began to roll back. Steering backwards was not part of the deal, so far as Julie was concerned, nor was the gathering speed of the vehicle. Looking behind her as she began her undesired descent, and just as she thought she might be about to die and was trying to remember how the Magnificat went – not entirely appropriate but the best she could do – she saw, in a moment of supreme hope, Nigel, on his pony, trotting out from a thicket of trees – and coming her way. Or rather, she was going his way. Fast. Perhaps he would dive on to the bike and stop her.

Fortunately, Marion's horse was some way behind Nigel and she only stood at the edge of the trees and watched the bike and its occupant whizzing downwards. It was, as she would say later, all over in a trice. Julie grabbed at Nigel as she flew past him and – a quad bike being no higher than a pony – she managed to pull him down, hold on with both arms and get free of the contraption – which continued downwards. The pony, thinking it was a great game, got up speed to keep up with the – now empty – bike – and Julie – happily not too close to the animal's hooves – let loose from Nigel – probably from shock – and rolled after it. Nigel was thrown, or rather slid, and then slumped, dazed, eyes closed against a mound. Only then did he realise that it was not a bird that he heard, nor a creature of any wild variety, but the sound of Marion Fitzhartlett screaming and screaming before jumping down from her horse and running across the grass to where he lay silent. Odd, he thought, as he opened one eye – for though Marion was no longer screaming but merely stroking his hair (as she would a startled horse's mane) the screaming, though farther away, continued. This time it was Julie. Rolling onward and onward, Spindle Tor being a very steep place, and only eventually coming to rest against one of the lower mounds. Where she kept up her howling for some minutes, as one might expect.

Interestingly, though she could no longer be seen from the village, Julie could certainly be heard. As indeed could the rumbustious noise of a quad bike breaking into what sounded like a thousand pieces on the stones below. Peter, merely guessing, and who had been standing at the door of the pub enjoying the view (this was a lie, made to himself, for he was scanning the Tor for a sight of his barmaid) suddenly leapt into action and

– some said afterwards – flew to Julie Barnsley's aid, terrified that she might be dead. Which quite took away any residual pain he might have felt on the death of his much-loved quad bike. The last thing Julie remembered, as she would tell her grandchildren one day, was the sight of Peter running towards her, his face streaming with tears.

The vicar sat perched in one of Sir Roger Fitzhartlett's wing armchairs. Large chair, small man, which may have been deliberate. Orridge brought in a tray of coffee and put it down on the table that was set between Lady Dulcima Fitzhartlett and her husband, and their guest.

Orridge had not yet forgiven Sir Roger for requiring to be carried home from the Old Holly Bush and the clatter as the tray was put down made everyone wince. Not least Orridge, who had been compensating himself with a bottle or two of Royal Oporto Tawny pre-phylloxera (1870, £750 a bottle and why the hellhound not?) in a less than sensible way. Despite his ill-wishes, Orridge knew what was what and the tray was placed, you could say, like a barrier between the gentry and their vicar and defined their status.

The vicar was well pleased. Very delicately he picked up the cup and saucer and gave Orridge a nod as he exited the room. The vicar sipped the dark and perfect coffee the very taste of which showed good breeding. Nectar. 'Ah,' he said. 'It's Monsooned Malabar.'

'Has it really?' said Sir Roger, whose mind was on other things such as his guns and his birds. 'Never been there myself.'

Lady Dulcima showed the merest flicker of amusement before giving the vicar a stern eye. 'Why?' she asked. 'Does she want you to conduct such a thing?'

'I'm not entirely sure,' said the vicar uncomfortably. He had raced away from Molly full of excitement and pleasure at the thought of something so unusual, where he would be the focus, something so rare in that wretched pulpit, but now he came to it, he could not, for the life of him, think why he had felt so joyful. It was that archaeologist girl. She had a way with her, a definite way with her. 'I think it's because such a ceremony will be a meaningful marking of the moment for the girl, and she will reveal to us all that she has found up there at the same time. And I will be the spiritual guidance. She says I can stand on her trailer. So I will be seen . . .' He gave his patroness a look. She responded with a look of her own and a plate.

'Biscuit?' she said. 'Build yourself up? Shortcake . . .'

The vicar took one, looked at his patroness again – but could discern nothing untoward. 'Thank you,' he said.

'Why is she asking our permission? It's Miles's hill, after all.'

'I think she wants you there as leaders of the community.' Even having said this the vicar knew he had been wrong to quote Molly.

'Good God,' said Sir Roger, jumping up. 'Makes us sound like a pair of ruddy commissars. What community? Is she a socialist?' Mind you, he was thinking, it would be a good place to have a go with one of his stickier guns – up high like that. All the guns seemed sticky at the moment. He longed to try something new. Life was empty of meaning nowadays if you couldn't take a shot at something.

'I think the vicar means the *village* community.' Dulcima bit thoughtfully on a biscuit.

'Perhaps,' said her husband with hope in his heart, 'we could give a volley or two? A gun salute?' He could take a pop at something. 'My wife must decide.'

Both men turned to the wife in question. Who continued to think for a moment. The vicar thought how elegantly she chewed her biscuit and Sir Roger thought she had never looked lovelier. Dulcima nodded and turning her eyes upon the man of the cloth asked if there was a precedent for an out-of-doors service?

The vicar swung his legs as he considered this. Dulcima looked at him with irritation. He wouldn't have to lift those legs if Mrs Webb was vacuuming around him. Why they had to appoint someone of such short stature, such a pity – it really was very, very annoying. Short men were not the most sensitive to others.

Seeing the look on his patroness's face, the vicar hurriedly said that he thought there was. 'It must be within the parish, I think, but certainly it is within the remit of the parish church and its incumbent. I think . . .' He was not looking entirely comfortable with that answer but the recipient of the news looked splendidly pleased.

'Excellent,' said Dulcima. 'And it is a Sunday on which we are to celebrate whatever it is we are to celebrate. So that will be the Sunday service over and done with. Yes?'

The vicar could tell this was important and nodded enthusiastically. 'The date falls on a Sunday, Your Ladyship.'

'In the morning?'

'Absolutely.'

'Over by lunchtime?'

'Easily.'

Dulcima leaned back on the sofa and looked pleased. 'Then we agree. We will come. And we will have a little drinks party here afterwards and ask some of the young men around about. Marion has been learning to –' she did not want to use the word socialise in case it caused Harty to explode again, so instead she said – 'get along with them. And who knows, vicar, you may be conducting another kind of ceremony altogether before the year is out.'

'Oh good,' said the vicar, quite at sea but happily so. Perhaps she meant the blessing of a new pulpit?

'Might see a pigeon or two up there,' said Sir Roger, thoughtfully. 'Big hill.'

'Roger!' said his wife sternly.

He said no more on the subject of birds. He began to think how peaceful and easy life was when she used to make those little trips to the cellar. 'How about a little sherry?' he said, with hope. The vicar rubbed his hands and swung his little legs again. But Dulcima rose from the sofa and held out her hand to the vicar, who took it and was immediately aware of being pulled up out of his seat. And before he knew it, with the polite sound of Her Ladyship's 'So good of you to come' in his little ears, he was shown the door.

'Are you never going to drink again, Dulcie?' said Sir Roger.

'Never,' she said confidently. 'Never again.'

Outside the door the heart of Orridge sank to his bootstraps. As did, on the opposing side, the heart of Sir Roger.

Donald, leaving the house for the surgery, looked up and saw nothing on the Hill except the covers and some figures darting about. One of which was his wife. If he screwed up his eyes he could just make out a familiar bottom in its rather fetching dungarees. He smiled contentedly. He thanked his stars she had found sanity. It was, as he said: a woman without anything to do tends to go peculiar. Pity she didn't find kitchen stuff enjoyable any more but he'd rather have her sane and out on Pound Hill than in the kitchen getting tight and flinging teapots about. Besides, the best chefs were men. He was a man. And his daughter, Charlotte, who had never had two words to say to him that were not of criticism, had actually said on the phone last night, 'Well done, Dad.' Tonight he would master macaroni cheese. It looked easy enough on the television. He opened the door to his car and was just about to get in when he saw Dryden Fellows coming down the street. He looked unwell again.

'Dryden, my dear chap! You look like you've seen a ghost.'

Whereupon, much to his amazement, Dryden Fellows burst into tears.

Donald Porlock would once have thought this showed lack of control and sissiness. Now, strangely, still fondly thinking of the macaroni cheese and the new lease of life he had embraced, he found his arm going around the shoulders of his unhappy patient, and heard himself saying, 'So sorry. An unfortunate choice of words. Want to slip into the surgery with me again, old fellow, and let's have a talk about it? Yes? I've got a bit of spare time.' And off they drove together, with Donald cheerfully telling Dryden how much better a cook he was than ever Winifred had been.

'Taken me all these years to find out that I've got a touch of the Master Chef in me. I love it. And Winifred is very good about clearing up the kitchen, very good. Not my thing, really. What's good enough for the television chefs is good enough for me.'

Dryden did not seem very interested in macaroni cheese, though when Donald got him to the surgery he thought he would give him a stiff noggin of medicinal brandy. They could both have one. Poor chap. Donald gave him a sideways glance. My, he did look pale. A wee drop of five-star would help. Donald found it did him a great deal of good when he was creating in the kitchen. He had come to think of it as a heart-starter. Strange how many dishes he cooked had alcohol in them, too. Great fun, this cookery lark. Great fun. Cheese dishes, so he read, benefited from an additional dash of kirsch. So would he.

Miles returned to his sitting room and slumped into his armchair. Sometimes one could feel quite alone, he thought. And even if Dorcas had been here with him, and not up with those two women, he would not have been able to share his thoughts for they were not – he knew – the most acceptable. Too much was talked about community and social responsibility, in Miles's view, far too much. An iron hand was what was needed. People being told what to do. And self-reliance. Miles brought his fist down hard on the arm of his chair, which made a loud puffing noise. He felt chilled, even though it was June – it was so early that the sun had not yet shone into the sitting room.

Montmorency, in his customary place curled on the seat by the (unlit) fireside woke at the unaccustomed disturbance. Normally all there was to be heard in this room was the gentle tapping of Dorcas's keyboard, and Miles's voice and pacing feet. The cat opened one eye. He was weary. He had been out for most of the night and he needed his sleep. If human beings went on hitting things, how could he catch up? He stretched, he yawned, he put out both sets of front claws, admired them, and then retracted them as he slid down to the floor. In a trice he had jumped on to Miles's lap and curled himself up again. Miles balanced the knowledge, recently learned, (BBC Radio 4, *You and Yours*), that a sleeping cat on your lap gave out an impressive amount of wattage and should be employed by poverty-stricken pensioners, with his total lack of warm feelings for the creature. In the end the latter won. Miles stood up, shedding Montmorency (who was quite ready for the drop for a cat knows when a lap is at rest and when it is not) and went upstairs. He would put on another jumper. It was June. It was a warm day. He was getting old.

In his bedroom he first went over to the window and peered up the Hill. There was the Gnome, grinning down at the village as usual – or was he grinning? Was he looking quite so full of himself now that his – er – appendage was under the tender mercies of Molly and Winifred (*Winifred?*)? Or maybe it was just earlier than usual and the light made him look a little less gung-ho?

Miles shivered again and turned away from the view to the chest of drawers from which he selected a thick jumper. He slipped it over his head and was about to close the drawer when he saw the little box. Go on. Just a little peep. Just a little feel. His talisman. While he held the diamond the world was in his control. He took it out and opened the box and immediately felt better. A diamond that size was worth a lot of money. He rubbed it on his sleeve and saw how it sparkled against the black velvet in the box. As so often, the sight of this stolen asset made Miles feel warmer and much better. Sometimes he just gazed at his investment statements – and they cheered him up immensely, too. What good would this ring have done Dorcas anyway? She mourned Robin, she had no money to speak of, and she was better off in the Squidge at a peppercorn rent and working for Miles. Apart from anything else – he shivered again – it cost very little to keep her place warm. Unlike here. He longed to be settled in the matter of his ownership of Robin's assets. Red tape. Always red tape. But at least he knew that he was officially the next of kin. Very lucky that Dorcas had not married Robin before he went off to South America. Very lucky.

He gave the diamond one last look, closed the drawer, and went back downstairs feeling much more cheerful. He would just have to wait for Dorcas to report back to him. Nothing more to be done. He slipped this morning's teabag back into a cup and poured on some boiling water. He had never liked strongly flavoured drinks.

Pinky was at the library in Bonwell – libraries, he had suddenly realised, were cathedrals of knowledge – and he was deeply engaged in reading a book called *The Good Parenting Guide*. He might have gone out and bought the book but he did not want any evidence left around at home. Just in case. It would not do to be proved wrong.

Susie was having her hair done. She was having the purple bits removed and the whole fluffy mass of it thinned and controlled. Pinky reminded her that when they first met at the 77a bus stop, she was turned out the usual sort of way: a pair of jeans, a jacket that hid her bum (he'd tried to gauge its rough circumference and couldn't) and pixie boots. Nice and simple. Her hair was longish and smooth – though she did wear a beret. Come to think of it, he should have been a bit wary of the beret. But – generally – she showed no hint of the forces that were to unleash themselves – in every way. So Pinky plucked up the courage to say that these purplish effects had created difficulties for him in the bed department, her explosion of curly hair so often got up his nose and in his eyes and it took his mind off anything else, and her clothes did – yes, he dared to say it – nothing for her. Or him.

Susie had fixed him with a pondering look and shed a tear or two, before visiting her crystal garden for guidance. So far Pinky was not entirely sure what the crystals had suggested but it was looking good. And since the absence of visits to the Gnome in their lives, and the apparently somewhat reduced nature of his power now that he had a couple of women in dungarees crawling all over him, Susie said sadly that she feared he was not as powerful as she'd first thought. When she returned from the crystal garden Susie's eyes were dry and she said very firmly, 'I think that it might be the place itself that is alive with ancient forces, rather than – well – *that*. Possibly.'

Pinky was overjoyed. He had no problem with the landscape being anything she wanted it to be – it was certainly full of tumuli and stuff. But the Gnome might have no power? Suddenly their future together opened up in a glorious landscape of ordinary daily life. They would go for walks together without his footsteps being directed towards that bloody Pound Hill. His wife had even left off the patchouli at night, which helped his breathing no end. His customers said he looked like a new man and his pipework was becoming the talk of the area as his name was passed from household to household. He loved his Susie all over again and in every way. And if he was right – he smiled into the book – then this was the result. And bollocks to the Gnome, large as you like. Vile, vulgar and gross creature. What man would want to carry a thing like that around with him all day? Why, you'd go faint from loss of blood to the brain. It made him feel queasy for the Molly girl and the doctor's wife who were constantly being exposed to it all up there; he hoped they were not becoming tainted. That was why Susie gave them the flowers – mind over matter, was how she put it. Though the Molly girl said that she took a very straightforward view of the site. Apparently when you were up close and digging you never saw what you were digging as a whole, just a bit of it, a part of the jigsaw. Then they had both laughed at the appropriate use of the term *jig*.

Susie entered the library. 'I've had a text message from that archaeologist girl. She wants me to ring her back. I wonder why?'

Pinky tucked *The Good Parenting Guide* beneath *Plumbing for Cowboys* and smiled up at her. 'Won't know until you find out,' he said.

He looked at his wife admiringly. She looked wonderfully ordinary. Beautifully ordinary, in fact. And completely devoid of pretension. I am, he told himself, a man of water and of sewage, a man with no pretensions either, a man who does *not* think that if you suck a dandelion it will make you urinate but who merely makes a flushing receptacle available should it be so. I do not need to be helped along life's way with ancient herbs and incantations. Therefore, the more my wife straightens herself out, the more I love her. I hope she will not abandon everything that adds a touch of magic and mystery to her, because those, too, have become a part of her – but a man can have too much of it. Getting rid of Susie's crystal garden and planting something useful like veggies, now that would be an achievement. The crystals, as he muttered over his plumber's flux from time to time, had not grown very much anyway.

Susie, in a moment of supreme restraint, had not gone off on one at her husband for keeping this all to himself for so long. But if only he had spoken out they would have saved themselves a lot of bother. She stood there, looking down on Pinky's little pink bald spot and she wondered what was a woman to do and why had he not spoken out? He always seemed to like the exotic and she had obliged. Susie was not one to be perverse – if he wanted straight, she would give him straight. It was all the same to her. It did not damage the inner spirit. But she did wonder, as they left the building quite happily together, why they – like so many others before them – and many to come, no doubt – had only found harmony after stumbling over the rocks of unexpressed desire in the darkness of repression until finally they found the light switch.

'I wonder what the archaeologist girl wanted?' said Susie, neutrally. Much safer.

'Let's find out,' said Pinky. Ditto.

Up on the Hill, crouched next to Molly and Winifred, Dorcas looked into the trench and the opening they had dug. Dorcas gasped. It was not an empty space and it was directly under where the cushiony part of the phallus ended. But now, where once had flourished the Gnome's greatest accoutrement, there was a dish-shaped dugout and in it, not yet entirely emerged but very recognisable nevertheless, were a pair of skeletons that seemed to be in an embrace. Scattered near them were more of the shale beads.

Molly gripped her shoulder and said softly – 'Most extraordinary . . . Most unusual. A grave for two . . .' Her voice softened.

'And you can just make out what they're doing. I've never seen anything like it in my life before . . . It speaks down the ages. It tells us something rare about our ancestors. It tells us how they *felt*.'

But Dorcas was scarcely listening. A lump had come into her throat and her eyes were a little wetter than the wind up on Pound Hill might have caused them to be. 'It's beautiful,' she said. 'Quite, quite beautiful. They are beautiful.'

Molly put a finger to her lips. 'Say nothing for the moment.'

'Cross my lonely heart,' said Dorcas.

Below them, Nigel set off from Beautiful Bygones in the direction of the Old Manor. He was whistling and walking with the cheery air of a man at one with the world – a man, thought his father, watching him go, who had nothing but happiness in mind. Dryden Fellows also noted, with great relief, that Nigel did not so much as turn once to spy on the Molly person up the Hill. Which was, perhaps, the best news of all. And if, by the time he turned on to the gravel drive of the fine old house he remembered that he had not looked for her before he set off, he did not seem very concerned. Much more concerned, was he, with the way Marion came running up the drive to meet him, her green eyes full of enquiry about his poor bruised face and body.

Two

FOR THOSE WHO may be wondering what was the other bit of good news that Molly might or might not be able to give to Miles and Dorcas, it was decided by that young lady that she would, after all, bide her time before bestowing it upon them – and therefore we will respect her caution and put thoughts of it to one side for a while. With such things, she knew, you must be certain. And so, since Dorcas seemed content to think that the news was something to do with the half-excavated grave on the Hill, which she had found wholly enchanting, and since Miles was content to think it was to do with something wonderful in the treasure line that had been found on the Hill, there were no more questions.

Molly also had other things on her mind. Now that she had posted up a notice about it in the pub, she and Winifred must finish their work and be ready for the ceremony due to take place on the Sunday in question. It was then that everything that Molly had set out to do would be accomplished and announced. It was now very clear that where she and Winifred had dug was the place that grandfather Bonner had dug before. And she supposed it was a marvel – or Marvell, as he wrote it in the notebooks – what they had found. How pleased she was to have vindicated him and the project he was unable to complete due to a bullet lodged in an archduke's jugular in Sarajevo and its miserable aftermath. And how pleased, too, to have proved herself worthy of her grandmother's faith – and to have achieved something in her own right. She allowed herself one small spurt of pride.

*

That evening, Molly tapped on the door of the small bedroom along the passage from hers, in which lay Julie Barnsley. Although there were no bones broken, Julie was much bruised from her ordeal, still shaken, and not keen for anyone to see her. A barmaid with a black eye and a swollen lip was not an appetising sight and might put Nigel off even more. So when Peter insisted that she stay at the pub, tucked away until she was quite recovered, she agreed. She tried, unsuccessfully, to glare at Molly. Glaring is not easy with a damaged cheek and eye socket. While she knew that Molly in her dungarees and old T-shirts was not likely to be seductive to him, Molly in her dungarees and old T-shirts compared to a woman who looked as if she had just gone three rounds with Mike Tyson might just have the edge. That Molly herself seemed unaware of the tensions she caused did not help either.

Julie Barnsley could cheerfully have throttled her in her seemingly happy ignorance. How unfair to be so balanced. How unfair. Nevertheless, she managed to smile at Molly and say, with difficulty, 'You should see the other guy . . .' To which Molly responded that – if the state of the quad bike was anything to go by – the other guy was not a pretty sight. A large tear formed in Julie's shut eye. 'Nor am I,' she said. And while this might be the opinion of many in the village who had seen Peter Hanker carry her semi-conscious body towards the Old Holly Bush, it was not the view of everyone. Not by a long chalk. Peter Hanker privately thought that the sight of his barmaid, her bruised head laid against the snow white pillows (courtesy of Bonwell's laundry, fortnightly) of his single room (with h/c and w/basin – £28 b&b per night) was pleasing. Very pleasing. Even more pleasing was that Nigel had not been anywhere near Julie, not even with a card to wish her well. A state of affairs that Peter did not find at all surprising and which he hoped might make an impression upon his barmaid's bruised and battered brain. Apparently not.

That evening, just before he opened up, the patient asked Peter, in an oddly meek tone (odd for her) if anyone had enquired about her. And Peter said that *everyone* had. Which did not seem to cheer her up very much. Now she transferred her enquiries to her visitor.

'Have you seen Nigel?' she asked Molly and Molly replied that she had not. Molly said this with such an air of detachment that Julie breathed a sigh of relief.

'Do you find him interesting?' asked Julie. Molly looked at her in amazement.

'My grandmother used to call my mother's cooking *interesting*,' she laughed. 'And you should have seen it. The one joke my father ever made, and he often repeated it, was that since he was married he had not put on an *ounce*. And my grandmother said it was hardly surprising . . . Interesting? Nigel? Well, not really. I mean – he's very *nice*.'

Julie relaxed completely. Eat your heart out, any hopeful lover, for being called *nice* by the object of your love is tantamount to being called *sweet* and therefore, in the privacy of your own consciousness, should make you want to smack them. The next thing you know she will be saying that you are her *very best friend* – which means, though it is possible that the likes of Nigel would miss the point, that there will be no carnal knowledge.

This statement, that Nigel was very *nice*, was greeted with a look of profound relief on Julie's part, followed, though she tried to hide them, by another large tear or two. Molly thought for a moment and added, 'Nor do I fancy Peter – in case you wanted to know that as well. My interests in that department lie elsewhere. Very elsewhere at the moment,' she added grimly. 'And with a shockingly bad communicator. Two lines of straightforward information and that's it. You try reading between the lines where there's only two of them.'

Molly laughed, seemingly at herself. Julie blinked out a couple more tears though she was uncertain why they should come at the mention of Peter. 'You've had a shock,' said Molly. 'You'll need rest. But you'll have to be better soon – we love Mrs Webb's cooking but we can't *stand* hearing about her naughty little gnomes and what she thinks they get up to. And it's not helped by mine host's long face, either. And anyway, you must be better by the time we have the ceremony up the Hill. I once fell down a shaft in Wiltshire – went all the way from the Roman level to the Mesolithic – talk about your previous lives passing you by – but I was all right eventually.' Julie shed another tear at this. It is never helpful when one whom you seek to despise shows you kindness.

Molly closed the door of the sickroom behind her and went to her own place. Here she sat at the table that stood beneath the window, from which she could look out at the Gnome and the Hill. The evening sky was a clear, deep blue, most of the tarpaulins were folded and gone, with just one stretched taut and fixed over the grave. The trailer had been taken down the Hill for the last time and emptied and now stood near the top cleared, cleaned up and ready for the vicar. And the stars were just beginning to appear. Rabbits, deer and birds were apparently at rest.

Nothing stirred up there. It seemed it was a hill in waiting. Somehow, though she could not explain it, Molly felt she had won. She picked up her grandfather's notebook. If the Gnome wished to make his presence felt to one whose plans had caused his most important attribute to be hidden from view, he would have to do more than glower down the Hill at her lighted window. For Molly's head was bent over the last few pages of her grandfather's last letter to her grandmother. The section began: '*I wrote of the Marvell. You will know precisely what I mean by that. Marvell is overcome, then. And I have proved it. But let me say these are <u>grave thoughts</u> and leave it at that until we meet. When I might be allowed to give you the truth of it. Does it help for you to ponder on the name of the village? Lufferton Boney? Try that. If you cannot – then you must wait until we are together again – and all is well and all will be revealed. Just a few more weeks, my love . . .*'

Molly had pondered and pondered these words, and wondered and wondered why – when they ran off to be married – her grandmother did not immediately make him tell her exactly what he meant by it all. I would have been desperate to ask, she thought, I would not have rested until I *had* asked and been answered. But her grandmother had not done so. Women in those days, so her grandmother told her, even young, forthright and feminist women, were nowhere near as liberated as women were today. If a man decided to remain silent on a subject, then he remained silent. Or you became known as a nagger and a scold. Besides, as her grandmother delicately put it, for Molly was very young then, they had other things on their minds than digging up bits of England for old artefacts and solving riddles. Running away to get married then was much more radical than nowadays. And – yes – once they were married they had more enjoyable things to pursue. Newly married things. And little time in which to indulge them before he went away to war. What was the making of holes in a little bit of hillside when they had these other considerations in their lives? It was all going to be over by Christmas, that war. It was only after his death, so she told Molly, that she realised, from his notebooks and letters, how much the discovery meant to him and then it was too late. Yes, she regretted it, but no, she did not think herself foolish for not asking – she was a very young woman in love, they were lovers who had just eloped: why would she even think of the Gnome of Pound Hill?

Molly looked at the reference to it being a marvel again. It was awkward and strangely constructed, and the syntax was not quite right, and she was as confused as ever by it. It seemed so slight a reference, a love-letter thing rather than a thing of significant archaeological reference – and yet . . . something niggled away at Molly. Her grandfather was the writer of perfect copperplate – and his spelling was good throughout. Until this. Niggle, niggle went the thought. It was extremely vexing.

You could say that our Molly Bonner was a victim of government education policy. At her school they had concentrated on the national curriculum – and also on the government's dictum that science was supreme. One way and another, Miss Bonner the archaeologist's granddaughter had missed out on a liberal education – arts had not featured greatly – with only a sprinkling of English literature as required by law. It is therefore not surprising that it should take an older woman, one who had been educated in the old way and by teachers who were unafraid to stretch their pupils' minds further than the settled median standards, to realise what it was that grandfather Bonner was hinting at to his beloved, and to explain it to Molly. But, for yet another night, Molly was left in ignorance. On her bedside table was the letter of two lines (well, actually, three if you included the signature which did have the grace to include several xxx's) from exotic parts, in response to hers and which added to her feelings of excitement about the way the world was unfolding.

Up at the Manor, Marion's father and mother exchanged a questioning look; they had just heard their daughter making her way up the stairs, laughing and singing to herself. 'She's gone potty,' said Sir Roger.

'In a way,' said Dulcima. They listened again.

'What is she singing?' asked her father.

Dulcima listened. 'James Taylor.'

'Never heard of him.'

The soft, slightly out of tune sounds of 'How sweet it is to be loved by you-oo' floated downwards.

'Yes you have. They've been going through your records in the games room. You used to sing this to me . . .'

'Did I?'

'You did. How swee-eet it i-is . . .'

'Taylor, Taylor – do we know him?'

Dulcima was about to admit that he was American but she wanted Harty in a good mood. So she said, quite truthfully, 'Lives in Berkshire – parents southern Scottish – old family.'

'That's all right then.' Sir Roger hummed the tune.

'Yes. It is.' Massachusetts and the American deep south did not need to enter into it.

'Good shooting on those estates near the Nith. Damn fine.' Her husband hummed on. Orridge, who had been listening both to Miss Marion's warbles and his employers' conversation, appeared with a hopeful look on his face. 'Will there be anything else before I retire?' he asked. Sir Roger was not one to sing unless in his cups. Yet again the answer was no. And yet again, in avoiding the dogs who were splayed around the room, Orridge tripped over a spare footstool on the way out.

'Oh Harty,' said Dulcima. 'Those dogs.'

'Oh Dulcima,' he replied. 'Those footstools.'

The door closed silently and disapprovingly. Above him, floating down from her room, came the voice of Marion who had moved on to 'All You Need Is Love'. Some of the records were very old indeed. Orridge made his way along the corridor to the green baize and another miserable night with only himself to drink with. It was hardly worth the effort of going down the cellar steps. Life had become empty and meaningless. Meaningless. All they seemed to do nowadays was put their heads together about Miss Marion – and all *she* seemed to do was either go out with that Nigel person who knew nothing of billiards or tennis, let alone fine wine, or go around the house laughing to herself and singing. Humbug.

It did not help that Orridge had a double reason for being at odds with his employer. On the night he had huddled by the steps of the Old Holly Bush to wait, Mrs Webb, having finished with her kitchen duties and departing the public house, spied him and, taking pity on him, took him into her home to warm up with a noggin or two. Not the best brandy, it was true, but a kindness nevertheless. Alas, he had made the mistake of admiring her gnomes next to her path that night, on his way to collect his master, and she had insisted that he call and be introduced to them in daylight hours. Twice he had received the summons by telephone and twice he had found an excuse. But he felt he could not go on finding reasons not to go – not least because a man craved a drinking companion, dammit, especially when the bottle he had in mind was a very nice '83 Cornas.

Marion mused on the forthcoming ceremony. Nigel had confessed to having fantasies about knights and ladies. And she then confessed to having the same little thoughts. In the end she attached her handkerchief to Nigel's wristwatch, which made them both laugh and say, 'Aha – my lady's favour.' He had not given the handkerchief back to her when he went home this evening and she wondered, as she pulled the curtains in her room, whether he meant anything by it. She looked into her mirror to try and gauge what Nigel saw when he looked at her. Not so bad, she thought, still humming as she undressed. But when she caught sight of her nakedness she thought of the Gnome again, threw her nightdress on immediately and stopped humming. Instead she shivered, diving under the covers and pulling them well over her head. That would never do, she thought, but all the same, she could not – quite – stop smiling at how the handkerchief had fluttered every time he looked at his watch.

In Chrysalis Cottage Susie was snoring. Snoring so loud that Pinky imagined it was not unlike sharing a bed with a navvy. Good, good, he thought, nodding to himself – that's right – that's just how it should be, that'll be the upper airways narrowing. And, having rearranged his earplugs, he fell soundly asleep. Susie slept on, quite oblivious, and dreamed of a chocolate lake that was warm and thick and sweet as love.

In Beautiful Bygones' upstairs rooms father and son lay in their beds in their separate quarters. On Dryden's face sat a beatific smile of full satisfaction – though he kept his eyes closed in case he should see what he did not want to see. Nigel lay in his bed and felt – well – quite as confused as Julie – who was also lying awake in her little bed in the pub. He had put the handkerchief under his pillow – only for safekeeping he insisted to himself, and 'Molly, Molly, Molly' he mouthed as he usually did before falling asleep, 'I love Molly'. But somehow the pleasure he once enjoyed at the saying of her name did not quite knock in the dowel for him now and he found his thoughts straying to getting up very early and continuing his work on the sporting gun and how interested Marion had been in the process when he described it to her. In his dreams, when he eventually dropped off, instead of Molly he saw Sir Roger Fitzhartlett's face, full of smiles and good cheer, as Nigel knelt in front of him and presented him with the Churchill. He had a feeling, in the dream, that this ceremonial took place on Pound Hill – which seemed extremely odd. Why would Sir Roger be up there? He had not shown the slightest interest in the work, or the lovely Molly. But that's dreams for you. They never get it right. For example, now that the dream-scene had moved to a new frame, he was kissing – not the archaeologist's granddaughter – but the Baronet's only daughter, and – what's more (he tried to wake and could not) – he appeared to be enjoying it. And not half as much as she was.

The vicar was so excited at the prospect of an early morning ceremony on Pound Hill – and the splendid freedom the occasion brought him for a modern Sermon on the Mount (the New Beatitudes, he thought, with his own particular example of Blessed Are the Generous or maybe Blessed Are the Little Men) – that he had quite forgotten to be annoyed by the height of the pulpit. On the Hill he could stand above them all – placed on the trailer – and look down on them without the indignity of what Her Ladyship would insist on calling tippy-toes. He would preach of loving thy neighbour, of course, but he would also preach that humility was a very good thing. Maybe that would make its mark on the Fitzhartletts who should take him, though small (and his earthly needs), more seriously. Love and humility. Excellent combination. Now – what to wear to cut a dash?

Miles lay in his bed reading *The Complete Tutankhamun* by Nicholas Reeves with an introduction by the 7th Earl of Carnarvon. Good sense told him that what was found would not be so grand as that – couldn't be, for the size of it – but something had excited the Molly girl, he could tell. And such excitement could only mean a find of substantial value. He might have climbed up the Hill to take a look tonight except that the person in question was sitting, yet again, at her lighted window in the Old Holly Bush and was bound to see him. He wondered if the wretched girl ever slept. It crossed his mind that, unlike Susie, Molly Bonner might really have second sight – or witch blood in her veins. She always seemed to know when Miles wished to be on the prowl. Well, as long as her gift took her to where the treasure lay, who was he to complain. He skipped most of the chapter about the various calamities that befell various members of the Carter team. All nonsense. Lord Carnarvon died a few weeks after the discovery of the tomb but people died all the time: Howard Carter's pet canary was eaten by a cobra – but cobras probably liked a bit of poultry. And what if Carnarvon's brother died a few months later, too? Such was the way of things. Miles smiled to himself, not entirely unhappily – *he* should know about brothers. No point in getting all emotional over things like that. He passed over the pages. There would be no such calamities here.

Winifred was sitting up in bed with indigestion. Perhaps it was not such a good idea to let Donald loose in the kitchen. Macaroni topped with grilled goat's cheese and flavoured with something that was oddly cherry-like (she did not like to ask) was probably not the best meal to go to bed on. And, truth to tell, her joints were feeling a trifle stiff now – the bending was pretty acute on the site in these last days of careful cleaning for they did not want to disturb even the tiniest item – and she was not – she told herself but no one else – she was not as young as she once was. Donald seemed to have got a second wind. How interesting it was, she thought, that providing he could be seen to be The Best at something, he would do it. Shades of the man she had married, only then she had seen him as honourable, a fighter for the world. Winifred smiled. She would always be her husband's *sous chef*. Better not to rail against it any more. The Hill provided a great lesson in what was important and what was not in a marriage. Presumably gritting one's teeth had been part of it since time immemorial. At any rate, he seemed to be laying off the bottle nowadays, and thank heavens for that.

Beside her, also lying on his back, Donald slept serenely. She realised that her arm was draped across her belly and that Donald was holding her hand. We are, she thought, comforted despite the whizzing and popping in her gastric regions. We are in exactly the same pose as the Arundel Tomb. How appropriate . . . And she searched her mind for a bit of lost poetry. Winifred had loved poetry .as a girl and poetry was part of the pattern of schooling, but Donald was a medical man and poetry was not part of his cure for anything. He should, really, redress that – for poetry, she thought, can mend much. She remembered Larkin's line . . . 'What will survive of us is love . . .' Not what might, not what could, not what should – she nodded sleepily – but what *will* . . . But of course, she thought, as she drifted off to sleep, but of course – that is what the Hill is all about.

And Dorcas – Dorcas who knew the secret of the Hill and yet had to stay silent – how was Dorcas that night? Well, despite being privy to the secret and feeling, rather cheeringly, that she was one of the trusted inner circle, which always makes one feel loved, that night Dorcas was very, very sad. Sad, yes, that is how Dorcas was. She did feel loved, being in the inner sanctum, but not loved entirely in the way she would like to be loved. And although she slept in a little narrow bed which, in its single-ness gave a comfort, nevertheless, that night, she did reach for someone, for the grave on the Hill had made her remember, and when she reached, of course, there was no one there. It was almost as if she had never, really, been cured of Robin – and that she still loved him exactly as before. Suddenly, and for no reason she could think of, she remembered the feel of him and the way he smiled and almost, almost she could remember the smell of him. That is what was unearthed in Dorcas when Molly and Winifred showed her what they had found and that is what had made her sad that night.

With a moonbeam settling on the empty Spode dish, eventually she slipped away to sleep. But her dreams were filled with people running away from her, and always when they turned around in the distance they were Robin. And, like a parody of Cinderella, all she had to hold on to in the dream was a scuffed old boot. Which is, she thought, when she briefly awoke in the night, what I have now become – both the lost one, and the one who has lost. *Some tame gazelle, or some gentle dove: Something to love, oh, something to love!* Dorcas, self-taught, also liked poetry. It came in small books that could be slipped in the pocket when you were on your travels. And thinking about gazelles and doves she, too, fell asleep.

Montmorency, not privy to poetry of any kind, not even Eliot's cats, staggered back across the silvery street to Hill View House and flopped, exhausted, into the basket in the kitchen. So that was what that yowling he found himself doing was all about. He slept.

Three

THE LAST TOUCHES of work on the Hill went smoothly and the weather remained fair. And even though she had neared the end of the project Molly still refused to let Miles come anywhere near the site.

'I am the owner of the Hill,' he said. 'And I should see what you have found before anyone else.'

But Molly was adamant. 'We have an agreement,' she said firmly. 'And I would ask you to keep to it. If not . . .'

Dorcas agreed solemnly with Miles that the girl was playing with him, dangling his hopes over a cliff-edge. But when he asked Dorcas what he could do about it, Dorcas replied that she could think of nothing. She spent so much more money, she told him, on attempting to get Molly to impart information in the pub, but none was forthcoming. He did not dare break the undertaking, not so close to the end of the job and he knew that he needed her goodwill in order to progress his plans. He stayed away. Thus, apart from the odd grunt of delight or surprise or confirmation, the two women worked on the Gnome in happy silence while the skylarks larked above them and the squealing kites went round and round in the clear blue yonder.

The last few days of tidying and setting up the excavation for visitors were days of pleasure – of easy work, slow and method-ical, without any difficulties. 'I think,' said Molly to Winifred, as they walked down the Hill with their mission complete, 'that I shall probably never unearth anything quite so profound. Or beautiful.' Winifred nodded and wondered why she was close to tears. She had been laughing with Molly not five minutes ago. She supposed it was partly because of what they had found, and partly because it was over, or nearly. Soon she must go back to being the doctor's wife, betwixt and between in the village, with even her role as head cook and bottle washer undermined. She might, she thought, be forgiven for feeling wistful as the final Sunday drew near.

Dorcas met them at the door of the pub and the three went in together, looking maddeningly delighted with themselves. Miles, standing at his window opposite, felt a rage he could scarcely contain at such a display of feminine conspiracy. However, he would not risk transgressing and so he remained where he was, sipping a glass of inferior sherry while in the Old Holly Bush the three women raised a glass of good wine to the success of the enterprise. Then Dorcas said to Molly, 'And now you'll be waiting for your explorer man to come home, yes?' To which Molly, looking even more mysterious than she usually did at the mention of Freddy, said that she certainly was, oh she certainly was. 'Here's to the wanderer's return,' she said, to which they all agreed.

Julie Barnsley, now restored to her place behind the bar, nearly all traces of her bruises having vanished, raised her glass of lemon barley water to the sentiment. When Molly bloody Bonner was safely re-stowed into her young man's arms, then perhaps Julie Barnsley could reapply herself to Nigel. At the moment he was safe enough playing silly arses with Marion on their travels around the area as they followed that old map. Julie would not interfere with that. Nigel looked so stupid on his pony that even Julie had difficulty watching him, let alone anyone else.

She tried not to think badly of being attached to such an idiot for life. But still. Needs must, as she had told Peter, who had merely nodded and said, 'Yep.' If Julie wished for a stronger response from her boss, she did not get one. Just as well, she told herself. Julie would not like a difficult scene when she returned to her own home. She would take her wedding magazines and depart very soon. Another bonus was that by staying away from her intended she had achieved, she knew, one significant advance – Nigel's father no longer looked at her with that glittering eye of his, or sometimes went pale like a man who has seen a ghost and wishes to murder it. If, indeed, you could murder ghosts. Anyway, even he had a rosy, benign look about him nowadays and managed – occasionally – to smile at her. I'm not dead yet, she thought, smiling back, even though I came close. And she shivered at the memory of the broken quad bike.

The announcement that Molly had pinned up in the pub to the effect that the villagers were welcome to come up and see the results of her work on a certain Sunday in June was noted and approved of by many. At last, they said. And now it was nearly done, nearly completed, and this should have been a time for Molly to celebrate. 'Amen,' said Molly. But as the three women sat together in their usual place, Molly, toying with her glass, had a faraway look in her eyes. 'Are you thinking about your man?' asked Dorcas, wistfully.

'No,' said Molly. 'As a matter of fact, I was thinking about something that just will not stop niggling away at me. Something my grandfather wrote. I can't get a handle on it. He was usually so clear in his writing, though I think he liked puns, according to my grandmother.'

'Ah,' said Winifred. 'The Victorians liked all that sort of thing. Parlour games and plays on words. What's this niggling thing?'

'Might as well,' said Dorcas, 'see if we can help.'

'It's such a small thing,' said Molly, feeling embarrassed.

'Go on,' they said.

'Well – he wrote this thing about the excavation on the Hill

300

and that it would "displace the Marvell" – or something like that, only he spelt it wrong and anyway, I don't understand it. And he'd underlined something about grave thoughts . . .'

Dorcas and Winifred understood the significance at once. They nodded at each other and winked. Molly, still confounded by the thought, did not notice. It was not often, in the case of the Gnome of Pound Hill, that Winifred and Dorcas knew more than Miss Bonner.

'Any thoughts?' asked Molly.

'Maybe,' said Dorcas.

'Tomorrow, perhaps?' said Winifred.

Molly was on the point of tipping her drink over them both, which would have interested Dr Porlock who had just entered the pub in search of his wife for the coq au vin was awaiting them (Waitrose, two portions, £6.60 and he was going to lie about it, which was Dryden Fellows's suggestion and a good one). Cooking, he now knew, was exhausting to *think up*. Winifred had never complained about it and he took his hat off to her for never giving him the same meal twice in a row.

'Winnie?' he said.

Both Dorcas and Winifred stood up to leave.

Molly, who for so long had kept the villagers at bay, would now have some of her own medicine.

The day of the Sermon on the Mount, as the vicar insisted on calling it, arrived clear skied and already warm.

He rose and thanked God for the sunshine before taking his breakfast in his nightshirt. It would not do to get porridge (summer and winter, Scotts rolled oats, £2.30 a kilo) over the new and beautiful vestments he intended to wear. He had purchased a nice white alb over which he would place a green cincture. Very appropriate. It was, he thought as he stirred in his sugar, a great pity that the date fell in Church Ordinary – so that green was all he could aspire to.

How much more delightful it would have been for it to have occurred in Easter red or Lenten violet. Ah well, he would show his patrons how – nevertheless – he could shine. Then they would surely see the value of him. 'I could give you sermons like that every day,' would be his line to the Fitzhartletts, 'if only I could see my congregation.' And then he would request, once more and with great feeling, a new pulpit. There was a very fine one on which he had set his heart (Victorian stonework, the circular section body with a pedimented niche to the front and bands of quatrefoils and naturalistic foliage above an open arcade raised on cylindrical columns all raised on a drum base and polygonal foot, with stone steps and gilt metal handrail. £16,000. He loved the grandeur of Imperial Victorian). At a pinch, there was always carved oak.

He sang in the shower. 'In heavenly love abiding, no change my heart shall fear . . .' Why that popped into his head he did not know, but he sang it with gusto. God moves in mysterious ways his wonders to perform, he thought. '. . . and He will walk with me-ee.' Short, tall, medium – He would not judge a man on the length of his thigh bone.

Sir Roger, who was never one to rise early except on hunting days, tottered across the room and knocked on Dulcima's door. Dulcima continued to refuse to sleep in the same bed with him, which was not quite so necessary now that she did not tend to take a little snifter to bed with her, but still . . . Her husband, as if offering her the crown jewels of England, had reluctantly suggested that for her the dogs could remain downstairs, but still she demurred. Occasionally, but not very often now that his wife seemed rather more alert, the Master of the House (which Orridge called him with a very sardonic smile) sneaked one of the dogs up to his room, which, he found, soothed his loneliness considerably. If he remembered rightly, and he could just about do so, he used to stroke Dulcima like that. And pat her. And sometimes she growled. And sometimes – she didn't.

Dulcima was already up, sitting at her dressing table, sipping what smelled to her husband like an infusion of old straw. The sunlight played about her head making a halo of light as she brushed out her curls – and her neck looked as long and delicately curved as a snipe's. 'Ah,' she said, 'you are up. Well done. Looking forward to the Sermon on the Mount?'

Her husband grimaced and then growled. 'I'd like someone to mount him, puffed up Godbotherer. What's it all about?'

'Now Roger,' said Dulcima. 'Go and get dressed and then we'll walk up the Hill together. Marion, of course, intends to ride. Though whether she will actually go up the Hill or not, I couldn't say. She says she'll try. If Nigel will go with her.' He stomped back to his own room. 'Oh and Roger –'

He turned, he growled. 'Yes?'

'No dogs.'

The door between the two rooms slammed shut.

'And no guns.'

Nigel put the last of the polishing equipment away and surveyed the gun. Then he slipped it into an Emmebi soft case in Albu leather (£200) which he took the liberty of extracting from Sir Roger's stores since he seemed to have several all the same with no guns to go in them, these having been stamped on. According to Marion her mother had bought her father one of these every year for yonks and never remembered that she had. Nigel slid the beautiful Churchill inside the case and stroked the leather. Perfect.

He had not told his father that the gun was finished; he had not even told him he was working on the gun. His father thought he was working on a nineteenth-century armoire while his father restored a nineteenth-century mahogany partners desk with three drawers to frieze. The Churchill, so his father had said, had lost some of its relevance and could wait. Nigel seemed to be doing well enough without it. Well – it had not waited and now it was done. Nigel would surprise them both, Sir Roger and Dad, and also show his mettle – but to whom, exactly, he was not entirely sure . . . Once upon a time, of course, it would have been Molly he wished to impress. The thought never entered his head.

As Nigel propped the gun up against the wall and hung his waterproof over it, Dryden Fellows appeared at the top of the stairs. For a moment, in the gloom of the passageway, as Nigel looked up at his father, Dryden thought he was looking down upon Lottie. He put his hand to his heart and gave a little moan. But the fear was dispelled the moment Nigel called up and said 'Anything the matter, Dad?' And, in the usual way, Dryden covered up any emotional confusion by shouting to his son that he wished he would not hang around in dark places and nearly give his father a heart attack. Nigel, quite used to such a response, paid no attention.

Lottie had been appearing rather less since Dryden's visits to Dr Porlock's surgery. Although she had not entirely disappeared, she was beginning to look a little more cheerful. Well, maybe not cheerful – but perhaps not quite so sad. If you could say that a spectre had a bit more colour in its cheeks, then Lottie did. But still, and always, there was that twinge of doubt, twinge of guilt, twinge of fear every time he saw her – or it. He longed for her to smile and wave and say goodbye for good. But how to effect this, Dryden had no idea. Porlock, reading to him from a medical book he had purchased precisely, he said, for Dryden's benefit, said that he had to go through the experience until its meaning was clear and then he could resolve that meaning –

and it would be over. The problem was, whatever the meaning was, he had no idea about that either. Still, it was unlikely that she'd follow them up the Hill. Lottie had not approved of the Gnome and thought it ought to be removed. She called it an alien, and Dryden had laughed at her stupidity. Mistake. Big Mistake. How many of those had he made over the years, and now she had come to haunt him for it. He always felt a little lurch somewhere above his stomach when he thought of her all alone in that graveyard – but he rather wished, all the same, that she would stay there.

Miles Whittington did not need to rise early, he was already awake and up and about and making what Montmorency considered an unnecessary noise in the kitchen. Cats need their sleep even if human men do not, and Montmorency was never one to forget his feline rights. There were silver linings, though; nowadays Miles invariably put too much milk in the saucepan, a rare oversight producing even rarer waste, and then left it on the draining board for later use. Montmorency always obliged . . . He needed it to keep his strength up.

Taking his toast and tea over to the window, Miles sat where he had sat when Molly Bonner first appeared in this room and made her heart-stirring offer. He looked up at the Hill, still morning-shadowed, and felt a tremendous stab of excitement. Today was going to be a day to remember, he thought, he could feel it in his bones. Why – he looked down at his toast and considered – why – he might put a bit of butter on for a change – maybe even some marmalade (Winifred Porlock, two years ago, Seville and ginger, free as no one at the Bring & Buy had wanted to) – and with a song in his heart and a clatter in his activities he set about creating the feast.

He returned to the window seat and began to visualise the gate at the entrance to the Hill, the tickets being issued for the exchange of notes, the path upwards and the roofed and door-wayed structure that housed the find. Doors that would be locked against anyone who did not wish to pay to see the sight. So – that was two fees before he had even started on the franchise material: one to gain access to the remarkable Hill itself, and two to be privy to the Hill's most notorious image – and whatever else it was that they had found up there. Obviously the treasure would not be left *in situ* – that would be his – but the site itself could stay as a reminder of the joy of discovery. He just wished he knew what he was fantasising about. What it was those three witches had discovered. And – he looked at his watch – he soon would. Only a little while longer and all would be revealed. All. Why, he might even have a second piece of toast – he looked longingly at the crumbs on his plate, but no – better not. It didn't do to get carried away with things. Let the vision of the future be good enough to fill him, mind and body: control of the Hill, control of the Gnome, control of whatever it was they had found up there, and income. Money. It was impossible for Miles not to rejoice secretly in Robin's disappearance now. None of this would have been his, none of it. He would have gone on sleeping in the small back room, while Robin had the large room at the front (now Miles's) – and even if the back room *was* no smaller than his brother's – it felt like it. Now he had the whole house, the whole universe that he looked out upon – everything, everything was under his control. Including Dorcas. It felt marvellous.

Montmorency was deeply, deeply surprised to be woken by the stroking of an unfamiliar hand on his ears. He opened his eyes, took one look, thought, *Why this is hell, nor am I out of it*, and closed them again. It was too much to bear. Where was his beloved Dorcas when he needed her? Come to that, where was his true master, Robin?

Strangely at that hour, having knocked gently on the door,

Dorcas was being ushered into the Old Holly Bush. Fortunately she had had the good sense to check if Miles was stationed at his window and to wait until he was out of sight. Dorcas did not want Miles to summon her before she was up the Hill and away. But she did need to speak to Peter Hanker first, to reassure him of something.

In she went. Her conversation was short and to the point and left all three of them – for Julie too was there – giggling rather naughtily. Sometimes, thought Dorcas, living in Lufferton Boney was like being back at school – with Miles as the wicked headmaster. The three of them did their best to stop the naughty giggles and just about managed it so long as they did not catch each other's eye. It was not very suitable behaviour for a day such as today, as they all concurred – but impossible to resist. For Miles, who had smiled so obligingly at the suggestion, thought that the little party Peter Hanker suggested should be given after the trip up the Hill was to be paid for by Peter Hanker. Instead, Dorcas had instructed the landlord to send the bill, made out to Miles, to her for payment, and she would pay it out of the emergency fund. This emergency fund, about which Miles had – strangely – forgotten – was set up a couple of years ago when Miles had to have his carpal tunnel operation and could no longer sign cheques. It was therefore necessary for Dorcas to be able to go to the bank and remove cash.

'So let's make it champagne,' she said as she left. 'It's not every day you discover something so beautiful . . .'

Before either of them could ask her what she meant, she was across the road and knocking on the door of Hill View House and encouraging Miles to set off in half an hour. 'And not a moment before, Miles,' she said as she left. 'Or that girl will have your guts for garters and send you back down again.' Although it sounded very much as if she were joking, nevertheless Miles felt it sensible to do as Dorcas said. He was still in his dressing gown so he would have time to make a careful toilette. Good.

Dorcas walked over to where Molly waited for her and Winifred. You could, thought Molly, feel the pulse in the air that morning, feel the pulse of all the blood pumping in the village, waiting, waiting for the half-hour to be struck by the church clock so that doors could open and the people of Lufferton Boney could walk up to the Gnome and see for themselves what the diggers had found.

It was, thought Molly Bonner looking all about her, so good to be alive. Which is why she wore the very same outfit she had worn when she first arrived in the village all those months ago. The circle of past and present had very nearly closed. 'Though I am bound to say,' she told her companions, 'that climbing up the Hill in this outfit feels ever so slightly ridiculous.' She shot a little sideways look at Dorcas's clothes. 'Has anyone ever told you, Dorcas,' she said, 'how much cornflower blue suits you?'

And Dorcas said that yes, indeed, somebody once had. Winifred, too, was wearing something colourful and pretty. Including lipstick, which matched the red of her dress and which, so she said as they climbed, had astonished Donald, an effect that pleased her very much.

'When are you two going to tell me?' asked Molly as they climbed.

'About what?' they both said, all innocence.

'What he meant.'

'Who?'

'You know who. My grandfather and this "marvel" thing.'

'When we get up there,' they said. 'And not before.'

Had they turned to look back they would have seen quite a little gathering now assembled at the foot of the Hill. And, looking peaceful and picturesque, they would also have seen Marion Fitzhartlett leading a pony and riding Sparkle down into the village, very slowly, very carefully. If a riding rhythm can be said to be a thinking riding rhythm – then that is what Marion was doing: thinking. Gently she brought the horse to the bottom of the Hill. Nigel was already there, with his back to the village, his gaze following the women as they walked on up to the Gnome. The breeze caught the pink of a skirt, the blue of a dress and the red of another skirt. Above them loomed the figure, cleared now, bright as new, almost winking in the morning sun. Marion saw it as if for the first time. She could not do it. She just could not. Her parents had not yet arrived, which she found a great relief. What she wanted was to return home with Sparkle and hide.

Another odd thing was happening at the foot of the Hill. Julie Barnsley, who had arrived there with Peter Hanker, looked – there was no other word for it – like a floating blancmange, in pink organza. Pinker, she thought with satisfaction, than Molly's. She, too, was staring up the Hill at the disappearing figures. Julie, disengaging her arm from Peter's, called Nigel's name. He turned – and then he saw Marion. So Marion turned – and quite suddenly Nigel was running after her, one arm protecting the gun bag, the other arm held out towards her. And there was Julie's face, quite a picture, the foreground of which might be surprise, the background of which was most definitely confusion.

'Don't go,' called Nigel and ran towards her.

Marion remained where she was, still holding the lead to the pony, Sparkle shuffling anxiously. She shook her head at him. 'I can't, I can't,' was all she said, over and over again.

'You can, you can,' said Nigel.

This went on for some time and eventually Julie, becoming rather fed up with it and not quite knowing what was going on, went over to the pair. 'Come on Nigel,' she said, tugging at his elbow. 'We're all waiting.' Then she turned to Marion and said, more kindly, 'Why can't you?'

But Marion was shaking all over.

'She had a fall there – you know that,' said Nigel, and put his free arm around Marion's leg, the only part of her available to him.

'Well I had a fall, too,' said Julie. 'And I've been up the Tor since. Of course you can.'

But Marion would not be budged. The Gnome winked and winked at her in the sunlight and she was not going anywhere near him ever again.

'Look,' said Peter, who was getting as impatient as Julie. 'Why don't you wait at the bottom here? Then, if you suddenly feel that you can come up with the rest of us, you can.'

It seemed the best solution. So when Nigel offered to stay with her she said firmly that he should go because he wanted to give her father the gun, and anyway, there was no reason for him not to go. He could tell her all about it later. Julie, with a light in her eyes that was the beginning, but only the very beginning, of the dawning of understanding, put her arms through both men's arms and pulled them towards her. And off they set. By the time they were halfway up to the top Julie was perfectly clear about what had happened. She had kept her eye on the wrong ball. The way Nigel turned every two yards and gave Marion a little wave, the way Marion gave a little wave back – the more she knew – definitely, definitely the wrong ball. Now what could she do? She looked at Peter who was looking upwards, carefree as anything. There was no way Julie would ever be able to compete with an aristocrat. Dryden Fellows, who was already up ahead of them, would see her under the floorboards of Beautiful Bygones first. He'd cheerfully turn her *into* a beautiful bygone, rather than lose a Fitzhartlett connection. So it was all over.

On the three of them walked but Julie was no longer quite so puffed up with magnificence. True, she was still wearing the floating blancmange, and true it was as fluffed up and Ginger Rogers as possible, but the person within its folds had a certain shrunken quality about her. And that is, indeed, what was happening. Julie was shrinking. Julie was back to feeling inadequate. The term bogtrotter came to mind. She thought she had buried it for ever but now it came back to haunt her. Uncivilised bogtrotters, they had been called. And now this . . .

Dr Porlock feared the worst: what with Winifred and her skirt and sandals and all that lipstick it was enough to give him a seizure. He had so hoped for a quiet and unprofessional day of it but now Peter called him over and it was – he could tell at once – another case of physical disturbance through mental stress. 'Now Julie,' said the man of medicine to the trembling woman. 'What exactly do you think started this?' Julie shook her head and her eyes were dark with fear. 'I don't want to be called a bogtrotter,' she said, and looked pale enough to faint. Dr Porlock fought his way through the organza to get to her and felt her forehead. It was cold and clammy. Oh, he pleaded, please do not say you have seen a ghost. Not another one. He sneaked a quick sideways look at Dryden but he seemed to be all right. You never knew. Oh, thought Donald Porlock, oh for a nice sprained ankle. Julie crumpled like a collapsing pavlova and Peter crouched down beside her. 'Anybody calls you a bogtrotter,' he whispered into her ear, 'and I'll thump them.' 'Really?' she said weakly. 'Really.' That was more like it, she thought, passing into the momentary comfort of blackness, that was what she needed to hear. Though she knew very well that Peter Hanker, whatever else he *did* have in his nature, he did *not* have an aggressive bone in his body. And perhaps that should be enough? He was not likely to thump anyone. Including, of course, her.

*

311

Nigel, edging away from Marion in a strange and regretful hopping motion, saw Sir Roger and Lady Dulcima arrive in the village street and wave rather anxiously at their daughter. Nigel wanted to be up there and in place when they reached the top. He gave Marion one last wave, and she him, as up and onwards he went.

Dryden was quite oblivious to the fact that Nigel had left Marion at the foot of the Hill. Last seen, the two were together and looked set to ascend together. He was beyond any thoughts other than the joys of making such a good match. That boy of his, who would have thought it? Well, perhaps Lottie had been trying to tell him that Nigel was better than he thought for all these years, but nevertheless – he had to hand it to the boy – he had done most of this on his own. He must tell him that he felt – yes – very proud of his only son.

Dryden was perfectly and wonderfully lost in thoughts of his future in-laws and dreaming of a By Appointment sign on the shop, one with feathers for preference (they could do that, these people, they had influence with royalty). He was well up the slope by now and scanning the distance with his hand shading his eyes, looking to see if Orridge was driving the Fitzhartletts or if they were walking. And walking it was. As he stood there he saw them turning along the lane that led between the church and Beautiful Bygones: they were taking their time – which was utterly fitting. They would probably be the last to arrive – perfectly, perfectly fitting. He did not wish to be seen to be watching them so he turned his face Gnomewards and continued on up.

Much heartened by Nigel's continuing concern and smiles of encouragement, when her parents arrived Marion insisted that she was absolutely fine, fine – that they must go on without her. Her mother looked at her with sad eyes. 'I had hoped you'd got over all that,' she said. But Marion merely shrugged. 'Maybe,' she said, 'in time.' Her oddly set eyes flicked up towards Nigel and she smiled.

'Hmmm,' said her mother. 'Are you absolutely sure you won't come with us?' But Marion shook her head (the hair of which was once again being scraped back any old how and comfortable for riding).

'Not yet,' she said, firmly. But her parents must go, she insisted. They had a position to uphold.

Marion insisted that they went. Marion was extraordinarily firm about it. Dulcima was surprised by her daughter's sudden attack of self-confidence. Despite her fears and refusal to budge, Marion looked oddly radiant. They left her as she requested.

'Do you think she's sickening for something?' asked her father as he and Lady Dulcima marched forth.

'Yes,' said Dulcima. 'I rather fear that I do. You did ask the Hescott Brown boy for today? And Toadie Logan's younger brother? He's nice, isn't he?'

'Wet,' said Sir Roger.

'Wet in this instance is good. He's agreed? And the others?'

'Yes, yes,' said her husband. 'The lot.'

'Good. And I've asked Orridge to do the drinks. Mrs Webb is doing her finger foods for us.'

'Finger foods!' said Sir Roger disparagingly. 'Roast beef and Yorkshires is what she does best.' He let his thoughts drift lovingly back to the meat.

And then, as if by magic (or angels, perhaps?) and quite dispelling Sir Roger's happy mood, the vicar appeared at their side. Pink and puffing a little and, even on such a hot day, wearing a very ordinary, very large, very dull brown cloak.

'Shall we?' he said beatifically, and extended his hand. Up the Hill they climbed together. Conversation was not indulged in as neither the little man, nor the big man, could do more than puff. And Dulcima was lost within her own thoughts, which were largely of her daughter and that thing called love. If she had been a white rabbit she might have started muttering something along the lines of *Oh dear, Oh dear, Oh my ears and whiskers.*

Above them was Miles. He *had* intended to be first up to the spot, of course he had, but just as he was coming down the stairs, Montmorency was tottering up them (an unheard of liberty, in Miles's opinion. The only kind thing to do to himself, in Montmorency's. It was a bed he needed and there were plenty up there and unused, he knew). Montmorency's timing was unfortunate, which was due to the immense languor filling his body. He needed to sleep. He had been told – shown, even – by the ladycat at the pub – that humans' beds were extremely nice places to rest upon. It had never occurred to him before. And it would hurt no one. But instead of the joys of a sprung mattress he got halfway up the stairs and was tripped over by the so-called Master so that they both tumbled to the ground. Disgraceful. Why did he not look where he was going?

Miles had no time to chastise the cat, though he wanted to, by golly he wanted to – but he needed to change his shirt which was torn from the rapid journey down to the hall. Hence he was late. Hence the smile he had determined to wear all day today if necessary was overly toothed and betokened nothing benign whatsoever. He had expected to be privy to what the Hill and the Gnome held before anyone else, naturally enough, and due to the infernal cat it was not going to happen.

For the occasion Miles had put on his best black suit and now wore his second-best white shirt. The suits and shirts he kept for funerals and committee meetings. He looked like some strange, thin Gothic creature, thought Molly, as she watched him climb the Hill. But he was smiling, looking up and smiling, which was a rarity and although it was hardly a melting butter kind of smile, it helped dispel Miss Bonner the archaeologist's granddaughter's slight sense of anxiety where Miles was concerned. She *thought* today would be one of the best days of his life, one way or another. He would, naturally enough, be disappointed about what she had found on the Hill, but she had something else lined up for him that would more than make up for it. More than. In fact, it would make more than one person's day. Possibly their lifetime. Nevertheless Molly continued to feel a slight sense of foreboding which made her give a little shiver as Miles arrived at the top and took her hand. 'Well done, well done,' he said. He turned to feast his eyes upon the spot and was disappointed to see that Molly had fixed a tarpaulin across the – er – top of the Gnome's – cr –. 'I was hoping,' he said, still showing far too many teeth, 'to see what you have found. Now.'

And Molly, overcoming her sense of foreboding, and the teeth, said, 'Not yet, Miles – we must wait for everyone to be here. Everyone.'

The Fitzhartletts and the vicar finally arrived. But where were Pinky and Susie? Molly shaded her eyes and looked down. 'Oh,' she said, 'I do hope they haven't forgotten. I need them, or rather Susie, to be here. 'Susie, Susie!' she called. The others looked among themselves and then turned back and said, 'She's not here.' Molly looked dismayed for a moment, and then she spotted Pinky. 'Where is Susie?' she asked. And he laughed out loud. 'You're almost looking at her,' he said, and laughed again. There was a rustling from within the crowd and a woman appeared at its edge – quite an ordinary-looking woman wearing a pair of loose linen trousers of that hue sometimes known as beige and lovingly described by fashionistas as taupe. She also wore a very straight pale blue shirt above which her nice, round face wore a smile. There was not a hint of kohl around her eyes. Her hair was neat and short and beautifully cut, and she wore no jangling jewellery, nothing but a simple pair of pearl earrings. The only slightly strange thing about her was that she carried a forage basket brimful of those same yellow flowers.

Everyone looked at the woman for a moment, familiar and yet not familiar, and then they realised that it was Susie. A new Susie, a changed Susie – actually a Susie who looked a great deal less frightening than usual. 'Don't worry,' she said to Molly. 'All is well. I would have been up here to see the dawn rise but I've been feeling a little bit icky recently. Still, better late than never . . .'

Pinky said nothing, just rocked on his heels and looked pleased with the world. He loved being up here now.

The clock on the church started to chime the hour and the ceremonies could begin. It was going to be a beautiful, beautiful day. In all sorts of ways, thought Molly. Winifred smiled at Donald, and then winked at him. A gesture that he found, in this desert of sanity, strangely comforting. It was a definite wink, he told himself, and not a twitch. It looked absolutely sane and – if he said so himself – rather alluring. As did the fluttering of her skirt. So he winked back.

As they all huddled together at the top, Nigel managed to manoeuvre himself next to Sir Roger and said, in a disturbingly hoarse tone, delivered, even more disturbingly, from the side of his mouth, 'I hope you will find this useful, sir. I renovated it entirely by myself, with you in mind. I know you like a good Churchill.'

Sir Roger looked at him cautiously. The last time he had been spoken to in that manner was at Newmarket when a toothless man crept up to him and gave him a tip for the three-thirty. He had not taken the tip and it won by a head. So perhaps . . .?

He smiled a little nervously and took the gun case and peered into it. For the first time that day his face lit up. 'But this is magnificent! This is wonderful, wonderful my boy.'

He, too, spoke from the side of his mouth. If sotto voce was the way to play it, so be it. His wife nudged him. She had no knowledge of toothless seers at racetracks and wondered if Sir Roger had been at the sauce already. She was finding being on the dry side very tedious and it did not cheer her very much to think that her husband had not supported her in this. Her thoughts went to Marion. And then to Orridge. Had putting him in charge of the drinks been a good idea? No matter, Mrs Webb would keep an eye on him.

Nigel was happy. The gift had been well received. Success, his very own success. His father had not noticed. His father – opposite him – seemed not to be noticing very much but merely smiling in that dreamy way he had taken to lately. Nigel hoped he wasn't on the turn. It'd be all he needed just when he wanted to show his father how clever he could be. He watched Sir Roger lean the gun in its case against his leg so that no one would really notice it. And he was patting it like a dog. I have jolly well gone and done it, he thought. I have fixed the gun and fixed my life. Nigel nearly shouted for joy. He realised, in a moment of pure ecstasy, that he was in love with the right woman and the right woman was in love with him and how could he ever have even *thought* he loved Molly Bonner? Or Julie Barnsley. He looked across at them both. They were both very pink. Not his sort at all. Even with those boots. If only Marion had made it up the Hill he would have sung like a lark.

The clock below finished its chimes. It was time for Miles to give a little speech.

Four

MILES HAD HIS hand on his heart as he spoke. He looked the picture of inspired fervour. 'None of us know, not even me, what lies beneath that cover, but you may be assured that it is a rich and rare discovery effected by our own dear Molly Bonner here . . . She has assured me that we will be thrilled with what she has found.' He turned to Molly and took her hand in his. For one dreadful moment it looked as if he were about to propose to her, or kiss her palm, something of the sort – and Nigel was considering stepping in to stop it – but then Miles let go of the hand and continued.

'As she told us all when she first arrived, Miss Bonner, Molly, had her own reasons for wanting to complete the task her grand-father began, and we can only be delighted at her dedication. Our village of Lufferton Boney and myself as the eternal curator of this Hill and all it contains –' he paused here as if to make quite sure everyone got the message of who was in charge, of who held the keys to the kingdom – 'will be forever thankful to her for the heritage she has left us. I am only sorry that my dear brother, Robin, cannot be here to see this day. He loved this place.' Dorcas thought she might be about to be sick but fortunately Miles started to clap and that took her mind off the prospect. Bastard. Bastard. Bastard.

Then Molly turned to the vicar, who stepped forward. He was still wearing his brown cloak and it seemed as if he might shrink away to a puddle of grease so hot was the weather, so hot was he, but this was his moment. He let the cloak slip from his shoulders and stepped forth looking, as Winifred (who was a keen if slap-happy gardener, or had been before Molly's time-consuming proposal) said afterwards, like a little green and white leaf bug. He had had the foresight to stitch up the hem of his green garment a little so he would not trip and he made a good show of being at the centre of a ritual as he walked the short distance and stepped up and on to the trailer.

'I can see everything from here,' he said happily. And he put up both his hands (empty, alas, but, oh for a bishop's crook) in a gesture of blessing, and took a deep breath, the better to project his voice. Molly looked rather anxious. 'Could you wait for a moment, vicar?' she said. He closed his mouth and tried to smile.

'Why?' he asked.

'Well we haven't actually revealed our findings yet.'

'Ah,' he said, and jumped down again. 'No, I had quite forgotten that aspect of the day.' And he trotted back to her side.

'Quite,' said Molly. Behind her Dorcas whispered, 'Unbelievable.'

And Winifred said sardonically, 'Our brother in Christ.'

Susie stepped forward. 'Where do you want me?' she said, and held her basket aloft. The flowers glistened waxy and bright in the sun.

'You do look different,' said Molly.

'Don't you worry about that, dear. There comes a time in every sensitive's life when she must put down the trappings and get on with life. I know what I'm doing.'

'But you are still Druidical?' Molly asked.

'Oh yes, dear, and even more ancient than that,' said Susie cheerfully. She glanced at the vicar. 'But you do not need to dress up in all that comical gear to prove it.' And she gave the vicar a long, considering stare which made the vicar blush and many smile.

'Good,' said Molly.

'It was the nearest I could think of and appropriate, I think,' said Susie. Dropping her voice a little she went on: 'I didn't want to offend the vicar but – really – it was all before his time. Who knows how long.'

Miles came up and leaned over the little wooden wall that surrounded the plastic-covered site, and pulled at the covering. Molly put a restraining hand on his arm, and he withdrew his. 'This has gone on quite long enough,' he said brusquely. 'Show us *now*.' He found himself looking at the admonishing digit of Molly Bonner.

'One more thing,' she said, 'and then we are ready.' Miles stepped back. *Purse strings*, and *never let* and *a woman* came to mind, but he said nothing. What was a minute or two more? Keep your head, Miles, he told himself, for soon you shall have it all.

Molly turned to Winifred and Dorcas. 'And now, perhaps you will kindly tell me what it was that made the two of you so amused last night? And if you delay any further –' she pointed to the covering sheet – 'that may not be the only example of such a thing that is found here in years to come.'

At which the women gave in. 'Shall you?' said Dorcas to Winifred. 'Or shall I?'

'Let's both,' said Winifred. 'Just the relevant bit.' And so they stood by the edge of the trench and began to recite, very quietly, almost as if they had practised, which, of course, they had:

> *. . . But at my back I always hear*
> *Time's wingèd chariot hurrying near;*
> *And yonder all before us lie*
> *Deserts of vast eternity.*
> *Thy beauty shall no more be found;*
> *Nor, in thy marble vault, shall sound*

> *My echoing song: then worms shall try*
> *That long-preserved virginity:*
> *And your quaint honour turn to dust;*
> *And into ashes all my lust.*
> *The grave's a fine and private place,*
> *But none, I think, do there embrace . . .*

There was a smattering of polite applause from those near enough to hear, though the gathered looked as sheepish as any gathering of British on British soil will when poetry is invoked without due warning. Except for Julie, of course, who being Irish was quite used to it.

'Andrew Marvell, dear,' said Winifred to the astonished Molly. 'To His Coy Mistress.'

'Seventeenth-century poet. English. Mid-seventeeth century, actually. Metaphysical,' added Dorcas, trying to look ponderous.

'He also wrote a poem called "The Unfortunate Lover,"' said Winifred, quite mercilessly. 'Which might ring a bell.'

Molly sat down in puff of pink skirt, all at once and in a heap, right at the side of the dig. 'All there in the notebooks. So he *did* know what was there. But he wanted to write it up properly. And the reason he didn't want it made public was that he wanted to know *why*? Just like I do.' She thought for a moment. There was a groan from the crowd, and she held up her hand as if to say, soon, soon, soon.

'Well, I think I can make a decent guess,' she said aloud. 'No wonder he was amused, given what he and my grandmother were up to.' Molly Bonner looked completely happy. Miles, on the other hand, appeared to be having some kind of fit – he was hopping from foot to foot and very red in the face.

'Time to do the honours,' said Molly to Winifred and Dorcas. 'Or there may be another death.' And they obliged.

*

The cover was pulled back to a great swelling breath of excitement and everyone crowded forward, peering downwards. Fortunately the low wooden fencing protected the site so that no one would damage it with their feet.

'The veil was rent,' said the vicar sonorously, his green and white garments flapping in the breeze, but when he too peered and saw what was revealed he, like the rest of the villagers, was suddenly silent. 'Good Lord above,' he said. And appeared to mean it. Yes, even the vicar was moved at the sight. And who could fail to be so? Who? Well, there was one. But for the moment we will ignore his crimson, baffled face.

And what did they see, the gathered of Lufferton Boney? They saw that, where once had risen the extensive corona of the Gnome's mighty maleness, lay a grave – stark, simple, unadorned – in which lay two skeletons. The skeletons faced each other, their skulls close as if kissing, their arms outstretched and holding each other tight, their legs entwined. Scattered near each neck, as if they had both worn the same decoration, was a handful of shale beads. If bones could show love, then these bones showed it. 'A fine embrace,' said Molly. 'And an undoing of Marvell.'

Five

No one spoke for a moment and then Molly stepped forward. She addressed Dr Porlock. 'I wonder,' she said, 'if you could confirm the genders of the pair?'

Donald, who felt rather moved by the sight considering he had spent a large amount of time surrounded by skeletons one way and another, knelt down and studied them for some time before standing up, brushing down his knees and nodding. 'As you might expect, I would judge that those are young bones. Maybe in their mid- to late teens. The one on the left is male, the one on the right is female.' He took out a handkerchief and blew into it very noisily. 'And I would say that they are *in situ* as they were laid in the earth.'

'Thank you, Donald,' said Winifred. 'That is what we thought.'

'Can you say what they died from?' asked Dorcas.

Donald knelt again and studied the pair. Winifred looked at the back of her husband's head and found that she just *had* to reach out and touch it. He went on studying the bones for a while. Then he stood up. 'Without proper analysis I can only say that I see nothing to indicate foul play,' he said. 'Nor that they were buried alive. If that had been the case they would not be embracing so peacefully. My guess – only a guess, mind – is that they died from natural causes – certainly not from anything painful. Poison is possible but it would be some kind of narcotic, there has been no struggle. Perhaps they died of the same illness.'

'And you agree that the bones are old?' said Molly.

'Very. But how old I could not say. I leave that up to you.'

'Considering that life expectancy seems to have been about thirty-five years, they were in their prime,' said Molly. 'They look too perfect together to be anything sinister. I suppose they could be a sacrifice but then I'd have expected to see more grave goods – special pots, or maybe decorated beakers or other symbols of their status. You see the grave,' said Molly, 'is a little larger than the usual Iron Age grave. As expected, it is a well-cut oval pit (2.58 metres long by 2.68 metres wide by 0.55 metres deep) with vertical sides and a flat base. The skeletons have been placed in the grave very carefully, their arms placed around each other in an act of love. It is as if they were laid there so that they might be united in death for ever.'

Someone in the crowd gave a little sobbing noise. Oddly, it was found to be Dryden. And it was Dryden who found the sob most strange. It came straight out of him, no messing, without a by-your-leave, just out it came. 'So they would each have company,' he said miserably. And gave another sob.

Nigel looked at his father in perplexity. Donald gave him an encouraging smile. He knew exactly what Dryden was thinking. Lottie. What Lottie might have thought, had she been anywhere in the ether, was that these were the first tears he had shed for her.

Molly continued, 'Each of the skeletons wore a necklace of twenty-four perforated and polished shale beads, Kimmeridge shale, brought here for the purpose of making decorative items. The female skeleton's necklace has lost three of its beads – we have found two and my grandfather found one, which he gave to my grandmother. Who knows how they became detached: animals . . . land movement. And they both wore armlets of Kimmeridge shale as well. The jewellery and the fact that there is a grave here at all indicates that these are the bones of very well regarded people . . .'

'A prince and a princess?' asked Dorcas, a faraway, dreamy note in her voice. 'Star-crossed lovers?'

'Unlikely,' said practical Molly. 'More likely they are ordinary people made to be significant. There's not enough wealth to indicate a grand burial.'

'Wealth?' There was a sudden howl of something: Rage? Pain? Disappointment? It was all three. It was Miles. He fell to his knees. He pointed. He seemed momentarily beyond speech. Then he began. 'These people buried here? Is that it?' Miles peered down at the two embracing skeletons with some distaste. Why on earth were they so thrilled to find these? A long-dead pair of old skeletons. He had imagined treasure trove. He had been led to believe it was something wonderful, wonderful. Gold, perhaps. Lovely artefacts that he could sell, or put on show for good ticket money. He said, with hope, 'You don't *know* that they weren't important people, now do you? A prince and a princess? It might be a king, perhaps? And a queen. High-ups. Celebrities of their day?' Already he felt better for he could imagine how such a story would up the stakes. Something had to. But to his chagrin Molly shook her head.

'I doubt that they were anything like that. If, as I think, this is a shrine – and this is the highest of all the hills which only faces in its full gradient one way and in the direction of what we know was an area of very well farmed Iron Age sites – then, perhaps – probably – they were an ordinary pair of lovers made special by being chosen for this grave. If it were a richer grave I'd be less sure of myself, but with these simple grave jewels on them, it's almost certain. They do not represent grandeur. I think they represent love, or at least the heart of a people.'

The assembled were silent. The Hill was silent. Molly explained that she based this summation on what all archaeologists know. 'The evidence for human burials or other funerary practices is lacking for large parts of Britain in the Iron Age,' she told them. 'Some burials have been found, but these were the exception, not the rule. In most parts of Iron Age Britain funeral rituals did not include burying the dead person in a grave. Individual human bones were sometimes found on Iron Age farms, hill forts and villages. More rarely, the complete skeletons of a small number of people were found placed in pits, postholes or in ditches. A grave like this is very special. Marked out. I've certainly never seen anything like it. The evidence suggests that when most ordinary Iron Age people died they were placed somewhere until their body had rotted away, leaving just the bones – similar types of funeral rituals occur in many places around the world today. In Iron Age Britain some of the bones left behind were later buried around the settle-ments. Any ritually buried human remains found on settlement sites probably came from from human sacrifice and other rituals. Our two skeletons are different. It is a type of burial quite unknown . . .'

'Does that mean it's valuable after all?' Miles had broken out in a sweat.

'Oh shut up, Miles,' said Dorcas, so that he stared at her his eyes popping, his jaw sagging. Right, my girl, he thought, you are out of my house, out of the Squidge, and out of a job from this moment on.

'Go on, Molly,' said Winifred. 'Pay no attention to him.'

'Well, at certain times in some parts of Iron Age Britain, a tribe or community would break with the traditional ways of treating the dead and, instead, bury them in graves. This was the case in the West occasionally where the dead were buried in stone-lined graves for much of the Iron Age. In the South-West it was not so common, but not unknown that from about 100 BC until after the Roman conquest, some crouching burials were performed. Many late Iron Age dead were cremated before being buried. Urns were sometimes used. I have seen one or two of those, and Winifred's film, made some years ago, shows that a wide variety of burial methods were used around about the area . . . This part of the South-West is extremely ancient and sacred. But with nothing, so far, like this . . .'

'Why are they buried up here?' asked Nigel. 'When Marion and I did our ride-about, the graves as marked on that map were all over the area but these are the only ones on Pound Hill.' He stepped back, slightly embarrassed. Dryden looked at his son in surprise.

Molly said. 'Exactly. That is exactly what we asked ourselves over and over again. 'Why here? Why these two? What is so special about this one hill? And then the answer came to me. The Gnome, originally, must be Roman. And cut into the Hill not long after they arrived.'

'Good Lord,' said Sir Roger, coming out of his reverie about the Churchill and forgetting to pat his gun for a moment, 'I had no idea the Romans brought their garden decorations with them. Just like the Webb family today. Roman gnomes. Traditions. Excellent.'

'Darling,' whispered Dulcima, 'I don't think she means they were used as something so innocent as garden ornaments.'

But Sir Roger did not mind being corrected. All he was thinking was that it had been a very long time since his wife had called him darling. He hugged his gun to his side all the tighter or he might have found himself hugging her. And in public, too. Good Lord!

'No,' said Molly kindly. 'It wasn't originally a gnome. I'm pretty sure it was a Roman god of sexuality.'

'Priapus?' said Pinky, without thinking. He was often in the library if he finished early.

'Clever thing,' whispered Susie.

'No, love,' he said. 'You are the clever thing.' And he very tenderly placed his bright pink hand (the blush always spread everywhere) on her blue-bloused belly and left it there. One day they would travel to Florence and he would see the Arnolfini portrait for the first time and it would remind him of this tender moment.

'Quiet for now,' said Susie softly. 'Let Molly tell us.'

'Not Priapus, I don't think,' said Molly. 'Because he was impotent.'

'What?' said Peter Hanker, before he could stop himself. 'With one that size. Bloody hell.' In need of a moment of levity, everyone, or almost everyone (Miles was on another planet of pain) laughed. Peter gave Julie a squeeze and she did not seem to object. Progress, thought Peter Hanker. Possibly progress.

'Impotent. Yes. He could, so to speak, get it up, but he could not, so to speak, fire live bullets.'

Sir Roger found his hand immediately and automatically reaching for the Churchill's trigger. But just then Dulcima slipped her own hand through his free arm and Sir Roger smiled contentedly. Who needs to shoot at anything at a time like this? He might surprise her later, though.

'So I have looked elsewhere,' Molly continued. 'And I think this might be the answer. It could be a combination of Priapus and Faunus. Faunus was extremely lively in the matter of sex, much given to doling out fertility. And this Priapus, as you see, had an enormous, erect member that would be seen by any of the tribes who lived at the bottom of the Hill. Just like yourselves. Settlers.' A ripple of mirth spread through the people of Lufferton Boney. Settlers? Us?

Above it all in the bright blue sky a pair of rooks cawed in apparent glee, echoing the amusement below them. 'Shoot the buggers,' muttered Sir Roger, but Dulcima gave him a nudge. Maybe later. He patted the gun again. Definitely later.

'Now the problem to consider is: why here? Why not on one of those other hills over there where it would be seen by far more settlements? It has to be because the Hill was sacred.

And that the figure was designed to oppress and suppress through desecration. We might find it amusing now but then – you'd have to imagine England being invaded today and the first thing the invaders did was to plant a figure like this over Princess Diana's grave – or Winston Churchill's. This Roman figure was cut over the most sacred of graves, deliberately, so that it would lower the morale of the rebellious population. It's a foolish tyrant who forgets the power of satire and laughter to undermine belief, and the Romans were good at that. But it is also a foolish tyrant who underestimates the native response.'

A ripple of pride went through the group. Just for a moment they saw themselves as the descendants of warriors – which, of course, they were.

Molly continued. 'There is enough archaeology here to show that what we now see as the Gnome's hat could easily have been a pair of horns – which would fit the theory. And his outstretched arm that seems to be nothing but gestural once held something that – if I'm right – was a flagellator. Faunus liked nothing better than to see naked women whipped by his followers in the – so they say – belief that the more you whip a woman, the more babies she will have. Hence the rather muddled thinking about fertility, perhaps.' Pinky felt profoundly relieved that he and Susie had not previously known *that*. 'No wonder,' he said, 'that he turned into something else over the years. You wouldn't want to live with that on your doorstep.'

They all agreed that this was so. In a strange way each of them began to look more kindly on the Gnome. When you think of what he might have been . . .

Miles blenched. And then righted himself. The prospect of knowing the true meaning behind the view from his windows was dreadful, to say the least. On the other hand – he perked up again – if it were such a dirty business – well – nothing sold like sex – so if it brought in the ticket money . . . At the bottom of the Hill, Marion was looking up in silent tableau. Despite the perfect weather and the curiosity she felt, she could not, could not go up the Hill and join them. Nigel, who was glad she had not been close enough to hear Molly's explanation, thought he would go back down and join her. Dulcima stepped forward and placed a kind but firm hand on his arm. 'Leave her,' she said. 'Let her make up her own mind.' And she gave him the kind of look that he, personally, thought would have quelled a Roman invader any day of the week. He stayed put.

'These were lovers,' said Molly, pointing at the grave. 'This is not the pose of good friends or a brother and sister. And I think their importance was that. Love. It is what makes them so special, so unique. For the first time in history as ancient as this we can see how our ancestors actually *felt*. Up until now we have known how they lived, what they wore, how they worshipped, what they made, ate, drank – but we have never known how they *felt*. This is proof that they *loved*, too, just as much as us if not more than us. We assume our civilisation nowadays is on a higher plane, and clearly –' she looked down at the embracing skeletons – 'clearly we are not. In fact, we are often quite the opposite. Even here in this village you have to look very hard to find an embrace as loving as this.'

The people of Lufferton Boney suddenly found themselves considering this, considering the truth of it, considering the very bones of their lives and feelings. It made them all feel quite uncomfortable. All except Miles who was too busy doing calculations in his head.

Winifred, who was now filming the proceedings, panned her camera from face to face and there was not a smile among them.

Winifred, had she been asked, would admit that she wasn't feeling too proud of herself, either. In fact, nobody was.

'Would you,' she said to Molly, 'say clearly why this particular hill was chosen. Look to camera, please.'

'Pound Hill is quite free of anything – except these lovers. Everywhere else is full of graves. Therefore Pound Hill is likely to be the most sacred place of all hereabouts. There are no lynchets, no signs of grazing, no disturbance of any kind. Perfect if you want to invade the locals' psyche with a desecrating figure like this.'

'Date?' asked Dulcima softly.

'Well – probably around the time that the Romans arrived. I can't be more exact. This area was one of the most rebellious in Britain. It took a lot of quelling. The Romans, never ones to hold back, were ruthless. So they would need to find a way to crush the local tribes.'

'But I thought,' said Peter, 'that the Romans were good at letting people carry on with their traditions and sort of worked alongside them instead of doing it all with a mailed fist.'

'Up to a point,' said Molly. 'But Pomponius tells us that people didn't just roll over when the legions marched in – they fought back. Particularly the Druids who were the recognised rulers of Britain: they made the laws and they were said to know everything including the shape and size of the world, the movement of the stars and the will of the gods. The Romans were accommodating once they'd *conquered* them but they would not tolerate any supreme rivals in the form of deities or knowledge. Some of those British tribes certainly took some taming.'

'Good show!' called Sir Roger.

'It was nearly two thousand years ago, Roger,' said Dulcima, but kindly.

'We still have our pride,' said her husband.

Molly laughed. 'And you can take even further pride, Sir

Roger, for I'm fairly sure that the strangeness of the shape of the end of the phallus, that rather odd angle it sits at, is because the Romans themselves did not cut the figure. I think they made the local tribes cut it. An even more shaming loss of honour. They were to put the great end of the shaft right over their sacred lovers. So – what did they do? They could not refuse because that would almost certainly mean death. Instead, being intelligent and also understanding the art of subversion, they made it so that it did not quite fit, not sit right – they rebelled in the only way possible short of committing suicide, they created a phallus that was a double cross, less powerful than peculiar in its droop. You do not necessarily need slingshot and arrows to win a victory. I'd like to think that when it was completed it made those locals smile.' This time a smattering of clapping broke out.

'Hurrah!' shouted Sir Roger who was overcome with joy and pride. And, since Dulcima had removed her restraining hand, he held his new gun aloft as if to prove it.

Now that the sun was higher in the sky the outlines of the barrows and cysts and circles were even more apparent in the surrounding landscape.

Miles was still trying to work out whether a shrine was a good thing or a bad thing. He decided that very probably it was a bad thing. Sex (he did not like to dwell on the word) sold things. Not shrines. Much better if they could weave a story around the skeletons. The lovers might be the uncouth Romeo and Juliet of the Iron Age, perhaps. That could be marketed very usefully. 'Nonsense,' he said. 'This is no shrine. These are two young people who were probably put to death by their own people – maybe they were from different tribes – maybe they crossed the line, did what they shouldn't do. Much more likely. After all, the doctor here thinks they were very young. Underage.'

'There's not a mark on them,' said Donald crisply.

'Oh shut up,' said Miles peevishly.

Winifred, standing close to him said, 'Shut up yourself, Miles. This couple were probably considered quite mature if you popped off in old age at about thirty-five. Much more likely that they represent the deepest sentiments of humankind.'

'In the Iron Age?' said Miles incredulously. 'They just painted themselves blue, couldn't write and lived like animals. Primitives of no consequence.'

Winifred, who had, like Molly, grown fond of the couple in the grave, handed the camera to Dorcas, took a step forward and gave Miles a look. Donald, who had been thinking that his wife looked rather nice in that skirt and those shoes, and very professional in the way she dealt with the camera, winced as she bent down and picked up a large bowl containing slightly muddy water. Oh, not again. He knew what was coming. And he was right, for Winifred then proceeded to tip the contents of the bowl over Miles, with a joyous smile. 'Fool,' she said, with satisfaction. Miles, with water streaming down his face, gasped for air and looked like an astonished fish. For once, Donald took her point. Indeed, Donald Porlock thought that had he another bowl containing a similar fluid, he would follow his wife's suit and do exactly the same. 'Oh Winifred,' he said. To which she, slightly surprised, replied, 'Oh Donald.'

'Oh dear,' said the vicar, looking down at the puddle on the ground and the dripping, gaping, furious Miles. 'That was the holy water.'

'Never mind,' said Susie. 'We can bless them with a shower of these lovely flowers.'

The vicar gingerly picked one out of the basket.

'It's Chase-Devil, vicar. Just what we need. The perfect name for a flower that is known to keep darkness away. You can bless these if you like.' The vicar looked helplessly in the direction of his patrons but, like the rest of the group, his patrons were staring at Miles Whittington with astonishment.

Miles, wiping the streaming moisture from his eyes, turned to Molly and said, 'There is no proof of anything that you say and it doesn't exactly hit the mark in terms of impact. Just a pair of lovers in a grave is hardly going to get them queuing round the village. You promised . . .' And then he stopped. He had a vague feeling that he had said too much as, through the bleariness of his wet lashes, he saw Molly come towards him with her hands on her hips. She did not look sympathetic.

'Oh good,' whispered Dulcima. 'She's going to hit him.'

But Molly did not hit Miles. Instead she stood in front of him, hands clasped fast to her hips, chin jutting, and said, 'And if that is what you really think, Mr Whittington, may I suggest you just turn again and go home?' There was a loud cheer from the assembly. 'Because they did *not* just paint themselves with blue and go about like animals. They had a sense of community, a sense of loyalty and protection of each other, a sense of *love* that we could do with a bit more of nowadays . . . And they were not Tinseltown celebrities for you to exploit. They were lovers. And these are the lasting bones of lovers. Which is almost certainly why the village is called Lufferton Boney.'

Miles took a step back. He went very red in the face, opened his mouth, and then closed it again to stop the filthy water dripping in. He reminded himself that whatever the girl said, *he* was the owner of the Hill, he was the person who would control and market and do all the things necessary to make the Hill and its contents – even if it was a mere pile of bones (oh why couldn't they be wearing gold torques?) – somewhere for people to come and pay their dues to see the sight. Therefore he would bide his time and remain silent. Miles had the upper hand and he knew it. Very well, he would wait.

The vicar said, rather tentatively, 'Well, they were heathens. Without a religious path in their lives. They took quite a lot of persuading to come into the Christian fold.' He pursed his little mouth and resembled one who had sucked on a lemon. Disapproval radiated from every pore. He smoothed his green garment and lifted his arms again. Had he but known it he was doing a very good impersonation of how a Druid greeted the sun. But now it was his turn to get the full Molly stare. Now it was his turn to wonder if he was going to be hit. Molly advanced towards him and pointed to the landscape, letting her outstretched hand move slowly in a circle as if to encompass all they could see.

'I should have known,' she said, 'With a name like Lufferton Boney and with a public house called the Old Holly Bush – such an ancient fertility symbol – I can't think how I missed the clues. St Etheldreda's, of course, is part of the whole. It was built on a previous church so before that it was probably something else. Even something pre-Roman.'

The vicar looked rather shocked. He hoped very much that there was nothing in the building and naming of his church that was connected with such wickedness. Peter Hanker, on the other hand, looked rather pleased at the idea of his being in charge of something connected with ancient rites, sexual or not. Though he drew the line at whips. He looked at Julie and winked. And Julie thought, maybe second best can become first when you take everything into account. He'd been kind to her. No one else had shown such kindness. The Old Holly Bush was doing well since the Molly person had come to the village, it had begun to feel like home – and – come to think of it – now that St Etheldreda's was mentioned, she thought that Peter, with the sun on his head and the glow of his fair skin in the sharp light, looked a bit like the stained-glass image of the desirable Egfrith so often admired in the church. She was also, though she would not wish to say it, moved at the sight of those lovers' bones locked in their eternal embrace. Love for all time. It counted for a lot.

Molly continued. 'What you are looking at, as far as the eye can see, vicar, is the route these so-called heathens with no path of spirituality made from one place to another and which they used over thousands and thousands of years. And along the way of it they buried their dead in careful and caring ritual manners, according to the dictates of the time – cremations, inhumations, crouching, in urns, with beakers, without beakers – grave goods and no grave goods – sometimes the whole skeleton, sometimes a part of it. These careful burials are placed all along this sacred route of theirs for hundreds of miles. As you can see if you look out from here, it was as crowded as your own graveyard at St Etheldreda's. In fact, it looks very much to me as if the church is right on their route. Very probably it was a place of ancient sanctity long before Jesus was a twinkle in his Father's eye. Oh yes, they had a religion – and we can call it that for it was a belief in something other than the living human world – like you, they believed in a life beyond – for thousands of years. How long has Christianity existed, vicar?'

Molly might not have had a broad liberal education that encompassed Andrew Marvell but she'd learned enough from history to be quite daunting when she set her mind to it. The vicar, answering like a caught-out schoolboy, said 'Two thousand, er-um.'

'A mere baby, then,' she said, keeping the glint in her eye, the flint in her tone. 'And another thing –' Molly advanced again. The vicar retreated until he felt – what?– something poking him in the middle of his spine. For one frightening moment he thought it was a gun held to his back and he put up his hands – but it was only one of the handles of the trailer. Though it should be said that the mistake made by the retreating vicar was a considered reality for a moment as it crossed Sir Roger's mind.

Molly continued to advance. 'But vicar,' she asked, 'why are you done up in all that church mummery?'

'Well, er – this is the correct colour and these are the correct garments for Church Ordinary. Green.' He gave a little twirl, without meaning to, which added to Molly's wrath.

'And do you think the white alb and the green sash' (green brocade with a hand-worked Celtic cross £95) 'with its golden embroidery is any less bizarre than a blue face? They are, after all, ritual garments in ritual colours, yes?'

The vicar nodded. 'Point taken.' And then said nervously, 'Do you still want me to bless the – er – unfortunate couple?' He gave Miles's dripping form a regretful glance. And looked appealingly at Sir Roger and Lady Fitzhartlett. Lady Fitzhartlett said, 'We do, vicar. We think it would be nice. A little extra duty for you to perform. Do it well and who knows what might not happen with your pulpit.'

The vicar beamed. He would give those bones a mighty good send-off. Perhaps one of the best he had ever given, and he had buried a few over the years. Susie nodded and came forward. 'And then I will give a little Druidical blessing as well. Just to be sure.'

'Well, that will all be very nice,' said Dulcima, casting a covert look at the vicar who did not, if his expression was anything to go by, agree with the sentiment. 'Then we must hurry off home for we have a little party waiting for us.' She did not catch the hopeful eye of Nigel.

Dryden was looking thoughtful. 'But would they – I mean the Romans – think of it as obscene?' he asked. 'I mean, they were a bit more up front about what they wanted their gods to do in those days, weren't they? It may be that they thought they were being *helpful* by adding someone with – that . . .' Words failed him. But a voice from the group said 'Big knob?' At which Dryden went quiet, the crowd turned to see who had made the disgraceful – if slightly funny – comment – and saw that Peter Hanker and Julie Barnsley were doubled up on the grass, clutching each other and laughing uncontrollably. In the manner of their clutching one another they did not look a million miles away from the lovers' bones. 'Oh go on,' said a voice. 'For goodness, sake *kiss* her.' The voice proved to be that of Dorcas Fairbrother. Who was usually so – well – the Lufferton Boneyites might call it buttoned-up. Not that there wasn't a very good reason for it. To lose the love of your life and only have a boot and a hat to remember him by – that must be hard.

Peter did then kiss Julie, and Julie – without even thinking – kissed him back. Bang goes my being a lady, she thought, but who wants to be one of them—? On the whole, she also thought, I am truly Irish – and I wish to have some fun.

Pinky and Susie applauded them, remembering how it used to be for them on this very grass. And when Peter and Julie scrambled back to their feet, Julie suddenly gave Molly such a smile, a heavenly smile, a smile of total friendship and kindness, that for a moment Molly was without speech. How strange – only yesterday she had refused her breakfast porridge on the grounds that it had a strange smell to it and Julie was so insistent that she should eat it all up like a good girl that Molly had the distinct feeling there was something of the Borgia in her enthusiasm. Now she realised this was very wrong of her. Perhaps some of the discord in the village had begun to work on her? Well, that must stop. How wrong she had been. Julie was perfectly all right.

*

'So you think the Romans feared that the spirit of the lovers' grave up here would strengthen the locals' rebellion?' said Dryden. 'It's a compelling theory.' It took a lot to permanently penetrate Molly Bonner's eternal joy and optimism with the world. But just at that moment, Miles made a very good attempt. Ignoring Dryden's statement (for he was, in truth, only a tradesman when all was said and done) Miles moved to the very edge of the grave and looked into it. 'It could be that the Gnome came first. We don't know.' His lip curled. When he thought of the powerful draw the Gnome *intacto* would be – when it was put back together again – it was no contest. 'I'll have to ask you to restore the Gnome to his full masculinity,' he said. 'We can't move this project forward with only half of his a – um . . .' Peter was very helpful with his anatomical suggestion yet again.

'Ah no,' said Molly. 'The archaeology proves it was the other way around.'

'If the lovers were there first,' said Dryden, 'then we should *not* restore it. The Gnome, I mean. He's a crude usurper.'

'Now just a bloody minute,' said Miles. 'I've got to have the Gnome put back the way he was – or no one will bother to come here. We'll just move the grave a little way. Who's to know? A bone is a bone, after all.'

Molly was enraged. 'You will not move the grave, Miles Whittington, those lovers will stay exactly as they are. They have held each other for two thousand years – and I will not allow you to change them. But you are right, the Gnome must be restored, too, if we are not to get into trouble with the authorities. Don't worry, I'll think of something.' And the Lufferton Boneyites thought to themselves collectively that they had absolutely no doubt that she would.

'And now,' said Molly, 'I think we should give the lovers their blessings.'

*

The vicar, who had recovered a little from the jibes regarding his appearance, and who wished to impress his patron and his patron's lady wife with his articulacy under any circumstances, stepped to the edge of the trailer and prepared to begin. But Susie intervened. 'Druids before Christians, I think,' she said. 'We got here first.' And standing at the edge of the grave she gave it her best ever blessing of all. Pinky thought she was magnificent, she could even transcend beige.

> *May the light of love*
> *Shine brightly in your hearts*
> *May the light of understanding*
> *Shine in your minds.*
> *May the light of harmony*
> *Glow in your home*
> *May the light of service*
> *Shine forth from your hands*
> *May the light of peace*
> *Emanate from your being*
> *May your presence*
> *Light the lamps of peace and love wherever you go*

The hush that descended after this was broken only by the sound of the church clock chiming again. Molly looked at her watch and then down the Hill towards the village below. And smiled. She had faith.

It was now the vicar's moment. In a flurry of garments and nerves, he stepped up on to the trailer. Looked down on them all and beamed. Now that was more like it. 'We will,' he said, his face shining with determination, 'bring these poor heathen souls back into the light from the outer darkness in which they lived. They will be born again.' The vicar, untouched by rural considerations and with no notion of evangelism but liking the grandeur of the statement, was quite unaware that this phrase was anathema to many traditional churchgoers since it required kissing your pew-neighbour, and vicars playing guitars. Sir Roger very nearly shouted Not On My Turf, but managed to restrain himself. Even he was rather taken with the way the archaeologist girl conducted herself. He would not interfere with the proceedings. Molly opened her mouth to say something but Winifred laid a restraining hand on her arm. 'Short men, dear,' she said, 'Some, though not all, can be a bit Napoleonic.' And so, unchallenged, the vicar began. And though the speaker might be suspect, the words were very fine, all agreed. Even Susie, who had a very different view of born again, too.

> *Father of all mercies*
> *And God of all consolation*
> *You pursue with untiring love*
> *And dispel the shadow of death*
> *With the Bright Dawn of Life . . .*
> *Bless these our countrymen in their love*
> *And hold them in peace in Your arms.*

Everyone was absolutely silent as they stood and stared into the grave and a little ripple of movement went through the gathering, a drawing together. There was the sound of clapping from behind the group. And a voice, confident, masculine and quite unfamiliar to all but one of the assembly, called out, 'Bravo, my Molly. Bravo. Beautifully done.' The clapping intensified.

'Freddy!' called out Molly, and immediately dropping all sense of formality she flew from the graveside, her long black boots jumped the wooden barrier, her pink skirt fluffed out all around her, her red hair flew out from her head like a fire – all in the most winning of ways – and she flung herself into his arms. 'I thought you would *never* get here.'

At which, entirely overcome by emotion, what with rebellious Brits and nasty Eyties apparently making mincemeat of them all over the place, Sir Roger Fitzhartlett, fifth Baronet and extremely lousy shot, released the trigger on his new Churchill and fell backwards to the ground, apparently shot through the heart and stone dead. Everyone rushed to help, but Dulcima was on her knees beside him before anyone else. She pushed them away with her hands. 'Let him breathe, idiots,' she said. 'It's probably kickback. Some fool didn't adjust the mechanism correctly.' But there was blood, all the same, and she did not sound wholly convinced.

'Is he dead?' asked Nigel from quite far away and fearfully. And then he fainted. Not so much at the sight of the blood as at the sight of his father's – not to put too fine a point on it – enraged face. He fainted right in the path of Donald Porlock who, not in the least knowing what had happened – for who did? – was on his way to offer help when Nigel passed out. It is a doughty doctor who can step over an unconscious man. He knelt to see what was what.

All around the body of Sir Roger the group came closer again, peering and whispering. 'Give him air!' yelled Dulcima. At last they moved away. But one figure remained crouching by the now moaning Sir Roger. And a voice in Dulcima's ear, another unfamiliar voice, yet – oddly – also a familiar voice, said, 'I'm a doctor. Can I help?' And it was not the voice of Donald Porlock.

Six

THE PERSON WHO said he was a doctor dealt smoothly and efficiently with the injured Sir Roger. He loosened his tie, he loosened his clothes, more importantly he loosened his grip on the
trigger of the smoking Churchill. He said nothing, this doctor.
He kept his back to the crowd behind him and did what he had
to do.

Dulcima, crouching next to him as the others looked on from
a distance, had but a moment to take in the wiry brownness of
the new doctor's bare arms, the dexterity of his sunburnt fingers,
the weathered lines on his cheeks. They did not look like the
fingers of Dr Porlock, she found herself thinking, nor did they
look like the cheeks of Dr Porlock, nor the arms – but he seemed
to know what he was doing. At any rate he seemed to have
staunched the flow of blood; if there had been a flow, that is.
Dulcima noticed that there was nothing to indicate a wound
anywhere on her husband's chest or shoulders – just a bit of a
nasty cut on his ear. It appeared to be bleeding very cheerfully
into the grass as he lay so still and peaceful with his arms by
his side. Surely he was not dead?

Dulcima was paler than she had been since Marion's little
accident. Fear gripped her. Love gripped her. And then her
husband suddenly made a very loud noise in his nether regions,
a noise that Dulcima long ago had decided was the last and
very giddy limit of what a wife in bed had to put up with. He
broke wind. But now she loved the noise as she loved life itself.

'He's alive, he's alive!' she cried in delight.

'Of course I'm alive, old thing,' said Sir Roger who tried to sit
up and in doing so made a similar noise to that made previously.

He looked nervously at his wife, who was looking down at him with such an expression of tender concern that he wondered for a moment if farting were the way forward . . . but decided, despite women being the most perverse of beings, that it probably was not. Then he looked up at the face staring down at him.

A brown, ruddy face, with bright blue eyes and curly reddish hair (what was left of it) and a very familiar look. Sir Roger decided to close his eyes for a moment. He was obviously having delusions. It would pass. 'Oh Roger, I thought I had lost you,' said Dulcima. 'Would you have cared?' he asked, rather surprising himself with the perspicacity of the remark and opening a tentative eye. She put her arms around his head and tenderly kissed his bald bit. 'Madly,' she said. '*Madly.*'

'He'll be fine,' said the new arrival, standing up. 'Porlock can do the rest, it will only need a bit of disinfectant and a plaster.' And he moved away. 'Hip pocket,' whispered Sir Roger faintly to Dulcima. 'Hip pocket.' He tried to move but seemed to be pinned to the ground. Dulcima felt around his shooting trousers until she found the correct pocket and drew out his Great-Uncle George's silver flask. She opened it carefully – while her husband lay there with his mouth open and ready – then she tipped back her head and took a decent gulp of the brandy and made that little noise that he loved so much which was something between a gasp and a cough. 'Now me?' he said.

'But only a little. Only ever a little, Roger dear.'

He nodded. He was happy. 'Damn fine gun, that, Fellows,' he called. 'Damn fine son, too.'

Marion heard the shot. Saw her father fall. Then saw the villagers all crowded about him. She steeled herself. She must ascend, Gnome or not. This time she would not fail – this time she would make the journey. She was a grown woman and she was needed . . . Up she went as if the wind was with her – Sparkle happy at last to be on Pound Hill which he and Coco had discussed many a time over a manger of hay as being just the best place to have a real run at it but they never got the chance.

On, on, Marion rode until she came to rest and slid off the horse into Nigel's waiting arms. Oh, it was just like something out of King Arthur, he thought. She did not have time to think for she threw herself at her father – and mid-throw was surprised to see him sitting up with a hip flask and smiling at her and Nigel in a way that said he was not dying at all. Though there was some blood on his shirt. 'Just a little cut to the ear,' said her father when she asked. 'Bleed like pigs, ears do. Don't they, doctor?'

The stranger nodded and stood up, peering over the heads of the crowd. He looked familiar to them all and yet . . .

Nigel clasped Marion's hand, Marion clasped Nigel's hand, their smiles split their faces and Dryden, who had heard Sir Roger say he had a damn fine son and was in ecstasy again, was jolted out of his ecstatic state by the sudden appearance – standing a little apart from the crowd of Lufferton Boneyites as she had always done in life – of Lottie. The wraith that was his dead wife was still pale, but a pair of roses of a delicate pink bloomed on her cheeks now. And she was smiling. Dryden smiled back, tears coming hot and fast. And such a smile was Lottie's. If Julie Barnsley had smiled the smile of warmth and friendship upon Molly and surprised her, how much more surprised was Nigel to see his father's smile bestowed (so it seemed) upon him. Dryden did not take his eyes from Lottie's little faded, quivering face. Her smiling continued. So did his. Then, tentatively, Lottie put her thin fingers to her pale lips, and blew him one loving kiss – a kiss of affirmation, a kiss of forgiveness, he thought. Dryden's eyes again filled with sadness: so this was what might once have been his and was now beyond his grasp? So this was loss. Dryden put his earthly fingers to his lips and blew her a kiss in return, a loving kiss, so tender that she smiled to see it. And then, with one last wave, a true goodbye this time, she was gone.

Dryden refocused on the world of reality only to find his son staring at him in wonder with his fingers on his lips and, it should be said with some embarrassment, blowing his father a kiss in return. While slowly at Nigel's side, his beloved Marion, suddenly realising what she had done and where she was – so near to the Gnome – fainted.

While the little matter of his patient and his patient's wife enjoying a social drink together was being re-established, the stranger bent over to brush grass and bits of chalk and whatnot off his knees. He was therefore quite unprepared for what happened next. Which was that the Hill, which had earlier been privy to the flying femininity of Molly Bonner, which femininity was now entwined in Freddy's arms while the pair looked on at a proper distance from where Sir Roger was being ministered to, was suddenly privy to something similar all over again. More flying femininity. The flash and blur of a blue and white frock was catapulted from the back of the crowd to the front and, on arriving at its goal, jumped with arms and legs akimbo into the earlier noted very brown arms of the stranger. With a cry of 'Robin!' Dorcas Fairbrother buried her head in her captive's neck, and howled – a noise that was almost drowned by the response of the Lufferton Boneyites who could not believe it, just could not believe it.

'Steady, steady,' said the captive who did not seem to mind too much about the wetness of tears and possibly dribble that was attacking his shoulder. 'Any more tears and I might start to shrink.'

Then he looked up, smiled at everyone and said, 'Home at last.'

Miles Whittington, who had been staring at the vision in front of him, and who finally managed to croak out, 'Robin?' suddenly made a dash for Sir Roger and grabbed his gun. Happily Nigel was not yet the best of gunsmiths – no, not at all – and everything was wonderfully jammed, try as Miles might to get the trigger back and put a bullet into his brother's heart. Miles then fell to the ground weeping with laughter. And fainted. Joining Marion Fitzhartlett, who was still out cold despite Nigel's attempts to rouse her, and Sir Roger who was lying in a state of bliss next to his kneeling wife.

'Good grief,' whispered Peter Hanker to Julie Barnsley. 'If anyone else goes down it will begin to look like the ancient burial place it apparently never was. Which had the result of making them both roll back on to the ground, yet again, with laughter – such is the *joie de vivre* of youth. Robin might have returned from Hades and his brother might have tried to kill him, but a joke, after all, is a joke to someone under thirty.

If you have ever seen a picture of happiness you have never seen one like the picture Dorcas and Robin made as they clung to each other by the side of the Gnome, who did not look quite so grand or powerful with his part removed.

'But *how*?' said Dorcas.

To which Robin replied that it was all to do with Freddy. And a certain young woman called Molly Bonner. And that he would tell her everything when he had been back down to his home, had a decent bath and a stiff whisky (he was British, after all). He set Dorcas back down on the ground (for he was not entirely himself in the strength department yet) and beckoned the vicar over. The vicar made a reasonable job of jumping down and felt rather sad to be so short again.

'St Ethel's still fit for a wedding, vicar?' he asked. The vicar, wincing at the abbreviation but wisely ignoring it, thought it would be the best possible ceremony for the sanctifying of his new pulpit. 'Oh yes,' he said enthusiastically. 'If you can wait a few weeks they have promised me that all will be well and that I shall be able to see properly. I'm not quite able to do so at the moment you know.'

Robin did not like to comment on the vicar's remarkable mobility, given his lack of sight. Instead he took Dorcas's hand in his and looked down at her fingers. 'But where is your ring?' he asked. 'I thought you'd always wear it for me.' Dorcas was about to say that she would have done if she could but she didn't know where it was – when from behind them came a terrible, gut-wrenching, tooth-grinding groan. And Miles said, with a smile on his face that was foul enough to shame the gargoyles of St Etheldreda's with its ghastliness, 'Just keeping it safe for her. Knew you'd be back. Just *knew* it.'

Miles, trembling and ashen faced, stood there with the slightly perplexed vicar who was beginning to feel just a little foolish in his embroidery and robes, though he could not say why. And as they both stood there and looked about them they saw a very strange thing. They saw that every one of the Lufferton Boneyites was holding his or her partner in exactly the same way as the lovers in the grave held each other. Except for Dryden, of course, and Dryden was smiling very contentedly at the sight of Nigel and Marion locked in an embrace that had little to do with horses and much to do with humanity. And, just to add to the moment, behind them, having followed Marion up the Hill, the pony sidled up to Sparkle and rubbed her female muzzle against his. Size wasn't everything, as had been pointed out with the Gnome. It is to be hoped this was duly noted by the vicar and made up for the fact that the thoughtful newcomer, with embarrassing gallantry, had taken his arm and led him down the Hill making loud comments about any obstacles in his way.

At the Old Manor, Orridge and Mrs Webb sat with the assembled young men and held forth on the trials of life – while helping themselves and their young companions to the Veuve Clicquot (well, it would do for them) and quite forgetting about the cold collation waiting and drying out in the warm air of the kitchen. Some hours later, when the Fitzhartlett family returned from the Old Holly Bush and the celebrations there (with hot mini roast and Yorkshires as Sir Roger had dreamed) they found a group of snoring young men in tweed in their sitting room, several empty bottles – and no sign of Orridge or Mrs W. The mystery was solved some time later when it was observed that the upper window of Mrs Webb's cottage remained curtained despite the evening sun, and that all the gnomes in her garden had been set to face the one Great Gnome of Pound Hill. And they appeared to be laughing at him, or dancing, or cocking their gay little legs.

Down below and back in the village, comfortably ensconced under the bar counter of the Old Holly Bush, the pub cat, simply known as She, was giving birth to her kittens. If I am to be tipped out at night to apparently hunt for rats and mice, was how Montmorency put it to himself some weeks previously, then I might as well go over the road for a bit of comfort. He had been agreeably surprised at the comfort offered him once introduced to human bedding by She – but he accepted it graciously, and, being a gentleman cat, he always left at dawn. However, recently, on stepping over to visit, She had remarked in a hissy sort of way that if he wouldn't mind clearing off, she would be very much obliged. And now she was just getting on with it.

Simplicity itself, being a cat. Compared, she thought, to the complexities of human beings. They seemed to be forever chasing their own tails, forgetting everything they knew, not knowing what they wanted and getting nowhere whereas She, Montmorency and their kind kept to their own territory, knew exactly what they wanted, took only what they needed, and on the whole lived very well on it.

In the surrounding landscape the breeze had dropped, the sun shone, the ancient shadows remained still and deep and the Gnome, or the god, or the mammoth bit of Roman graffiti – whatever the figure be – had the look of one who is not very happy but can do nothing about it. Bloody lovers, he thought. Always something going on up here to remind him of all *that*. And he without even the art of lifting his manhood above his ankles (Sappho, paraphrased, c. 590 BC). Below him Mrs Webb's gnomes winked and shone and twinkled in the warm light. He glared all around him, as he had been designed to do, but no one paid him the least attention. The earth was still for that moment, love was let in and even the rooks were quiet.

Postscript

IF THERE WAS one thing about Freddy Rathbone that Molly Bonner had to acknowledge it was that he was even more tenacious than she was. If you said to him in a letter something along the lines of, '*I do not think you will be able to help but you might. This young man called Robin Whittington who is in the same neck of the woods as you and has been lost presumed dead for nearly five years. I doubt you can help to find him, but – just supposing – here are all the details of the case* . . .' Despite the careless dismissal of several hundred miles (*same neck of the woods* being scarcely true), if Molly Bonner knew anything about anything, it was that he would try – and if there were a Robin Whittington out there to be found – he would find him. And he did. Doctors being rather thin on the ground among the outlawed of those parts, and the outlawed of those parts very often needing the administrations of a good medical man, Robin was an unwilling guest for the duration, though a Hippocratically useful one, and very glad to be rescued.

That first night, having overcome a certain amount of disbelief and shyness which had naturally led to activities of a private and personal nature, Dorcas and Robin, naked and happy, lay in each other's arms and marvelled – and Marvelled – at how, despite time passing, love could remain constant. Dorcas asked, perhaps with just a hint of censure, 'Did you ever try to escape?' And Robin said that of course he did. Dorcas then asked, still with the hint of censure, 'Did you ever refuse to do what they wanted?' To which Robin said that of course he did not. He reminded her that, given the situation he found himself in, he was, first and foremost, a doctor, and that no doctor worth his or her salt would – even though a kidnap victim – refuse to help an ailing man, woman or child. Of whom there were many in the place where he was kept. And Dorcas, pressing up close to the body of the man she loved, and it had to be up close because they were in her bed in the Squidge which made any other such position perilous, decided that was the reason she loved him. 'But I don't think I'll be going abroad for a while,' he said comfortably. 'No,' said Dorcas, showing a spirit that had seemed lacking in recent times. 'You most certainly will not.'

Now the dig on Pound Hill was well and truly over – the tarpaulins and the plastic were all gone – and everything had been put back exactly – well, almost exactly – as it once was. Except for one very clever thing. Molly kept her promise. The Gnome's mighty member was restored and rested once again across the grave of the lovers, as the council and the heritage people insisted it must, but with one great difference. At the point at which the Gnome's mighty member lay across the grave of the lovers, instead of grass and chalk, a sheet of laminated glass was placed there, so that all who came up to look and pay their respects to the Lovers of Pound Hill could do so by viewing them through the transparent panel. As Robin said, 'From now on we can look at love through and beyond the vulgar attempt to expunge it.' The vicar had nearly eaten his little heart out at this line from the inaugural speech, for he wished with all his little heart that he had said it; more, he wished within his little heart that he had *seen* it and recognised it. He felt unusually uncomfortable and vowed to try harder. Why, he was wearing the most ordinary, humble clothes that day, which, he felt, was a start.

Molly approved. She might not know her poetry – something

she intended to put right, much to Freddy's amazement and amusement – but she did know her history, and her historians. Their words transcended time. As Tacitus, or Livy or Plutarch knew, men (and presumably women, though they kindly do not say) and their worlds crumble when they forget to recognise and respect the lessons of history. And there on Pound Hill, she thought happily, is the truth of this. No more dismissing love as an unknown, or a convention, or not experienced until modern times, no more forgetting the value of it now as then. The Lovers of Pound Hill had seen to that. A lesson for us all, she thought, and Yes, yes, she really must read some poetry.

Winifred had edited their Lufferton Boney footage so that it was perfectly professional. Molly would take this new evidence to London along with her grandfather's notebooks and he would be accorded the correct honours. Molly would take second place. He had led her there and he had told her, more or less, how to go about things. He was the real star, not her. The letters she would keep along with the shale pieces and the electroplated button. Her spoils. She left the village more fulfilled than when she arrived there and who, she said to Freddy, could say fairer than that? They packed up all the cumbersome hardware and her beautiful tools, and placed the bosing mallet and the lump of wood in pride of place. Who knew if she would use it again? For the moment there were things of a more personal nature to concentrate on. Being Molly Bonner, you may be sure that she would.

The vicar's delight knew no bounds. Two prospective weddings. Two! 'You will be raised up,' so Lady Dulcima had said, and the vicar thought, Who can deny the honour of an aristocrat? He was only waiting, somewhat nervously, for the adjustments to start on the pulpit, as promised. He went away to stay with his sister in Filey, at the suggestion of Dulcima, for a little break. He was very excited. Raised up at last.

Lady Fitzhartlett, who was one to keep her word and who had never intended to knock down old traditions – even if they were a touch uncomfortable for their vicar – selected the highest of the footstools to present to him when he returned from Filey. He would be easily seen over the beautifully carved pulpit rim once he stood on that, and it would make Fitzhartlett happy to lose at least one of them, and she liked the idea of making him happy again. The other footstools would make excellent wedding presents as they were finely worked and rather beautiful. It would please her very much to give Dorcas another gift from Beautiful Bygones. She vaguely remembered the Spode dish and how it had made her smile. Now that Robin was back perhaps she would be able to spend some time putting her feet up so a footstool would be just the thing. And then there was the christening present for Pinky and Susie. Oh yes, she would find homes for them all. Waste not, want not. Dulcima sighed with pleasure. Even Nigel seemed more manly nowadays. He was not Dulcima's first choice, it is true, but he was what her daughter wanted and her daughter seemed to be exactly what he wanted. ('Lady Fitzhartlett, I would not change a hair on her head' – which was rather a blow). Nowadays Marion went up and down Pound Hill without so much as a squeak. How nice it was the way everything worked out in the end. Harty would come round eventually when Nigel learned how to shoot properly – or even adequately. Let us face it, thought Dulcima, Sir Roger never has.

In the Old Holly Bush Julie Barnsley was crouching under the bar and stroking She. And She was purring. Both felt an immense sense of achievement. The kittens slept. 'We'll give one to Miles,' she said later to Peter. 'He'll need a bit of company now he doesn't have Montmorency.'

Pinky and Susie sat side by side at the kitchen table. They had their backs to the open window and the Gnome. On the table was the rudimentary plan of a vegetable garden. They were now considering where to put the herbs. 'Probably where the crystals are now,' said Susie, without so much as looking up. And Pinky replied, quite smoothly and easily, 'I agree.'

On the day of Molly's departure, Robin and Dorcas climbed to the top of Pound Hill and looked down on the van and the trailer as it made its way along the winding road out of the village. Of course Molly Bonner would be back, Dorcas knew, for she had several weddings to attend. And a baptism, or christening, or Druidical baby blessing. Happy things to come. As Dorcas raised her hand to wave at the slowly disappearing vehicle, the sun came out from behind a cloud (there were not many in the sky that day) and caught, like a tiny fire, the diamond on Dorcas's finger. It flashed its light and sent a wink across the landscape. And, as if to answer the wink, the laminated glass that covered the grave of the Lovers of Lufferton Boney also caught the sun, and also winked. Which seemed, to anyone who noticed in the village below, to be a satisfactory phenomenon. Back down the couple came, slowly, laughing again at Robin's mistaking the vicar for someone who was blind. Though privately Dorcas wondered if that was very far from the truth.

In the Squidge, and unaware of the furry feline gift that he would one day receive, which might prove the making of him – and might not – Miles sat motionless and miserable in an armchair, staring out and up at the Gnome. As the sunlight caught the glass that covered the embracing bones of the eternal lovers, Miles saw how Dorcas's diamond winked and flashed its message across the landscape and into his tiny, narrow, dark sitting room. That Molly Bonner, he thought. That archaeologist's granddaughter with her full purse and promises. She had well and truly done for him. Somehow, somehow, he had always known, from the very first time he saw her bouncing her way down the village street, that she would. All that shocking colour, that startling pink and red and whatnot, could only do him harm. Like the Gnome, Miles was now a creature undone. 'I lift up mine eyes to the Hill,' he said aloud, 'From whence cometh my help.' But sadly for Miles, it did not.

The so-called Lovers of Valdaro, also dubbed the 'Valdaro Lovers', is a pair of human skeletons locked in an eternal embrace discovered by archaeologists at a Neolithic tomb in S. Giorgio near Mantova, Italy in 2007.

Archaeologist Elena Maria Menotti led the excavation. Scientists believe that the lovers are a man and woman no older than 20 years old and approximately 5'2" in height. They were removed from the ground intact and sent to Musei Civici in Como where they are undergoing tests.

Author's Note

PARTLY THIS BOOK is all my daughter's fault for rekindling my interest in ancient landscapes – through her involvement with a Jurassic Museum on Purbeck – and partly it came about because, living in the beautiful south west of England, there is no escaping our ancestors. It must have been like Piccadilly Circus, particularly in the Iron Age, with groups of people tripping over each other all the time – virtually no hill was left without a human settlement or fortification. And then there is the Cerne Abbas Giant – that unashamedly masculine figure cut out of the Dorset landscape with no one quite knowing by whom or why or exactly when. He's certainly a shocker. I was playing around with these ideas and the way we feel we are so sophisticated and advanced in our ways now compared to the superstitions and rituals of the past, and thinking that for all their being thousands of years old those rituals and superstitions seemed to be very powerful and exact and full of meaning. I went on the Internet to see where I could read up more about these things and – quite suddenly – I was staring at a picture of two neolithic skeletons, very young, male and female, held together in a loving embrace that had lasted for five thousand years. For the first time in anything so ancient that I had seen, here were our indigenous ancestors showing us that they knew all about love in quite the same way that we did. Perhaps even more so than now, given the current somewhat fickle and transient nature of love affairs (if *heat* magazine is anything to go by). Out of that came a novel that put together the two ideas of the Cerne Abbas Giant and the apparently all-powerful supremacy of his bigness, and the underlying, undermining sweetness of the two young eternal lovers.

The Italian archaeologist, a woman, who discovered the skeletons in Valdaro was absolutely determined that they should never be separated, even when taken away for investigation. And they were not. Only an Italian . . .

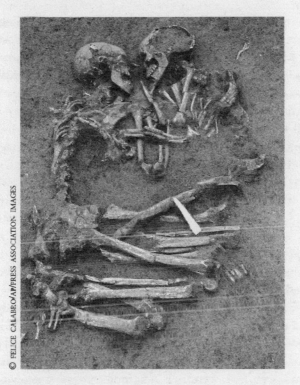

© FELICE CALABRO/AP/PRESS ASSOCIATION IMAGES

ACKNOWLEDGEMENTS

Particular thanks to Martin Green, farmer and winner of the Pitt-Rivers award for independent archaeology, who let me loose on Down farm in Cranborne Chase (which must be one of the most dug-up areas in England) and took me through 10,000 years of chalkland history. If you want to be inspired, as I was, read his book *A Landscape Revealed* and understand a little bit more about your far-off ancestors. I should also thank Steve Etches, amateur palaeontologist, whose Jurassic collection is of global importance, and who set the whole visit up and came along and shivered with us. Without men like these, the honourable amateurs, we'd know very little about the teeming past.

THE POWER OF READING

Visit the Random House website and get connected with information on all our books and authors

EXTRACTS from our recently published books and selected backlist titles

COMPETITIONS AND PRIZE DRAWS Win signed books, audiobooks and more

AUTHOR EVENTS Find out which of our authors are on tour and where you can meet them

LATEST NEWS on bestsellers, awards and new publications

MINISITES with exclusive special features dedicated to our authors and their titles

READING GROUPS Reading guides, special features and all the information you need for your reading group

LISTEN to extracts from the latest audiobook publications

WATCH video clips of interviews and readings with our authors

RANDOM HOUSE INFORMATION including advice for writers, job vacancies and all your general queries answered

Come home to Random House

www.randomhouse.co.uk